THE MERCY OF THE NIGHT

ALSO BY
DAVID CORBETT

THE MERCY OF THE NIGHT

A NOVEL

DAVID CORBETT

Published by Thomas & Mercer, Seattle

www.apub.com

Amazon, the Amazon logo, and Thomas & Mercer are trademarks of Amazon.com, Inc. or its affiliates.

ISBN-13: 9781477849446
ISBN-10: 1477849440

Cover design by Salamander Hill Design, Inc.

Library of Congress Control Number: 2014952440

Printed in the United States of America.

For my wife, Mette

Changeling

In the predawn darkness the forest smelled peaty with mushrooming rot. She hacked a path through sword ferns and redwood sorrel and coiling blackberries spiked with thorns—a long-haired girl, eight years old, light-headed from little to eat for three days and stripped naked, shackled to a broken chain.

She feared crashing through the woods in hopeless circles or, worse, just plunging deeper into the tangled undergrowth, lost for good. From time to time, glancing up through a feathery opening in the pine and eucalyptus branches, she stared at the drifting canopy of mist and felt abandoned by the moon.

Then gravel, like bits of broken glass, stabbed the soles of her feet. She tripped on a jagged lip of asphalt—she'd reached the road: curving, two-lane, dark.

Hugging herself for warmth—how long before she heard a car? Minutes, maybe, warped into hours.

The thing rumbled up the fogbound hill, headlights a smeary glow then breaking the turn, and she stepped out onto the blacktop, breath visible, hands splayed.

The car braked and lurched to a stop. Engine throbbing under the hood, tailpipe with its dervish of white exhaust.

She realized it might be him, coming back. The man they'd identify as Victor Cope but to her was simply the creep, Mr. Menthol Meth Head—what if she got free and stumbled all this way only to make it easy for him?

He'd chase her into the woods, take her down, grab her by the hair and drag her back to the moldy house—and then? He hated her enough already. She wasn't like Marina, his little blossom, his perfection.

The driver-side door creaked open. The ceiling light gave birth to a silhouette beyond the headlight glare. A man. He dragged himself from behind the wheel, got out.

"Jesus H. Christ . . ."

He edged closer. Some kind of redneck longhair—lumberjack shirt, thick black beard, scuffed boots. Voice like a chain-smoking folksinger.

"Are you—Jesus fucking hell—you okay?"

He took off the shirt, wrapped her in the thick coarse wool, warm from his body. Put his arm around her, then just as quick snapped the arm away, like he'd been bit. Cautious. Caring. He led her to the passenger-side door.

"Go ahead. Get in. I'm not gonna hurt you."

Ten years later, she'd wonder how she knew to trust that.

An old El Camino, kind of car Richie, her brother, would cream over. Inside it reeked of cigarettes and black coffee, while Mardi Gras beads dangled from the rearview and the radio glowed, the music faint, nighthawk soul or some kind of R & B.

He got in, slammed his door, reached for the gearshift. Stopped. Turning toward her, he stared for a second, like she was a fawn, an elf, a changeling, sitting in his car.

"You're that girl," he said quietly. "The one got took up north."

No, she thought. I'm the other one.

"What am I thinking?" He slapped his head. "Get us the hell away from here." Throwing the El Camino into drive, he roared off down the curving mountain road. Velocity seemed to suit him. Glancing once his way, she saw his jaw was set but his eyes were calm, steady, and she took comfort in that.

He switched off the radio. "Must've had you holed away in one of those houses back up the ridge." He shook his head. "There's coons and mountain lions and ki-yotes up in there. Lucky one of them didn't spot you, slink on down in the dark, drag you off."

"I'm not afraid of raccoons." Her first words in . . . how long?

He chuckled. "Boy, you're a tough one, aren'tcha?" He stopped at a T in the road, looked both ways. A sign read "Bonny Doon—1 ½ miles" with an arrow pointing right. He turned left. "Weren't really the raccoons I was talking about."

"I know."

That seemed to tickle him even more. A muted kind of laughter in his eyes. She liked that, liked him. She needed to.

"I'm taking you down into town, get you to a hospital. That be all right?"

The word "yes," it caught in her throat. Scared her. She nodded.

"Well," he added, "maybe not directly to the hospital."

Pulling the heavy shirt tighter, she eyed the chrome door handle, then glanced out through the windshield, looking for the next spot he might slow down.

"Don't worry, I'll make sure you get looked after and all. I just mean I can't get myself tangled up with the law. No cops, no questions." He nodded, as though to confirm the end of an argument he'd been having with himself. "It's complicated. Let's just leave it at that."

It wasn't till then she realized he'd not mentioned his name.

"I'm Jacquelina Garza," she said.

"Nice to meet you." A nod, like a gentleman tipping his hat. "Seriously, let's leave it there."

He drove down the winding hillside road until they reached a main drag leading south into Santa Cruz. At a little diner called Bernadette's he pulled into the parking lot, killed the ignition, glanced at his watch. The diner glowed like a spaceship serving breakfast.

He turned toward her, arm perched on the steering wheel, eyes warm but wary. "Here's how it is," he said. "Got me a friend who works here, great lady, name is Dawn. I'm gonna go in, let her know I found you up in the hills, then hand you over to her so she can get you seen to. Gonna be a lot of hoopla surrounding that and it's just not what I'm into. Right? I'm glad I could help, real glad. Happy you're safe. And you are, you're safe now."

His hand reached out. She stiffened, not ready to be touched. But he didn't touch her. He dug a cigarette pack from the shirt pocket, tapped out a smoke, lipped it, thumbed in the dash lighter.

"I need you to forget me now, okay? Forget this car, forget my face. A stranger picked you up, saw you standing there by the road about two miles east of the Bonny Doon cutoff on Woodbriar Ridge—remember that, they're gonna need to know the spot so they can backtrack, find the house you escaped from." The lighter popped, he plucked it from its socket, touched the red coil to the tip of his cigarette. That intimate hiss as it singed the tobacco. "This stranger, one who found you—some kinda holy roller, let's say, do-gooder type, no reward necessary—he dropped you off around here, you stumbled into the diner on your own." He exhaled a long plume of smoke. It smelled like him. "Sorry to make it complicated, but it's for the best." He smiled with a wary sort of kindness. "Think you can do that for me?"

Of course she could. And she did.

She gave him back his shirt and let the woman named Dawn bundle her up in a big soft sweater as the El Camino drove off, and she sat at a table inside the diner with some buttered toast and a cup of hot chocolate till the highway patrol arrived. She never mentioned the stranger in the El Camino who'd appeared out of nowhere, though from that day on she'd envy his ability to become invisible. She said a man in a suit and tie and glasses picked her up, prayed when he found her and prayed as they drove off down the mountain, praising the Lord and his mysterious grace and refusing to accept recognition for his good deed—that would be unchristian, he'd said, the sin of pride—leaving her within an easy walk of safety.

She lied, the first in a blizzard of lies, until it became the easier thing, the truth so unforgiving.

Part I

1

Phelan Tierney made his way around the palatial Nordic monstrosity housing the center and followed a winding gravel path lined with Japanese maples—the graceful, meticulously tended trees in winter silhouette—continuing back to the sprawling garden, where he finally spotted the woman he'd come to see, Lonnie Bachmann, kneeling in mud.

Dressed in a hooded yellow parka and shapeless jeans, she neither greeted nor even acknowledged him as the crunch of his footsteps stopped. Bracing himself against the blustery cold, he watched as she submerged one gloved hand in a bucket of slop—he could smell it from where he stood: coffee grounds—while the other smeared the gritty black muck around the base of a freshly planted azalea.

"Lonnie?"

Startled, she flinched, then turned to glance up, nudging back the kerchief securing her blondish hair. The face possessed a weathered loveliness, evidence of both her homespun youth and twenty years chasing the crack dragon, turning tricks to pay the freight.

She spanked her gloved hands together, creating a small cloud of black specks. "Well, well. The man with two last names."

How many thousands of times . . . "I thought I'd explained that."

"You did." The ghost of a smile. "I'm teasing."

His mother's maiden name was Phelan. She'd been, perhaps, over-attached to it.

"Thanks for coming so quick," she said. "Mind if we talk out here?" She gestured to six or seven unplanted azaleas lined up along the swerving flower bed, each with its own predug hole, root balls mummified in burlap. "I'd like to get these in the ground before the rain."

A major storm front was moving in off the Pacific, only the second this winter. Good news, given the drought, and despite the threat of landslides, overtopped levees, and flood plains turned into lakes.

He said, "We can chat wherever you like."

They'd met at a fund-raiser for her little operation here, and Tierney had taken an instant liking to her. They shared, in a sense, the same reason for being.

Lonnie had turned her life around at the cusp of forty, the prodigal beauty, steadying her legs beneath her through five years of rehab, battling relapses, gradually acquiring a wise gentle strength.

She started working with teens and women trapped in the same circle of hell she'd escaped, proving good at the work, exceptional by some accounts, and with something of a reputation established she cobbled together enough grant money to transform the old Norse American Hall, with its hulking, neo-Viking timber and stone, its hillside view of the Napa River watershed and the North Bay wetlands, into a halfway house where working girls, struggling to stay clean and straight, could hole up, gain strength from one another, learn some job skills, visit with their kids.

Tierney, who'd gained an almost encyclopedic knowledge of the building trades through twenty years litigating construction defects, first became involved with Lonnie's venture by helping her negotiate with the contractors needed to reshingle the Gothic roof, replace the dry-rotted staves and cross braces, regrout the stacked exterior stone. More than once he managed to protect her from the old change-order shakedown, and in the span of nine months the place transformed from ruin to eyesore to local gem, enjoying the same kind of turn-around promised to the young women who came to live there.

She called it Winchinchala House, from the Lakota word for girl, though some of the less enthusiastic neighbors dubbed it the House of Whores, or Casa de Crackhead.

Trudging on her knees along the flower bed—two troughs of flattened grass in her wake—she reached for the next azalea, cut the twine, tossed the burlap aside, then combed loose the root ball with gloved fingers, showering the ground with potting soil.

"You've been working with Jacqi Garza, preparing for the GED, am I right?"

Recently he'd transitioned from construction guru to tutor, something he seemed strangely good at, dropping in twice a week to help the girls with their practice tests.

"Jacqi and a handful of others." He plunged his hands into his pants pockets, balling them into fists, not just because of the cold. "Is there a problem?"

She dropped the plant in its appointed hole. "You got along with her okay?"

"I suppose you could say that." One of the trickier aspects of volunteering in a place like this was that the women could foster attractions, or grievances, which amounted to pretty much the same thing if they decided to start talking about you. He'd sensed no such problem with Jacqi. She took the prep work seriously, had reasonably good reading skills, and didn't think of math as some tedious, draconian kind of magic.

"She's not in some kind of trouble," he said, wondering as well: Am I?

"I don't know." Lonnie plowed loose dirt into the hole around the azalea's roots, patted it down. "You've lived here in Rio Mirada how long?"

Where's this heading, he wondered. "Six or seven years."

"Just curious if you know her story." She looked up at him with a kind of defeated concern. "Jacqi's, I mean."

Realizing, finally, he wasn't the one under scrutiny, he smiled. "I tend not to pry into the private stuff."

"Reason I asked," she said, "about ten years ago, when she was eight, Jacqi was all over the news."

"I wasn't aware of that, no."

"One day she was walking home from school and just vanished off the face of the earth." Lonnie met his eyes again. "Sure you never heard about it?"

He searched his memory—Jacqi Garza, or Jacquelina Esperanza Garza, as she signed her name on the practice tests. It began to ring a bell. A somewhat distant bell. "Remind me," he said.

"Two girls disappeared in a six-week period. Jacqi was the second. In a lot of ways the girls were almost identical. Physically, at least."

She turned toward the bucket of coffee grounds, which now lay out of reach. Tierney collected it for her.

"Both girls were slim and pretty and olive-skinned, big brown eyes, long dark hair." Lonnie extracted a helping of grounds and smudged them around the base of the plant. "But the first girl, Marina Bacay, was by all accounts a little angel—did well in school, made friends easily, good home."

Tierney, sensing a cue, said, "Jacqi, on the other hand . . ."

Lonnie glanced up at the sky for a moment as overhead a ragtag flock of herring gulls circled and shrieked, the birds heading inland ahead of the storm. "Jacqi was different." She brushed her hands on her pant legs, then moved on to the next plant, the next hole, same knee-march through the grass as before, this time clanging the bucket alongside. "But that difference didn't matter much to the man who took them both."

No, it wouldn't, Tierney thought, following slowly along. "I think I remember this now," he said. "She escaped. Jacqi, I mean." Adding to himself: Physically, at least.

Lonnie nodded. "After three days. A local cabdriver named Victor Cope took her to a house in the hills near Santa Cruz, kept her chained up in the cellar. But then he left her alone for a few hours and she found a way to get out."

He pictured Jacqi as he knew her, slim but strong and still growing into her beauty, tried to imagine her ten years younger. He cringed at how casually he'd misjudged who she was, what had happened to her. "Pretty brave for a girl that age."

"Our plucky little heroine." Lonnie smiled ruefully. "Her father was in prison—Corcoran or Soledad, I can't remember which. Her brother—he was thirteen at the time, I think—was already involved in gangs, some *norteño* clique."

"I suppose that explains her pluck."

"Yes." Lonnie scratched her cheek with the back of her glove, leaving a streak of dirt behind. "Fair to say she came pre-equipped for dealing with trouble, especially in the form of men." She turned the azalea this way and that in its hole, trying to determine which side should face front. "Mother's no picnic either. Met her just once, but Jesus."

"Raised by wolves," he said.

"Queen of Mars, more like it."

O for a muse of fire. "And the other girl, the angel?"

Lonnie seemed content with the plant's orientation now and began backfilling the hole. "Marina was never found."

Of course not, Tierney thought, sensing the shape of the story now. The wrong girl came home.

"So," he said, "skip ahead ten years. Jacqi starts using, her dealer becomes her boyfriend and then her pimp, something to that effect. And one day she winds up here."

"Yes," Lonnie said, "lucky for her."

She reached for the next azalea, took its thin trunk in hand, and knee-marched ahead. Once again: cut the twine, tear away the burlap, pitch it aside. She picked off a few brown, hardened leaves.

Tierney waited, then said, "There was a problem."

She stopped her fussing and just knelt there for a moment, silent, her gaze a thousand miles away.

"Lonnie?"

"Yes, sorry." She tugged at her gloves, tightening the fit. "You're right, there was a problem. And now it seems our plucky little heroine has disappeared again."

2

Jacqi pressed a washcloth hard against a gaping cut on the big man's massive brow. He sat on the edge of the bed, spellbound by the minibar.

His name was Michael Verrazzo but she called him Fireman Mike, the one repeat trick she had so far and, if she played it right, a possible frequent flyer. He'd sprung for a real room tonight, just a Marriott but still, way better than the usual jump joint. Or his car.

He'd texted ahead, told her to do herself up, look nice, a little catnip for the captain. So she'd put on some black tights and her one good dress, a low-backed slate-gray sheath with a cinched waist, slipped on her one pair of heels. He'd come decked out himself in his dark dress blues, striped epaulettes, gold piping. Fresh from a city council meeting, he'd said, making it sound like a brawl—or a farce—which no doubt explained the drinking.

Big fella tugging away at a flask as he drove them here, and that just a chaser from earlier. Hey, you're head of the firefighter's union, you can get away with crap like that.

Correction. Ex-head.

What you can't get away with is being so tight you miss the curb and swan-dive onto the sidewalk. Head wounds, they bleed like crazy. Made for an interesting check-in.

"Turn this way," she said. Every light in the room on. "Stop fidgeting. Christ . . ."

"Just press, don't rub."

"Don't be such a baby. It's still, like, oozing."

"Here, gimme it." He snatched the washcloth, stood up. Like a refrigerator rising to its feet—shoulders and arms like a powerlifter, grip like a slammed door—but Christ, that was what firemen did all day, free weights and machines, strength and cardio, got paid through the nose for the privilege too.

Snorfing back a throatful of phlegm he shambled to the bathroom, dragging his Frankenstein feet in their shiny black shoes. Bracing himself, one hand on the doorframe, he glanced back over his shoulder. A wolfish smile, not unkind.

"You look nice, Jackalina."

She sighed. "I asked you not to call me that." She used Volanda when working.

"Right, yeah." A wink. "Like I don't know who you are."

Not really the point, Buckwheat. "I have my reasons, okay?"

Reaching up, he gingerly touched his gash, inspecting the thread of blood his fingertips took away. "You're a total smokeshow in that dress, know that?" That complicated smile again. "Look like a real lady."

Don't act so surprised, she thought.

"Could pass for twenty-one easy, older even."

Quietly, she said, "Thank you." Thinking: That's kinda, like, the point? She didn't do the sexy little girl bit. For obvious reasons.

He squinted up at the ceiling. "Kill some of these lights, Jesus." Turning back toward the bathroom, he gathered himself. "Let me take care of some business," he said. "Then we'll, you know, take care of business."

• • •

Once the door clicked shut she got up, turned off the overhead and two other lamps, then settled in on the bed, slipping her shoes on and off, taking in the décor. Even with mood lighting, it was meh. Bet every room in this place, she thought, every room in every Marriott across the world had the same fake maple TV cabinet, same torture-to-sit-at desk, same watercolor landscapes of nowhere. You could fall asleep in one room, wake up in another, how would you know the difference?

It gave her the willies, but then Fireman Mike snapped her back by hurling up his last five meals beyond the bathroom door.

Long-distance call on the big white telephone. Looks like it's gonna be a while, she thought, snapping open her purse to collect her phone.

Checking the chat rooms she used for clients—BlueMoon.com, MeetMe.com—she found no hits on either and felt both disappointed and relieved. Glad not to be bothered, needing the money.

She'd have to go out north of town tomorrow and work the river road, hope for a drive-by, a trucker or two. And the forecast was rain, for once. Lots and lots and lots of it.

She'd saved a little under two hundred already, not bad for just one week, the benefit of not pissing it all away on wine coolers and crank— God help me, she thought, remembering that night they arrested her in Browner Park, jackhammer heartbeat, head full of snakes, bruised and bloody and screaming.

Tricking again was degrading enough, but she'd rather set herself on fire than go back to being that strung out. She had no illusions about the undertow. Death by a thousand bumps. And everybody's got one. Just for you.

Give Lonnie Bachmann her due. Got me clean—okay, I'm grateful—but the woman had an agenda. "I'm here for you"—such a crock. I Play Favorites, more like it. Well it's my life, queenie, not yours, not Terrible Tonelle's, not Momzilla's, nobody's.

How dare you ask me those questions. How dare you let them go at me like that.

She figured once she had two thousand, she could make her move, put this town behind her forever. If two grand ended up leaving her short, she'd work it out when she got there.

The point was she had to go, leave here, leave her miserable freakish past, everybody wanting to know all about it, again, forever, thinking they had a right—which prompted a switch from BlueMoon.com to the Lonely Planet web page.

The place was named the Costa Chica: a long bright stretch of empty white sand starting forty miles south of Acapulco and continuing all the way down to Oaxaca. One spot in particular, Playa Ventura, called to her, and she scrolled through the pictures again.

A town with just three narrow streets, a few beachfront hotels and restaurants shaded by palms, simple and friendly, nothing to the west but blue water.

She'd live in a thatched *palapa* and hustle up work, make herself useful, folding laundry, scrubbing floors, collecting firewood, whatever. Her Spanish was rusty since her *abuelita* died but she'd get it back, and her English could prove a plus, always useful, even off the major tourist track.

If that didn't work out she'd head farther south, Playa La Bocana, where the Rio Marquelia meets the ocean. She'd sleep in a hammock hitched to coconut palms near the food stalls on the beach, find work at the hotel, clean out *cabañas* along the lagoon.

She knew what people would say if they knew. Okay, so sue me, I have this thing, this hope—hear that, people?—call it a dream, fine. I need it. Or I think I just might die.

There's a place where nobody knows me and nobody asks. A place where I'm just the new girl, the quiet girl. A place where, for the first time in my life, I'm free.

The screen on her phone went dark. She thumbed it back so she could exit out of the page. Lonely Planet. Got that right. But not forever. Nothing says it has to be.

The bathroom door blew open and Fireman Mike stood there, tie tugged loose at his mangled collar, face flushed. He offered a slack grin as his big legs steadied beneath him and from somewhere miles inside his gut he dredged up a ripping belch.

He made way to the bed and dropped like a buffalo on a trampoline, bouncing Jacqi upward.

"I'm so outta here." He dug the flask from his pocket, unscrewed the cap, a ravenous lip-lock and chug. Beads of sweat glistened across his meaty face. "Got myself a whole new situation, captain's post in Visalia, start next week."

"Yeah," she whispered. "You told me in the car coming here."

"That's why I went down to the circus tonight," he said, "give a fond farewell to the fuckwads. Citizen Pinhead, Angry Joe Blow. Milquetoast the Mayor and the Council of Cunts. You wanna make me the scapegoat for the city going belly-up, hey, have at it. Place you oughta be looking, though, is straight into a goddamn mirror."

He wasn't talking to her so much as some invisible anybody, the stenographer in his head. He went away for a second, behind the invisible curtain, then just like that he snapped back, peered one-eyed into the flask, a little shake to hear how much was left.

"Time to hit the minibar."

Knock yourself out, she thought. "I'm good."

"Gonna make me drink alone?"

Like me and an army could stop you. She shrugged, remembering to smile.

He studied her for a second, that lurid, friendly grin of his. Then he did the strangest thing.

3

It was almost ten by the time Tierney returned to Winchinchala House. He stood on the floodlit porch and pressed the bell, listening to the stately gong echo beyond the thick stone walls. Footfalls approached on the slate entry floor, then a shadow darkened the peephole. A scramble of locks, the door swung wide.

A twentyish black woman stood there. Catlike, muscular. Shaved head.

"Kinda late to come a-tutorin, ain't it?"

Tierney smiled. "Good evening, Tonelle. I'm here to see Lonnie."

She eyed him cagily. Schooling's just racist indoctrination, she'd told him once, keep the niggers under the boot. Diploma's just a new kinda chain. None of which meant much. Tonelle just liked to argue.

She waited a beat, just to emphasize she could, then stepped back to let him pass. "Go on through, Tooder. She in her office."

The study room hummed with a quiet intensity as the young women suffered over their studies. A few curled up in beanbag chairs and plowed through dog-eared paperbacks with torrid covers. Across the hall a handful of others watched TV, the volume a respectful murmur. Several greeted him with lazy waves as he headed toward the back.

Reaching Lonnie's office, he glanced in at the doorway before knocking. She sat at her desk, a massive oak monolith turned caddy-corner at the center of the room, the better to fill the vast, high-ceilinged space. A gooseneck lamp cast a focused glow on a blotter full of paperwork.

Rapping his knuckles on the doorframe. "Got a minute?"

She glanced up as though from a miserable dream, then smiled, seeing it was him. The smile faded quickly. "No luck, I take it."

She'd been to a function earlier, judging from how she was dressed, navy blazer and gray herringbone skirt, the jacket unbuttoned, revealing a jabot blouse.

He took a seat. "I haven't tracked her down as yet, no. But I've been busy."

Lonnie sat back in her plump chair, outside the cone of light. "Tell me."

He took note of the wariness in her voice. "Spent the afternoon at the courthouse, plowing through case files. The Cope thing, in particular. Came to nine volumes, with the trial transcripts."

She cocked her head. A small, dispirited sigh. "Don't take this wrong, but was that really the best use of your time?"

"You don't just want me to find her," he said. "You want me to persuade her to come back, right?"

"Yes. I told you that."

"I don't want to come off like a simpleton when I talk to her again. And I don't want to get sandbagged."

She reached for a paperweight on her desktop, something to hold, fuss with, then dipped back out of the light again. "I suppose I see your point."

"After the courthouse I checked out the library—street kids like to hang there, it's warm and dry, it's safe. Spent some time on the computer, waiting to see if she might turn up, got a little more background off the web. When she didn't show I went to the mother's house—you're right, she's, well, interesting. And unhelpful." He shrugged. "Then I drove around for a while, circling the usual places in case, you know, Jacqi's working again."

In a small voice: "Thank you."

"There's still a few things I'd like to get a better handle on. You said her dad was in prison when Cope took her."

"Still is, I think."

"Don't think. He's doing twenty-five to life. Felony murder. He was the driver in a jewelry store heist that went sideways, the shop owner and one of the crew got killed."

He waited for a response. She shrugged. "I'm not sure—"

"That's not just some random fuckup," he said. "That's heavy. It tells you something. About the home Jacqi grew up in."

"I thought I made that clear—her home life, I mean. If I didn't, I'm sorry."

"I also tried to follow up on the brother, the one you said was with the *norteños*."

"That was the rumor."

"There's hardly anything on him. What's there is minor, drug stuff, theft. And all of it goes away. He's never been convicted of anything."

She leaned forward, far enough for the light to harshen her features. "Phelan, I'm not sure where you're going with all this, but the point I was trying to make is that when two girls went missing in just six weeks, it felt like the city was cursed. Then Jacqi escaped, and it was like a miracle. The curse got lifted."

"But not for long."

"No. This is still a small town in a lot of ways, no matter how big it gets or the kinds of problems it has. It didn't make headlines, more like a whisper campaign, but the issue of her family just wouldn't die. People weren't content with just Jacqi back, they wanted Marina too, they wanted Jacqi to lead the police to her, and when she couldn't, well

. . . There was some resentment. That's all I was trying to get across by bringing up her dad and her brother."

"Okay," Tierney said, thinking: Let it go. "I also checked out Jacqi's files. There were four—razor thin, nothing but the complaint inside."

"That's not unusual. She's a juvenile, the rest is sealed."

It's not all that's sealed, he thought, not by a long shot. But he was saving that to talk over with Jacqi.

He said, "She's been tagged with soliciting and public intoxication—no surprise, since she wound up here—but there's also two assault charges, one against a teacher, a second against a gentleman named Gerald Anthony Manzello, who just happens to be with the Rio Mirada police."

"Are you surprised?"

"Can you fill in the blanks a little? She's always been pretty tame with me, but if she's going to take a swing, I'd like to be prepared."

Lonnie sat back in her chair again for a moment, rocking a little, then got up, went to the door and closed it. Sitting back down, she said in a lowered voice, "Jacqi's something of a unique case, but a lot of the girls here have been abused. Most, actually. None who've been abducted, okay, but plenty who've been through some pretty awful stuff. You know Tonelle, nice-looking black girl, bald?"

"She greeted me at the door," Tierney said. "I use the term 'greeted' somewhat loosely."

"Tonelle never, ever has nothing to say."

"That's pretty much my experience."

"But she's got a story, too. Break your heart."

"I can only imagine."

"Anyway, you go through all that, a childhood like that, then hit puberty and the hormones kick in? It's weird to begin with, for everybody. But abuse means depression, and some girls go inward, others act out—turn mouthy, pick fights."

"We're back to Jacqi now."

"Not just her. They all get into drinking or drugs or both. And they get sexually active way too soon—I know, after the abuse it doesn't make sense, and yet it does."

Todestrieb, Tierney thought. Freud's term, the repetition compulsion, rooted in Thanatos. The death instinct.

"Odd as it sounds," she said, "tricking can give you a strange sense of power. It did for me. Anyway, the drugs, the sex, the acting out, all that happened with Jacqi by the time she was sixteen. Became a terror at school, and she was hardly a model student before the Cope thing. Started picking fights, ugly ones, not just with other kids."

"The thing with the teacher," Tierney said. "And Officer Manzello?"

"I don't know about that specifically. But she was living on the street for weeks at a stretch, which meant run-ins with the cops. They hate her—I know a bunch of them here, grew up with some, got to know the others through work. I even know Manzello, but I never heard about this. Anyway, they can't understand. 'She got her life back, now look at her, throwing it all away.' One guy told me cuffing her was like trying to put a headlock on an explosion."

"What about the most recent thing? The one that brought her to you."

She glanced at the distant wall, its array of plaques and commendations, as though to reassure herself of something. "Six months ago somebody spotted Jacqi wandering around in Browner Park, no shoes, just a tank top and cutoffs, cranked out of her skull. Paramedics took her to ER, and they piped her so full of droperidol and olanzapine it's a miracle she didn't slip into a coma. Turns out she had her gear with her when she was found and that just enhanced the parole violation. She was looking at lockup but juvie probation came in, contacted me, we got her diversion instead. That's how she ended up here."

My star pupil, he thought, bit of a joker but quiet, attentive, pencil chewer, all bouncing knees and awkward elbows. "It seemed to be working out," he said. "At least, from what I could tell. She was work-ing hard—"

"She got scared. Scared enough to turn the corner. Cleaned up, stayed clean the whole time she was here. I was proud of her. And I'm worried for her now. I hate to think she's falling back into the life. She really is a sweet, strong, pretty girl. And smart. Wicked smart."

Interesting way to put it, he thought. "You still haven't told me what went wrong. Why she left."

Lonnie sat there a moment, looking at him with that same sad, helpless concern. It was beginning to seem a bit like a mask.

"She couldn't deal with group. The girls and me, we sit in a circle, we talk. It's not enough to be honest with yourself. You have to learn to be honest with others. But Jacqi couldn't go there. Ask her what was going on, she'd say she was fine, maintaining, whatever. Try to delve into what happened with her, the abduction, how she's dealing with it, she'd rattle off details like she was reciting her trial testimony. Ask her about why she used or tricked and she'd say it was behind her now, so no big deal, and don't waste your breath asking about her family. Nothing to tell, she'd say. I mean, really. Finally some of the girls called her on it. I called her on it. Tonelle seriously got in her face."

"So no secrets," he said. "No privacy."

"That's not how it works. Privacy is one thing. But secrets are for users."

She stood up suddenly, idly searching through papers on her desk-top, as though in hope of some kind of validation. Proof. He wanted to tell her to sit back down, it was okay. There are a thousand ways to get greedy, being greedy for the truth is hardly the worst. But before he could say that her hands fell still. The mask of concern fell away.

"I should have stepped in," she said. "Protected her better."

4

Of all the things I saw coming, Jacqi thought, this wasn't one of them.

Still sitting close beside her on the hotel bed, Verrazzo rummaged around inside his jacket, searching the pocket over his heart, then dug out a little felt box and handed it to her. "Go ahead," he said quietly. "Open it."

The box was soft, furry to the touch like a hamster, warm from the drunken heat of his body. The hinge was tight but Jacqi worked open the lid, snapped it back.

White satin inside. Gold chain with a hummingbird charm.

She knew what gifts meant—you ended up paying for them one way or another—still, she smiled. It was pretty.

"Jeez," she said. "Thank you."

She held up her hair and he put it on her, fumbling with the clasp at her nape, and she indulged a momentary daydream of being rescued by him somehow.

"Maybe you can come down, Jackalina. Visalia, I mean."

She said, "I don't know where that is," feeling a need to stall.

"What difference does it make? It's down south. Got my own condo—sauna, steam room, pool. You can keep me company."

She tucked her hands under her thighs. "And your family?"

"Family's not coming." His eyes went flat, then he rechecked his flask, like it might have magically refilled. "Family's staying put. I'll come back up on my off days."

Not likely, she thought, judging from his tone.

So why not say yes? Why not let him get you out of this town, put you up for a while, take care of you?

Because it's not the plan. The plan's not to get kept. You already know what it means to get kept.

"Here's the thing," he said. "Me and you, Jacqi, we got something in common, know what I mean? All those people out there"—pointing with the flask—"they need us. Need us to hate. They hate me because I refused to buckle under. I refused to cave. I was stronger than they were, until, you know. And they hate you because . . ." He turned to look at her. "Well, you tell me."

I got tired, she thought, tired of proving I deserved to live.

"Nothing the losers would love to see more," he said, "than to watch us dig our own graves. So they can push us in. I'm not sticking around for that. You shouldn't either." He reached up and gently stroked her chin with his thumb. "So what d'ya say?"

"Can I think it over?"

"I leave next week." He took back his hand. "And what's to think over? You like selling your cooze? Just another corner cunt."

"Don't talk to me like that." The tiny gold hummingbird quivered against her breastbone. "It's not polite."

He smiled like he couldn't believe she'd say such a thing, and yet his eyes warmed. "Sure," he said. "My apologies."

"It's just that I'm saving for something."

"Yeah?" Flicker of mirth in his eyes. "Saving for what?"

"Something important. To me."

"Don't tell me it's a sex change."

Oh, you wit. "Yeah. I'm getting neutered."

"You want money." Nodding, like he should've seen it coming. "Not enough I offer you a safe place, roof over your head, food in your belly."

"That's not it. Look, don't get mad, okay?"

"You're shaking me down."

"I'm not—no, no."

"I'm trying to be a nice guy here."

"Stop, okay? It's just . . ." She stuffed her hands in her hair as her voice trailed away. She swallowed. It felt like a rabbit's foot lodged in her throat. School, she thought. Tell him it's for school. "I'm just saving for something, okay?"

"So you want, what, an allowance?" He stood up from the bed. "Pocket money, mad money. And once you've saved up a nice tidy nut, what then? 'Tough luck, sucker. Adios.' That how you show your gratitude?"

"I just asked if I could think about it."

"Sure. Yeah. Do that. I'll think about it too."

From inside his jacket his cell went off. He patted his pockets, searching out the hum, found it, pulled out the phone. He read the text he'd just received, eyes hardening. "You sorry fucks . . ."

Slapping the phone closed, stuffing it back in his pocket, he spotted his reflection in the mirror over the desk and ran his hands through his bristly hair, tightened the knot of his tie. Looking for his hat, finding it. "I gotta go."

"What's wrong?"

"Nothing's wrong, I just gotta be somewhere."

"Is this those same guys from back east?"

He'd taken a call once before when they were together and gone into a mood like this. A couple of union *jefes* from DC had come out here to monitor the bankruptcy and they were hammering him over something.

He snapped his head toward her. "What was that?"

31

"I just wondered—"

"Look at me." He waited till she glanced up, then locked on her eyes. "Let's get one thing straight. Whenever we're together, whatever gets said, if it don't involve you and me?" He ticked his finger back and forth. "You forget about it. Never happened."

Then don't tell me, she thought, but just murmured, "Okay." Unconsciously, she'd started knocking her knees together, then crossed her legs to make it stop, a whisper of nylon from her tights. "So you wanna rain-check on tonight?"

Patting his pockets for his keys. "Yeah, sure, whatever."

"And what about the room here?"

"It's paid through till morning. Spend the night, you want."

"You coming back?"

"No!" Like he was sick of her, done with her. Pest. Then just as quick, the eyes warmed again, a hint of regret. "What's tonight, Tuesday? I'm all booked up tomorrow but I'll call you Thursday morning, I'm wide open then, we'll go out, have breakfast. Talk about what we just talked about. You coming down. Visalia."

Once he was gone, she went to the curtains and looked out the window to make sure he made it to his car okay. The storm was already blowing in. Date palms lining the hotel grounds, lit from below, rattled and swayed in the wind.

Two men got out of a car. Verrazzo turned as they slammed their doors. They wore blues but didn't look much like firemen. They looked like muscle.

How did they know he was here?

The men converged. One guy crossed his arms and held back, the other got up in Verrazzo's grill, spearing a finger into his chest. Jacqi glanced around the room for the phone, in case she needed to call down, get security out there, then turned back to the window and chewed away her lip gloss, watching the three men go at it.

They barked and snarled, toe-to-toe, till finally Verrazzo with his mitt-sized hand shoved Mr. Finger out of his face. The guy tumbled back like he'd been smacked by a wrecking ball, windmilling into his buddy, but just like that he caught his balance and charged forward again, fist clenched, arm cocked, till the buddy reached out and snagged him, wrapped him up and spun him away.

Some more gestures and yelling, spittled with hate, but no punches. Saving it for later, she thought, someplace else. Then as sudden as it started the thing broke up. The two sides parted, crowing at each other across the parking lot. Verrazzo dragged himself to his car, got in, the others did likewise. Then the screech of tires as they all drove off.

She was turning away from the window when another guy appeared, drifting into the frame like an afterthought—hooded sweatshirt, jeans, emerging from the shadows somewhere along the hotel's front. Like he'd been waiting out of sight.

He stopped at the edge of the parking lot, gazing at the cars as they tore off, like he was trying to memorize their taillights, then thumbed at his phone. So what's your story, she wondered, just as he turned and glanced up.

Like he knew exactly which room.

She stepped back quick from the window and crouched. Close the curtains, she thought—no, it'll just give you away. Feeling behind for the bed, she found it and perched on the edge, waiting for what felt like forever, expecting any minute to hear a fist at the door, pounding like a sledge, a voice demanding she open up.

And in time she did hear voices—a pair of men somewhere down the hall—so she crept to the door, pressed her ear to the wood, trying to catch words. She thought about peering through the fish-eye peephole but feared someone might be right outside, staring back. Then they'll know for sure you're here, she thought. And whatever they started with Verrazzo they'll finish with you.

She stood there, flush with the door, light-headed from taking shallow breaths and listening to the murmur of voices, then a pair of doors clattered open and promptly boomed shut. The voices trailed away.

She stood there a moment, wondering if that was that, when she felt it—an eerie silent presence, just outside. Only the door between them.

She stared at the door handle, expecting it to move—he'd test it, see if she'd left the thing ajar—but nothing. She considered reaching up, throwing the security latch, but again feared the telltale sound it would make, no matter how careful she tried to be. Meanwhile, that same strange gravity, the sense of another body inches away.

She closed her eyes, wishing it would go, thinking of a thousand ways to say it: please please please just leave.

In time she felt it, like a loosened grip. Whoever had been there drifted away.

She went back to the bed and sat on the edge, watching the digital clock on the desk blink through the minutes. It felt like a lifetime before she relaxed. Venturing up from the covers finally, she inched toward the window, peered out from the edge. Whoever the guy in the sweatshirt had been, he wasn't out there anymore either.

What now? Before hooking up with Fireman Mike she'd cleaned up at Bettye's, the hair salon where she'd been staying the past week, let in the cat for the night. Nothing to do on that front till morning. Why risk getting followed—or worse—just to go back to a strip of foam in the storage room?

It'd been a week since she'd left Casa de Crackhead, slept in an actual bed.

And despite all the extracurriculars, there was still a chance Fireman Mike might come back. One big moody dude. He might want company, everybody does, specially after a fight. If he did show up, she'd want to smooth things over, make peace.

Visalia. Just a temporary stopover. Or a major mistake. How to tell?

She got undressed. Clutching the hummingbird to her chest, she tucked herself between the sheets, so crisp against her skin they felt like paper. She was stuffed inside an envelope, a letter headed somewhere south.

5

Tierney's headlights carved a tunnel in the rain, the windshield hazed with fog. The clock on his dash read quarter past twelve—noon, not midnight—the storm front draping itself across the green coastal hills, shrouds of mist hazing the marshlands and the dull black gash of the river.

He slowed to the curb, smearing the wet glass with his hand, wipers a rhythmic thump and squeak as he peered out at the women huddled inside the bus shelter. Three of them—stomping their feet for warmth like ponies, clouds of breath veiling their faces.

One seemed ancient, rail thin, a comical black wig perched atop her head. Mattie, if he recalled the name right—Lonnie Bachmann had mentioned her—oldest woman working the streets in the North Bay, something of a local legend.

The second was thirtyish, hefty, big-thighed, raking her Afro with a pick.

He recognized the third with a twinge of grateful sadness, lowering the passenger-side window, waving her closer.

She leaned down, framed by the open window—raccoon eyeliner, neon lipstick, a glob of concealer lathered over a pimple on her chin.

She seemed thinner in heels and was going at a wad of gum like it'd hurt her feelings.

"Jacqi, hey. I heard you left the center. Thought I'd make sure you're okay."

She stood there frozen. Like he embodied some thoughtless mistake.

"Lousy day for being outside," he said. "Want to join me for coffee somewhere?"

She cheeked the gum, pushed the wet hair off her face. "How'd you find me?"

"It wasn't easy."

"She send you?"

"Nobody sent me. Lonnie told me what happened, yeah. She feels bad about it, feels like she let you down. But I'm here because of you, not her."

Fifty yards ahead a streetlight flashed red above the rain-swept intersection like a robot in distress, its copper wiring gutted by thieves. "That's nice, but you still gotta pay for my time." Her hands did a quick wet tom-tom on the windowsill—she was like a performance piece, part awkward teen, part juvie-hall hustler, part street pixie. "Twenty-five for lunch, fifty for dinner. Don't wanna eat in the car, room's on you."

How many ways, he thought, is this girl going to break my heart? "Sorry, that's not even close to happening."

"Then we got nothing to talk about." She straightened up, turned to go.

"Jacqi, you've violated a court order by leaving the center." Easy, he thought. Don't scold. "If the next car that stops has two guys from SCU inside? It's not going to be the catch-and-release you're used to. More like ninety days in county, minimum."

The city had finally scrabbled together enough money from federal and state grants to reassemble the Street Crimes Unit, which meant working girls and corner crews were back on the radar.

"If money's a problem we can talk about that. I don't want anything and I'm not paying for anything. But maybe I can help out if you're strapped." He leaned across the car, opened the door. "Come on," he said, "get in. Cup of coffee, lunch, whatever."

Jacqi shot sidelong glances at him as they drove back into Rio Mirada proper, trying to crack the code, figure out the real reason he'd come looking for her. Not that she minded his company.

The last joker on the scene had pulled up in a rust-bucket Dodge, seventy if he was a day, all wrinkles and bones, yelling out his lowered window, "I'm gonna tear that pussy *up!*" Only Mattie had the stomach for him, and she came back quick.

Tierney resembled an actual man, even if he was, in fact, Lonnie Bachmann's errand boy. He had the voice of a professor but the shoulders of a goalie and those eyes, Christ, malamute blue with sleepy lids. Reminded her of the kinda guy you see in a movie, not the star, the guy just beneath the star, the wily sidekick who takes a bullet for the home team and everybody cries.

He pulled into a parking lot just off the main drag, a place called Javarama—smart choice, she didn't get shunned like a leper here. The place offered a kind of homespun funk, free Wi-Fi, an oasis in the ghost town called downtown. He nosed the car against a wall of whitewashed brick and killed the engine.

"Look," she said, "before this goes anywhere, let's get something straight. If this is about me going back? Ain't gonna happen."

He sat there, rumpled and handsome and sad as a map. "I'm not sure that's wise."

"I've made other plans."

He nodded, like he was turning a page inside his head. "I'd like to hear about them," he said, jangling his keys from the ignition. "Your plans, I mean."

She felt the smile form slowly, wickedly on her lips. "Yeah? Well, gee. I'm not sure that's wise."

He chuckled, lifting his hip to stuff his keys in his pants pocket. "Well played."

"Look—"

"Know why I liked working with you? You not only got it, you enjoyed it. Most of the others, it's like thinking is physically painful. Don't tell them I said that."

"I'm not telling them anything—know why?"

"You've got promise. I don't want to see you backslide."

"It's not your problem."

"I don't think of you as a problem."

He sounded like he meant it. It scared her. "What's your story?"

"How do you mean?"

"We talked about it, me and Angelica especially. She's got, like, an apocalyptic crush on you—you know that, right? You're too smart, too good-looking, you dress too nice—no way you're just a *tutor*. So what's your story?"

He took way too long to answer. "I like tutoring."

"That's not what I asked."

Tierney already realized that she'd smell out anything short of honesty and use it as an excuse to blow him off. He also sensed she probably thought of honesty as the consummate sucker move and would blow him off regardless. Still, it was worth a shot.

"I was a lawyer in San Francisco for a while."

She chewed on that for a second. "How long's 'a while'?"

"About twenty years."

"That's a pretty stiff while."

The Honda's windows were dotted with rain and fogged from the warmth of their breath, but through the blur he watched a woman in an oilskin and wellies leash her black Lab to an iron table, then disappear inside the coffeehouse. The dog stared after her like if it concentrated hard enough he could make her come back quicker.

Jacqi said, "Were you any good? As a lawyer."

He smiled. "I spent a couple years right out of law school in the prosecutor's office in San Francisco and couldn't have been lousier at the job."

"How come?"

"I lack a killer instinct when it comes to putting poor people in jail."

That earned him a grin. "What about after? The next seventeen years."

The span of her lifetime, he realized. "I joined a firm that specialized in construction litigation."

"Any better at that?"

"The people who needed to know who I was, knew who I was."

She seemed vaguely impressed. "Huh."

He shrugged.

"So why'd you give it up?"

He looked out again through the misted window at the lonesome dog, ears pricked, waiting in the lousy weather. We're all dogs, he thought, we're all trying to figure out the mysterious creature at the other end of the leash, trusting in the simple logic of: if I give her what she wants, I deserve something back.

Go ahead, he thought. Tell her.

6

"Little over three years ago," Tierney said, "they found what they called a complex mass in my wife's ovary."

"You don't wear a ring." Jacqi nodded at his hand. "We all noticed, trust me."

"My wife didn't make it."

"Oh." She looked more chastened than sorry. "It's that kinda story."

"There's a test called a CA-125 that can help determine whether ovarian tumors are malignant or benign. The day the results were due I was in trial."

"That doesn't sound like you." She pulled her legs up under her, settling in for her story. "I mean, just from what I know."

"I was different then. And Roni, my wife, was okay with it. It was an important case."

"Important to who?"

Exactly, he thought. "My firm was defending a developer named Hank Kitson, major player, one of the three biggest builders west of Chicago. He'd slapped up a hundred oceanfront townhouses down in Half Moon Bay that were, to use the technical term, junk. Every time the wind blew they had another problem. Homeowners sued and the case should've settled—throw out a number, offer to mitigate, done. But Hank Kitson, he wasn't the kind of guy you told what to do. So-called self-made man. They're always the worst."

She seemed to enjoy that, and he felt a sudden wave of protectiveness toward her. She was still growing into her bones, and despite the tough-girl attitude a certain helplessness lingered in her face. Her eyes showed the strain of working hard not to be so young.

"So we march into trial hoping to turn catastrophe into mere disaster. The jury's not terrible and we're feeling mildly optimistic as plaintiffs start to put on their case. A construction expert for the homeowner's association, this empty suit from Phoenix, takes the stand and it's my job to destroy him on cross. He's halfway through his testimony when my cell goes off."

"Your wife," she guessed.

"If her CA-125 comes back under thirty we're in the clear, the thing's benign and they can scrape it out—debulking, they call it—chemo and radiation for good measure. Things suck for a while but life goes on. The text, though, just says: *Sixty-seven*."

"That's, like, bad—right?

"A death sentence. And I just sat there, numb, holding my phone."

Like I could make the number change, he thought, if I just stared hard enough.

"That sounds more like you," she said.

"Meanwhile plaintiffs counsel has wrapped up his direct and the expert's sitting there on the witness stand, twiddling his thumbs, waiting for me to stand up and start my cross. But I'm on the moon. Everybody's staring, including Kitson, who's planted on my left, fuming. Finally Larry Bohn, my second chair, pops up, asks for a recess. The judge looks at me, reads my face, and though trial's barely started we get our break."

The black Lab's owner reappeared from inside the coffeehouse and the dog shot up like a missile of joy, yipping and wagging its paws.

"In the attorney lounge Kitson wastes no time. He knew my situation, it was hardly a secret. He comes up, nose to my chin, says, 'I don't care if the bitch is on fire—in here, right now, your time belongs to me.'"

"What a scumbag." Jacqi tugged her legs a little closer. "Hope you decked him."

He sat there a moment, lost in the memory. "I broke his jaw in three places."

Her face lit up. "Get outta town."

"I'm not proud of it. Christ, I don't even remember it. One minute I'm smelling his breath and feeling his finger poking my tie and the next he's on the carpet, writhing around like he's trying to swim. My hand's clenched tight and it's throbbing like hell."

"Good for you."

"No. Not good. Yeah, I was pissed." He took a deep breath. "So what?"

"You had a right to be. Guy was a dick."

"It wasn't just him. I was pissed at fate and cancer and God, pissed at Roni for having to die, pissed at myself for not being there with her. And to the extent I was ticked off at the great Hank Kitson, it was largely because at that moment he was a perfect stand-in for everything I hated about my life."

He stared blankly through the hazy windshield at the white brick wall.

"Just a guess," she said, "but seems to me you were out of a job at that point?"

He chuckled. "Pretty much, yeah."

"You go to jail?"

"No. My firm worked that part out, plus the stuff with our E&O carrier, all that. I had other things to worry about. Like taking care of Roni, helping her die. By the time that was over I was pretty much in a perpetual daze."

A sudden gust of wind raked the car, a patter of rain.

Jacqi said, "Sounds like you really loved her."

Unfortunately, he thought, love doesn't cure cancer. "That I did."

"Why not go back to being a lawyer now?"

"My bar card's still in limbo. Ethics board tends to frown on clocking clients."

"So what do you do for money?"

He knew better than to go there with her. He'd help her out—he'd already offered—but she didn't need to know the rest. "I get by."

"Doing what?"

A wry smile. "I tutor wayward women." He glanced out at the low winter sky. "I'm about ready for some coffee. You?"

7

Jacqi felt a welcoming jolt as soon as they stepped inside, assaulted by the heady scents of nutmeg, espresso, candle wax, cheese. The café bustled lazily, lunch crowd, not the usual morning bunch, all those jittery gargoyles thumbing their gizmos. Jacqi ordered a double cap, Tierney a macchiato, and they moseyed back to a table in a paneled nook out of general earshot.

Lifting her napkin, she spat out her gum as daintily as possible, then emptied four packets of sugar into her cup, stirring until bitter and creamy and sweet all blended. Tierney watched her like she was giving a demonstration.

"Getting back to the subject of stories," he said, "I feel a bit foolish not knowing yours. It wasn't my place to pry, but still, I should have recognized your name at least."

Please God, she thought, don't go there. "I'm grateful you didn't. Made it easier for me. If I wanted to talk about all of that I'd be back at Winge-and-Holler House."

He smiled behind his cup. "Is that what you guys call it?"

"It's what I call it. The others, I dunno, probably think a winchinchala's some kinda mink."

"Would it really be so terrible, going back?"

She lifted a foamy spoonful to her lips, puckered and blew, like it was soup. Other people in the café were stealing glances—no surprise, given how she was dressed. And she was known here. One mope in particular—white kid in dreads, floppy Rastafarian hat—tried to hide his fascination by pounding away at his Mac.

I'm just so goddamn interesting, she thought. Like a parrot.

"You're in a stronger position than you realize," he said. "Lonnie knows she let you down."

"Had a wack way of showing it." She licked the foam off her spoon.

"She's willing to cut you some slack in the group sessions."

"Wow. That's white of her."

"You don't have to talk about what happened to you if you don't want. Just ease back into the routine, get off the street, catch your breath."

"That my problem? I'm short of breath?"

She whipped around, mad-dogged the wannabe Rastaman—sure enough, he was staring. He dropped his head, tippy-tapped on his keyboard.

Turning back, she offered Tierney a timid smile. *Maybe I can help out if you're strapped.* Hotshot lawyer fallen from grace—with a ghost on his back—but doing okay from the looks of him. Play this right, she thought, you might be able to hit him up for the whole nut, full ride to Playa Ventura. Meaning no more need to humor Fireman Mike and his dream of a detour to Visalia.

"How much do you know? About what happened, I mean. To me."

"Just what I've read."

"Which is?"

"Some stuff on the Internet." He drained his cup, set it down. "I took a look at your case file."

The hair on her neck stood on end. "You read the case file?"

"It's public record."

"Said like a lawyer."

"Former lawyer."

"Disrobed lawyer."

He smiled. "Disbarred, I think, is the word you're after. Though even that's not quite right. But point taken."

"You don't get it, that's why I liked you. You didn't know or didn't care and that made it easy for me. I could relax with you. Well, congratulations. No going back now."

"I wanted to understand—"

"You can't. You won't." She shot another glance toward the goof in dreads but he was too weaselly to get caught staring twice. "I told you already, it's not your problem."

"I'm not trying to box you in to anything. I just want to help."

"Yeah. I get that a lot."

"Look—"

"Know how a do-gooder says 'Fuck you'?"

He sat back and sighed. "You've made your point."

Not by a long shot, she thought. "I mean, if you and Lonnie don't like the idea of me being back on the clock, there's an easy fix. You wanna step up, help me out on the money front, like you said . . ."

Christ, she thought, could you have said it worse? Why not just roll him?

"We can work something out," he said, a bit more stiff than before. "I mean that. But, again, there's a court order involved, you can't just—"

"I told you already—I've made other plans."

"That won't square things with a judge."

"I'll be long gone before that becomes an issue."

He cocked his head slightly. "Gone where?"

"Someplace safe."

He nodded, not buying it. "Okay."

"You gonna help me or not?"

"That depends—gone where?"

"I need two thousand dollars."

His eyes tightened. "Really."

"Really."

"To disappear—where?"

She stared into her cup, turning it in its saucer, a little this way, then that, like she was working a combination. The magic door. To Mexico. "I'd rather not say."

"But you know the price to get there."

"I need some distance," she said. "More than anything. Someplace different."

"I can understand that."

She glanced up, tried to read him, tried to read his eyes, so coldly blue behind the half-mast lids. It dawned on her then just how much she wanted him to like her. "Meaning what, you'll help me out?"

"You're running away."

"I'm starting over."

"You sure about that?" He sounded vaguely fed up. "Nine times out of ten, people who run end up right back where they started. Ask Lonnie about it."

"Lonnie can drop dead."

"You're wrong about her."

"She had the most famous screw-up in town right there, palm of her hand. Turn me around, clean me up, oh man, gotta be some good ink in that. Pick up the phone, make some calls, hit up her donors—"

"That's what you think this is about?"

"You gonna help me or not?"

"To run away? No."

She felt like pitching her cup at his head. "I'm running *to* somewhere, not *from*."

"The way I see it? That's a distinction without a difference."

It's not so much to ask, she thought. Help me. Like me. "Then I guess we got nothing to talk about." She snatched up the napkin with her gum inside and pushed back her chair. Why couldn't she just grab his ankles, flip him over, shake till the money just dropped? "Good news? There's somebody else willing to step up. Not just talk about it."

"Someone with all the best intentions in the world, I'll bet." His voice was calm. It made the mockery worse. "Only wants what's best for you."

"He's more honest than that." She began to get up. "It's what I like about him."

Before she was out of her chair he pulled several sheets of notebook paper from his pocket. "You ever see this?" He unfolded the pages, set them down on the table near her cup. "I found it in your case file. It was sealed by the judge on his own motion, which is relatively rare. Usually one party or the other has to petition for that. But this is a letter and it's addressed to the judge and so I guess he just decided on his own—"

"If it was sealed, how'd you get it?"

Poker face. "Let's just say I borrowed it."

"And that's like, what, a crime?"

"That's not your problem. To borrow a phrase."

"A letter? Who from?"

"Victor Cope."

The chair seemed to tremble. In her mouth, a sour taste. "Why show it to me?"

"If the judge doesn't want it . . ."

She stared at the lined yellow pages, the spidery scrawl, the jagged edges where the paper had been torn from the tablet. "Did you read it?"

It seemed like forever before he answered. "Yes."

"And?"

"It's pretty much what you'd expect."

"Yeah? What would I expect?"

"It's a lot of self-serving nonsense, poor me, blah blah. My lawyer won't let me take the stand, the evidence is trumped up, the whole trial's a travesty."

"What's he say about me?" She barely got the words out.

"He said he picked you up hitchhiking—"

"That's a lie."

"I know it is, stay with me here. There was something else—"

"Oh, I bet."

"He said you told him a friend of your brother . . ." His voice trailed away. He swallowed nervously, then nudged the pages slowly toward her across the table. "You're entitled to your secrets."

He might as well have reached across the table and fished under her skirt.

"They're not my secrets."

"The point—"

"He's an *asshole*." She was shaking. Everybody but the yokel in dreads glanced over. "*Assholes* talk all sorts of shit. It's what makes them *assholes*."

"Let's say you don't quite make this great escape you're planning. Let's say you get picked up and thrown back inside instead. Maybe the judge changes his mind, he decides to unseal this. Yeah, the original's gone now, thanks to me, but I know enough about courts and courtrooms to know there's a copy tucked away somewhere. Imagine the press getting their hands on it."

"It isn't *true*."

"That doesn't matter." He tapped his fingertip against the pages. "It's just a little too specific. He didn't say your brother, he said a friend."

"You wanna believe some psycho pervert instead of me, then pretend you wanna help? You're an even bigger prick than he is."

"Who are you trying to protect?"

"Listen to me." She stood up, leaning into the table. "Victor Cope shoved me in his trunk, he took me to that house in the Santa Cruz hills—the one he'd scoped out, his love nest—he chained me up in the basement for three days. Not my brother, not some friend. Him. That's the story. If it's not good enough for you, Lonnie Bachmann, the bitches she herds over, Rastaboy over there, who-the-fuck-ever, it ain't my problem."

"Your mother says no one in the family's seen you in ages. Not her, not your brother. She didn't know you'd left Winchinchala House. You never talk to her. She figures you're living on the street, shacking up in squats—"

Backing up unsteadily, she muttered, "You and my mother can both go to hell."

The next thing she knew she was across the room and through the door. Outside in the rain she kicked off her shoes, grabbed one in each hand, and started to run.

8

She kept going till her lungs gave out. Hands on her knees, soaked to the skin, freezing cold, she half expected to see Tierney tooling up and down the wet streets in his foggy beater, trying to track her down, win her back, all "So sorry" and "Let's try this again."

That sealed it. When Fireman Mike got in touch she'd tell him straight up: Visalia? I'm in. Wherever the hell it is, middle of the desert, fine with me. Just get me outta here. Can't be gone soon enough.

The rain had softened into a needlelike mist, and she climbed the three cracked marble steps of the old Redman Hall to huddle in the coved entryway, out of the weather.

A letter, Christ, a goddamn letter—from Cope of all people—and Tierney, the simp, he not only steals the thing but thinks I want it, like it's some kinda gift, oh babe, just what I always wanted. Takes a special kind of genius to be that stupid.

She realized then that she'd left it behind, the letter, sitting on the table like a confession, at which point the rest of it hit. A friend of your brother—Jesus fucking hell, no, no—and like a spell the scent of gasoline and plums arose from somewhere inside. Sure he was strange and nobody's idea of a saint but he cared about you, liked you, brought you plums from a tree near the Citgo where he hung out, cleaning tools for pocket money, doing odd jobs for the mechanics. Made you feel that maybe, just maybe, life could be okay.

But then that door of your life slammed shut and the next one opened and there you were, a cinder-block cubbyhole, the space tall enough so the other guy, the one who took you, the scrawny meth-eyed troll, could sit in his old wood chair, gaze at you like you were a TV made out of skin and hair, hours of that, something almost ancient in the lack of personality. Tied your hands, chained one foot to the wall, gagged you but no blindfold and you knew what that meant, staring back into the emptiness of his face. Then he'd go away for a while, leave you alone with the dark red carpenter ants and the mildew, this one small green-and-black spider hovering in its stretchy swirl of a web, hazing a corner.

By the time she snapped to, the rain had stopped. She'd fallen asleep, or maybe it was one of her episodes. Every now and then, especially when she felt stressed, time opened up like a wound and she slipped inside, taking comfort in the empty warmth.

Blame Tierney for the stress, she thought. The flashbacks weren't exactly new, they'd started up again at Winchinchala House, all that badgering—*Own your story, bitch*—but she'd gone most of the week since leaving the place blotting it all out. One thing she'd learned: you wake the dark genie, good luck stuffing him back in the bottle.

• • •

Come six o'clock it was pouring again, the rain slanting almost sideways in the wind. She scampered door to door, getting drenched regardless, heading for the steamy glowing window with its arching letters:

BETTYE'S BEAUTY MECCA
BRAIDING AND LOCKING—WEAVES AND WIGS

Dripping wet, she ventured inside. Bettye stood at the cash register, thumbing through twenties, tens, fives, singles, tip of her tongue between her teeth.

Jacqi took a seat. In a quiet, shivery cold voice she said, "Hey."

Bettye glanced over her shoulder but said nothing, just dropped the cash in her bank bag, zipped it up, locked it, then stuffed her arms into her fur-collared coat and hiked it onto her back. Snapping open her purse, she checked that the .38 was handy—she'd been robbed twice, once at the bank, once walking out to her car—then turned to go, glancing up at the ceiling as she headed toward the door.

"Don't take forever cleaning up, turn these lights out quick. Lectric bill damn near killing me."

It took a little less than an hour, brushing off the swivel chairs, sweeping up the hair, binning it, then picking up the jars and bottles and boxes—Murray's Black Beeswax and Dr. Miracle's No-Lye Relaxer, Duke Wave Pomade and African Pride Miracle Sheen—dusting each one, putting it back, label facing out.

The heavy stench of chemicals lingered in the air and it conjured the memory again, gasoline and plums, but she told the ghost to go away and in time, as she focused on chores, it obliged.

Once done up front she switched off the lights, all but the one above the wash station. The sink and chair basked in the downward glow like a ghetto throne. Above it, a needlepoint message, framed in gold:

YOU CAN HAVE ANYTHING YOU WANT.
SO LONG AS YOU DON'T WANT WHAT YOU CAN'T HAVE.

She left the storeroom door ajar for the sake of the wash station light, then climbed to the top of the storage racks, farthest corner, checking her secret stash, counting it out, $193, same as last time, good.

Opening a tin of cat food, she spilled it onto a dish, set it down, and cracked open the back door, chains still in place. She glanced out the gap to check for skulkers lingering in the alley. "Snickers! Get your butt in here. Food. Now."

The old mouser showed up in his own time, squeezing his orange-furred fat through the opening. Jacqi slammed shut the door, bolted up, feeling at last almost safe.

The cat stared up at her, blinking, then lost interest and chowed down, hissing after every swallow. Jacqi gathered the rolled-up strip of foam from its shelf, untied it, laid it down, and collected the gauze-thin sheets, shook them out.

As always, not even thinking, she checked for spiders or ants.

He'd left her alone for hours in the cubbyhole that first night, his footsteps a drumbeat above her. She shook nonstop, nothing but a scratchy, musky blanket between her and the rough concrete floor. When he finally came back he brought saltines, skim milk, a tin of Spam, set the plate on the floor, pulled the gag out, held a knife to her neck.

She choked on the crackers and greasy, oversalted meat but ate, and before she could beg for her life the gag went back, and he just sat there, eyeing her, one smoke after another, that sad-sack weary bit, like it was so damn tiring, being him.

Looking away as he finally got on with the rest of it, she saw the busy trail of ants against the cinder-block wall, this quivering stream of constant motion, whereas the spider in the corner never moved. And she guessed that was the trick. In time she hovered there too, watching herself from above. There but not there.

9

Tierney sat perched at the kitchen table, poring through documents he'd copied, *People of California v. Victor Cope*, when from behind he heard the approach of padded footsteps, a long-limbed stride, and then Cass appeared, finger-raking her mad red hair. She was naked except for one of his button-down shirts and a pair of thick white socks, scrunched at the ankles.

She worked oncology at Rio Mirada General: Cassidy Montesano, OCN. They'd met when Roni was dying, though they hadn't hooked up until two years later. He'd wandered back to the cancer ward from the wilderness of his grief to pay his respects to the nursing staff finally, thank them. Cass took him for coffee and let him know she remembered him well, him and his lovely, unlucky wife. They were nearing their six-month anniversary now, his first real involvement since the funeral.

Snagging a plate of chicken from the fridge, she shouldered the door closed and headed for the table, calling to mind the high-school hoops star she'd been—muscling into the paint, boxing out for rebounds, the killer fadeaway. She nudged back a chair with her knee and dropped into it.

"I'm bored with what I'm reading." Crossing her ankles, she lifted her feet and nestled them in his lap. Legs like redwoods.

"Sorry to hear that." He'd recommended the book: James Conway's *Napa: The Story of an American Eden.* "What seems to be the problem?"

She lifted a chicken leg from its whitish aspic of cold jellied fat. The skin crackled as she bit down. "I can't keep the names straight," she said, chewing. "Hard to follow who's who."

"The rich and the white," he admitted, "do tend to blur together."

"'Where the niggaz at?'—to quote a much funnier story."

He smiled. Gary Shteyngart, *Absurdistan,* the last book he'd loaned her.

She fiddled her fingers at the roasted bird. "Help yourself, by the way."

"Thanks." He made no move for the plate. The shirt, unbuttoned to her navel, slid down toward one shoulder. It looks good on her, he thought, nice fit. They were exactly the same height. In heels, she was Queen Maeve.

"Came in here an hour ago, you were staring at those same sheets of paper."

He was holding Cope's letter, the one the judge had sealed, the one that had sent Jacqi off in the rain like a rocket. Seventeen years old. Same age Cass had been when she'd made all-state.

"I screwed up today," he said, setting the creased pages down. To himself: I got greedy for the truth.

"Ah," she said, licking her fingers. "That explains it."

"Explains what?"

"You seem, I dunno, distracted." She offered a warm but thin-lipped smile, waving her feet lazily in his lap. "Been that way a lot lately."

The dog made his appearance, drawn by the scent of food. Some kind of Airedale mix, wiry and smart but mellow, old now.

His musk preceded him and his approach was sling-backed, the tender thud of his paw pads, the tick-tock-tick of claws. Shortly his snout appeared tableside, the twitching black peach pit of a nose, hazy cataract eyes peeking through scruff, the bumming tail wag. Breath to kill a rat.

"What rough beast," Cass said, tearing off a sliver of meat, tossing it. The dog snapped, missed, snuffled around the floor, found it.

"My mother always warned me," he said, "about women who quote Yeats to their dogs."

"Yeah? My mother always warned me about guys who won't come to bed."

The dog's face reappeared. She tore off a larger chunk of meat, held it up. "This is the last tidbit, Noble. Lie down." A finger snap. "Go on." The dog obeyed, watchful, "tidbit" one of those words. She dropped the meat between his paws and he lingered over it, licking it like a wound.

Watching him, she took another nibble of her own, lifting her head back as she chewed, shivering the hair off her face. "It's just that, normally, the one thing I can count on between us, you know? The physical thing."

He reached over, edged his fingertip beneath a blackened scallop of chicken skin—maybe he'd have some after all. Feed the hungry ghost. Inwardly, he cringed: the *one* thing she can count on?

She said, "Ever since this thing with the girl—"

"Let's not blame her."

Nudging the plate forward. Tempting. "You found her, right? Talked to her."

"Finally, yeah."

"Figured out why she took off from the halfway house?"

"You're not jealous."

"Beats distracted. Maybe you should give it a try." She dropped the bone onto the plate, a small thudding chime. The dog looked up, attentive. "What I am, my dear, is lonely."

It was like gravity suddenly doubled in the room.

"There's no reason to feel lonely."

They moved from kitchen to bedroom, stripping off clothes, sliding into bed alongside each other. For a moment Tierney just lay there, looking at her. With a whiff of atonement to the exercise, he felt ready to go. And they say the age of irony is dead, he thought. Somebody tell my crotch.

Leaning in for a kiss, he smelled her hair, caught a faint scent of pepper and rosemary. She offered a low, luxuriating moan, kissing him back, taking her time before rolling from her back onto her side, offering her tush to spoon. He nestled in, palmed her breast, bit the meaty curve where neck and shoulder met in a crush of freckles.

She bent to his touch as her breathing deepened and she nudged back toward him—quivering a little, pleased when she discovered he was ready. Arching her back, she reached behind, took him in her hand and guided him in. Simple as that. Home.

Pressed together, they started rocking. He lifted his hand from her breast to her mouth and she took the heel of it between her teeth and bit down hard, gave it to him, gave him what he deserved, a flash of pain, punishing him for making her wait this long, work this hard, and the rhythm between them grew deeper, shorter, strong.

How odd we must look to the angels, he thought.

Teeth still gripping his hand she rocked harder, pushing herself back against the plow of his hips, then a full-body shiver, her hand splayed, telling him: stop.

A hiss of breath, not quite a whimper, eyes shut tight. A few sharp twitches. Aftershocks. Her jaw relaxed, he took back his hand—throbbing—rested it on her shoulder. Finally, she turned, scooped back her hair. A look of gratified wariness.

"You okay?" Always the nurse.

"I'm grand," he whispered, Lucky Charms brogue. "Fookin' brilliant."

Her red-brown lashes fluttered. "I'm sleepy."

"Me too."

She lay there a moment, warm as biscuits. He stroked her flank.

"She still seem as smart as she used to? When you were tutoring her, I mean."

Like that, the sudden sad gravity again.

"Cass, please." He set his chin on her shoulder. "Don't."

She studied him, eyelids mere slits, a glimmering dark stare. Her breath slowed. "You sure you're okay? You didn't—"

"I'm fine. I'm happy. Go to sleep."

Through the blur of a frantic dream, Jacqi caught the hum of her cell. A jolt of waking dread, like being yanked from a hiding place, but then she got her bearings. The cat lay curled and warm between her legs. Bettye's wash station light glowed in the open doorway.

Blinking, she rose from the foam pad, pushed back the sheet, felt around, and finally palmed the vibrating phone: a text. From Verrazzo.

Tomorrow morning, 9 AM, meet me downtown, the old Odd Fellows Hall on Cullmore. We'll have some breakfast. Talk.

Well well, she thought, smiling as she lay back down. Fireman Mike. You're gonna come to the rescue after all.

Cass lay there fast asleep, a toasty stretch of deadweight against his flank, while Tierney remained wide awake. A streetlamp's glow hazed the curtains, giving the room a wash of filmy light. A sycamore creaked in the wind outside.

Shortly the rain returned, hammering the roof, the windows. He pictured the Napa River Road, imagined the girl out there, teetering up coltishly in high heels to a pair of slowing headlights.

Garza, he thought: Spanish for heron, a power animal, symbol of fierce independence, a loner. A knack for taking advantage. The capacity to change when necessary.

Jacquelina Esperanza. Jacqi Hope. The girl whose secret is a lie.

Part II

10

She had him unzipped and halfway out when the first rock hit the windshield.

Fireman Mike, true to his word, had picked her up downtown at nine. He hadn't brought up Visalia, not yet, or even breakfast for that matter, focused instead on agenda item number one, her face in his lap, but she wasn't getting out of the car without talking all that through. The thought of sticking around this town even one more week made her so depressed she could barely see.

The second rock hit while he was stuffing the bad boy back in his pants. This one left a nasty hole, spider-web fissures in the windshield.

Glancing up, she spotted the source of the trouble: four of them, hoodies and baggy pants, flipping off Fireman Mike, stacking hand signs, hoots and fuck-yous. They stood just beyond a raggy, six-foot hedge, fifteen yards away. Maybe they'd been hiding there, watching the whole time.

Another rock. Whistling miss.

He cinched his belt: "Look what they did to my goddamn windshield."

So like him. *My* windshield. Car belonged to the city. But guys with size, everything was theirs.

"I bet you know these fucks," he said.

Actually, she did. Two anyway.

Mo Pete Carson, hat kicked sideways, fat and scary, squint-eyed and dumb. Acne so thick your own face hurt when you looked at him.

Damarlo Melendez—D-Low they called him—skulky and sad, like a kicked dog, but catch his act now. Off the leash, howling.

The other two?

One was a *cholo*, all scraggly stache and banger tat and busting a sag on his Dickies. Sleek dude, like a razor, and that's when the name came to her: Chepe Salgado.

The fourth guy was tall, coffee-colored, that's all she could see, his face buried in shadow from the hood of his sweatshirt.

Misfit bunch, no gang ties binding them—if anything, they should've been at each other's necks. Strange, really, their being together like this, no logic to it at all, nothing but the opportunity, fireman in his shiny red car, getting a wake-up knob job on a drizzly school day.

She'd told him, not so close to the corner, Christ, not so close to the school—but listen? Fireman Mike, Mighty Whitey—even with that ridiculous gash on his head from two nights before, courtesy of his drunken face-plant on the sidewalk—nobody runs him off. Watch and learn, boys and girls. Behold Goliath.

Verrazzo threw open the car door and bulled toward the circle of rock tossers.

"Which one of you shitbirds pitched the rock hit my windshield?" He reached out, went to yank the hood off Damarlo's head but D-Lo ducked away. "Come on, you don't have to think about it—who?"

God, he had a voice. Tough as they pretended to be, the boys shrank back a little, like the guy was a wall of heat. Mike Verrazzo— Sicilian, not Italian, he'd told her once. One more thing to swagger about.

More kids came drifting through the yards, across the train tracks, up from the corner, down from campus, a dozen or more mulling forward, another dozen behind them, swarming from between the sad little houses and collecting beneath the elms and live oaks and chinaberry trees arching over the one-block street—shuffling little homies with backpacks, pierced girls in cornrows cradling their books, black and brown and trailer trash—responding to tweets and texts to check it out, fireman getting blown in his car by guess who, or just drawn by the catcalls and the flow, the laughing bodies.

How, she thought, gnawing at her lip, am I gonna get outta here?

For the most part the crowd gathered on the backside of the fight. She still had the same fifteen yards between her and most of the onlookers. Go on, she thought, crack open the door, slink away, if not now, when?

Then something out there clicked, like a thrown switch. She saw it in Mo Pete's eyes first, glowing with hate, then Chepe's. Finally the gaunt one she didn't recognize stepped forward and launched a haymaker from outer space.

Verrazzo, she thought, he called somebody a porch monkey, nacho nigger, fudge nudger. Something.

He took the punch like a drunk's kiss, grabbed the kid's wrist, bent it back, twisted. Kung Fu fireman. Like that could save him.

The gaunt kid howled, buckling, and the other three just stared.

Then another switch flipped.

The four newfound road dogs snapped to, rallied, jumped on Fireman Mike, circling fast, a blur of kicks, fists—

Wham to the lower back.

Thwack to the knees.

Pow to the back of the head.

Verrazzo gave back as good as he got, for a while anyway. Then one savage punch from Chepe, up under the rib cage—*boom*, like that, Fireman Mike keeled sideways, hobble-kneed. It left him wide open, and sad dog Damarlo wound up for a free kick to the jellies.

Even as far away as she was—bunkered inside the car, safe behind the windshield glass—she winced at the impact.

Verrazzo closed up like a knife, dropping to the asphalt.

D-Lo jigged and pranced, arms high: score!

The onlookers circled in tight now, screaming, egging the fighters on: *Light him up! Make him pay! Fuck him good!* Boys mostly, but a few girls too. Other girls stood in tight little knots, rolling their eyes, playing too good for all this, like it was some new clip on YouTube, not a ratpacked man right there.

I should honk the horn, she thought, get out there, do something. They're gonna kill him.

A lone guy drifted past the car from behind. Hoodie like the others but wrong style jeans and worn too high. Work boots, not kicks. How old, she couldn't tell. A slouch in his walk, ambling quick to where Verrazzo lay curled up on the ground.

The loner dropped to one knee, untucked his hands from the sweatshirt pouch. The rest wasn't real clear, the guy blocking her view with his back. Maybe he grabbed Mike's collar and shook, maybe he got in a few good licks, she couldn't tell. Either way, the crowd went nuts, hoots and cackles and cheers.

If you're gonna leave, she thought, do it now. Too stupid from shock to move.

The stranger got back to his feet, tottering a little. His whole body shuddered, like a current running through him had shorted out.

Mo Pete stood there, staring at Verrazzo, like a hole had opened up in the street, ready to swallow them all. Whatever he saw, it scared him so bad he turned around fast, pushed past Chepe and started to run.

All eyes turned toward Mo Pete then, the chunky big man pushing past anyone in his way and damn near losing his hat as he fled. After that, it rippled through the crowd, like a pulse—mutters and curses, finally screams—bodies scattered, pinwheeling every which way, down the tunnel of oaks and elms and chinaberry trees, back between the shabby houses, pushing through gaps in the fences or scrambling over, making for the railroad tracks and beyond—hoodrats and *cholos* and hangers-on, even girls in heels. Some, still, were laughing.

Verrazzo began thrashing on the ground, grabbing his neck with one hand, the other flailing around like he was drowning.

Get out of the goddamn car, she told herself, help him, finally reaching for the handle and yanking—the door was locked.

The loner stepped back from Verrazzo as the big man kept pitching back and forth in the street, then the guy pivoted, stuffed his hands back in his sweatshirt pouch and lurched back the way he'd come.

Through the spider-web cracks in the windshield, his eyes locked with Jacqi's.

For a second she recognized the emptiness, the savage lonely punk nada. Then it came to her. The other night, at the hotel, the stranger who showed up at the end of the fight, drifting out of the shadows—this guy?

With that, her own switch clicked.

The cool gold hummingbird quivered at her breastbone, she was shaking, but she finally managed to unlock the car door, got out, stood up, shouted. "What the fuck you do?" Her voice sounding strange and small and far off. "Answer me, asshole—what the fuck did you *do*?"

The guy glanced once her direction—the face still not clicking into recognition, long and bag-eyed and older than the rest of him, bony and thin-lipped—and for a second he hesitated and she thought to herself: Yeah, come on, finish it. But instead he just shuddered again, some invisible hand grabbing him by the neck, and he tucked himself down and kept moving.

It was raining now, a wind-driven mist, that metal smell.

Jacqi ran, knelt down in the damp street and pushed her hair back, turned Verrazzo toward her slow—he'd stopped thrashing around and now lay utterly still except for a kind of feverish trembling.

His eyes hovered in their sockets, pale and lifeless, like sick fish. His skin had turned a waxy blue-gray and a curdle of blood flecked his teeth as his whitish lips pursed around an absent breath. Several new gashes joined the one from two nights ago and a deep florid bruise marbled his throat, like some awful birthmark.

She started digging through pockets for his cell. "You're strong," she said, "strongest fucker I know, hang tough, come on." She found the phone, thumbed in 911. Dispatch came on, a woman. "Somebody here got jumped, Goldenrod, the cul-de-sac up from the Pay-N-Go on—"

The telltale beep in a blizzard of hiss. "Your name, please."

"He's Mike Verrazzo, fireman, you know who I mean. He's hurt bad."

"I need your name, miss—"

Jacqi thumbed off, dropping the phone like she'd been scalded. It clattered against the damp pavement.

"They'll be here soon." She took his hand, the thick palm heavy with calloues, icy, damp. "Can't stick around, Mike." Thinking of another voice, another time, her bearded Samaritan in the El Camino, the Santa Cruz hills. *I need you to forget me.*

His grip clenched, not hard. A tic. Then he launched into one last seizure—locking up, shaking so hard he inched across the blacktop like death was rousting him out of a deep sleep. The sleep called his life.

11

"I told you before," the woman said, fretted by shadow beyond the screen, "I haven't seen her, I don't know where she is."

A voice that could frost the lawn, Tierney thought: Nina Garza, late thirties, maybe older, raven-black hair in a wedge cut, part on the side, the face an impressive cage of angles, like you'd cut yourself going in for a kiss. Which apparently didn't bother the man standing behind her, buttoning his cuffs.

"I'm sorry if I bothered you the other night," Tierney said, "and I'm sorry to bother you now. I'm just concerned that if Jacqi doesn't come back to Winchinchala soon, something unfortunate—"

"I remember what you said." Behind her, like an usher, the man cleared his throat. She refused to turn, an almost imperial calm, tinged with disdain. Queen of Mars. "Now please remember what I said: she's not here."

"Could she be staying with her brother—Richie, right?"

A faint recoil, like who was he to say out loud the name of her son. "I don't know how else to say it—I don't know where she is. Are we through here?"

"Is there a problem?" The man stepped forward finally, a deft glide, easing the woman back from the door. Not tall, just compact, strong, wearing a violet shirt, pleated gray slacks, his thinning dark hair combed back.

"Mr. Garza?" Playing dumb. Tierney knew where to find Joe Garza.

The guy was still fussing with his cuffs. "What's your name?"

"Here." Reaching into his sport-coat pocket. "Let me give you a card."

"I didn't ask for a card. I asked your name."

Out of sight behind the door, Nina Garza let out an oceanic sigh.

"Tierney. Phelan Tierney."

Across the street, some Mortimer in an old Le Mans cranked the V-8 cold and revved it hard. Hillbilly tune-up.

The man at the door waited for the noise to die down, his face broad and flat, etched with worry lines but bright from a fresh shave, dark eyes bedded in folds of skin. A knot of cartilage creased the bridge of his nose.

"Okay. Phelan." The man smiled, like the name told him everything. "As I understand it, you've explained what the situation is. We appreciate that. It's the family's problem now. We'll take care of things from here."

"I'm sorry, I'm still unclear on who you—"

"Don't get clever." The man's smile turned strangely warm, as though he could respect a stranger with a devious streak. Another place, another time they'd share a drink, a raunchy joke, a slap on the shoulder that was secretly a dare. He stepped back, started to close the door.

"Look, I know I'm a pest," Tierney said, "but I really have Jacqi's best interests at heart. All I'm asking—if she gets in touch, have her call me. I need to talk with her."

"What you need," the man said, nothing but a voice now, a hash-marked silhouette beyond the screen, "is to pay attention to what I told you."

"If you shut me out, the only thing you'll guarantee is that in a few days or weeks it'll be the police standing here. If Jacqi's lucky, that is. I'm not so sure she hasn't used up her luck."

The man eased forward toward the screen, his features discernible again behind the mesh. "Know what I think? You talk when you oughta listen."

"Yeah. I get that a lot."

"From where I'm standing? Not often enough."

"Look, no offense, but I need to ask—are you the reason she doesn't live here anymore?"

He'd realized finally there was nothing to lose. These people weren't going to help except by ruse or accident. One rule he'd come to live by working in the law: never sacrifice the client on the altar of civility. And yes, he supposed Jacqi had become a kind of client. More than that. So shake the tree, he thought, shake it hard.

"I mean, if things were great on the home front, she'd come around, right? But she doesn't come around. She does everything in her power *not* to come around. Know how I learned that? I listened. To her mother right there, behind the door. Two nights ago when I spoke to her the first time."

He expected another burdened sigh from the shadows but none came. The man's gaze narrowed, like he was peering through Tierney's eyes to the back of his skull. It caused the knot of cartilage fusing his eyebrows to bulge a little more, like a knuckle.

"I'm not doing this to make a point," Tierney said. "She's never coming back here. We all know that. If you care as much as you say, you'll help me out. Talk to me."

Up the street, three kids in slickers, skipping school, trudged uphill beneath a canopy of rain-wet cottonwoods and laughed, pointing fingers, a listless shove.

"You're right," the man said. The cagey smile turned businesslike. His voice was calm. "Jacquelina, she's a troubled kid. Who wouldn't be with all she went through? And like you say, she's probably not coming back here, except—who knows? You wanna pin that on me, hey, have at it. Could be, though, you're missing a big piece of the puzzle."

Behind the door, Nina Garza coughed.

"That's kinda my point," Tierney said, thinking: Just keep him talking. "I'm missing something. I know that."

"You have yourself a real nice day."

The door shut a lot more gently than Tierney expected, but that didn't change much except the thud.

12

Jacqi stood at the end of the cul-de-sac, near a gash in the chain-link fence, an easy getaway over the railroad tracks and across the soccer field in the rain—but she wasn't too clear on how she'd gotten there. Maybe she'd had another one of her episodes, second in two days, which sucked. She hadn't had one in a while. Now all this.

Once again, she thought, I'm here but I'm not here.

She imagined herself back at Mike's side, kneeling in the street, brushing the hair off his face. Face of a guy she'd kinda grown to like. Face of a guy who walked into burning squats and dragged out the losers inside. Saved old folks in the Casa Mirada fire. And once, jaws of life and the whole bit, flipped car up on Hillcrest Road, smoke and flames and the mother hanging dead in her harness behind the wheel—he reached in, backseat, saved the little girl.

Not me, though, she thought. Never quite got around to saving me.

Most guys don't want you looking at them, they do you from behind or bend you over their crotch or some creeps even wrap a T-shirt around your head, right before they pound the crap out of you. Mike liked being looked at. Sure, as a kid, he was probably an ugly lump of a dude, teased by girls, mocked by boys. It turned him into a brawler. Pretty much stayed that way, she supposed. And the people in his life, from his enemies to his buddies to the women he didn't pay for, they saw what they wanted to see, his bull-like attitude, his cage-fighter smarts.

But I was the one who actually looked at him.

A pair of squad cars came howling up, first one then another real quick, gumballs flashing in the hazy drizzle. Two cops ran straight to Mike, one dropping down to his knees on the pavement at Mike's side, the other leaning over right behind.

She heard the spectral wail of more sirens careening in from all directions, getting close. The paramedics would roll up soon and take him away, and she pictured herself riding along in the ambulance. She'd cradle his face in her hand—*I'm the one who looks at you*—let him know: I'm here.

But she wasn't. She wasn't anywhere. She'd seen that scared hateful emptiness in his eyes and it was like a pair of hands reached out of the sky, pitched her down into that sneaky gap in time, the crazy nightmare fissure in the world she'd first discovered ten years ago. The day she became famous.

Tierney took out his phone as he walked to the curb outside Nina Garza's house, sneaking a picture of the Lincoln in the drive. Once he got behind the wheel of his Honda he pulled up the image, enlarged it till he could make out the numerals on the license. Memorized the sequence, hit speed dial.

Racheline, the receptionist, came on the line, quick as a hiccup, New Zealand accent. "Matafeo and Associates."

"Hello, happiness. Caffeinated yet?"

"If it isn't my favorite fella—Phelan! I trust you're well."

O she will sing the savageness out of a bear.

"I was just instructed to have a real nice day. I'm doing my best. You?"

A chuckle gauzed in a sigh. "Not quite peachy but pert near plum, as my dear dead nana was wont to say."

"Dead nanas do say the darnedest things." He leaned over the console, glanced back through the droplets on his passenger-side window at the small tidy house. California Craftsman, low-pitched gabled roof with overhanging eaves, transomed windows. The very picture of working-class rectitude, even in the rain. What are Mrs. Garza and Mr. Knuckle-Nose talking about in there, he wondered. Arguing over. Deciding.

He glanced at his watch, then told Racheline, "I'd like you to run a plate for me, my dear. Assuming Mr. Matafeo approves."

The paramedics came, tumbling out of their ambulance and onto the street to work their magic. A moment or two of fussing, some business with the jaw, then they hoisted Fireman Mike onto the gurney, slid him into the ambulance, and it took a moment or two, longer than Jacqi expected, but finally it pulled away, swirling red strobe, the siren only kicking in once they got around the corner.

Meanwhile one cop started with the scroll of yellow tape, marking off the scene like an animal pen, another directed traffic at the intersection. A third, some kind of sergeant maybe, pointed another two toward the houses on either side of the street and those two started working their way up the cul-de-sac, knocking on doors, talking to anyone dumb enough not to pretend they weren't home.

Even from this distance, she recognized a few of the officers, ones who'd arrested or hassled her, names a blur.

And no doubt they'll know me, she thought. What would she tell them once they figured out it was her in the car?

I was with him, yeah. We're, like, lovers. He was taking me with him to Visalia. He's done with his greedy slob of a wife—bet you didn't know that—nothing left but the movers and the paperwork. He's gonna sneak me onto his dental plan, major medical too, set up a little fund, my education, name me in his will, put me up in his tricked-out condo. Lightning strike me down, I'm lying. Gonna have me look after the place, weed the flower beds, sweep the patio, toss the junk mail. Come dinnertime I'll order us some Filipino takeout—he's crazy for *lumpia*, bet you didn't know that either—then I'll put on a lacy dress and gauzy white stockings so he can fuck me like a bride.

She licked her lips, wet from rain, and they tasted like greasy metal. A vibration stirred in her pocket, the telltale hum, and she took out her phone. A text:

Yr so-called tutor showed up again. Who is he really? If he bothers us one more time—

She snapped the phone closed, dropped it back in her pocket. Like I can do jack about it, Mother.

Both had coffee, neither drank.

He should've been gone by now, things to attend to, the casino guys from Thunder River to meet, work out a deal on the cash machines. But this nonsense with the girl, Jacquelina. Bad enough she was out there half-cocked, now they were coming for her. The hump at the door. Tutor my ass.

"Nina," he said, "I've told you hundreds of times. The things you've been through. Woulda broke most women straight down the middle." He traced the edge of his cup with a fingertip. "Not you. You stayed strong."

He sat across the table from her—minuscule kitchen, original tile, art-deco pink and green. Kinda place you expected to find somebody's grandmother. Nina wouldn't move. Sentimental, if that was the word. Stubborn, more like.

"Put your whole heart and soul on the line for that girl. But what's it gotten you?"

Stare a hole right through the woman, he thought, still she wouldn't look up. It'd come to that between them.

Quietly, she said, "I don't need you to tell me what I've done or not done."

He sat back. The woman could test the patience of a stone.

"Fine. You wanna take offense, your privilege. All I'm saying, I've seen it, I've been here, I know. But it's outta your hands now."

She glanced up, finally, and quick. Eyes like onyx. "What's out of my hands?"

"You know what I'm saying. No shame in it. She's messed up in the head. Totally understandable. But not acceptable."

"What," she said, "is out of my hands?"

"This doesn't affect just you. I'm in this just as much, more maybe. I'm not her old man, okay, I get that, but in everything but blood I've been the one who's stepped up. That means I have a say."

Her eyes dropped to her cup again. "When have I ever denied you a 'say'?"

Let it go, he thought. "Kid's like a bottle rocket, and that mouth. Just no way to be sure which way she'll go. She could say anything, just to get even with you. With me."

The business card lay on the table between them, a bad luck charm, nothing but a name, a PO box, a phone number. Phelan Tierney, what kinda name was that? Smacked of the chummy-and-clubby set—prep school, yachts and ponies and welcome to my vineyard—but the guy was built like somebody's sparring partner and he talked like a judge. Or a cop. Tell him "No," he hears "Try harder."

"I know some people out of town," he said, "people we can trust. Run a private school up outside Chico, about ten miles south of Mount Shasta, near the casino. She'll like it up there. Let them knock some sense into her head, teach her some manners."

"You think I haven't tried to teach her manners?"

"You got nothing to feel guilty about, Nina. But it's time for me to step in here. Past time, maybe. And if that's the case I apologize. Irregardless, what's it gonna be?"

From somewhere in the kitchen he caught a whiff of mold, fruit going bad in the basket over on the counter maybe. The one wrong note in the whole house. Including you know who. Day off from work, still she'd put on a white blouse, pencil skirt, stockings. Makeup like an etching. Woman didn't know the meaning of take-it-easy. That was the problem.

"Nina?"

She let out a ragged breath. "If you'd stop talking, I could think."

Couple years ago, he woulda backhanded her for that. Now he just felt tired.

"Have I not been good to you? Your kids? Joe, even."

He reached across the table and cupped her cheek and after a second, finally, she met his eyes. How many thousands of miles farther I gotta reach, he wondered, to touch what I want?

Three engine crews pulled up, two pumpers and a hook-and-ladder, firemen spilling out of them like paratroopers over a drop zone, then four more black-and-whites arrived, misery lights carving up the drizzled grayness. The street swarmed with cops and firemen charging around or huddling up, a show of force, solidarity, hail the fallen comrade—practically every uniformed mope in the city on the scene, plus a handful of mucky-mucks: mayor, couple council members, whoever the stubby guy in the trench coat was.

I need to find a good hide, Jacqi thought, grab my stuff from Bettye's, track down somebody willing to tuck me way. Christ, who?

She clung to the fence one-handed, fingers twined in the chain-link, soaked through now. Her hair clung to her face and neck. Do it, she thought. Take off. The cops going door-to-door edged closer to the end of the cul-de-sac, one glanced up her way.

But that wasn't what nailed her in place.

Distance didn't matter. He stood out—plainclothes, skinnier than she remembered but unmistakable, know him anywhere—fighting through the crowd to duck inside the tape, checking in with the sergeant on scene, making notes, a pat on the shoulder, then heading off toward the corner mini-mart.

Ten years, memory like a stab in the mind.

Skellenger.

He'd seemed a little kinder than his partner, but kindness is a trick—Christ, even Cope knew that—maybe the oldest trick of all. Sat beside her in the examination room, the hospital in Santa Cruz, asked her how she liked the cocoa, gave her a packet of Fig Newtons, adjusted the blanket around her shoulders. Smiled that fatherly fuck-you-up smile cops are born with.

Take your time, he said. But I need to know what he did to you.

What was she supposed to tell him? I was there, but I wasn't there.

13

Dim light washed down from the mini-mart's dusty fluorescents, one of them near the back flickering like a dying thought.

Skellenger, gloved up, dug through a cardboard box containing the behind-the-counter trash: crumpled pop cans, candy wrappers, used coffee filters thick with damp grounds, and a white takeout tub mulched with boiled cabbage, rich as a nursing-home fart.

A few feet away, Rahim Salaam, the storekeeper, watched from a folding chair, hands knotted into a single fist that he pounded softly against his chin. His beetle-browed eyes were dark but soulless, his smile a habit learned from an unhappy man.

"That was all there, I tell you, when I came this morning. All of it. You have questions, ask DeMontel, night shift."

Do yourself a favor, Skellenger thought, and stop. Sure enough, deep within the crud, the shiny telltale disk glistened. He felt pissed off and sad and lucky, finding it—how stupid does this chucklehead think we are?

The man must have waited too long, he thought, devil on one shoulder, angel the other, only getting the nerve to make his move once the squad cars pulled up outside, then too scared to haul the trash out to one of the bins around back, afraid he'd get made.

"Looks to me we have a decision to make here, Mr. Salaam."

The habit of a smile stiffened. The blank eyes fled further back into their emptiness. "Those criminals are my customers—understand? Every day, three o'clock. One half buys so the others can steal."

Amazing, Skellenger thought, how quickly an accent can fade. Not to mention the oily rectitude and deference that come with it. "I can bag this as is. Or it's possible this is all a mistake, it really was in the tray all along."

Hennessey, one of his uniforms, stood at the door, nobody in or out.

"Do you even listen? You want that disk, fine, good. Hey, good citizen, we love America. And the news comes on the TV, everybody sees, all those kids. See their faces maybe. And they know it was me, this store, with the camera. Think they're scared of me? Of you? How long before they show up? How long till, like you, they just come behind the counter, drag me out? Douse me with gas from my own pump, strike a match. You have what, with the bankruptcy, maybe eighty cops now. Used to be one-fifty. You'll protect me?"

A clipped, bitter chuckle. He dug deep at his eyes, rubbing hard.

"I'd like to take a look at this, Mr. Rahim."

Skellenger dropped the disk into its tray, pushed the load button, and waited for the outside feed to flicker off, the play function to take over. Once it did he maneuvered through, checking the time stamp till he found his way to shortly before the 911 call came in. He thumbed the tracking till he found the moment Verrazzo left the car, then went back a little more.

The Mercy of the Night

Reaching up behind the tails of his sport coat, he lodged his hands deep into the back pockets of his slacks, feeling bone where his ass used to be—he could barely remember what an appetite felt like, luxury from a forgotten time, the era of money and mucho OT, full staffing and happiness—gazing up at the monitor.

The image was grainy and distant and rough. But it is what it is, he thought, and it's all we've got. For now. The dead-end street seemed even drearier in the harsh black and white, the houses low-slung and drab, patched roofs and rusty gutters, stucco speckled with mold.

It was hard to tell where exactly the first group of kids came from. Suddenly they were just there, coming out from behind a wall-like hedge, pointing down the street. Four of them, saggy pants and hoodies, one in Raiders gear. And no sign of Verrazzo, just the RMFD Crown Vic, the kids ten to twenty yards away, huddled near the curb, stealing glances and thumbing at their phones.

He made a mental note: Get those numbers, track those calls.

Then one of the four picked up a rock, a knuckleball heave, direct hit, the windshield. That got them going. The others started pitching stones too. Meanwhile stragglers shuffled up here and there, through the fence near the rail bed at the cul-de-sac's far end. Others drifted in through the yards, between the houses.

Finally Verrazzo made his grand entrance, charging out of the car, plowing forward, and Skellenger couldn't help but think: You deserve what you got, you miserable prick.

Who else would bull-rush four dickheads all but screaming their gang colors as more and more other kids crowd around? How exactly was this supposed to end well?

Old Rahim was right, the force was down to almost nothing, ten cars on day shift patrolling the whole city. Now this. Mayweather, the watch commander, had already called out not just to the guys off duty but to neighboring cities too, manpower needed. Now. This case would bleed them dry, work every cop in the city to the bone, and for what? An arrogant ass-clown who didn't have the sense to let something go.

Verrazzo had been the one to dig in, lasso the unions together, push the city to the brink—dare the council to file for bankruptcy, thinking it was just one more round of chicken. Told his members: the city's lying, the general fund may be dry but they're hiding money in other accounts, they've got assets they can liquidate, land they can sell, they can honor our goddamn contract or face the wrath of God. Meaning him.

Even as the cops got smart, cut themselves loose and struck their own deal with the city, Verrazzo pushed on. Armed with some grand jury revelations about financial mismanagement—city hall filching from the sanitation department to keep the general fund afloat, borrowing from the water district to pave streets, shelling out millions to buy property for a solar panel farm that went nowhere, all culminating in five years of rigged books to make it look like the city was solvent—Verrazzo sweet-talked the IBEW into following him into the breach. God only knew why they agreed.

Donny Bauserman, head of the IBEW, always seemed better equipped to hang in somebody else's backdraft than take the lead, and Verrazzo told him there was no way they'd lose.

Finally the bankruptcy judge laid it out as plain as he could to all concerned: I'm about to rule on whether the city can void your contracts. And one side or the other is really, really not going to like the way things turn out. Not just you. This is federal court. My decision will have repercussions far beyond this case. Sit down, talk, work it out.

But Verrazzo had bullied the mayor, the council, the city manager for so long, mocked them, pussified them, outmaneuvered them, he became blind to the future. After so many years of ruling the roost he couldn't imagine this time might be different. He'd risen to the top with one credo: Hang Tough, Fight Rough. Why back down now?

Realistically, nobody knew for sure how the judge would rule. But when he did and the decision went against the unions, voiding their CBAs, it was like the floor disappeared. Everybody cashing a muni paycheck from here to Miami knew Verrazzo's name and either looked up to him like a figurehead, the union movement's John Brown, or hated him, not casually but with a special vengeance, knowing he'd made all of their wage and benefit packages nothing but smoke and a handshake. Cities wouldn't tumble into bankruptcy in a giddy rush, but it wasn't unthinkable anymore, either. The proof: Stockton, San Bernardino, Detroit. Mike Verrazzo had erased the future.

The firefighters cobbled together a contract they could live with—early retirements and transfers for the older guys, layoffs for some others, two-tier wage and bennies, the new guys getting pummeled—while the IBEW, with Bauserman at the lead, got told by the city the sad and bitter truth: last man standing gets screwed the worst.

Sure the fire crews took it in the teeth, but it was nothing compared to the pipe job delivered to Bauserman's guys, the carpenters, electricians, maintenance crews who actually made the city run. They had to carve four million a year off their payload to the city, which meant a bloodbath: layoffs, givebacks, hiring freeze.

Meanwhile the cops, even with the early deal they struck, still had to gut the force to half its former strength, sacrificing staffing to keep wage and bennie levels worth the bother, at least for the time being. Guarantees were nil. Crime had jacked up with fewer bodies to deal with it, and the foreclosure mess just compounded the problem, turning the city into a magnet for dirtbags—what the policy wonks prosaically called an Area of Opportunity. Stress had transitioned from occupational hazard to modus operandi—guys were chasing Xanax with vodka in their squad cars, and don't even mention ye olde home life.

That was Mike Verrazzo's legacy. Arrogant didn't come close, really. Now this. Taken out by a pack of teenage nitwits. Oh, the poetry.

14

"Hail Freedonia," Hennessey said, edging up behind Skellenger as he watched the video.

"Remind me, that's . . ."

"*Duck Soup.*" Hennessey sniffed at the freshened stench of cabbage and coffee wafting up from the trash basket. "Best of the bunch, except for maybe *Horse Feathers.*"

It was a running gag with him, comparing the day-to-day madness in the city with a Marx Brothers bit.

"Freedonia," Skellenger said, "that's the country that goes bankrupt, right?"

"Due to the Honorable Rufus T. Firefly. That fucking perfect or what?"

Hennessey had no more use for Verrazzo than anyone else on the force. Skellenger had little doubt the wisecrack would spread—he could hear it now in the locker room, shouted aisle to aisle: Who killed Rufus T. Firefly?

They watched the blurry screen as words went back and forth between Verrazzo and the hoodrats, some long-armed shoving, schoolyard stuff. Then the tall skinny kid on the right struck out, sidearm whiplash punch, lucky to land, followed by a feint and counterpunch from Verrazzo, dropping the kid hard, a bit of cringing from the others, then more barking, a swing here, a dodge there, Verrazo with his arms up like a boxer, protecting his head, a crushing punch landing underneath the rib cage and finally a circling, hammering flurry of blows until the four of them got Verrazzo down on the pavement and started to kick the living Jesus out of him.

"That's Mo Pete Carson, fat one on the left." Hennessey's hand appeared over Skellenger's shoulder, pointing at the screen. "Pretty sure."

"Javon Carson's brother?"

"Cousin, I think. Both of them Cutties, though, from Brickyard. I tagged this goof last year, knife fight at the Bump Room, Juneteenth, had a personal stash of Skittles in his pocket, Triple Stack Superman tabs. Should still be on parole for that. We've got free rein, search and seizure."

"What about these three?" Skellenger reached up, tapped the screen. "Recognize any of them?"

In the corner of his eye, he saw Rahim Salaam pretending not to pay attention.

Hennessey said, "Guys in SCU will, I bet. Could get lucky."

Let's hope so, Skellenger thought, thinking through how he'd phone it in to Mayweather. One assailant possibly identified, Mo Pete Carson, parolee, check gang log for legal name, affiliated with the Brickyard Cutthroat Killas, a.k.a. Cutties, prior arrest for assault and battery and possession of MDMA—Skittles, as the tablets were known, Triple Stack Superman a particularly popular brand, known for the signature S and shield on each pale blue hit.

Meanwhile Verrazzo's pounding went on. He lay there curled up, fetal fight position, shielding his head and crotch, smart man. The ordeal looked more painful than deadly, at least until a loner in a hoodie drifted in from the lower left edge of the screen.

A hulking lean to his walk, shoulders clenched, a deliberate pace, not quick. Like a stray nosing forward.

Hennessey—a soft, down-drifting sigh: "Fuck me. Who the hell's that?"

No sooner did he get the words out than the guy knelt down in the street beside Verrazzo and did something hard to see, sudden quick movements, head area. Shake him? Hit him?

Then the guy stood up, looking wobbly. That quick, everything changed.

Mo Pete Carson, Cutthroat Killa, fled like a girl. Everybody else took off right after.

"I'm never having kids," Hennessey murmured.

Wise man, Skellenger thought. This opened the whole damn mess wide open again. The four buffoons who'd started it hadn't finished it—apparently, maybe. Either way, if somebody didn't ID this DON—Dude Outta Nowhere—he became a stand-in for the thousands and thousands of unnamed souls who had every good reason to want Mike Verrazzo dead. Line them up from here to the moon. Even if these first four got nailed, dragged into court, put before a jury, they could always point to the empty chair. Look at the video, their lawyers would say: *Who's this?*

The suspects had just become limitless. In a town where resources were damn near nil.

Then the weird thing happened.

The DON was lurching back the way he'd come when a girl shot out of the car. Skellenger hadn't even noticed a second somebody in there—hard to tell, picture quality what it was. And not just any girl.

"That's Jacqi Garza," Hennessey said.

Skellenger shrugged. A flicker of dread rat-lined up his backbone. "Kinda hard to tell."

"No. I mean, I'm pretty damn sure. I've booked her twice. Jesus, what am I telling you for? You worked that case."

A smoke, Skellenger thought, just one. Scotch rocks. Someplace dark and quiet. What he wouldn't give. "Ten years ago, yeah."

"Jesus. I knew Verrazzo was a pussy hound, but this is new."

"Seriously, Sean?" Skellenger palmed a signal, *Keep it down*, glancing back at the storekeeper—Rahim Salaam wasn't bothering to feign oblivion anymore, he sat there riveted. "And let's not jump to conclusions, okay?"

She was going off on the guy, screaming like only she could—Girl with the Dragon Wazoo, her handle in the squad room—and as the young man turned her direction you could, for just an instant, almost make out his face.

Skellenger hit the pause button, peered in close. The guy'd tethered the hood of his sweatshirt too tight. Blow it up, maybe they'd get something.

Talk about wishful thinking.

No mistaking her, though, not now. Use the zoom, get the tech squad to enhance it, there'd be no doubt. Only a matter of time before the press caught wind of it, and betcha-gosh-golly-wow, wouldn't that be a story.

Outside, through the glass, he could see the ever-growing crowd, suits and overcoats, uniforms and umbrellas—police chief, fire chief, the mayor, council members, Alice Hazelton from the DA's office—plus a bunch of looky-loos drifting out of nearby shops. And damn near every fireman in the city. If it'd been a cop who'd bitten it, they would have had snipers on the roof.

The first of the TV crews was setting up too—a windblown blond in a raincoat gripping a microphone, the red Crown Vic in the background, Corporal Rusty Medaglia hunched inside with his powder and brush and cellophane tape, lifting prints.

Little doubt whose latents we'll get, Skellenger thought. The girl's sight line was clear, close enough to nail the stranger's face straight on, his hood not an issue from that angle. Rio Mirada's most famous witness. Again. Details at eleven.

Lucky us. Lucky me.

Hennessey softly clucked his tongue. "Bet my tin on it. That's goddamn Jacqi Garza."

15

Atop a narrow stair, stenciled lettering arched across vintage frosted glass:

MATAFEO & ASSOCIATES
GRADY MATAFEO, MANAGING OWNER

Tierney entered quietly. Racheline—humming to herself, back to the door and pitcher in hand—busied herself watering Grady's vast array of South Seas flora: wax-leafed crotons, feathery aralias, possum tail ferns.

"Did you get a chance to run that plate I asked for?"

She flinched and spun around. He expected a smile, would have begged for a wink. Instead she scooted behind her desk and sat, tucking her hands beneath her skirt.

"I believe you need to take that up with Mr. Matafeo."

No one called Grady "Mr. Matafeo" except strangers, fellow Pacific Islanders hoping for a favor, or people he frightened.

Tierney sighed. The girl was refreshingly wholesome—bright blue smile, deep red soul—plus that New Zealand accent that charmed every living thing. "Sorry if I caused you any trouble."

Tierney took his time, ambling down the wainscoted hall, admiring the wall art: to one side, a collection of Tongan tapa mats, intricately patterned, tastefully framed; on the opposite wall a series of hand-carved Maori *koruru*, ritual masks of eerie godlike menace. At the last office he stopped, knuckling the doorframe. "Room for one more?"

Every surface in the room sat covered in dusty stuff, to where it looked like an eccentric landfill. Grady rocked in his swivel chair behind his desk—pockmarked face, stately paunch, ponytail a bright black sheen—reading a deposition transcript the size of a suburban phone book. He'd worn one of his cowboy shirts today, deep blue with pearl buttons and white piping, plus his sharkskin roach killers.

The Samoan Six-Gun. Yippy-o-ki-a-lua.

Grady marked his place, then tossed the deposition onto his desk. "Why the sudden interest in Pete Navarette?"

Tierney removed a stack of case files in Smead folders from a plump leather chair, dusted the cushion and sat. "I don't know who that is."

"You had Racheline run his plate, yeah?"

"Ah." Tierney recalled the Lincoln parked in the rain. "You mean the curious gent I encountered this morning at Nina Garza's house."

Grady squinted meaningfully. "Run that by me again?"

"I told you I'm trying to help Lonnie Bachmann locate Jacqi Garza."

"Yeah, and that's on your letterhead, not mine."

Grady had convinced Tierney to obtain his own investigator's license, so he could contract out to anyone he pleased, given his hot-and-cold interest in work. The process proved disarmingly simple—having passed the bar exam a lifetime ago, he'd satisfied all experience requirements, and no one seemed to care about his bar card being in purgatory. As for the PI test itself, it proved to be the most nerve-rackingly boneheaded thing he'd ever sat through, a gift to the ungifted—ex-cops, mall militia, borderline simians—so they wouldn't humiliate themselves and flunk.

"It's not an investigation," he said. "It's a favor."

"You ran a plate. On my account."

"Bill me. I'll reimburse you. I'm not seeing the problem."

"If I'm gonna get linked to what you're doing, I'd like to know a little about it beforehand. Getting back to which—"

"I went to the mother's house this morning," Tierney said. "Jacqi's mother. It would appear she has a special friend. Not just that, he acts like he speaks for the family. I thought it might be wise to know his name. That's it."

Grady sat back and laced his fingers across his midriff, rocking gently. "Navarette's boning Nina Garza?"

"A gentleman never tells. But so I surmised. There something I should know?"

Grady was a kind of local savant and folk historian, at least in matters of crime. A gentrified roughneck from the Bay Vista projects who refused to discuss his life between the ages of twelve and twenty, Grady for years had been one of just a handful of North Bay investigators devoted to criminal defense work. Not only did he not shy away from gang cases, he embraced them, clear across the racial spectrum—Nazi Low Riders, Baymont Wet Crew, Southtown Krazy Raza, 415 Kumi, even FAIM, the Family-Affiliated Irish Mafia. Up here in the sleepy North Bay, all a prosecutor had to do was whisper that one word, "gang," and he could clock his conviction. Grady, to his credit, saw the evil in that. It was one of several reasons Tierney enjoyed his company.

"How much do you know," Grady said, "about Jacqi Garza's dad?"

Tierney recounted what he'd gleaned from his reading. "I understand he's in prison. There a link with Navarette?"

Grady shrugged. "Pete's an old-school dude, *veterano*, runs that restaurant north of town—Todo's? Supposedly scrubs a lot of *norteño* swag, but the hammer's never come down. Silent partner in a couple card rooms, too, same rumors there. They tried snitches, undercover, wiretaps. He's a very clever cat. Throws money at the Police Activities League, chips in big whenever a cop takes a bullet."

"No offense, but you lost me. The link to Joe Garza . . ."

"There was talk Navarette bankrolled the DeMartini thing."

"The jewelry store robbery."

"Then he circled the lawyers, made sure nobody rolled up on him, which took some doing, given how lousy it went. Paid everybody's legal fees, put a little bit aside for the families—mom, pop, wifey, the kids, even an *abuela* or two. Sent a message. I'll take care of things. Or, you know, we'll go the other way."

Tierney remembered the man at the door, buttoning his cuffs, so unfazed, so matter-of-fact. The kind of man who doesn't make threats. "There was something about him, about him and the mother together, couldn't put my finger on it. I just got the sense he's a big reason Jacqi never comes home anymore."

Grady chuckled. "The guy maybe responsible for your dad being in the joint's now playing hide the cassava with your mom—yeah, that might make the evening meal a bit tense." He lifted a briarwood pipe from its stand on his desk, tapped out the spent tobacco in an ashtray. "Mind if I ask a question?"

Tierney resisted a sigh. "Depends on the question, I suppose."

"Why are you so obsessed with Jacqi Garza?"

From the floor below, faint but clear, Tierney heard a familiar descending progression of chords from a well-tuned piano. Ms. Lovely in Leotards, the ash-blond bohemian divorcée who rented the studio space from Grady, gave lessons in the mornings, but this didn't sound like a student. The playing was lyrical and confident, with deft precision in the pedal release, a haunting gentle pulse in the left hand: Chopin, the E minor prelude. One of Roni's favorites.

He said, "I wouldn't say obsessed."

"People with obsessions never do. Should see your face when you talk about her."

Tierney wondered what Cass would make of that, then suddenly Racheline was there, drumming her nails against the doorframe, directing a penitent gaze toward Grady. "Excuse me, but you wanted me to remind you." She waved a message slip. "Telephone conference in ten minutes." She tiptoed forward like a balletic fawn, set the message down amid the desk clutter, then fled.

Tierney wondered if the message was a hoax. Old trick: you have a call.

"I'm just concerned about her," he said. "Jacqi Garza, I mean."

Grady squinted at the message slip. "You getting paid?"

"I told you. It's a favor."

That prompted a knowing smile. "Look. Maybe you think there's a different Jacqi Garza buried inside the Tasmanian she-devil everybody hates."

"I tutored her, remember? She was never that way with me." Until yesterday, he thought.

"You got lucky, trust me. Things I've heard—"

"Grady—"

"Permit me my lofty quote of the day. 'The doer is a fiction attached to the deed.'" He inspected the bowl of his pipe. "Jacqi Garza is what she does, and for most of the past eight years or so what she's done is pick fights, party hard, turn twists, and bite every goddamn hand that comes within a country mile. It's sad, given what happened to her. But it's not really your problem, yeah?"

How to explain it, Tierney thought. Maybe obsession wasn't off point, but he sensed something else as well, and it wasn't just the dirge from the studio below that made him feel that way.

About a year ago, he'd had a kind of revelation while thumbing through a magazine—an article on Caravaggio's *Supper at Emmaus*. It discussed the medieval lore of the Unrecognized Christ, the stranger who appears out of nowhere and offers unexpected comfort or hope, only to reveal his divine identity at the end: the young man in the white robe who greets Mary Magdalene at Christ's tomb. The traveler who joins two humble workmen from Emmaus on the long road home. And as soon as he'd read that, he thought: Roni was my Unrecognized Christ.

She'd appeared out of nowhere one day in Napa, down the bar at the Verasa Hotel, fussing with her cowl neck and reading Anna Akhmatova, and he'd known, somehow, that he couldn't turn away. He had to meet her. Had to invite her into his threadbare life. And everything changed.

The message was simple and terrifying: anyone you met could end the world and announce another. Anyone you met could reveal herself to be the very person who could save you. Maybe it was presumptuous to think he was the person to tell the girl her life didn't need to be the way it was—okay, sure, it was presumptuous—but it was also true that if anyone could use a change of direction, it was Jacqi Garza. If only he could gain her trust, prove he deserved it. Then again, for all he knew she'd be the one rescuing him.

None of which was the kind of thing you told a man like Grady.

Tierney stood up, shook out the crease in his slacks. "I will take what you said under advisement, Mr. Matafeo."

"Thank you, Your Honor." Grady reached for the phone, punched in a number, then pressed the receiver against his trendy cowpoke shirt. "You want work, by the way, I've got plenty, and not just stringer stuff. I like the thought of you gainfully occupied."

"Fine, sure." Tierney turned to go. "I'll stop back later, we'll talk it through."

"In the meantime, I'd keep my distance from the likes of Pete Navarette, yeah? That's a problem you want no part of, trust me."

16

"These are the best I have."

Nina Garza slid four snapshots across the tabletop—a booth in a small back room at Todo's, closed off for privacy. Navarette's men—Ben Escalada, the small one, and Hector Mancinas, *el bruto*—collected the pictures like some puzzling form of money, spread them out, studied them.

In the background, beyond the thin walls, the restaurant staff shifted over from breakfast to lunch—from the dining room, the click of flatware hitting starched cloth and the flap of fresh napkins; from the kitchen, the hammering chop of cleavers on cutting boards, the gong-like clamor of the steam table trays getting pulled for their change-of-shift washing.

"Which one's most new," the small one asked.

She pointed—the one from the girl's *quinceañera*, held at a country club in St. Helena. A hundred guests, four-star caterer, mariachis bussed in from San Jose. Such a disaster. The girl disappeared with three of her hideous friends, came back loaded on pills, drank herself sick, they had to send everyone home. Humiliating. And then trying to clean her up, that beautiful dress, all that satin brocade. The things the girl said.

Said? You mean screamed. Hissed. Like an animal.

The small one glanced up. "Like, how recent is this one?"

"Two years ago, almost three. She was fifteen."

"Not so recent." He turned the picture a little, as though a different angle might make it newer. "It's hard to make out her face."

"I told you, they're the best I have." She snapped shut her purse. "My daughter doesn't like her picture taken."

Not by you. Not anymore.

"It's okay. I mean, Hector and me, we've met her, you know? Here at the restaurant. These are for the other guys."

Escalada collected the photographs, shuffled them, tapped them against the tabletop, then tucked them away. Always trying so hard, she thought, this one. Typical. Small men, so afraid they won't be taken seriously. Whereas the big one, he was afraid he was always a step behind. Because he was.

"Mr. Navarette, he's told us to make it happen, no matter how many men we need. We'll find her."

She pictured a pack of unleashed dogs circling a feral cat. "All right. Thank you."

"I promise you, we won't—how to put this . . ." Escalada tapped his fingers against the tabletop, cheap rings clattering against the laminate. "She'll be okay."

Nina took a sip from the tumbler of ice water resting at her elbow. "My daughter will not be 'okay,'" she said, "until you have brought her to me. I know what you're saying, and I appreciate it. But don't fool yourself. She will do nothing to help you and a great deal to make your job impossible. I sense you are capable. I'm grateful. But let's be clear. Nothing you do to her—nothing—could possibly be worse than what will happen if she's allowed to go on the way she has."

The small one's face knotted up for a second, like he'd just been given permission for the impermissible—and he understood he'd never really be forgiven, if it came to that, no matter how well he performed.

Outside, in the parking lot, someone leaned on his horn. A pickup roared to life.

He pursed his mouth and nodded. "I appreciate you saying that."

Left alone, Nina leaned back into the corner of the booth and shut her eyes. The way you talk about that girl, she thought. People will think you're heartless.

People will say what they want no matter what. Besides, I said nothing, compared to all I could.

I've done everything I know to protect her. As a girl, always in the clouds, so easy to fool. That's why she was taken. And yes, I hate her for that. I know what she went through was beyond true hell and yes, one way or another, sooner or later, it's always the mother to blame. But there are girls who've been through worse. *Mucho, mi amor.* Get some perspective. Appreciate the fact you escaped, it's over. The world doesn't owe you anything because you've suffered. Everyone suffers. Open your eyes.

You don't desert your men—your father, your brother, the man who puts food on your table. The world has no pity, and sometimes men do what they must for the sake of their pride. Pride is the money of the soul. Strip a man of that, what then?

Nothing is given, you have to take, or watch it get taken from you. Not understanding that, thinking what you want matters, thinking the truth matters, that's the one unforgivable sin. What you think is the truth cannot be the truth and that ends the discussion. Your truth will destroy everything and everyone. You have to be strong and put aside your own wishes, grow up.

You think that creature who took you ruined your life? Three days, he had you. Try to think about what an entire life of being a prisoner feels like. Because that's what being poor is. And women who lose hold of their men wind up poor. There is no different world to live in. This is it.

The door reopened. Navarette ventured in. "I thought I'd check in on you."

From the scaffold of her face, she erected a smile. "That's kind."

He slid into the booth across from her. As always he'd rolled up his sleeves, left open his collar, revealing the thick arms, the bearish chest, reeking of cologne.

He said, "Try not to worry."

She bit back a miserable laugh. "Thank you."

"Ben and the others, they know their work. They'll find her. Bring her home."

"Yes. They assured me."

He reached across the table, took her hand. She let him.

"Stop punishing yourself. You have nothing to feel guilty about."

If only he'd stop talking, she thought. If only he never spoke again.

"It's called being a mother."

He smiled, as though what she'd said was the saddest, bravest thing. "When this is taken care of," he said, "when she's away in school and safe and under control." He squeezed her hand, lifted it to his lips. "When there's no more worries, we should take a trip. Get away."

Yes, she thought. Away. Where they take your money and let you live.

"I doubt I can take the time off work."

"Of course you can. I'll arrange it."

Outside, from a pen on the neighboring property, chained dogs were barking nonstop. She crafted a docile smile. "As you wish, *mi amor*."

Part III

17

Outside the ER entrance, vans from the local TV stations disgorged a scrum of busybodies, shouldering cameras or bracketing them onto tripods, uncoiling cable, setting up the light boxes. Time to tell the world: Mighty Mike Verrazzo is dead. Absolute last thing I want, Jacqi thought, is a microphone shoved in my face.

Easing up soggily from her chair, she stepped around the *vieja* with her scalded foot, murmuring to the woman, *"Con permiso, señora, buena suerte,"* then headed for the long white tunneling hallway, past the reception desk, deeper into the hospital.

She'd been shivering on and off so long it felt normal. The soles of her shoes chafed the endless linoleum and her wet clothes sagged. At the same time she felt strangely weightless, as though muscle and bone had turned to breath.

No matter how hard she fought them, memories kept boiling up from that night at the hospital in Santa Cruz, after she got away from Cope.

The intake nurse photographed the cigarette burns on her skin before dabbing ointment on them, then checked for shock and dehydration and hypothermia.

They called in a special nurse after that, one certified for sexual assault, to handle the rape kit.

Her name was Polly Bell and she was strong like a tennis player and strawberry blond with a firebird tattoo on the back of one hand. She had a soft husky voice, asking twice if she was pronouncing Jacquelina right, then continued murmuring reassurances in that same throaty alto as she went about her business.

She combed Jacqi's pubic area, furrowing the few downy strands of hair she had—early developer, in every way—hoping for a stray from Cope, then sealed the comb inside a plastic bag. Next she inspected Jacqi's arms, her chest, her back, her legs for blood or semen, using a special lamp, dabbing a couple places with moist gauze pads and sealing those away as well, jotting notes. That rough voice, the strong smile, her knowing hands—Jacqi, feeling both numb and on the verge of being sick, came within an inch of asking if she had a little sister, if not . . .

"This next part might hurt a little," Polly Bell said.

She needed hair samples and they had to be plucked, not cut, first the head, then between the legs. And it did hurt, but not bad. It wasn't the pain anyway. It was the shame of it, being naked and messed up and a pointless chore, a thing you had to probe and poke and catalog.

Next came the swabs, long as sparklers, that Polly used to take samples from deep inside, followed by the shiny speculum, lubed with saline, to check Jacqi's hymen. What to do? She almost blacked out, so scared, thinking: Tell the truth? Lie? Say nothing? Would even a nurse turn away in disgust once she found out what really happened: *There's something I need to tell you. About this boy we call Eastwood.*

As it turned out none of that mattered. Skellenger and his partner, Daddy-o, waltzed in. And everything changed.

. . .

She'd half expected to see Skellenger here, wandering around some-where, but maybe coming to the hospital wasn't part of the routine. No rush. The dead don't answer many questions.

She passed another long corridor all but identical to the one she was walking—how did you not get lost in here?—and spotted midway down the hall a crowd spilling out of a room, some of the men in firefighter blues, a few cops in the mix as well, some snoots in suits. A hushed urgency in the faces.

That's where he is, she thought. A sudden shock of sad longing. Poor old Fireman Mike. The man who said we were two of a kind, the kind people love to hate. And yet look at the crowd. Nobody knows you when you're down and out but, hey, everybody's your pal once you're dead. Bet the Wicked Wife of the West is in there too, sobbing away. Or maybe she'll save that for her close-up.

"Looking for somebody?"

She jumped and spun and Skellenger stood there, hands stuck in his back pockets, sport jacket pushed back at the hips, revealing the shield on his hip, his holstered weapon. Eerie, seeing him right there after just thinking about him. Like her mind had made him happen.

Why couldn't her mind make him not happen?

"Who says I'm doing anything?"

He looked unhealthy, way thinner than she remembered. Something in his face made her think of an empty house.

He glanced up and down the corridor, smiled and nodded at a passing nurse's aide, then took Jacqi's arm, not rough, and nodded toward a door. "We should talk."

"What's wrong with out here?"

"Humor me, okay?"

"I don't owe you."

"Look, this isn't the time—"

"Right, right. That's what Daddy-o always said. Your pal."

"It's Daddeo," Skellenger said. "And he was my partner, not my pal."

"Sue me. When *is* it the right time—ever?"

He squared himself, looking tired. Long day already. It was just past noon.

"There was a security camera at the gas station," he said, "at the corner of the cul-de-sac. It caught it all, the Verrazzo thing." Said like it was a scandal, *the Verrazzo thing.*

She swallowed a ball of air big as an egg.

"Pretty soon that video's gonna hit the news—we won't be able to sit on it forever—and then the questions start. I'm trying to help you here."

"That's another thing Daddy-o always said."

She meant it meaner than it came out, her voice weak. A camera. Of course. How could there not be a camera?

He found an empty room, gestured Jacqi in. She considered running, but where?

18

Skellenger closed the door quietly behind her. Two empty beds, neatly made.

"We're looking at a real mess here."

Jacqi said, "Who's 'we'?"

"This thing's gonna spin off in every goddamn direction you can name unless we put a lid on it quick. Your name comes up, that won't happen."

"Tough luck for you."

"Me? I wasn't the one working a twist in that car."

Like that, her face felt hot. "Go to hell—I'm clean, six months."

"Good for you. Like that's the issue, but good for you. Look. Once your name's out there, everybody in the world is gonna be looking for you. Understand?"

"I can handle the press."

"Maybe so. But you're not eight anymore. 'Whatever happened to little Jacquelina Garza?' There's a story. You're gonna end up the poster child for: ten years later—wow, bummer." His eyes softened a little. "It'll be a goddamn zoo. Way worse than before. You stood up once. I'm not gonna make you do it again."

"Such a nice guy."

"I'm trying to be, yeah."

"You're just scared I'll tell what really happened. You know. With Cope."

The soft eyes turned hard again and sank a little deeper into his face. "I've got nothing to be worried about."

"Oh yeah?"

"There was another girl out there, at least one, maybe alive."

"No, I get it, believe me."

"We had a duty to her, to her family."

"No duty to me."

"We nailed Cope, didn't we?"

"Thanks to who?"

"There were other girls at risk."

"*I* was at risk."

"You were safe at that point."

"No I wasn't, I told you. But you needed me. And here we are again. Say what you want, but I know why we're here."

"I'm trying to protect you."

She couldn't help herself—that was funny—and lowering her head she laughed. He didn't say anything, and when she glanced back up whatever had seemed comical wasn't anymore. Gotta give him credit, she thought, he's got the stare. Cop eyes. Cope eyes.

"So what happens if I agree? You gonna give me a Get Out of Hell Free card? Little late for that."

"Look, I'm sorry for what you went through, and I'm sorry it didn't work out for you after, but I'd say the blame on that lies elsewhere, wouldn't you?"

"You're so weak."

"Yeah? You wait until your name's out there again. You think the nightly news'll give a damn? How about every blowhard blogger and self-anointed genius on the web? You want to read the comment threads? Okay, I'm weak. But I'm not your problem."

A soft knock, the door opened—one of the janitors, a Sikh in scrubs with that prow of a turban, the soft black scraggly beard. He nosed in, garbage bag in hand, chestnut skin and the darkest eyes, bottomless. Jacqi wanted to dive in, vanish, hold her breath at the bottom of those eyes. But he was the one who disappeared—an apology, all murmur and birdsong accent.

Skellenger took out a notepad and pen, thumbed the plunger, clicked the tip into place. "Help me out, I'll help you."

She leaned back, rested her weight against the door. "Jesus—"

"I need names."

"I gave you names before. You had a chat with my mom, we came up with new ones."

"I told you, I'm sorry."

"And that just makes a world of difference, trust me."

"Who was the guy who walked up late out of nowhere? Came from the corner."

She thought back to the moment when they stood eye to eye in the street, the feeling he might be the same guy who'd been hanging around outside the hotel Tuesday night—and what about the two out-of-town firemen who'd ambushed Verrazzo in the parking lot? Maybe I should tell him that, she thought, throw him a bone, but what good would it do? Cops don't bring back the dead, and she had no stomach for the sideshow. She felt the sudden sense of puzzle pieces drifting together, a pattern slipping into place.

"I don't know who he is, never saw him before."

"Can you maybe describe him?"

Yeah, Jacqi thought, I suppose I could, conjuring the longish face with the tea-bag eyes, skinny lips, black hair. "I didn't get a good look."

"You stared straight at him."

She was shivering again. A camera, Christ. Talk about buzzard luck. "I was kinda out of my head at that point."

"How about race? A ballpark on his age."

"White guy. Early twenties, midtwenties, I dunno."

"Get a look at his hair? Eyes?"

"Yeah, yeah, I remember now. He had eyes. What d'you want? I wasn't focused on him. I wasn't focused on anything, I was out of it."

Skellenger tapped his pen against the notepad. "Who were the four guys who started it, the ones pitching rocks at the car?"

"Never seen them before."

"Stop lying. You don't need to be scared of those assholes."

"Oh yeah, way you guys chase your tail these days? And screw you, who says I'm lying?"

"Jacqi, you're thinking about this all wrong. I've got guys from Street Crimes poring over the security footage, trying to ID who was who. But it's blurry, far away."

"So how come you can make out me?"

"You're closer. And more familiar. Not just to me."

He waited for that to sink in. Yeah, she thought. Everybody knows who I am. Everybody and nobody.

"Look, help me out, then you can go wherever. I were you, I'd find someplace out of town. Wait this thing out."

"Great idea. Been my plan for a while now. But, you know, the whole money thing." She looked up into his sad hollow eyes. "How bad you want me to vanish?"

He cocked his head, like he thought she was shaking him down. Maybe she was.

"I'm supposed to be in rehab at Lonnie Bachmann's halfway house. I got tired of getting ragged on, I booked, but that's, like, some kinda violation of a court order."

Skellenger read her eyes, then prepared to write. "Who's the judge?"

"Stawicki. He's the one gave me diversion. He'll throw me back in for ninety days, maybe worse, I get caught out on the street. You'll fix it?"

"I can try." He thumbed his pen, click-click, nervous. "Give me something—"

"I told you—"

"The names of some of the kids at the scene. At least that. Maybe they'll step up."

A leaden weariness came over her. She almost felt like lying down in one of the crisp white beds. Go on, she thought. Give him something, make him go away.

She closed her eyes, tried to picture it. There were the twins, Symphony and Rhapsody, their surname a mouthful, DiGeronimo maybe? And Skeevy DeJuan and Toni Cake Face and Captain Emo and how many others she'd passed by briefly with her zombie-like stare in her fleeting appearances at the prison called school. She studied the impressions they conjured and in time a couple more names drifted up whole from memory, a kind of homeroom roll call of the mind, first one, then another. She murmured them to Skellenger, added a few bogus ones just to assert some control.

He wrote them all down, asked her to repeat them to be sure he'd gotten them right, then said, "Thank you," stuffing his notepad back inside his jacket pocket. "Look, like I said, even if I do everything to keep your name out of this, you are who you are and it makes a great story. In the event somebody does track you down, there's a way to play this so it's not so, I dunno, damaging, revealing. For you."

"You're a thoughtful guy—anybody ever tell you that?"

"You're kind of an open book. I've read the arrest reports. They're not flattering."

Strange, how dirty he could make her feel. "I told you, I'm not using. Besides, aren't those supposed to be sealed or something?" Like Cope's letter. Christ.

"I wouldn't put too much faith in that. Not once this gets rolling."

"So what are you saying?"

"There was a house on that block with the electrical rigged up to bypass the meter, jumper cables clipped to the power line and strung down to a junction box. My guys who did the house-to-house saw it. Probably squatters living there. You can say you knew about the place."

"Yeah? How would that happen?"

"You saw it on the way to school—"

"I'm not *in* school, I told you, I was holed up at Winchinchala House till—"

"You walked by, heard about it from somebody, whatever, you thought it was a fire hazard. You bumped into Verrazzo somewhere— not the corner store. The camera, remember. You bumped into him and you told him about this house and he asked you to point it out. That's why you were in the car."

It should've been funny, wicked funny. Once again: say this. Easier this way. Better for everybody. Especially, you know, us.

She felt her phone buzz in her pocket. A text. She brought it out, checked the screen:

Call the Bachmann woman. Get her to tell this Tierney
person to leave us alone, before he bothers Richie.

Yes, Mother. We must protect our men.

"Check it out. Greetings from Momzo. Anything you want me to pass along?"

Skellenger didn't take the bait. "I'd turn that off if I were you." He gestured for her to step away from the door. They were done. "Works like a GPS when it's on. Better yet, get rid of it, buy a burner, use that.

Because we're gonna clone that one there. Warrant's getting written up now. Every text, every call, we're gonna know about."

19

With a little creative surfing on the Internet and a pretext call or two, Tierney learned that Richie Garza worked for Sanitation and Flood Control, what used to be known as the Sewer Department. A half hour later he was getting directions down a dogleg of tight, low-ceilinged hallways to the bar screen area, where Richie ruled his own peculiar corner of the netherworld.

Tierney glanced through the square portal of an unmarked door, saw no one behind the service desk within, and tried the knob. Open. He ventured in.

A placard reading "Wall of Weirdness" marked a series of white wood shelves chocked with curiosities filtered from the city's wastewater by the mechanical screens meant to protect the treatment pumps. He'd read about this display in his web search—it was a common feature on field trips from the local middle schools—and yet, even forewarned, he wasn't quite prepared for not one but seven Barbies in various incarnations (Mexican, Harley-Davidson, Naked), all a little worse for wear, plus a vast and varied collection of cell phones, dentures, backgammon tiles, sunglasses, dog collars, shuttlecocks, knives. Reportedly they'd once found a live, twenty-inch hardhead catfish in the catch basin. At least twice, a fetus.

A brass hotel bell lay on the counter and he tapped the plunger once, resisting the impulse to bellow out, "Front!" He was about to try again, louder—the heavy thrum of the chopper pumps was everywhere, even here, though the stench of organic matter, as they liked to call it, seemed a bit less tart inside than out—when someone bellowed, "Hold on," and shortly came forward from an office in back.

Tierney marveled at the resemblance. Taller, of course, and a few years older—black hair combed straight back on the sides, a rakish dangling forelock, long-sleeve shirt buttoned to the collar and cuffs to hide his tats most likely—but put him and Jacqi side by side?

"I was wondering if you might help me out. My name's Tierney. I'm hoping to find your sister." He slid his card across the counter.

Richie Garza glanced down but didn't reach out to pick it up, just nodded heavily. "Heard you might come around."

Tom-toms pounding, Tierney thought. Pony soldier come. He offered an easy smile, took in the room. "Intriguing workplace. Real chick magnet, I bet."

"I don't have nothing to tell you."

"Have you seen Jacqi lately?"

Richie stood there, hands on the counter, gazing at the card. "I don't see her much. She's not welcome at my place."

"Because . . . ?"

"She's a fucking thief." He picked at a ragged bandage circling one of his knuckles, eyes flitting up to Tierney's face just briefly, then whisking off again. "Kicked her back to Mom, but she don't come around there neither."

"That's what your mother said. Her and Pete."

Tierney watched for the response. Richie nodded a couple more times and finally picked up the card, like he didn't know what else to do. Still not looking up.

"Mr. Navarette," Tierney said.

"I know who you mean."

"I didn't realize how close he is to the family."

Richie tapped the card against the counter. "Look, from what I hear, my mom's already—"

"I'm up here, Richie."

So simple a trick, but there: Richie glanced up at last and met Tierney's eye. Like he'd been frog-marched to the blackboard. Like his shirttail of a soul was sticking out.

The face was lean and finely boned like Jacqi's but harder edged like the mother's, a little darker too. A constellation of tiny black birthmarks dotted his cheeks, his brow. Eyes like knots.

He favored his right leg with his weight, not standing square, ready to swing from his left, though both arms looked relaxed. A kind of edgy lassitude about him, and despite the lithe build you could tell he lifted. Plus his hands were banged up, maybe from the free weights, maybe from wrench work in tight places, maybe something else.

Tierney said, "Your sister could use a little help. I'm just trying to do my part."

Richie almost guiltily broke off the stare-down. "Yeah. Everybody wants to help poor Jacquelina. 'Cept it's not your job."

"Funny how many people keep telling me that."

"Don't listen to them neither?"

"Look, I don't like bothering people. But I'm truly, honestly worried about your sister."

Richie puffed out his cheeks, like he was straining to be polite, or there was just too much to think about. Tierney wished there was a way to pop open his head, get in there, dig it out, lay it out on the counter between them so they both could marvel at it. Something for the Wall of Weird.

"Look. I gotta get back—"

"There's something in Jacqi's file I've been puzzled by."

Like before, with Navarette, there seemed no point in restraint. Richie Garza was telling him loud and clear, don't bother dancing around the issue. Go straight at it. One thing he'd learned over twenty years in the law: no second chances. You get one shot at a witness. Unpack him. And if that meant picking the scab off Jacqi's secret, bringing up the letter from Cope, he'd make it up to her somehow. Besides, the truth wasn't the problem. Fear was the problem.

Or, as Lonnie put it, secrets are for users.

"Near the end of the trial, after your sister testified, Victor Cope wrote to the judge and said that Jacqi'd told him that she'd had a run-in with one of your friends."

For the first time, Richie shifted his weight to the other foot. Maybe he led with his right after all.

"Know what? We're done."

"Any friends of yours ever express an interest in Jacqi?"

Ripple in the neck muscle. Fistfight eyes. "You're a sick twist, know that?"

"Just a question. If it never happened, fine. But then why get defensive?"

"How'd you like something like that said about you? Going around, putting that shit in people's heads. Who d'ya think you are, Dirty Harry?" A quaver in his voice, despite the hard eyes. "Yeah. Sure. Clint Eastwood, that's you."

"How come everybody sees me as the problem? Instead of the one guy willing to stick his neck out, help your sister? What's that about?"

"The story's a crock, asshole. And I'd lay odds my sister told you that."

"What friend are we talking about, Richie? What's Pete Navarette got on you?"

"Look, Eastwood, there's nothing to say. You wanna talk about sticking your neck out? We stood up for her more than anybody knows."

"Why don't they know?"

"Cuz it's nobody's business but ours."

"You mean yours. You, Richie. You stood up. It's your business. Why?"

Richie turned a little one way, then the other, unable to move. Show him the way out, Tierney thought. Make him the hero.

"How did you stand up? What did you do? Your sister cares about you—that came through loud and clear when we talked. What did Navarette make you do?"

Richie met Tierney's eye. "You're on city property." Struggling to say it quietly. "You been told to go."

"Why won't your sister come home anymore?"

"You're asking the wrong guy."

"I don't think so. I think I'm asking exactly the right guy."

Richie's whole face compressed, like it was all he could do to keep himself in check. Come on, Tierney thought, you're right there.

"No." A whisper, a headshake. "No." He turned, started walking away.

"Richie, come on. I know it's hard." It felt like a tremor buckling the floor. Failing. Failin' Tierney. "Help me help your sister."

Hand on the doorframe to the back office, over the shoulder, "Tell me how hard it is, Eastwood," then he stepped through the opening, closed the door behind him.

20

Sitting alone against the wall in the hospital cafeteria, Jacqi cupped her hands around a small ceramic pot of tea and, feeling warm for the first time in hours, inhaled the twiggy smell. So tired. Maybe she could nap here. Maybe she could sleep forever.

Her phone thrummed, a text:

I told u 2 contact the Bachmann woman. Tierney saw Richie @ wrk. Happy?

Like that, her skin turned cold again. Yes, Mother. She thumbed the delete pad, watched the text vanish in a swirling *woosh*. I'm thrilled.

Secretly, she was beginning to like Tierney again. You had to respect a man who could get Momzilla that jacked. But Richie. Jesus. As if things weren't bad enough.

She still caught herself sometimes turning suddenly at the shadow of a stranger in the corner of her eye, wondering if—maybe, finally—it was him. The freckled boy with the cockeyed face, the slanting smile. He'd come back from the nowhere that had swallowed him whole. No doubt he had stories to tell, but that could wait. For now he'd just walk up, brush the hair off her face, stammer hello. And she'd reply: Hey, Eastwood. Where the hell you been?

Tierney waited a full twenty minutes for Richie to reappear. When that didn't happen he found his way back through the maze of hallways and stepped out into the tangy air—like someone had mopped out a gargantuan outhouse, courtesy of several tipper trailers, brimming with haulage for landfills, backed up to the reject pond.

He crossed the parking lot, glancing across the acres of sprayfields, beyond which the green-gray spines and scarps of the Mayacamas range beckoned fragrantly. He was thumbing the bob to unlock his car when both doors opened on a Mercedes SL sitting a few spaces down.

The men were Latino, impeccably dressed, well-groomed—no garish boots, no bolo ties, no throwback sideburns. The driver called out, "Mr. Tierney." Barest trace of an accent.

Somewhere, Tierney thought, there's a textbook that explains in excruciating detail precisely what to do in a situation like this. Deny your identity? Bolt for the car? Put up your dukes?

He put his hands in his pockets and smiled. "That's my name, don't wear it out."

The driver was the smaller and better looking of the two, dapper and trim. The other guy wasn't exactly a lug, his suit tempered that impression, but it seemed pretty clear he tagged along to punctuate whatever the first one said.

"Can I share a word?"

Tierney glanced skyward. A dozen crows uttered piercing caws from their perches on nearby power lines. *O heavens, let the devil wear black.* "As long as the weather holds, sure."

The smaller one squared himself. "I understand you've been making inquiries. About Jacquelina Garza?"

Tierney resisted a chuckle. In-kwy-reez. "I'm trying to find her, that's correct."

"What you been doing is harassing people. Her mother at her house this morning. Now her brother inside here."

How quickly word travels, Tierney thought. "That's not how I'd describe things."

"And that ain't exactly up to you, is it."

The smaller one shouldered a little more into his jacket. Now that he stood closer, Tierney could make out the shiny whitish scars on his chin and throat, evidence of more than casual acquaintance with the angry end of a knife. And yet of the two he did the talking. That said a lot about somebody. Tierney wasn't quite sure whom.

"Look, no disrespect, but who are you guys?"

"We were asked by the family to have a word with you."

"The family or Pete Navarette?"

The two men glanced at each other. The big one's eyes retained their bearish emptiness, but the smaller one looked off, put his hands on his hips. "Look," he said. "We're trying to make this, you know, not complicated."

"That's great. I'm trying to make it professional. Either of you have a card?"

"Man, you are just not—"

"What is so damn threatening about someone being interested in Jacqi Garza?"

"The family's interested. They're taking care of it."

"They have a strange way of showing it."

Finally, the big one stepped forward. Tierney pointed to a vapor lamp on a pole nearby. "You guys know about the cameras, right? City's got them damn near everywhere now. The cops have monitors in their cars. They can scan and zoom in, peg a license plate like it's a billboard. Impressive, in an Orwellian kind of way."

He had no idea if there were cameras here, but the big guy looked up. The smaller one, the driver, kept his eyes locked on Tierney. "You misunderstood."

"The situation's rich in ambiguity. Look, I keep hearing the family's taking care of things. But all I've seen so far is you two guys and all I've heard is—"

"You're hearing what you need to hear. From me, right now."

"Honestly? I'm not." He held out his hand to count out conditions. "Until I hear a lawyer's petitioned the court to amend Jacqi's diversion—one. Two, until I've heard that order's been granted and she's been assigned a new facility. And three, until I hear she's agreed to all that of her own free will"—and fat chance of that, he thought—"I'll keep trying to find her before she winds up in jail. Or worse. Sorry, gentlemen, but that's the best I have to offer." He glanced face to face. "We finished here?"

The driver nodded his pal toward the car. "We appreciate your taking the time."

"Not at all. Glad we could work this out."

For the first time, the little guy smiled. "Take care, Mr. Tierney. You've heard the expression 'There's many a slip between the cup and the lip'?"

They got in their coupe, backed out of their space, and took off. Tierney waited till they were out of sight, beyond a turn in the access road, before feeling beneath his bumper, the most obvious spot.

He found it almost instantly, near the bracket—God, they must think I'm dumb—small metal box fitted with a magnet, size of a cigarette pack. Sliding back the casing door, he found the tracking device cushioned in cellophane, a little number called the Ranger if he wasn't mistaken.

He cocked his arm, ready to pitch the thing into the reject pond, then got a better idea. If the tracker stayed put they'd figure out he'd found it, left it behind. Squatting down, he tucked it up under the grill of the car parked in the slot next to his, right behind a bumper sticker that read: "I Get My Exercise Pushing My Luck." Depending on how closely Navarette intended to watch him, the trick might earn him a couple hours or a couple days. Regardless, if there was one thing this little episode had taught him, it was the importance of buying time.

21

At the hilltop Denny's overlooking the freeway cloverleaf, Donny Bauserman pressed his tie against his paunch and slipped into the booth across from Teddy Buker.

Bauserman glanced around, made sure no one was sitting close. "Did you see it?"

Teddy'd come dressed in this woolly zigzag sweater, some souvenir from a doper ski shop. He stabbed a wedge of pancake, pushed it around in his syrup. "See what?"

"You weren't there?"

"Where?" The kid made a face. "What are you talking about?"

Bauserman and Teddy's dad went back to the old days, the money days, when working for the city meant you were set. Ron Buker—master welder, stellar guy, solid worker—he'd joined the IBEW after the shipyard closed, became an inspector for the maintenance crews. He could've gone to work for the refineries for more pay but he liked the health-care package the union offered. Ironic, looking back. Ironic as in lousy.

His boy Teddy grew up down south with the mom, then come eighteen got sick of the latest stepdad and swung up here. By then his old man had the cancer. Little by little, like nibbling fish, it was eating his liver away, and with the bankruptcy the health plan givebacks started out brutal, then got worse.

By the time the IBEW had its shot, the well was dry. Ron would be leaning on his pension soon, but now voters in San Jose and San Diego had approved walk-backs on those, too. There was talk about putting the same thing on the ballot here, and lawyers in the Stockton bankruptcy were talking about going after retirement packages. Mayors all across the state were telling the legislature: without pension reform, we all go to court.

Promises meant nothing. The whole world was scared and pissed and the future was a joke. A joke nobody could stop telling, even though it wasn't funny.

"You've heard, right?"

Teddy wiped his lips with his napkin. "Jesus, Donny, what the fuck you talking about?"

The waitress showed up, dropped a menu on the table. "I'm good," Donny said, "just coffee."

She snatched back the menu and left. He waited till she was out of earshot.

"Mike Verrazzo's dead."

The kid looked up from his plate. Tunnel eyes.

"Got jumped over near the high school. Pack of kids, I'm hearing."

Teddy's eyebrows pinched together. "Dead?"

"I was halfway hoping you'd seen it go down. Could ID who did it."

When the IBEW got left holding the bag in bankruptcy, Bauserman developed a special hate for Verrazzo. Phony, gasbag, user. Led everybody down the primrose path, then pushed them over a cliff. Bauserman's membership especially. Worse, while everybody else slashed and burned their budgets, let guys go, cut back hours, Mighty Mike scooted out the back, found himself another trough of money in Visalia.

Bauserman knew about the hookers, figured it was even worse than the talk going around. Ron's kid, Teddy here, he'd started the apprentice program with the local but then got the same news as the others. Not enough work for the guys with twenty years in, let alone the youngbloods. He was shut out just as his dad was facing chemo, and Donny could tell from the way the kid carried himself, from the things that came out of him at meetings, he was pissed off too. Like a wasp in a jar, this kid.

So Donny put him to good use, had him tail Verrazzo—paid him a little, not much, cash out of pocket. Turned out the kid was a natural— kept a log of the corner hookups, the motel stops, Verrazzo going at it in the car with some tramp in a white wig at the back of the Rumpus Room parking lot. Teddy snapped pictures with his iPhone. Bauserman had a dream. He was gonna ruin Mike Verrazzo, cut him down to size, slam the door on that golden getaway. Make him face what he did to every worker in this city.

"I had a call this morning," Teddy said, "job over in Morning Crest, fix the sink. Nice little Spanish bungalow, but the pipes are shot. Brass is flaking away. Owner thought it was dirt. Like a tree trunk had punctured the main."

The waitress showed up with Bauserman's coffee, then tried to grab Teddy's plate—why make a second trip?—and the look on his face, like he might stab her in the neck with his fork. He still had his rashers and two bites of short stack.

She huffed away. The kid stared a hole in her back.

"So you didn't see anything?"

"Donny, listen to me, I wasn't there."

"Okay, okay. Cool off. Finish your food."

Bauserman fiddled with his cup, gazed into his coffee. The one time the kid might've seen something big, he was someplace else, head under somebody's sink.

I can live with that, he thought.

Teddy said, "You afraid somebody's gonna think you had something to do with it? Whole world knows you had a hard-on for the guy."

"Hypothetical hard-on." Bauserman sipped his coffee. It tasted like liquefied charcoal. "I wanted to humiliate him."

"You wanted to destroy him."

"Not kill him."

"Big diff."

Bauserman looked out the window at the knotted freeways, watching traffic speed west on 37 or north and south on 80. Highways always gave him the itch to go somewhere, all by his solo, no Maureen, no kids, pack up the car and head off late at night, nobody on the road but you.

"Verrazzo was a murder waiting to happen," he said. "Know what's ironic? Stop stuffing your piehole for a second and listen. What's ironic? Murder's too good for the guy. Gonna get played up like some martyr and, boy, there's a turd to swallow. I wanted him jobless and broke, wife on the warpath, blackballed, no fucking port in the storm. Wanted him to feel for himself the pain he caused everybody else."

"Little-known fact: they call that motive."

"Don't fucking say that. Yeah, I had motive. But I lacked opportunity. I watch *Law & Order* reruns too, smart-ass. I wasn't there. Had a meeting with Code Enforcement. Got witnesses who can testify."

Teddy pushed his plate away, wiped his lips, downed what remained of his juice. A clot of syrup clung to the front of the goofy sweater. He looked like he'd just stuffed it all down not even thinking, fill up some hole inside.

"Well, bottom line, Donny? I wasn't there neither. So I can't get dragged into this thing. And I can't drag you in with me. We good?"

22

Her appearance—business suit, silk blouse, cameo at the collar, black hair parted just so—made Skellenger think of something trapped in amber. "Thanks for agreeing to meet," he said. "I thought it best we talk about this in person."

They were in a café down the road from Todo's, Pete Navarette's place. Nina Garza, not glancing up, hypnotically stirred a cup of tea.

"I realize your daughter's been a handful the past few years," he said, "but this morning she really outdid herself." He laid the thing out, from Jacqi's being in the car when the murder went down to his chat with her at the hospital. "She says she didn't get a good look at anybody, but even if that's true, and I tend to think otherwise given what I saw on the video, it's not gonna keep her out of this."

The mother said nothing for a moment, just continuing slowly to circle her spoon through the dark tea cooling in her cup. Finally, she said, "I appreciate you coming to tell me all this."

"When she walked off the reservation over at Winchinchala," he said, "that made her an abscond. It's open season. She gets picked up for loitering, caught in a squat raid, she's back inside and I run out of options. Once she's processed the system takes over. Anybody can get to her—press, defense lawyers. Only gets worse if the DA decides she's a material witness, and you can pretty much bet that's gonna happen. She says she's been clean six months and I hope that's true. But she's obviously back on the street. Temptation's just gonna get worse. She starts using—"

"Is there a reward?"

Give the woman her due, he thought. She sees the whole board, thinks several moves ahead. "Not yet."

"But you assume there will be."

"Depends how quick we can wrap it up. We're not talking criminal masterminds here. But yeah, the city, victim's family, the local, the labor council, any one of them or all of them together could pony up. Then again, there were a lot of kids at the scene. They didn't do jack when the man was getting killed but wave some cash their direction? Even if Jacqi steps up, she'll be sharing the pot with God knows how many others. And nobody'll get paid quick."

The woman nodded thoughtfully, taking her time. "There's something else in this situation to consider."

Oh you bet there is, he thought. "Yeah?"

"The chance to be the center of everything again."

A tick of acid crawled up his throat.

"You're assuming," she said, "Jacquelina will think it through. That's not who she is. I love my daughter, Detective. But she's a seriously troubled girl."

She lifted the cup to her lips and Skellenger found it impossible not to watch—the clockwork movement, the glimmer and chime of bracelet, the pulse in her throat as she swallowed. A ghost of lipstick darkened the rim as she set the cup back down.

"What I mean," she said, "is that Jacquelina is impulsive. To a fault. And, as I mentioned, she craves attention. She misses being the person everyone is talking about."

Then do something, he thought. "I doubt the attention she's going to get in this is the kind she'll like."

"You really, truly do not understand my daughter."

He felt a sudden awkward pity for the girl. "Maybe not, but like I said, we spoke. She didn't seem too eager to step to the front of the class. I let her know if she took a breather, got out of town for a while, might be the best thing. She didn't disagree."

Finally Nina Garza lifted her gaze. Their eyes met. "Really."

"One reason I'm here, I was hoping you might help out on that end. I don't mean another halfway house. She'll have to register, and once her name pops up it's just a matter of time. But if she just gets tucked away. Someplace safe. For all concerned."

"As a matter of fact . . ." She glanced away, fist to her lips, clearing her throat. "There's a private school we've been looking into upstate."

How quaint, he thought, imagining the ivy and brick. Mistress Meany's Academy of Discipline and Deportment. "Victor Cope's upstate. Not exactly in school. Still, I'd hate to see him graduate."

"That's not a subject we need to discuss."

Actually it is, he thought, but we never will. A retrial. *C'mon, kids, let's put on a show.* Everything back on the table. Including my tin, my vestment, my pension.

"You do your part," he said, "I'll do mine. If I can keep her out of this, I will. But this thing's not just a nasty storm that'll blow over sometime soon. It's got its own climate. I can't guarantee anything."

She wasn't listening. Digging through her purse instead. "One more thing." She withdrew a business card, slid it across the table. "This man, he's bothering me, my family. Says he's a tutor at that place you mentioned—the Bachmann woman's center—he apparently worked with Jacquelina. Says he's concerned that she left but I get the impression he's after something else. He went to see my son. He asked questions."

Skellenger read the card, nothing but the name, a box, a phone number. Phelan Tierney. Sounded like one of those stuffed shirts on NPR. "What is it you want?"

"I met with the Bachmann woman, let her know I'd go after her license. Sue her. Ruin her. But it's unclear she has any sway over the man."

"He's a civilian. Questions aren't a crime."

"He has no right to the answers. You know what I'm talking about."

Yes, he did, more or less. He rather wished he didn't. "Has he made any threats, asked for money?"

She looked incredulous. "I *told* him to leave us *alone*."

Skellenger batted at the card with his index finger. Looking past her through the window, he saw someone in the parking lot lighting up a smoke. For the slightest instant he envied the match.

23

Face hidden deep inside the hood of her jacket, Jacqi returned to her seat in the cafeteria with a fresh pot of tea and a packet of rye crisps, some blueberry yogurt. Despite an utter lack of appetite she felt light-headed, and though she knew it was risky staying here with the news crews trolling the halls, she couldn't figure out where else to go. She lacked the oomph to move regardless. It took absolutely every ounce of strength she had to peel back the foil lid, dip her spoon into the bluish creamy muck and have a taste, tear open the packet of crackers and take one out, munch the rough dry tip.

It's okay to be scared, she thought. Scared is normal.

As though summoned by those words, Verrazzo's face swarmed up in her mind's eye—that empty dread in his eyes, blood on his teeth—and she pressed her hand to her mouth, feeling sick, clenching her eyes shut, telling herself: Don't think. Don't think. Just be still. Breathe.

She set the spoon down carefully, afraid she might drop it, draw attention.

Her phone thrummed inside her coat pocket. Ignore it, she thought, counting the murmuring pulses, five, six, seven . . . then still.

Just be still.

She wasn't sure how long it took—three seconds or forever, time had turned to soup—but gradually the follow-up hum brought her back, the nagging alert: the call had gone to voice mail. Digging the phone from her pocket she read the display: Mother.

She pressed her thumb to the throbbing red panel and lifted the device to her ear.

Jacquelina, mi niña. I've learned what happened this morning. Of course I'm disappointed. I had hoped you'd put all that behind you. But that doesn't matter now. It's time to put everything that's come between us aside. Everything. You can't bear this alone, the weight is too heavy, and no one can hide forever. I know you are afraid. Come home. I will take care of this. Te amo, mi amor.

An almost dreamlike loneliness descended, and she tucked herself so deep inside it she barely felt the hand on her shoulder or heard the birdlike voice—same attendant as before, the Sikh in his turban, those bottomless eyes—asking if she was okay.

Wipe your face. Pick up the napkin, blow your nose.

Whisper your thanks and tell him you're fine. Don't draw attention.

24

The daylight filtering in through the Gothic-arched windows in the Winchinchala office had a grayish cast. The sconces were lit, two per wall, but they weren't much help dispelling the shadows either.

Lonnie Bachmann sat forward at her massive desk, elbows on the blotter, head in her hands. "Phelan, please, you're being impossibly stubborn."

"They can't yank your license, Lonnie. Not over this."

Middle of the day, the center felt empty. A few of the residents busied themselves elsewhere in the big house, chores or schoolwork, the rest were off campus attending interviews: job counselors, custody mediators, parole officers.

"They can pull my certification," she said, "and then I'm just another name on an endless list. Money gets ten times harder to raise. Besides, it's not Health Care Services I'm worried about. Not compared to the family. That woman."

"Her name's Garza, Lonnie, not Borgia."

"Phelan, please, listen to me. I mean it. You weren't here. She came in like she already owned the place. And planned to burn it down."

He glanced at the clock—ten minutes more, he'd be late for his lunch date with Cass. "There's no chain of liability. I'm not your employee, I'm not your agent. I'm not even acting on your behalf, really."

"Like that's the issue."

"They can't realistically sue you because of anything I've done. That's the issue."

"Phelan—"

"Or me, for that matter."

"Stop thinking like a lawyer. It doesn't matter whether the family can win. They can make it damn near impossible for me to function. One call and next thing I know DHCS is here, turning the place upside down."

"You didn't kick the girl out on the street. She left."

"I have a duty to keep her safe."

"Physically safe. On the premises. Once she leaves, it's out of your hands."

"You're missing the point. This place exists on the good graces of people willing to grant me funding."

A siren howled past outside, third in five minutes, one more patrol car screaming down Bufflehead Avenue. Secretly he welcomed the distraction. "What the hell's going on out there?"

"You didn't hear?" She sat back, tugging her skirt primly as she crossed her legs. "Mike Verrazzo's dead."

It took him a second to place the name. "Really."

"Murdered. On the street, bunch of kids. Been on the news all morning."

"I had the radio off." Tierney harbored an aversion to the so-called information industry that bordered on malice. He preferred the Latino stations with their operatic *cumbias* and *rancheras* or just the silence of his thoughts. "Did you know him?"

Lonnie took a second before nodding. "IAFF sponsored a couple fund-raisers for us." She sounded more reflective than sad. "It was a little awkward, to be honest. There were rumors he cruised—couple girls actually knew him, or said they did. Anyway the local made us a lot of money and it's, you know, that kind of town."

It brought to mind some graffiti he'd seen a week or so back, scrawled across the side of a shuttered firehouse, ironically: *Rio Mirada—If You've Got the Lipstick, We've Got the Pig.*

That kind of town.

"Getting back to the matter at hand," he said, but then a reedy Latina with spaniel eyes—Angelica, the one with the nuclear crush, per Jacqi—appeared at the office door and timidly knocked.

"Miz Bachmann? Sorry to butt in like this but you got a man at the door. He's asking for Mr. Tierney."

The man was wiry like a middleweight and ash blond. Sunken eyes in a drawn face, hands stuffed in his pockets. A well-worn suit that looked at least one size too big, rain freckling the thinly padded shoulders.

He said, "Phelan Tierney?"

"That's me." Worried that Navarette's two humps had come around to complete what they'd left unfinished in the Sanitation Department parking lot, Tierney had convinced Lonnie to stay put in her office. Vaguely relieved he'd been mistaken, he extended his hand. "Can I help you?"

"My name's Jordan Skellenger." His hands stayed put in his pockets. "I'm with the Rio Mirada police department." He gave up two inches and maybe as much as twenty pounds to Tierney, rocking back a little on his heels, that cop sense of owning the room. "We've received a complaint from the Garza family. They say you've been badgering them. They want to be left alone."

First the dogs, Tierney thought. Now the cavalry. "Sorry, your name again?"

"Did you hear what I just said?"

"I did. But I'd like to be sure I have your name right. Spillinger?"

"Skellenger."

"And that was Sergeant—"

"Detective."

"Detective Morgan—"

"Jordan." A pissed-off sigh. "Jordan. Skellenger."

"Good. Sorry. Thanks. You were saying—"

"We take harassment accusations seriously, Mr. Tierney."

"Then you're probably aware of the legal standard. There needs to be a credible threat of serious harm."

"Mr. Tierney—"

"There's also a standard of reasonableness, and no reasonable person would think that anything I've done seriously alarms, torments, or terrorizes anybody. That's the statutory language. And the behavior in question has to serve no legitimate purpose. Not true here. I'm trying to find Jacqi Garza. You know who that is, I'd guess."

It took the man a moment to answer. No expression. "I do. Yes."

It wasn't till that moment the name clicked. "You worked on the Victor Cope investigation. When Jacqi disappeared."

Skellenger stopped rocking on his heels. "That's correct."

"Well, she's disappeared again. I'm trying—"

"From what I hear the family is handling the matter on their own. They didn't ask for your help. They don't want it."

"Have they reported Jacqi missing? To you, I mean. The police."

Another blank-eyed pause. "You won't be able to find anyone from inside a holding cell, Mr. Tierney, and that's where you'll end up if you keep hounding this family. They've been through enough. They have a right to be left alone. I trust I've made myself clear." Without looking, he reached behind for the door. "Good day."

When Tierney returned to Lonnie's office he found her leaning against the wall beside the window, staring out beyond the vintage muslin curtains at the drizzling rain.

Tierney said, "Well that was interesting."

She turned toward him but stayed put. "Who was it?"

"A detective named Skellenger. Ring a bell?"

"Jordie Skellenger?"

"You know him."

"I told you, I know a lot of the guys here. Occupational necessity."

"I mean it rings a bell from before, Victor Cope, Jacqi's kidnapping."

"Sure. I guess. What did he want?"

"He was contacted by the Garza family."

"Christ." A thin, shuddering breath. "Fabulous."

"Lonnie—"

"Have they reported her missing?"

"I had the same question. He didn't really answer."

"Phelan, you need to listen to me. I need you to stop. I need you to let go of this and just stop." She moved toward him, hand held out, as though approaching a strange dog. "I'm asking as a friend. I screwed up, okay? I screwed up by not reporting to the court that she's no longer here. If DHCS finds *that* out—"

"You don't have that obligation." He wasn't entirely sure that was true. Still, he'd read the relevant statutes, which were almost blithely moot on the subject.

"I didn't tell the mother either," she said.

"That was hardly reckless, given the history. Let alone wrong."

"The girl's seventeen. No matter how screwed up the family is, she's still a minor."

"You hoped she'd come back on her own. When she didn't, you turned to me."

"For God's sake, Phelan, will you *listen*? It should've been me who called the police. Days ago."

"You did what you thought was best. I had a good relationship with her, something her family sure as hell didn't. She didn't go home, probably never even thought about it. If I've confirmed anything, it's that. And you said yourself the cops hate her—why contact them?"

"If only you hadn't been so, I don't know, tactless."

"Excuse me?"

"I'll call Skellenger, straighten this out."

"If you feel you have to." *Tactless?* "But I still think it's wrong to just stop. Of course the family's pushing back—they're the problem. You said as much yourself—"

"Phelan—"

"If we give up, who fills the vacuum?"

"I get that, believe me." She returned to her desk finally and dropped into the chair as though manning a cockpit. "But whatever trouble she gets into is largely her own doing. She has to stand up for herself, Phelan. She has to want to be found." She wetted her thumb on a damp sponge and began ticking through a stack of message slips. "Girls go missing every day. If anybody understands that, it's Jacqi Garza."

25

Tierney reached the hospital twenty minutes late for his lunch with Cass. Entering the cafeteria, he performed a quick scan of the crowd and spotted her across the room, wearing a green mock turtle beneath her blue scrub shirt, her hair gathered back in a ponytail—tamed, to the extent possible, with a scrunchie.

She tapped her wristwatch as he approached.

"I know. Sorry." He brushed the moisture off his sport coat, then set it on the back of his chair. "Got held up."

She cocked an eyebrow, then sighed. "I took the liberty of ordering. Hope you don't mind." Ham and Swiss on rye for him, fruit salad with cottage cheese for her. "Your coffee's probably cold."

"I'll grab a refill. Anything I can get you while I'm—"

"I'm fine." She'd already finished half her meal. "Do hurry back."

He did. As he sat back down he saw the wisdom of a little conversational misdirection. "By the way," he ventured, "not sure if you heard the news. Mike Verrazzo's dead."

She glanced up as though he couldn't possibly have said anything more inane. "You serious? It's all anybody's talking about around here."

She filled him in on a few of the gaudier rumors floating around, her tone noticeably unenthused. Stabbing a wedge of melon, she smudged it around in her cottage cheese. "You know what Verrazzo means, right?"

Tierney feigned deep thought. "Verrazzo, Verrazzo . . . From *verus*, a genuine thing. A true thing." What good was a Catholic education if you couldn't strut your Latin once in a while?

"It means a guy who works with pigs," Cass said. "Male pigs. For breeding."

Noting her tone—she sounded upset—he said, "You know this how?"

"My *nonno*'s from Bonifati. Lotta stud hogs back in those hills. Anybody sticks a microphone in my face, that's what I'm gonna say."

Not upset, Tierney thought. Ticked off. "Now there's news I'd stay up to watch."

"I wouldn't stay up for any of it." She toyed with a slice of kiwi, nudged it aside. "I'm sorry the guy died but I also know there's people who aren't and I'm already sick of the whole business. Everybody drunk on their own bile, looking for someone to blame. Someone to hate. Hardly a surprise it came to this but that doesn't make it interesting."

Two black ladies—one plump and methodical, as though in pain, the other prim and gray-haired with a veiled cloche hat—sat down at a neighboring table. Tierney could smell their soup and the rain on their corduroy coats.

"You doing okay?"

Cass glanced up and gave him one of those looks that have turned men to stone for centuries. He was pretty sure he was crazy about this woman.

"This is just between you and me, okay?" She glanced up to make sure he'd registered that. "The guy gave unions a bad name. Him and his circle of hotshots, milking this town for every dime they could get while they laze around in their four-thousand-square-foot Monuments to Me in Orinda or Marin. God forbid they have to live in the sinkhole they created by robbing the rest of us blind. Drove the city into a ditch, then walked away from the wreck."

Behind her, the two black ladies closed their eyes, murmured grace.

"The bankruptcy had a lot of fingerprints," he said, "not just Verrazzo's. And honestly? I'm not so sure it wasn't a good thing in the end. The money is gone. First jolt of cold hard truth anybody's managed as long as I've lived here."

"Murder's a kind of truth, too. That how it is now?"

She resumed attacking her plate. Behind her, the plump black woman lifted her glasses, dabbed her eyes with a hankie. The one in the veiled hat patted her companion's hand. Tierney leaned forward, lowered his voice. "What's going on?"

"I don't know what you mean."

"Sure you do. You're angry."

She looked up, meeting his eyes with a strange sad emptiness. "I hate the way I feel about this. I don't like talking trash about some guy a bunch of creeps left to die in the street. And what I just told you, trust me, I'll never tell another living soul. Sure as hell not the press—they've been running around the halls quoting anybody dumb enough to open his mouth. I'm not gonna join the orgy. But that doesn't mean I didn't wish I felt different."

The nurses had gone out on a one-day strike three times the past year, no contract since June, negotiations going nowhere. Every nurse walking the picket line got death threats sooner or later.

"It's an ugly situation," he said, "and complicated. The man had friends and he made a lot of enemies. Not your fault you feel how you do."

She smiled weakly and shrugged. "First the bankruptcy, now this. Take a guess what either of our houses will be worth now."

"It's not that bad. We're a stone's throw from the Napa Valley, remember."

"Yeah, well, the stone just got a heck of a lot heavier." She sipped from her glass of iced tea. "When they find out who killed him—Verrazzo, I mean—is there any chance you'll wind up working for the defense?"

Ah, he thought. Now we have it.

"Hadn't even thought that far ahead, to be honest. Would you prefer I didn't?"

She nudged a stray red curl from her eye. "They're saying it's a bunch of kids, maybe gang-related. And that means, you know, Grady."

He recalled the offer from earlier that morning: *I like the thought of you gainfully occupied.* And if he knew Mr. Matafeo, the man was already on the phone, calling around, massaging those connections. Plum case, ton of publicity, milk those billable hours. Only a fool wouldn't want the thing.

"I like Grady, and I enjoy picking up work from him every now and then. He gets interesting stuff. But I can resist his sly entreaties."

"It just seems like this is going to get real ugly, real quick. And stay that way. Do we want that in our lives?"

He reached across the table and laced his fingers in hers. A buck-up squeeze. "I like to think I can rise above the fray."

"Maybe I wasn't talking about you."

26

She pretended to finish her lunch, he pretended to sip his coffee, both of them lost in thought.

"So how's your adventure with Jacqi Whozit going?"

He drifted back from his mental haze. "You really want to hear about it?"

"Any change of subject will do. But I thought I'd be broad-minded and indulge your obsession."

He smiled tepidly. "You're the second person today to call it that."

"First being?"

"Grady. Speaking of the devil."

"I could develop a serious crush on that man."

He wondered how much to tell her. God forbid he should be tactless.

"Seems like I've hit a dead end. But I saw the mom again this morning, found out she's involved with some guy named Pete Navarette. Name sound familiar?"

"I must confess," she speared a grape, "it does not."

"Apparently he's something of a local character. Grady says he may have been involved in the jewelry store job that put Jacqi's dad away."

Cass shook her head. "I feel for that girl. But this thing just gets creepier."

"Spoke to her brother too, and that was, I don't know, even more interesting. Given how much Jacqi claims to hate her family, I was expecting someone much different."

"Since when do people hate their families because they're *different*?"

She slipped off one of her clogs and rested a white-socked foot atop his shoe, inching a toe up under his cuff. A shy little glance. Speaking of changing the subject.

A phrase came to him, an Irish expression: stepping on stray sod. It meant the eerie sense of being lost in what once had been reassuring surroundings. Being afraid or confused by the thing that once made you feel safe. He indulged the play of her stocking foot against his calf and wondered if she didn't sometimes ask herself: Who is this strange man? How did he jimmy the door to my life?

She caught it, his being mentally miles away, and suddenly there was more than a table between them.

"Know what I think?" Removing her foot, slipping her clog back on. "This idea of yours, easing back into the legal stuff, it's not good for you. Plays on your worst impulses."

What an utter bonehead you are, he thought. "What impulses might those be?"

"Way you get into tutoring? You oughta go back, get your master's in math, maybe a doctorate. Teach. You'd be brilliant at it. God knows they need math teachers."

He contemplated apologizing for his distraction, but merely said, "I spent almost half my life mastering the illogic of the law. Seems a waste just turning my back on all that."

"Hon, you wasted it when you popped that billionaire in the snout."

• • •

Scanning the cafeteria again, he watched as an Asian family—a father, a daughter, two sons, no mother—wordlessly got up from their table, cleared their trays, tidied their chairs. Beyond them, visible only now that the family had left, the girl sat alone at a two-top, hunched over a pot of tea. She'd pulled her hood up over her head but he had no doubt. The coat alone he recognized.

It hardly would have startled him more if a wildebeest were sitting there.

Cass noticed the change in his face, turned to glance over her shoulder. "What?"

"Table over there, against the wall."

Subtly, back still turned, Cass froze. Like she was afraid of the look on his face, didn't want to turn back around and see it, not yet.

"Wonder what she's doing here," he said.

Finally she returned to her plate. "Go find out."

"You mind?"

She smiled emptily. "It's all good. Least now I know what she looks like."

Cass fought the urge to watch him walk toward the girl's table. That's the way it is, she thought. They develop their little fascinations, tell themselves it's not important, it's nothing. Then they leave.

She began to massage her eyes, trying to hide the obvious—she was doing everything in her power not to turn and look—and shortly found herself remembering a day from two years before, near the end. His wife had become delusional from the morphine, her thoughts mixed up from the chemo, and she was getting harder to talk to, harder to understand. Cass imagined the woman's thoughts going off in her mind like jagged flashes of lightning in a sea of fog. Roni Tierney's name had been up on the patient board for a month by then, nothing but lousy news. Everybody was ready for an ending. Well, maybe not everybody.

The pain team wanted to change her regimen, and Cass came in with the new vial, ready to hook it up to the drip. She blathered the usual chipper nonsense, got no response. The sad lovely woman sat in the bed like a mugged nun. Cass tried to attach the drip to the port in her chest and got for her trouble a windmill of arms, a whimpering cry.

Roni Tierney wouldn't be touched.

Cass tried again, then a third time, but the resistance only grew more intense. Phelan was there, trying not to interfere. She told him, "If she doesn't cooperate, we'll have to restrain her." Another nurse, Arturo, loomed in the doorway, ready to help. They'd lash her hands and ankles to the bed, despite the fact she was already scared. They'd force her to do what they needed her to do.

Phelan asked to be given a minute. He sat on the bed beside her, took her hand. "I have an idea you think this is something it's not." He said he realized she believed they were all there to kill her. The new drug wasn't a higher dose of fentanyl but some kind of poison. Everyone was lying. She was being put down like a dog.

"That's not happening," he said. "I won't let it happen."

He kept talking, the gentlest voice imaginable, at one point pressing her hand to his cheek, then his heart. Her gaze remained dark and empty, but she listened. In time she nodded, agreeing to be hooked up.

Cass, as she stood there watching, thought: Someday I want a man to care enough to talk to me like that. Walk me back from my terror, even if I'm crazy. Promise he'll never hurt me, never let anyone else hurt me. Never.

27

It wasn't like Jacqi didn't know he was there. She just thought if she didn't look up from the table maybe he'd drift away.

"Hey," he said. That smart, rumbly, whispery voice. "Are you all right? Did something . . . happen?"

Clutching her cup like an anchor. Yeah, she thought. You could say that.

"What I mean is, are you here because you're hurt, or did someone you know wind up in here . . ."

She didn't know how much time had passed since her strange bout of tears, but ever since then she'd been lost in place, trying hard not to think about much of anything at all, especially not that, him, Fireman Mike. A busman had come and gone, clearing away the yogurt and crackers, neither more than half-eaten. She took a slug of cold tea.

"You've made a real impression on the mom unit, know that?" Change the subject, she thought, glancing at her cell. "Been blowing up my phone, telling me I need to do something, get you to back off."

Someone moaned loudly from a nearby table, not from pain. Something else.

"Yes, well," Tierney said, "that seems to be the general message all around. I didn't mean to get on her bad side. But my focus is you, not her."

Despite her own best instinct, she glanced up. The man had absolutely the world's saddest smile. And Christ, those eyes.

"Don't take it personal. Mom likes being disappointed in people. It's her reason for getting out of bed."

"I'll stow that away for future reference." The kindness came off him like too much cologne. "Anyway, seriously—are you here to see someone?"

The words dissolved into sounds, drifting around in her mind, like her head had become a snow globe. "I just wanted to get outta the rain. And I'm crazy about the oolong here." She reached under her hood to tuck a strand of hair behind her ear. It felt like straw, finally dry. "What's your excuse?"

"Lunch with my girl." He turned to point her out, but the table his hand aimed for was empty. At the far end of the room, a lanky redhead in a scrub shirt and white slacks, stride like a puma, cruised to the bus tubs, tossed her plate and silver, stacked her tray. No glance back as she left.

Oops, ouch, and over. That's what you get, Jacqi thought, for getting mixed up with me.

He tried to cover by checking his watch, but his eyes were someplace else. "She's due back at work. Upstairs. RN, oncology clinic."

"Busy busy."

"Anyway—"

"Yeah, I came here to see somebody. Not anyone I know well. Just, you know, around."

"I'm sorry. Everything okay?"

"It's a hospital. How can things be okay?"

"I meant relatively speaking."

"Relatively speaking, four million dead is 'okay.' Better than four million one."

"I forgot." He pulled up a chair and sat. "You've got a head for numbers."

For some reason, that made her laugh. She tapped her teacup, watched her reflection vanish in the dark ripples. "You're funny, Phelan Tierney."

"I'm here through the weekend. Don't forget to tip your waitress."

It hit her then, the thing he'd said, or the thing beneath the thing. "Your wife died of cancer—and you're dating a nurse?"

If she wasn't mistaken, he blushed just a bit. The sad smile turned uneasy. "She was one of the nurses in the cancer ward, actually, when my wife was here. Roni passed away upstairs."

I was wrong, she thought. He isn't funny. "And you come back here, like it's some kinda shrine." In love with his misery, she thought. There's probably a word for it. "God, that's so like you."

He looked right through her. "Given what you know," he said. "About me."

"I know enough." She wiggled her fingers, a conjurer of knowledge. "You're, like, an easy read." It was such a lie—the man baffled her—and judging from the look on his face, he knew that.

"Yes, well," he said, "I've been learning a great deal more about you as well. How popular you are, in particular. Since last time we talked, I've had several unique encounters. Just a little while ago a detective named Skellenger got in touch."

The lingering taste of her tea went sour in her mouth. "Imagine that."

"You know him, I understand."

"Could say that."

"Seems he's heard from your mother as well. Not to mention Lonnie, who had the distinction of an actual visit. Your mother makes quite an impression apparently."

"You have no idea."

"I had a visit, too. Couple of characters tracked me down to give me the news."

"What news?"

"About your family stepping in, taking care of your problem with Lonnie."

The room suddenly felt smaller, colder. "Two," she said. "Big guy, little guy?"

"Exactly. Slapped a GPS on my bumper to bring the point home."

"Smaller one's Ben Escalada." GPS, she thought, glancing at her phone to be sure it was off, remembering Skellenger's warning. "The moose is Hector Mancinas."

"So you know them."

"Oh yeah."

"Can I assume that means it's okay, then, the fact they're looking for you?"

"Do I look like it's okay?"

He studied her across the table, and for just a moment she wished he'd get up, come over, put his arms around her. She would've given anything in the world.

"No," he said. "You don't look like it's okay."

28

Tierney sat there, waiting for her to say something. She couldn't meet his eyes. It was like some kinda spell he had. Cancer nurse for a girl-friend. Jesus. Meanwhile the unseen moaner from earlier broke into soft, muffled sobs.

"If you're not going back to Winchinchala," he said, "and given how the wind's blowing, I've got a pretty strong sense you're not, what exactly do you intend to do?"

She opened her hands around her cup, a shrug. "Any suggestions?"

"There's still a court order to worry about."

No there isn't, she thought, thanks to Skellenger. "Yeah. Whatever."

"You mentioned a man who was willing to help you. Is that still an option?"

Her eyes started to burn, she could feel the tears welling in her eyes. No, she thought, biting her cheek, digging her nails into her palms. Don't you dare.

"I haven't heard from him in a while."

"Are you all right?"

"How about I camp out at your place? Just till I sort things out."

He chuckled, this far-off look. A *vato* sleeved in banger tats pushed a stroller past. "Uh, no. That's not going to happen, sorry."

"Yeah." Give the man a prize for being honest, she thought. Except there is no prize for being honest. "You see my problem."

"You should've seen your face just now, when I brought up those two men—Mancinas, Escalada."

Good memory, she thought. Tierney the tutor. "So why not front me the two grand I asked for?"

Like she'd told him she was carrying his kid. "We've been through this."

"You've got the money."

"Do I?"

"Look, you're right, there's a lot going on. A lot of, I dunno, pressure. All of a sudden. And I need to get out of town. Not soon, not later. Now."

"Why all of a sudden?"

"Trust me, the less you know—"

He reached across the table, took her wrist, not hard. "Why . . . all of a sudden?"

Go on, she thought, tell him. He's an all-right guy, for a mope.

Jesus, no. You nuts?

"Let go of me."

He took back his hand. "I'm sorry."

"You don't touch me, understand?"

To his credit he didn't shrink back in his chair, look around, see who was watching. His eyes remained fixed on hers. "Yes. I understand."

"What's happened," she said, "is just, you know, something out on the street. Nothing, you know, major, but I was there. I'm a witness, I guess."

He sat back in his chair, looking puzzled, like something had changed. About her. About them. "Witness to what," he said, "exactly?"

To the crap in my head, she thought. Can't get it to stop. "Nothing. Everything. I see a lot out there. You'd be surprised."

"No doubt," he said. "But this one thing in particular."

"It's nothing. Really. I shouldn't have brought it up."

"Does it have to do with the friend of yours who's in here?" He gestured toward the corridor. "The one you came—"

"Seriously. It's nothing."

He looked at her like she was about to catch fire. "This have anything to do with Mike Verrazzo getting killed?"

"No, no, Jesus. Look . . ." Her voice quavered. She swallowed, telling herself to calm down. "Please. Just . . . drop it. Okay?"

His fingers did a little dance on the tabletop. "Maybe this is off topic, maybe not, I don't know. But I spoke with your brother."

For just a second, she thought she might puke. "I heard."

"He got a little testy when I mentioned I ran into Pete Navarette at your mom's house earlier this morning."

She started to tremble. *Come home. Te amo.* "What's that got to do with me?"

"The two goons who told me to take a hike, they work for Navarette, am I right?"

"What difference does it make?"

"You okay with him hanging around your house?"

Like it's up to me. "Compared to who, the other weasels in my life? You?"

"How long has he been involved with your mom?"

No. Not going there. "Your nurse left in a huff. How're you gonna make up?"

"What's Navarette got on your brother?"

"Gonna come clean about us, honey bear?"

"Whatever it is, he's using it against him, against your mom, you—"

"You high? My mom doesn't get used."

"You saying she's in on it?"

She snatched up her cell, dropped it in her pocket. "I gotta go."

"Witness to what, Jacqi? Something happened. Not just out there on the street, not just this morning."

"You misunderstood."

"Explain it to me."

"I already did."

She pushed out her chair. He reached out, grabbing her sleeve this time.

"Let go of me or I'll fucking scream."

"What's Richie's thing with Clint Eastwood about?"

This time she really did think she might heave. The walls buckled in. Buckled out.

"What'd he say?"

He didn't answer, just drilled her with those arctic eyes. She heard a voice from somewhere. Her voice. "What did he say about Eastwood?"

"He said not to be surprised if you looked the way you do right now when I brought it up."

She snapped to, shook off his hand. "That's a crock." She shot out of her chair.

He stood too, but only so he could lean in, lower his voice. "Maybe I'm wrong, but despite all the lip service, all the phony concern from damn near everybody—and yeah, I'll even throw in Lonnie with the rest of them now—it seems I might just be the only friend you've got."

"You're my friend? Loan me two thousand dollars."

"*Loan* you? That's funny."

"How about one thousand, a couple hundred—"

"Tell me about Eastwood. Who is he? What is he?"

"Eastwood, Eastwood, Eastwood. It's a word. It's nothing."

"What's Pete Navarette got over on Richie? On you. You're angry because you're scared. What is it? What are you so scared of?"

"Leave me. The fuck. *Alone!*"

She snatched her arm away like he was trying to eat it. Heads shot up and turned—everywhere, all across the cafeteria. Insomniac moms. Leg-kicking kids. Pill-zonked *cholitos*. Don't make a scene, she thought, not here, not now.

She moved in close to whisper. Make it look like a spat. They were family. Letting off steam. It's a hospital, for chrissake.

Meeting his stare, fending off the voodoo in those eyes: "What am I scared of? Guys like you."

Part IV

29

Skellenger's cell started buzzing as he hit the squad-room door. Flipping it open, he checked the incoming number—his wife—then gestured to Dick Rosamar from the SCU that he'd be a second.

"Hey, what's up? Kinda crazy here right now."

An uneasy pause, crackling with static, not all of it the kind you hear. Lot of tension between them lately. Life didn't feel like life anymore, she'd said. It felt like a deck of cards always getting shuffled, never getting dealt.

"It's Ethan," she said, sounding like a roof had collapsed. "They sent him home from school. He had pictures in his backpack. Drawings. Very elaborate drawings, if you get my meaning. Male and female both."

Ethan was the artistic one. Emily the pragmatist, obsessed with becoming a vet. Three more years, hopefully, they'd both be out of the house. Maybe he and Rosellen could slip back into the old routine, something that felt more like a marriage, less like a root canal.

Who was he kidding? Kids didn't move out anymore. This economy?

"They'd be impressive," she said, "the drawings I mean, if they weren't so . . . unsettling."

It hit him then. Not just women.

"Listen, seriously, I don't know if you heard—"

"About Mike Verrazzo? In an hour he'll still be dead. It's one of those times, Jordie."

"It's gonna have to—"

"I know staffing's down, but you're the only guy down there?"

He glanced up and down the hallway, a sea of blues and browns and off-the-rack suits—cops from nearby cities, deputies from the sheriff, troopers from the highway patrol in their flying-saucer hats—humps and helpmates, gluttons for overtime. Here and there an honest-to-god cop.

"I'll see what I can do. If I can, I will."

He slapped the phone closed, put it away, but then stood there a moment, held by a fleeting thought, not of elaborate nudes or dead firemen but Bovoni Bay on Saint Thomas. Two years after the wedding, delayed honeymoon, before the kids. Last real vacation they had, snorkeling in water so clear you wanted to breathe it. Shimmering walls of fish. Ash-white beach and scalding sun and the constant churn of the surf. At night the rickety tin fan whirred nonstop on the cabana's wood table, and despite the sunburn they couldn't get enough of each other. Rosellen slim-waisted but big-hipped, high-chested, ashamed of her thighs. He'd never desired anyone so much, and told her so.

The words appeared on the squad-room whiteboard, upper left corner, testament to a training session in ethics the state had forced upon the whole force six months back:

Heave the Fat Man

An adjunct professor from Sonoma State, mumbler in tweed, attempted to explain—between pushing up his glasses and coughing into his fist—the inarticulate, often unexamined sources of morality.

The professor posed what he called a classic problem: you see a trolley coming, and the brakeman has suffered a heart attack. The trolley is barreling toward a group of five tourists who don't see what's happening. You stand by the switch. If you pull it, you can save the five tourists. But along the trolley's redirected path is another unsuspecting soul, who will surely die. What would you do?

Overwhelmingly, research showed that people—including on this occasion the roomful of cops—believed the right thing to do was sacrifice the one for the five. Animal math. Unfortunate but inescapable. Right but not easy.

But imagine now you're not on ground level but perched atop an overpass and can't reach the switch in time. There is, however, a heavyset man standing nearby—so heavy that, if you can bench-press his heft and hurl him down onto the tracks, he'll act like a well-placed baby whale and bring the trolley to a messy but fortuitous stop.

In the abstract, the moral calculus remained the same: the sacrifice of one life to save five. But research showed most people didn't think that way. They recoiled at physically laying hands on another human being and causing him gruesome deadly harm, no matter how many others were saved.

The adjunct professor wrapped up with a nod and eyed the room with a pinched smile, hoping he'd made his point. A puzzled, cross-armed silence greeted him, until a voice in the rear of the room crowed out, "You kidding me? Heave the fat man."

So much more vivid than "Whatever It Takes," the motto it replaced.

Meanwhile, in the whiteboard's lower right corner, much more modest in size, another epithet appeared, fresh from this morning, Hennessey's penmanship:

Who Killed Rufus T. Firefly?

30

Dick Rosamar, Denny Copenhaver, and Marion "Don't Call Me Sherlock" Holmes, all SCU guys, were gathered around a monitor watching, rewinding, watching again the security footage from the Pay-N-Go at the corner of Goldenrod and Buckeye.

Skellenger had probably ten more years on the job here than any of the others, an occasional point of tension. A wedge existed between the older cops, younger cops. The old guard, with its laid-back culture of "Blue Is True," had been a little too close to the bikers in town, too prone to think of black neighborhoods as Indian Country, too cozy with their CIs. The younger ones were better educated, more professional, and their pay had always been generous, no need for side work as bouncers and such. That had all changed with the bankruptcy, of course, creating even more friction. Skellenger, something of a tweener, was usually considered okay, young enough not to be tainted, but too old to genuinely trust.

In particular, he and Holmes had never clicked. Ichabod Negro, some of the older crowd called him, but Skellenger liked to think of himself as more evolved than that. For him it was just a clash of styles. Holmes had been a star power forward in high school here, went off to Fresno State, collected splinters on the bench, but came back just as cocky. Lanky build, bony face, tiny ears. Ugly as he was, women still threw pussy at him.

Girls like Ethan too, Skellenger thought, or so it'd always seemed. Maybe the kid just didn't like them back. Or not enough.

Male nudes. When it fucking rains.

He eased up from behind on the crew, leaned in toward the TV, squinting for a better look himself, the figures grainy, like video of Sasquatch.

"How we doing?"

Rosamar—thickset, black-haired, matinee smile—pointed with a pen. "Hennessey was right. This here's Mo Pete Carson, Brickyard Cutthroat Killas. Raider gear's the giveaway, white sideline snap especially, that's BCK."

"The Hispanic kid?"

"Most likely he's Chepe Salgado, Southside Punk Stoners."

Skellenger loosened his tie a little more, the room warm. "We know this how?"

"Been tickling Elmo," Rosamar said. "Summoning all CIs. Bit of a gym rat, this Salgado nitwit. Stomped that kid at the Deer Valley game, sent him to the ER, eye socket crushed. Couldn't nail him for it but, hey, we know. And he knows we know."

Skellenger, still unsure: "What the hell are these guys doing together?"

"Ah. Time for this week's puzzler."

"Not real clear yet," Holmes said. "But one of Dick's guys—"

"Not solid as a rock," Rosamar said, "but I think he's good on this."

"Said a shot caller for the Nuestra Familia inside Folsom flew a kite on Jimmy Palanque, Southtown Krazy Raza? Not paying his taxes. He's split for places unknown."

"Means there's a vacuum," Rosamar said. "Cutties and Punks, their turf butts up against the SKR's. Our numbers where they are, the goofs are rolling and tolling, nobody wants to mess that up. Peace means profit. This was something of a conclave, midlevel lieutenants, way to feel things out, manage the transition—brothers keep thizz and coke, *cholos* get crank and skag, pot goes where it goes."

"The other two toads," Skellenger said, "they're who?"

"Tall dude on the edge." Copenhaver finally chiming in—thin as a whistle, shortstop eyes. "First guy to throw a punch?"

"Arian Lomax," Rosamar said with a smirk. "Otherwise known as Itchy Homo. Booked him on his last pop. Kid was any dumber he'd have antlers."

"Guy here beside Lomax," Copenhaver said, tapping the screen, "we hear he's named Damarlo Melendez."

"Yeah," Skellenger said, "but who *are* they?"

Copenhaver shrugged. "They're kinda from nowhere."

"Itchy Homo ain't hooked up." Rosamar, still grinning.

"But the Melendez kid, what's his name, Dumbardo?"

"Damarlo." Copenhaver shook his head. "Not really nailed that down just yet. I got a name and a guess from my guy. That's all he had."

"They could be our ticket." Skellenger wondered when one of the men would bring up Jacqi Garza. He'd been mentally rehearsing. "If they can hang a visual on the last guy in, the one who finishes it, they've got an ace to play."

"I'm not so sure," Rosamar said, "I'd jump to conclusions just yet on who finishes what. This Damarlo kid, he's flying wild. Kicks like a chorus girl."

Copenhaver chuckled. "Putting in work."

"More to the point," Rosamar said, "he's up near Verrazzo's head, his neck. Coroner's still being cagey but he admitted the COD is most likely a crushed trachea."

"I heard the same thing," Skellenger said, "from one of the paramedics at the hospital." He fished out his notes, thumbed through pages. "Said Verrazzo already coded by the time they reached the scene. Trachea crushed, couldn't breathe. Load and go."

"They got there in what," Holmes said, "six minutes?"

"Five. They knew who it was. So no beefs about response time. Figure he had maybe four minutes tops after the windpipe caved in. More like three. No way an ambulance could've gotten there that fast. En route to the hospital they tried to pass an ET tube, couldn't get it through the ruptured cartilage, so they took out the needle and did a quick crike. Surgeons went at him another twenty minutes in ER, so nobody could say they gave up too soon. Waited for the wife to show before coding him for good."

Rosamar, cocking an eyebrow: "You talk to the lovely bride?"

"Yeah." Skellenger tapped his notepad against his knuckles. Gina Verrazzo—fortyish, plump, blond with dark roots, peach-colored sweats. Called Mike a man of the people. "She took the time to put on lipstick before getting to the hospital."

Rosamar grinned. "Pucker up, buttercup."

"There's rumors," Copenhaver said, "she and Mike, they'd packed it in."

"Yeah, well, this point?" Rosamar pointed at Verrazzo on the ground. "I'd say divorce counsel's off the clock."

Copenhaver acquired a bemused, studious look. "Skelly," he said, "you think the wife might be good for this?"

Skellenger sighed. "Do I think the grieving widow hired a pack of teenage porch punks to whack her faithless fuck of a husband? Not really. But I'll keep an open mind."

"What if she hired the last guy up, the one we don't know?"

"That's a different matter."

Rosamar shook his head. "I still say, look at this Damarlo kid—"

"Vid ain't gonna prove diddly," Holmes said. "Make it say damn near anything."

Copenhaver sighed. "Slow it down, frame by frame, blow by blow."

"Gonna come down to who says what." Holmes again. "Best shot we got, grab these first four melonheads, stick 'em in the rooms, see who gets down first."

"Mo Pete, Chepe—sheets they got?" Copenhaver crossed his arms. "They're gonna lay this off and fast. Put it on one of the nobodies."

"My boy Itchy," Rosamar said, "he's not quite nobody. Two strikes. And he ain't a juvie."

"Good," Skellenger said, nodding. "That's good."

He thought it through, weighing the angles. Despite the tensions—younger cops with Skellenger, all of them with Verrazzo—the motivation level in the room felt good. Nobody wants to look flat-footed, so to speak. They'd put aside their contempt, their resentment, rise above it all and close this thing if only to prove they could. Mike Verrazzo, the man who all but killed this city, would not himself die in vain. And that was just about a million times better than he deserved.

True, they'd need every one of these juvenile jokers in the courtroom. Nobody'd walk, but it'd be open season, each man for himself. The thing was in play. There were options. "We got warrants yet?"

"They're moving, first four anyway, ones we know." Holmes hit fast-forward till the Dude Outta Nowhere appeared at the bottom of the screen, hunched forward, hood pulled tight, plodding forward. "This fool's still a mystery."

They watched as the nameless stranger shuffled up to the melee, knelt, did whatever—three quick blows? Try to slap Verrazzo conscious? Shake him? Then Mr. Nameless wobbled to his feet, stared down at Verrazzo. Mo Pete Carson reacted to something he saw, turned and ran. That quick, the other three astronauts panicked, everybody else followed suit, all except the stranger, who just turned and started humping back the way he'd come.

"Tried to blow this section up," Holmes said, "but the thing just falls apart. Can't make out any detail on the face."

Copenhaver said, "Techs in Video Forensics, they'll perk it up."

Holmes shrugged. "Gotta hope so."

The door of the red Crown Vic flew open, Jacqi popped out. Despite himself, Skellenger flinched. Rosamar said, "And now, ladies and gentlemen, the star of our program."

Holmes adding, "We rely on her, we lose. Turn this into a god-damn circus."

"Like it's not already," Copenhaver said. "Anybody catch the news?"

Skellenger froze. News?

Holmes stretched, those albatross arms, palms touching the ceiling panels. "Michael Dominic Verrazzo, former head of the firefighter's local, major mover in the city's misfortunate bankruptcy, treats his big important self to a tasty little eye-opener."

"Making the scene with our favorite teen," Rosamar said.

Skellenger tasted bile in the back of his throat. "They're saying that?"

"Not yet." Holmes retracted his arms from the sky. "Matter of time."

"Fucking Mike Verrazzo." Copenhaver unwrapped a stick of gum, plowed it into his mouth. "Guy was a total muff missile. If it had a pussy and a pulse, he launched."

Holmes shrugged. "Maybe he was trying to turn the girl around."

"Only reason that fat fuck ever turned a girl around," Rosamar said, "was to nail her from a new angle."

"True connoisseur of corner cunt." Copenhaver popped his gum. "Living the dream."

They watched Jacqi confront the stranger, scream at him.

"Whatever's going on between her and him, there's heat," Holmes said. "She's howling." Shaking his head. "We gotta get out in front of this."

Copenhaver: "Jordie, you know her, right?"

"Not well." Skellenger stared at the screen. At her. "Not anymore."

"Any chance you could put the touch on her, bring her in for a chat?"

Everybody turned.

"Like I said, I don't know her that well anymore." Changing channels: "Any word on the house Stritch and Manzello ID'd in their door-to-door?" He fanned the pages of his notebook, looking for the number. "On this block, jerry-rigged electrical—"

"Didn't pan out," Holmes said. "Place was trashed but empty."

"How recent the tenants leave?"

"Can't say."

Oh fuck me, Skellenger thought. Didn't mean it couldn't still be useful, though. Only Verrazzo and Jacqi knew what they were doing there, one was dead, the other soon to be gone—hopefully—that meant it was anybody's guess, and Skellenger had every intention of keeping that hole card close.

"As for all the other kids," Holmes began.

Rosamar: "The ones standing around?"

"Not standing around," Copenhaver said. "Cheering. As a man gets pounded."

"Too bad we ain't got guys posted in the schools anymore," Holmes said. "We'd have more names than we would handle by now."

"I may have something." Skellenger found the page in his notebook, read off the names Jacqi had given him.

Holmes wrote them down. "Where'd all this come from?"

"You guys aren't the only ones tickling Elmo." He flipped the notepad closed, tucked it into his pocket. "And we're gonna need plenty more. Everybody put a hat on a hat. Somebody out there knows who it is we want." Jacqi was still on-screen, kneeling beside Verrazzo. Calling to mind how she looked at the hospital, that red-eyed ten-mile stare. "They're kids, they talk to each other. Christ, it's all they do." That and draw unsettling nudes. "Get in on the conversation. We need names."

31

Stopping for a moment in the arched entrance of the chemo unit, Tierney looked at the high-backed vinyl recliners, some discreetly obscured by curtains, most open to view. Maybe a dozen patients sat hooked up to their infusion pumps—medicinal poison dripping into their blood, like nods to a fix—drifting in and out of various states of distraction, some napping, some lost in thought, others trying to read or watch the TV perched high in the corner.

His eye gravitated to the chair Roni had always preferred, near the window, so she could look out at the oat fields coursed with winding sloughs, the first of the valley's pear orchards, the westerly sky. No one sat there today.

He smiled at those who glanced up as he passed, then found Cass poring over a chart at the nurse's station. Big Red, he thought. My girl.

"Hey."

She glanced up, face like a stone apache. "What brings you here?"

Patting his pockets, "I seem to have misplaced my melanoma."

She closed the chart and tossed it onto a nearby stack. "Clever." The nurse's aide beside her struggled against a grin.

He nodded toward the hallway. "Give me a minute?"

• • •

Out in the corridor she leaned against the wall, arms crossed. "I'm kinda busy, we're short a nurse."

"I'm sorry."

"It's okay, it's just that things are—"

"No, I mean I'm sorry about what happened earlier."

One eye shuttered slightly as she took that in. "Okay."

"I shouldn't have just left you sitting there. It was rude."

"I told you it was okay," she said.

She began slipping her foot in and out of its clog, reminding him of his botched response to her affection. The articulations of his guilt seemed endless.

She said, "Wanna know why I left before you came back to the table?"

"I can imagine. But yeah, I'd like to hear."

Her eyes shifted, as though searching out some critical detail in his face. "I know you've got a job to do, or that's how you're thinking about it. And I know sometimes, even when you tell yourself it's just a job, there's somebody who, for whatever reason and for however long, steals your focus. I've been there. Happens a lot here, actually. But sooner or later you gotta snap back, see the bigger picture, or you're being unfair."

Glancing past her into the clinic, he saw the sad, stoic patients lashed to their medicine. "I don't mean to be unfair," he said.

"Doesn't matter much what you mean. Hardly ever. It's what you do."

He resisted an impulse to reach out, stroke her cheek. "If it's any consolation, not even Jacqi wants me in her business anymore."

Almost imperceptibly she leaned a little deeper into the wall. "Yeah?"

"Down in the cafeteria, let's just say we failed to reach a meeting of the minds."

She seemed to turn his words over a few times, began to say something, checked herself. A moment later she couldn't look at him anymore and glanced back toward the clinic doorway. "And that means what—you're gonna drop it for good or dig in that much harder?"

"Cass, I came here to apologize."

"I get that. But the part that comes after—the part that goes, 'It won't happen again'—that part I'm not hearing. Not really." She pushed off from the wall, turned back toward the clinic. "Gotta get back to work. It's Thursday. Couple minutes we start the pediatric clinic, and I gotta get ready for my kids."

She'd told him about it, the sad parade of young ones, some still reasonably healthy, some little more than drawn skin and withering bone, all coming in for their toxic promise. How trivial his preoccupations must seem, he thought, next to hers.

"Talk about this more tonight?"

She glanced back. "And say what?"

32

Tom Pendergast—public information officer, shirt and tie, sleeves rolled up—sat perched on the edge of the chief's vast desk, staring at a TV on a roll cart in the corner, the screen locked in freeze-frame: grainy blowup of Verrazzo lying motionless, small in the background, the Dude Outta Nowhere caught in midstep trudging toward the camera as Jacqi Garza, standing beside the car, bellowed something: an insult, a dare, a name?

Pendergast said, "The press situation's getting hard to control."

Skellenger glanced back and forth—Pendergast, the chief—then shrugged. "Tell them to wait. What're they gonna do, leave?"

"Jordie," Pendergast said, "the spin's getting ahead of you."

"Investigation's what, five hours old?" We're marginally smarter than criminals, he thought, but guess who has to be perfect. The speed, though, every day faster.

"We're going with the video," the chief said, hands tented, enthroned in his chair, all done up in his best dress blues.

"An edited version," Pendergast added.

"Edited how?"

"Ten seconds tops. Near the beginning of the fight."

So that's it, Skellenger thought. Things had to be skewing weirdly haywire if forty kids standing around laughing as a fireman gets kicked to death is the better story.

He walked over, tapped on the glass, the stranger, the wild card. "What about him? We know nothing about him. He could be anybody. He could be a pro, he could be a skeleton out of somebody's closet, the mayor's, some councilman's, anybody with an ax to grind." Gina Verrazzo, he thought. One of us.

"It's talk like that," the chief said, "we're trying to avoid."

"What if it's true?"

"You've been busy," Pendergast said, "and may not have a full grasp of what's happening in the background."

"Come on. Tom, trust me, we fuck up the front end of this thing, the back end's gonna make whatever problems you've got now look like a bachelor party."

"Let me show you something." Pendergast dug out his cell phone, then thumbed a key, lifted the display so Skellenger could read it. "The thing's blowing up. You got reporters at the scene, the hospital, Verrazzo's house, here in the building. They're posting every rumor they trip over. Worse, you got the Topix site with a comment thread, and the yahoos can't type fast enough. Same with Facebook, Nextdoor. Like they opened up a sewer."

"It's cancer," the chief said.

Skellenger could only imagine, with Verrazzo murdered, the kinds of things people were posting. During the bankruptcy cops became nigger-bashing night riders, firemen wannabe mafiosos and shakedown artists, together they turned public safety into a protection racket, while the sex lives of every council member got dissected in vivid, skin-crawling, homoerotic detail.

"There's a protest planned," Pendergast said.

The chief: "Pitchforks and torches."

"Plus a counterprotest. We get hit with a riot, manpower shortages we've got?"

"We've had calls from four lawyers already," the chief said, "representing our elected friends. They want a stop to the slander. Like we're to blame. One of them actually said 'lynch mob.' Point is, we've gotta get ahead of this thing. Stop the speculation. Give people something to look at and say, 'Oh, *that's* what happened.'"

Skellenger rapped at the TV screen again. "Back to this guy. What're you gonna say about him?"

"For now," Pendergast said, "nothing."

Skellenger waited for more. None came. "That's gonna look like a cover-up."

"Not if we handle it right," the chief said. "He's just one more body in the crowd."

For a second it was like a group scan, everybody's eyes tracking everybody else's. Then Pendergast cleared his throat, wagging his phone.

"There's something else. You've got these little corners of the web, semiprivate comment sites, on Tagged or Path or Highlight or Roamz. There it's kids talking. And everybody knows it was Jacqi Garza in Verrazzo's car."

Skellenger's stomach plunged five stories. For the last several hours, he'd dealt with nothing but hassles, insults and lies, dodges, innuendos, lined up like dragons. But this was the first time he'd felt truly worn down.

He knew the cop who'd probably come up with all this—new recruit, specialized in Internet crime, spent at least a couple hours a day impersonating twelve-year-olds looking for "someone who understands." Everyone on the squad called him Tiffany. Now this. What else did he know, Skellenger wondered. What were kids saying?

"What's your point?"

"We don't need another sideshow," the chief said. "Press latches on to her and you, it's all they're gonna talk about."

"Which is an improvement maybe," Pendergast said, "over the political angle, everybody thinking city hall put out the hit, but not by much."

They're kicking me off, Skellenger thought.

"Look, Jordie," the chief said, "it's politics driving this. I've already fielded calls from the mayor, Congressman Rinehart, a couple county supervisors, and just about every numbnut on council. Bankruptcy was bad enough. We turn back the clock to Cope and the whole kids snatched off the street business—"

"Not to mention," Pendergast said, "what's she doing in the car?"

"As it is we can't float a bond to save our souls," the chief said. "Add this? We won't see new business here for a decade. Property values tank. Taxes dry up. Staffing gets axed even worse and God only knows what happens to pay, never mind benefits."

If the city's still around, Skellenger thought. Could be nothing but meth labs and tumbleweeds by then. Hail Freedonia. "I'm not sure what you're asking."

The chief said, "Can you solve this thing without her?"

33

Skellenger was turning to go when he saw the two blue uniforms at the door, strangers waiting to enter. Jesus fucking hell, he thought. What's it gonna take to get outta here, dynamite?

The first of the two came forward, crew cut, barrel-bodied, plowing the air with his hand—toward the chief, not Skellenger. The second, tall as a ladder and weak-chinned, shadowed behind.

"Chief," the hefty one said, "apologies for barging in, we're kinda pressed." He gestured over his shoulder with his thumb. "Your secretary said we should come in once your meeting here wrapped up."

He smiled emptily at Skellenger, nodded vaguely toward Pendergast. How much had they overheard?

"I'm Nick Dugan, this here's Mike Bernardo, we're out of DC, representing the national offices for the hearings up the road in Sacramento. Got wind of what happened to Mike Verrazzo and drove right down. Only take a minute of your time."

The unions were making the rounds in the capitol, pushing mandatory mediation before a city could file for bankruptcy, hoping to forestall the kind of bloodletting that had happened here. Otherwise, it would've been curious, these two being local. Maybe it still was.

"I've spoken with the executive board," Dugan said, "and they're stepping up, as I knew they would. This is a terrible thing, and we intend to send a signal. We're offering a hundred-thousand-dollar reward for material testimony that leads to the arrest and conviction of Mike's killers."

Skellenger glanced at Pendergast, who, from his expression, was suffering the same thought. "That's a lot of money, especially this quick."

Dugan turned slowly Skellenger's way, like the turret on a panzer. "Hi," he said. The hand. "Nick Dugan."

Like I'm the help, Skellenger thought, taking the hand. "Thing is," he said, "there was anywhere from thirty to fifty kids watching as the thing went down."

Dugan turned back to the chief. "It's a lump sum. We'll divvy it up once the issue's settled after trial. Material testimony. Leading to arrest and conviction."

"We're just saying," Pendergast offered, "given what little we know just yet—"

"Person or persons," Dugan said. "Come one, come all. I don't see the problem, to be honest."

He can't be serious, Skellenger thought. A reward that size, this town especially, Pendergast and the chief already grousing about the online chatter. Wait till this hits the wire. Every moonrock who can count on his fingers and toes is gonna be hitting the hotline. In particular, Jacqi Garza. She'd all but hit him up for money so she could skip town. If the mother didn't wrap her up before this news went out—and the girl had a knack for slipping through nets—she might well sit back and ponder the odds.

Dizzying, really, the turnarounds. Just a moment ago he'd been told to pretend she didn't exist. Not just that, the chief had his back. Now they were throwing money at her.

"I still think it might be wise," Pendergast said, "to hold off mentioning the reward for now. We've got a bit of an information overload as is."

"And we're already ready to make some arrests," Skellenger said. "Why throw your money away?"

Dugan turned to the chief. "May I speak frankly?"

Without asking permission, the quiet one, Bernardo, went and closed the door.

"Perhaps I'm not making myself clear," Dugan said. "One of our own was murdered in this shithole today."

Some kinda gall, Skellenger thought. Guy comes from DC.

"I know there's tension here between you and the fire department," Dugan continued, "but let me make this plain as fucking day. There are no issues for us. None. I had my differences with Mike, we were both very honest and open about that. But come something like this? The ranks close. He was my brother. You don't want to tell people about the reward? Fine. There's a roomful of reporters out there. They're waiting for somebody to say something. I'm happy to oblige. Am I getting through?"

34

Skellenger went downstairs, retrieved his vest from his locker, shook off his sport coat and donned the bulky Kevlar, decade old at least, strapped up the Velcro, shouldered back into his jacket.

Climbing the stair to the main floor, he noticed how much the walls needed paint—the scuffs and cracked grout, the riverine cracks and powdery gouges in the plaster, they all acquired an almost hallucinatory clarity—then all of a sudden the light closed down, the air felt close.

He suffered a sudden blizzard of zagging dark spots—clutching the handrail, waiting a moment for his head to clear. Instead a space opened up in his mind and a memory slipped in to fill it, the night of his last drink, the Malibu drifting at high speed from the road like an angry dream as his head lolled on his neck and his eyes shuttered, the car fishtailing across the slick grassy downslope, almost rolling, then slamming into a surprisingly sturdy, noisy, thrashing mass of cattails before thudding to a stop in the drainage-ditch muck. That eerie, ticking silence, like God's clock. Ice-cold water ripe with stench seeping in through the door cracks, soaking his socks and shoes, and glancing down he noticed his slacks and boxers bunched at his knees, unable to recall how they'd gotten that way but pretty sure he hadn't been taking a crap as he drove, then noticing the blood, slathered on his hands and lap, wondering in a sick panic of guilt if he'd severed an artery—his? someone else's?—or cut his own throat, causing the accident, then the thunderclap awareness of pain in his face and he realized he'd crushed his nose on the steering wheel.

Minutes later the humiliating slur of words into the flashlight of the first cop on the scene—guy named Bertsler, working somewhere upstate now—the whirling red and blue of his squad car's strobe atop the incline. Back at the station, the tidy little cover-up commenced. With its big condition.

Shaking his head, he snapped back to the here and now, thinking: You need to eat. Instead he found a pack of gum in his pocket, slipped a stick into his mouth, waited for the jolt of sugar to kick in.

Hundred thousand fucking dollars, he thought. Call center's gonna explode.

Outside the dispatch center he gathered with Holmes, Rosamar, and Copenhaver, passed out warrants and divvied up uniformed units, a final brief on who they were after.

"Don't turn a blind eye to what's in plain view," he said, "but this isn't a scavenger hunt. We're after four guys. Keep it simple."

On his way out to the car he passed the door to the briefing room—filled to overflow: firefighters, city staff, reporters, TV cameras. Pendergast stood at the podium, brow dotted with sweat, squinting from the glare as from somewhere in the back of the room a voice pumped with attitude called out: "We're hearing from various places that Jacquelina Garza was with the victim, Mike Verrazzo, at the time of the killing. Could you comment on that?"

35

Tierney stood in the ER waiting room, face raised to the TV, joining everyone else assembled there, the whole room mesmerized.

He'd been having trouble dragging himself away from the hospital. After his tête-à-tête with Cass in the cancer ward he'd come away sensing that he'd only made things worse, and so he'd meandered a bit, trolling the endless hallways like a ruminative maze rat, finally landing in the canteen, where he'd sat for the past thirty minutes or so, sipping the execrable coffee, working his phone, answering calls and e-mails and texts, trying to feel productive.

Finally, he'd risen and headed on out, making way past the ER desk toward the electronic doors, when he'd spotted the scene in the corner of his eye, through the doorway, the roomful of uplifted faces gazing at the TV screen.

A kind of gravity nagged at him, telling him to stop, drawing him in.

Local news, a network affiliate, North Bay bureau. The screen showed a grainy video of maybe a half-dozen kids kicking six shades of hell out of a curled-up figure on the pavement, framed by a tree-lined cul-de-sac.

Other kids rimmed the scene like a chorus—ghostly, pixilated, edging in and out—egging the brawlers on or just milling around, a party, a laugh, a goof. A fire captain's car with its distinctive red gum-ball sat midway up the block.

The crawl read: *Firefighter's Union Head Murdered in Rio Mirada . . . Key Figure in City Bankruptcy.*

Then the video cut away to a still photo, and Tierney felt a haunting jolt—the image a decade old, the slender fox-eyed brown-haired girl, scrappy little heroine.

The scene switched back to the cul-de-sac, live now, a male reporter, fluttering parka, wind-mussed hair, notes in one hand, microphone the other. The ER staff had set the TV's sound to murmur level so Tierney had to edge forward and lean in to catch the words.

". . . won't confirm or deny just yet that she was at the scene, but the Internet is literally *on fire* with comments linking Jacquelina Garza to the incident, saying she was in the car when Verrazzo stepped out to confront the crowd—the crowd you just saw in that disturbing footage. If that's true, if she was at the scene, it adds another intriguing element to this already shocking story, Gwen. The girl whose testimony proved so crucial ten years ago is back. And once again she may find herself on the witness stand in a case that could rock this city to its bankrupt core. Reporting live from Rio Mirada . . ."

Tierney noticed again the gutted streetlight flashing red in the northerly haze on the river road. The same storm system lingered over the bay, a low shifting mass scudding in across the coastal range, turning the afternoon air a steely twilight blue. In the distance, an intrepid cyclist pedaled toward Napa.

No Jacqi in the bus shelter, but the old girl was there: Mattie, skeletal and wigged and wearing nothing but a red, long-sleeved sheath, canvas slippers.

He stopped, got out of the car.

She greeted him flatly, "Hey there," the voice slurred from ruined teeth. "Aren't you handsome."

He collected his wallet, fingered a twenty, reconsidered, decided on twice that.

"Not out here, hon." A birdlike hand reached out to cover the money, the dark skin soft and deathly cold. The stiff black wig pivoted as she glanced up and down the two-lane road. Other than the faraway cyclist, no one.

"I'm looking for Jacqi Garza," he said, and tucked the folded bills into her palm, wrapping his warm hand tight over hers so she'd feel some sense of kindness and know as well the money was hers to keep.

She glanced up, met his eyes, a quiver in her chin—lipstick patchy, thick here, gone there.

In an idle moment on the web, taking time off from his searches concerning Jacqi, he'd pulled up Mattie's arrest records and discovered her real name was Buttonwillow Hazeltine, and she'd been born in Flowood, Mississippi. He wondered who she'd been back there, back then, how she'd looked and talked and felt when she'd been a girl like Jacqi.

"She's in kind of a spot. It's important I find her as soon as possible. Any idea where I might look?"

She lifted the money to the hollow nook that served as her cleavage, stuffed it inside her tatty bra. "There's other men's looking for her too, you know. You ain't the only one."

36

Taking in the welcoming tang of freshly cut limes and jalapeños, Jacqi ordered her food at the bar from Ilena, the matronly cook, then collapsed into the nearest booth.

Her favorite place, Los Guanacos—hole in the wall, beer signs glowing in the misted window. Christmas lights rimmed a Salvadoran flag above the bar.

She slipped off her shoes, rubbed some warmth into her sore feet through her tights, then tucked her legs up under her.

Rudolfo, Ilena's brother, stocked the bar, thumping boxes on the dark hardwood, clanging beer bottles into the fridge, getting ready for the dinnertime rush—and every now and then a glance up at the corner TV as he worked.

She followed his gaze and caught the end of a Viagra spot snapping into a newsbreak, and quick as that the screen went from a gray-haired couple riding horseback along a sunset lake to a grainy clip, like a postcard from a nightmare: Mo Pete and Chepe and Damarlo and the fourth guy she didn't know stomping Fireman Mike.

She untucked her legs and slipped her shoes back on, feeling naked suddenly. Feeling a need to run.

The footage, she assumed, came from the camera Skellenger had mentioned—well at least he hadn't lied about that. Small comfort.

Then the clip cut off and guess who.

There she was, on-screen, ten years younger. The girl I'll never be again and can never stop being. The girl I hate. The girl I miss.

Now absolutely everybody knows I was there, she thought—how'd it happen so quick? No time to regroup, get her mind around the thing. They're gonna come after me, Mo Pete, Chepe, maybe even the cops—Skellenger can't pull off every dog.

Then the kicker: a reward. A hundred goddamn thousand dollars. How far could you go on that? Far enough. Long enough. Mexico. For good.

Yeah, like you'd live long enough to collect.

She felt a humming buzz in her pocket. Her cell—she'd forgotten to turn it off after checking it last. Stupid. Dangerous. She fished it out, checked the display—a text:

Why haven't you answered my messages? It's all over the news.

Don't be fooled and go to the police. It's a trick, the money. You know how they are. Do what they want and they'll just make life miserable for us all.

The TV chingados have shown up outside. Don't come here. Call me, talk to me, tell me where you are. I'll come get you. We know a place where you'll be safe.

Jacqi found herself staring at the words, as though they were a kind of optical illusion. Look at them this way, they appear to be *this*. Then turn them like so—see? Now they resemble *that*. Except they didn't resemble anything. They weren't, in any actual sense, even real. They were there but not there.

So much for *Come home*, she thought, snapping the phone closed. Let alone *Te amo*. Now turn the thing off, like you've been told. Or go to the door and chuck it hard and far. Cuz they're out there looking for you, all of them, this minute. Hunting you down. *You know how they are*. Yes, Mother, I do. Just like I know what "we" means.

The restaurant door opened with a rattle and a chime, and despite herself she jumped. A man. It took a second, the light behind him, but then he stepped forward, got close. The silhouette acquired a face.

"Okay if I join you?"

Tell him you're leaving, she thought, but then Ilena arrived with her food. Busted. Wiping her hands on her apron, the plump *salvadoreña* glanced toward Tierney, and he gestured he was fine. Ilena trundled back to the kitchen and he just stood there, waiting.

She had trouble looking up at his face. "What are you doing here?"

"I saw the news."

"You know what I mean. Why are you *here*?"

Rudolfo lowered the TV volume and began humming some nameless *corrido* behind the bar, letting them know he was watching, wary of trouble.

"The friend you went to see at the hospital," Tierney said. "I guessed right. It was Mike Verrazzo."

That's how easy it'll be, she thought, for the whole damn town to put two and two together. And come up with whatever they want. "Answer my question."

"He was the man you were hoping would step up, help you leave town."

She swallowed what felt like a wad of wet hair. "What if it was?"

"You watched him get killed. That's a hard thing to go through." His voice was gentle. "I felt concerned. Thought it wouldn't hurt to have someone to talk to. If you'd like that." He gestured to the other side of the booth. "Mind if I sit?"

She wanted to believe him. So tired of being lied to. So tired in general. "First you gotta tell me how you found me."

"If it's any consolation, this is the fourth place I looked."

"Yeah, I'm so consoled. Who—"

"Don't be mad at her."

Her, she thought. "That'll depend."

"Mattie. The older—"

"I know who she is."

Rudolfo, apparently mollified, turned the TV to a soccer match and notched the sound back up—screaming crowd, breathless announcer with a voice like a gong.

"If you're going to get mad," Tierney said, "get mad at me."

Yeah, she thought, you'd like that. "Sure, fine, sit down, whatever."

37

He shouldered out of his coat, nudged it into the corner and slid in across from her, nodding at her plate. "Smells good," he said. "Go ahead and eat."

She looked down at the grilled *pupusas* with the shredded pork inside, the steamy pool of puréed black beans plopped with sour cream, the toasted chunks of yucca—how, she wondered, can I be this hungry and still feel like I'm gonna hurl?

"By the way—you may find this interesting—know what Mattie's real name is?"

Granny Snitch McCumglutton? "No. Tell me."

"Buttonwillow Hazeltine."

He looked pleased with himself, explaining how he'd dug it up on the Internet, court records. Yeah, she thought, you must love that, digging stuff up. "You coulda been some twisted slasher dipwad, wants to cut me open."

"But I'm not. She got that. I think you do too."

Oh go take a jump. She unwrapped her fork and knife from their paper napkin. The plate seemed big as the table. "You want some of this? I don't think I can eat it all."

"You should try," he said. Then, pointing. "I'll take one of those." He reached over, plucked a slice of fried yucca off her plate.

"What you should try is some *pupusa*." She cut off a corner, speared it with her fork, passed it to him. "It's pretty yummy."

He took the fork, hesitated.

"I'm not worried about your cooties," she said. "If you're worried about mine, I haven't used the fork yet."

He blushed and smiled and plucked the morsel daintily off its tines, using his lips, not just his teeth. Oh, how bold.

"Wow," he said. "What's that flavor?"

"It's called *loroco*." She tucked her hair behind her ears, get it out of her face. "It's, like, this little flower pod." She cut off a bite of *pupusa* for herself, shmoodged it around in the black beans and sour cream. "So old Mattie handed me up."

"Don't take it out on her." He'd moved on to the yucca, holding the toasted wedge like a magic coin. "I think the old girl's got a soft spot for you, to be honest."

"Like you. Two of you got something in common. Maybe you should hook up."

"I've got that base covered, thanks."

"Not from what I saw." She remembered the lanky redhead, the nurse, bolting the cafeteria.

Ever so slightly, his face colored again. "Point is, if I can find you this easily, anybody can."

"So you get why I'm pissed at Old Mattie."

"Maybe it's not such a bad thing, being found. If it's up to you how you're seen. And by who."

She looked at him, chewing. "Wow. That's, like, deep."

Don't be such a snot, she thought, digging into her food some more. The *curtido* tasted crisp and vinegary but not sour. Behind the bar, an ecstatic buzzing cry from the TV crowd, the announcer dragging it out: "*Goooooooooooooooooooal!*"

"I wasn't being philosophical," he said. "Mattie told me there were some other men, two in particular, who came around, asking if she'd seen you. They had a picture."

Jacqi glanced up, gripping her fork a bit tighter, feeling the pulse in her throat. Ben and Hector, Navarette's hammerheads. "She give them the same info she gave you?"

"I don't think so. She said she didn't."

"She just, what, liked your face?"

"Like I said, I think she realized I wasn't out to hurt you. But it might be wise not to stay here too long."

As though on cue the door opened again with the usual rattle and clang. In unison Jacqi glanced up, Tierney spun around.

Two young *jornaleros* entered, their hair wet and the shoulders of their jackets dark with rain. They nodded shyly and dropped into the first booth as, from the back, over the TV, Ilena crooned, *"Momen-TI-to!"*

38

Jacqi relaxed back into her seat, only then realizing she was gripping her fork like a weapon. Tierney turned back around, offered a buck-up smile, and leaned closer across the table.

"Getting back to what happened this morning," he said. "I'm guessing that derails your plans about leaving."

Jacqi cut off another morsel of *pupusa*. Her hand trembled. "Nope."

"It should."

She affected a shrug. "None of your business, to be honest."

"You asked me for money."

"And you said no way. Change your mind?"

She glanced up. That face, she thought. He should rent it out for funerals.

"Not exactly," he said. "But I've been thinking about something else you said, about staying at my place."

Jacqi stopped chewing and locked her eyes on his. He didn't seem to be making a play, given the kind of come-on she was used to. Still . . .

"The house I shared with my wife is largely empty. I stay at my girlfriend's house most of the time now."

"The nurse," she said, thinking: Most of the time. Not all.

"Her name is Cass. I just go over to the old place to pick up mail, get a change of clothes if I need it. I can make sure the pilot for the water heater's on, crank up the furnace. You'll be safe there, or as safe as anywhere else, while you figure out a plan—"

"I don't need a plan. I have a plan. I told you—"

"You're a material witness in a major homicide."

"I didn't see anything."

"That's called a finding of fact, to be determined at trial. They'll be looking for you everywhere."

"Not where I'm going."

"You don't have the money, you told me that, what, an hour ago? Think. There's a hundred-thousand-dollar reward out there now. You don't step forward then your whereabouts become an issue and anyone who hands you up has a legitimate claim to part of that pot. Besides which, the headlines in this thing? No lawyer on either side can afford to phone it in, and you can bet, on top of everything else, somebody's going to sue somebody else for negligence or wrongful death, the wife especially, loss of financial support, loss of consortium—which is a joke, given what I know about this guy—but the numbers at stake will be huge. If there's even a hint of gang involvement, the city and county may try using asset forfeiture to cover their own exposure. Long story short, ten years from now they'll still be litigating this thing, which means it'll be worth someone's while to track you down no matter how far you run."

She pictured it again, Playa Ventura, saw in her mind's eye the narrow, hoof-marked, sand-drifted streets, the ramshackle hotels along the volcanic beach, the relentless surf. No way they'd find her there—how would they even know to look?

Then she remembered—Skellenger said they'd be cloning her cell. They could track her web search history, all those Lonely Planet hits.

It was enough to make her weep. Where's a guy like Victor Cope when you need him? He'd know how to make her disappear.

"Know what? I'm sick of saving people. I saved this city, remember? Testified against the monster. Look how fabulous that turned out. Now seems like they want me to do it again. Whole new monster. Well, fuck them. Fuck you. I can't give you whatever it is you want. Just leave me alone."

"If I thought that was your best option," he said, "I would."

He had the whole sincerity thing nailed, had to grant him that. "So what makes me safe at your place?"

Tierney glanced briefly at Rudolfo, then over his shoulder at the two workmen, nodding thoughtfully as he came back around, as though gearing up for a long story.

"This goes back before you were born, but I assume you've heard of the O. J. Simpson case."

That one came outta left field. "I'm not stupid."

"I didn't say you were. There was a friend of Simpson's named Al Cowlings."

"The white Bronco guy."

"Exactly." He seemed modestly impressed. "Nickname was AC. He was with Simpson during the drama on the freeway—kind of like you in the car with Verrazzo. That entire situation gave 'media circus' a whole new meaning, and the trial was even worse. But Cowlings never got formally charged and he never testified at trial. Hardly anyone knows who his lawyer was. Because he wasn't out to milk his client for publicity or cash in on the back end. His name was Don Re. The one lawyer in that whole mess who seemed to understand what his job was. I know a few guys in the city like that—Tony Tamburello, for one. I'd trust my life with Tony."

"It's not your life we're talking about, though, is it."

"You can rely on him."

"To do what?"

"He'll probably have you surrender, make bail if they decide to charge you—"

"I didn't *do* anything."

"I've explained this to you. You violated a court order when you left Winchinchala House. You didn't remain at the scene to give a statement. As for what was going on in the car—"

"*Nothing* went on." We didn't get that far, she thought.

"Regardless, he'll probably have you take the Fifth unless they promise immunity. Even if they do, Tony can make it so both sides realize they've got more to lose than gain by putting you on the stand. I assume that's what you want, given your attitude."

"What attitude?"

"You haven't stepped up and told what you saw, despite a reward."

"Rewards are a joke."

"Have it your way. My point is, Tony's smart. He'll protect you."

Meaning you'll protect me, she thought, finally beginning to see his angle. "And who's gonna pay for all this?"

"Knowing Tony, he might take it pro bono. If not, I can help out."

"Get real, he's gonna want something, right?"

"I can't speak for him, but—"

"So you'll pay for that but not front me two thousand so I can just disappear."

He sat back, sagging a little. "You won't disappear, that's the point. Not for long. And it's not about the money."

"What's it about then—Eastwood?"

That stopped him for a second. "It was wrong to push you like that. You don't have to tell me anything you don't want to. Especially now."

"Got that right." Inside her head, a sound that wasn't a sound—a screechy howling silence—raked across the darkness. She wanted to let it out. She didn't dare. "So I stay at your place instead."

"Until Tony gets up to speed, yeah."

"Know what?" She leaned forward, squared herself, took a second to lock in. "I spent a couple days at some guy's place before. Not for long. Waiting for him to get up to speed, so to speak. See where I'm going with this?"

It was like she'd pulled a plug. The color drained from his face and he sat back, started to say something, checked himself. She could almost hear the gears turning inside his skull.

"I can protect myself," she said.

"Not by running."

"What is it with you? You're my tutor for the goddamn GED, for chrissake. No, wait, you're some hotshot lawyer with, like, connections, except you're also tracking me all over town like some skeevy bounty hunter for Lonnie the Liar. God knows what else. Your nurse girlfriend storms out when you come over to talk to me, what the hell is that about? But 'Hey, crash at my place, it's cool.' I'm supposed to *trust* you?"

I'd like to, she thought. If you'd just stop trying so hard. Christ, back off and I'd kiss you. Shoving her plate away, she said, "You're making my head hurt."

He had that look, so strong, so soulful. So full of shit.

"Sorry," he said, sounding like a drunk trying to donate blood.

39

Tierney, feeling spent to the bone, doubted he'd ever worked so hard to such humbling effect. And yet the girl seemed somewhat ragged as well. Maybe, he thought, we're actually getting somewhere.

She sat across the table, staring at her plate as though hoping to move it through telepathy. Fussing with her hair. Nodding.

"So you're really not interested in hearing about Eastwood anymore?"

Tierney chuckled to hide his surprise. You had to hand it to her, the girl had a major-league curve.

"I said I don't need to hear about it, not now. You've got more immediate worries."

She glanced up. "It's not what you think."

"I'm not sure I think much of anything. I mean, except that it's important somehow, given how everybody's acting."

She began picking at a protruding edge on the strip of ridged aluminum rimming the laminated table.

"Eastwood," she said, "was this friend of my brother's, that much is right. He was four years older than me and he used to come over to the house to visit Richie and I kinda, I dunno, had a crush on him.

Schoolgirl stuff, embarrassing really, looking back at it, I mean. I was really into *Smallville*, the TV show? He was, too, and we'd talk about what we liked, what we hated. He hung out at this gas station where there was a plum tree around back and he'd bring over these bags of plums."

Her nodding became a little more earnest, as though the memory had convinced her of something.

"Honestly, that's all there is to it. But when I was outta my mind scared with Cope, I must've said something—I'd seen on TV where it's harder for a killer to follow through if he can see his victims as human beings. And so I just started talking this one time and he must've taken it, you know, like Eastwood and me had some kinda thing going on. But that's just sewage from Cope's sick head. It's got nothing to do with me or my brother. I need you to hear me on that, okay?"

Her voice cracked a little at the end and her eyes seemed uneasy, like she was expecting an argument. Tierney said, "If that's all it is, your brother's reaction seems, well, rather extreme."

"Nobody in the family wants Victor Cope back in our lives."

"Of course, but—"

"He gets wind anybody takes him serious, about this or anything else, he'll find himself a jailhouse lawyer and file some goddamn motion and next thing you know—"

"I understand," Tierney said, thinking there was more, maybe a lot more, still left unsaid, but before he could think of a way to get there the girl stiffened, her eyes turning hard as she looked past him toward the door.

Turning, he saw the familiar black Mercedes convertible pulling to a stop out front. Navarette's men, Little Monster and the Moose. Ben Escalada, Hector Mancinas. Apparently ol' Buttonwillow had told them after all.

Jacqi slid quickly out of the booth. Tierney reached for her hand. "Wait—"

She yanked the hand back, eyes flashing, but then seemed to calm down and nodded toward her plate. "Pull that over to your side, like it's yours. Tell them you came to find me too but I wasn't here, you decided to grab some chow." She backed away, eyes on the door. "I'm gonna go hide in the ladies'. Let Ilena know when they've left and she'll come get me."

She hurried down the hallway beyond the bar toward the restrooms, ducked her head into the kitchen, caught Ilena's eye. *"Mi amigo pagará mi comida."* She pointed toward the rear of the restaurant. *"Afuera?"*

Ilena, using tongs to arrange shredded *curtido* on two plates, glanced up wearily, then nodded.

Beyond a clutter of mops and brooms and hanging coats, Jacqi spotted the door leading out. She headed straight for it, threw the bolt, shouldered it open, felt the damp cool air on her skin.

A narrow alley with a high brick wall, stitched with vines, ran in both directions. She gathered her bearings, pulled up her hood and headed west, toward Bettye's.

Digging into her pocket, she took out her phone and finally turned it off, realizing that wasn't how Escalada and Mancinas had tracked her down but understanding now, better than ever, how easily she could get found.

She hit the side street and pictured Tierney still sitting at the table, left to deal with the situation alone, like some chump she'd tricked into taking her to the prom so she could hang with the guy she actually liked. She felt bad. Not terrible, but bad. The man was jinxed. Rotten luck followed him around. Very rotten luck.

Next time you see him, she thought, apologize. Till then, remember: you're the girl who gets away.

40

Tierney sat there toying with the cold plate of food, detecting a faint soap-like scent he ultimately traced to the cilantro. He'd gotten up and taken the girl's place once she trundled off, wanting to face the door when it opened.

He'd considered priming his cell to 911, ready to thumb the call button, but he thought better of involving the police just yet, seeing the wisdom of first wrangling up a lawyer for the girl. Hearing the car doors slam out front, he turned and caught the barman's eye, saying matter-of-factly, "There could be trouble," then the front door swung open with a rattle of blinds and the chime of its small tin bell.

Tierney pretended to eat until the two of them reached the table and stopped, the small one walking point, the hulk watching his six. Glancing up, he offered a smile.

"Well slap my ass and call me Spanky, look who's here."

Up front near the window the two *jornaleros* shrank into their meals, trying to become even more invisible as the small one, Escalada, glanced around. Finally his eyes landed on Tierney, not happily. "Where is she?"

"Who do you mean?"

"Don't play. Where is she?"

Tierney speared a piece of cold yucca with his fork. "I have no idea. I came here hoping to find her, like you two, but that didn't pan out. Nice place, though." He glanced around appraisingly. "Figured what the hell, might as well grab a bite."

Escalada narrowed his gaze, like he was struggling with the small print, then turned to the mammoth, Mancinas, nodding him toward the back.

The big man started lumbering that direction and Tierney slid quickly out of the booth, shot to his feet, and snagged an arm, the muscle hard as a lamppost beneath the suit-coat sleeve.

"Don't bother these people. I told you, the girl's not here."

Mancinas tried to shake off the hand but Tierney held tight. He figured the buster for two and a quarter, a fifty-pound giveaway, but you could tell from the shuffling footfall he wasn't quick. Built like a freezer, just less agile.

The guy's opposite arm came around high, a meat-hook round-house aiming for the skull, but Tierney had a month to block the punch, then he grabbed both lapels and jerked hard, delivering a head-butt that drew blood fast from the big man's nose.

Mancinas dipped at the waist in pain and Tierney ducked under him, centered his leverage, hooked an arm beneath one thick leg, lodged a shoulder into the big fella's midriff and lifted him up, off his feet, then dropped him onto the floor like a big sack of thunder. Not quite the perfect snatch single takedown, Tierney thought, but sufficient to the day thereof. *I will kill thee a hundred and fifty ways.* If this had been a match or an honest-to-god street fight, he'd have gone to the floor to finish it, but the smaller one, Escalada, reached inside his jacket, drawing Tierney's focus, just as the bartender hammered the top of the bar with a maple timber baseball bat he'd pulled from a corner.

"Out!" He raised the bat to his shoulder like an ax. "*Todos.* The girl no here."

The two *jornaleros* were the ones who moved, dropping their forks and scrambling out as another voice—the woman's, Ilena's—shouted from the kitchen doorway. "The girl, she go." She gestured behind her with a nod. "That way, the back." Slowly wiping her hands on her apron. "Now go. You leave us in peace."

Mancinas struggled to his feet, eyeing Tierney with school-yard hate, one bloody hand cupping his nose, while Escalada slipped past quickly and nudged Ilena aside, went back to check the restrooms—doors screeching open, slamming shut—then through the kitchen to the rear.

No one else moved, Tierney momentarily stunned that the girl had fled, feeling vaguely comical. *I can protect myself.*

Escalada hurried back, pushing past Ilena and heading toward the front, not wasting a glance on Tierney, just nodding for Mancinas to follow him out. But the big man lingered, tottering a little on his feet as he mad-dogged Tierney one last time—puckering his lips, a wink, a surprising choirboy tenor. "Catch you on the flip side, *gabacho.*"

It talks, Tierney thought, as the two men headed out, then he pulled out his wallet, hands trembling from adrenaline. "How much do I owe you?" He pointed toward the front table, where the two workmen had sat. "I'll pay for them as well." Neither Ilena nor the bartender spoke. He counted out five twenties, set them on the bar, then raised his hand and said, "We'll leave it there. My apologies for the trouble."

41

Jacqi stuck to backstreets and headed for Bettye's, wind ripping off the river down the jagged weedy concrete as she slinked shadow to shadow, hood pulled tight, listening for sudden cars.

Night already, barely five o'clock. No rain yet, but she could smell it coming.

If she'd been paying more attention, not lost in thought, she wouldn't have blundered right in.

But there she stood, nailed in place as she finally glanced up, halfway in, halfway out, hand on the doorknob, barging in on Mo Pete Carson, plopped in one of the styling chairs like he'd come to get his braids washed out and retwisted.

Bettye. She'd watched the news, made some calls, put two and two together.

Time feeling stuck, like a snapshot.

Two other Cutties behind Mo Pete, thugging it up, arms crossed, one thin as a rail, the other chunky but solid, not fat like Mo Pete, hat kicked right, brim cocked.

Mo Pete with one hand deep inside a knapsack—my knapsack, she thought—the floor littered with socks, tights, blouses, undies.

The clincher: Bettye, off to the side, thumbing through a money roll.

My money: $193.

Next snapshot—*click*—everybody glancing up, turning her way. Theater of eyes, dumbstruck stares. The moment like a punch, a rocking silent pulse of air.

She ran.

Get off the street, she thought, hearing the two hoodrats bang out the door behind her—not needing to look, not wasting the time, pushing herself to full speed, arms and legs pumping like skinny pistons, darting down the nearest side alley and feeling the little fist of food in her belly clenching, working its way up through a sour backspill.

Pools of misty lamplight. Caves of shadow.

She ducked into the first space between garages, almost hitting the trash can, giving herself away.

Holding her breath. Trying not to upchuck.

The two Cutties barreled around the corner, passed her spot, figuring it out too late. She darted back the way she'd come.

Seeing the hand reach out, corner of her eye, she swatted it off, batting at it, spinning out of its grip, aiming for the street and flying.

What was it some kid said from the edge of a fight she'd been in, middle school, kicking the shit-and-chickens out of Junalta Cuthbert? *Damn, check it out, yo, that Garza bitch, she's wiry but she's strong.*

Strong enough to fly.

She dodged a downhill bus, the thing pitching to a stop to miss her, all headlights and screeching hiss and lunging silhouettes inside. She hopped a fence, heading for the next alley over. This one darker, much so, safer.

Into the maze: window lights. Barking dogs. Jabbering TVs.

Pathways and landmarks fired in her memory—she was tunneling like a rat, reminding herself: this is your domain, not theirs, your one advantage. Go.

Quick glance over the shoulder—there they were, both of them, Thinman in front, all knees and elbows, Chunky lagging, gripping his hat, but both on the come.

She headed for the trapdoor she'd thought about, planned for, thinking she might need it someday: back of the old Odd Fellows Hall, the ladder to a fire escape. Grab it, climb fast, pull it up behind. Safe. Scramble to the roof and catch your breath, think things through. Plans B through Z.

She turned the corner, alley funneling toward the spot, and she sprinted, lungs burning. Then the sudden curious heart-stopping sense: No. Wrong.

The ladder was gone.

Somebody beat her to it, they'd pulled the thing up. It beckoned out of reach, a practical joke.

Thank you, God. Why do you hate me?

The pounding flap of sneakers behind. A quick glance back.

Taking off, burst of speed and her throat aching now, chest aching too, mouth dry as stone from sucking in air, like inhaling bleach, legs tightening. A thumping quiver in her right thigh. No no no, please no.

Whimpering grunts behind as Thinman closed ground, edging nearer, pushing himself, hurtling toward her, a human blade.

The alley broke open at the street and she was angling left when the hand reached out again, pawing at her first, then catching hold, the hood, some hair, snapping her back.

Unthinking, a spin, a kick, nails to the eyes, scraping at the damp dark skin. But he didn't let go, he threw a tight punch of his own, clocking her head as he spun with her and she only vaguely sensed the thing, the mass of metal, not braking in time.

Off-balance, they toppled into its path, the car missing her by an inch, maybe less. The dull snap and breathy thud of his body slamming against the headlight and fender, the wet shriek of rubber gripping pavement, then he jackknifed under the thing like a broken doll dragged by an unseen hand.

The tire crushed his leg, and he screamed like a boy.

Kept screaming.

Time broke again, like a shattered window.

Rhythmic swoosh of the windshield wipers. The driver, small, gray-haired, slumped, hands gripping the wheel like the top rung of a ladder.

Jacqi thinking: If you hate me, God, why do you spare me? Or is that just part of the hate?

The other one, Chunky, burst from the alley, thudding to a clumsy stop. Chest heaving. Staring at the ground first, pop-eyed, the screams, his friend, then up at Jacqi, gaze empty, back to the ground—bending his knee, stopping himself, clutching his head.

She ran.

Part V

42

They'd come and gone throughout the middle of the afternoon, her little ones. Thursday, pediatric cancer clinic. The last of them left at four, some happily responding to treatment, some sunnily brave despite their ghostliness, some quiet, worn down, and scared. The parents were just as various, mothers mostly, everything from stoic to shrill. All, on some level, numb.

Even now, more than an hour later, Cass had yet to tug off the motley jester's hat she wore for them—perched atop her tumbling red hair, each floppy velvet point (green, black, yellow, red) tipped with a tiny silver bell. I just may, she thought, wear the damn thing home. Make Phelan fuck me in it.

Usually the clinic bustled this time of day, five to six, patients transitioning from work to home, with a detour for treatment in the jagged crack between worlds. Today, though, only two patients sat in the infusion chairs.

There'd been more than a few cancellations. The whole town seemed in shock, asking or fearing to ask: What next?

The first patient was Mariko Detwiler, forty-two, Stage III metastatic breast cancer, Adriamycin and Taxotere. Birdlike, square-faced, an artist—specialized pottery, fine ceramics—she paged through trashy magazines, tethered to her drip.

The second: Ron Buker, Stage II hepatocellular carcinoma. He was getting systemic chemotherapy too—same drug even, Adriamycin—because he didn't qualify for hepatic artery infusion. Bad luck on that front. Systemic chemo was a long shot for liver cancer, but what else was there—leeches?

His hair had turned patchy but he'd yet to make the bold move to shaving his head, preferring to comb strategically what was left, his pale head furrowed with wispy dark strands. Once hard-muscled and oxlike, now he was wasting, fifty pounds lost in the past six months. He admitted fatigue and mouth sores. Bruises mottled his fleshy arms.

His son, Teddy, twentysomething, a tradesman like his dad, had come along as always. Today, though, he seemed mesmerized by the TV in the upper corner.

The Verrazzo thing. Every ten seconds, it seemed, an update.

They'd already made some arrests, the news bits picking up pace. Teddy seemed particularly mesmerized by the video of the kids kicking Verrazzo to death.

A blogger for *Rio Mirada Spotlight*, an online zine that reported whatever the local paper wouldn't touch, had been wandering the halls like so many other newsmongers, and apparently he'd latched on to the Bukers somewhere between the lobby and here, chatting them up, following them in.

The guy's name was Doug Zordich—out of some awkward courtesy, he'd handed Cass a business card—and he sat with the father now, recording their conversation on his phone, an interview for some kind of podcast related to the murder.

As Cass cycled through, checking the older man's infusion rate and reservoir level, she caught a little of the back and forth.

"Correct me if I'm wrong, but you guys, the IBEW, you were left with scraps."

He wore his graying hair long and combed straight back, like a cartoon maestro. Herringbone sweater draped on a stick-thin frame.

"CBA got tossed, yeah." Ron took in a ragged breath. "Health care got cut from fifteen hundred a month to zip. Overnight. Obamacare chips in now, but there's always talk about repeal, or cutting it back to squat. Death by a thousand cuts. I'm buying generics against my doctor's advice because I can't afford the seventy-five-dollar copay."

"Your pension doesn't cover your costs?"

"Who said pension? I'm stuck on disability."

"You're not retired?"

"Got five years before that kicks in. If it's still there. Or I am."

Cass, sensing it was time, leaned down, hands on knees. "Mind if I butt in here for a sec?" Bright smile for the patient. "Hey, big stuff. Tell me. Feeling okay?"

Their eyes met, and his rancor melted. A smile of almost boyish welcome. "Hey." He shrugged. "I'm okay." He nodded at her headgear. "Love the hat."

"Thursdays. I'm Cass the Clown. How's the nausea?"

The eyes went inward, dragging his voice along. "Gotta be rough, those kids."

"It's all rough. What about the nausea?"

"Same." Another shrug, eyes still elsewhere. "Pretty much."

"Pretty much as in a little better, little worse?"

"Can't really tell, to be honest. Try not to think about it. Let's just say same."

"Okay." She stood full height amid the tinny racket of jester bells. A warning glance at Zordich. "Let's keep things calm." She smoothed an invisible sheet.

• • •

Trooping back to the nurse's station, Cass glanced once toward Mariko and her glam mags, once toward Teddy still hypnotized by the TV, cocked an ear.

Ron turned back to Zordich. "I know how you guys think. Like we were robbing the store. Well get this. You work thirty years, scrimp and get by, banking on that money, your pension. Then you get to where you need it. And it's a joke, a lie."

"Not a big believer in pension reform, I take it."

"Reform for who?"

"Well, you've got to admit there were abuses. Workers spiking their wages right before retirement, air time, even felons getting payouts."

"I'm tapped out. Down to the fumes on my savings. My boy, Teddy, over there, he's kicking in. Good kid. But there's no work for him up here, neither."

"Economy's pretty rotten all over."

"You're not hearing me. Our promises we kept. But theirs?"

Teddy, having caught his name, finally pried himself away from the TV, drifted a little closer toward the conversation. Sizing up Zordich, his dad: "Everything copacetic?"

Zordich sat back, pushed his glasses up his nose, eyes still focused on the father. "What about the politics that got us here?"

"That was Verrazzo," Teddy said. "Look where it got him."

"You think his killing's some kind of payback?"

Teddy bridled. "Little-known fact, pal: what goes around comes around."

"I'm hearing some people think your guy, head of the IBEW, Donny Bauserman—they think he's feeling pretty good right about now, given how Verrazzo—"

"What the fuck you know about it?" Like that, the kid looked ready to have at it. "Ass-hats like you—carpetbaggers, yuppie fucks—you think you know everything, but guess what? You don't know jack, not about working people, not about us, not about what—"

"Teddy." His dad breaking in. "Don't let this character—"

"Bauserman wasn't anywhere near Verrazzo," Teddy said. "He had a meeting this morning, Code Enforcement, he—"

Zordich: "And you know this why?"

Caught up short, the young man blinked. Then a wince, like he'd been bit by a tricky thought.

Cass slid from behind the nurse's station, took up position between the two, a referee. "What did I say?" Her eyes moved face to face, and only then did she realize she was still wearing the ridiculous hat. She considered yanking it off, but then thought: Why? There was something to be said for a six-foot redhead wearing jester bells who could shut these fools up. "You keep it down," she said. "Or you leave."

Teddy shot Zordich one last look, then turned away, edged back to the TV. Zordich nodded guiltily, glancing at the floor. Ron sank back into the infusion chair.

"Better," Cass said. She glanced over at Mariko, who seemed even more Zen-like with her magazines, then dragged herself back behind the nurse's station.

Dropping into her swivel chair, she finally tugged off the hat.

43

In time Zordich left and the clinic fell quiet except for the TV murmur. Mariko snagged a pen and notebook from her purse and began sketching savagely. Ron Buker napped while his son once again stared up at the news, transfixed by the coverage.

Cass caught herself every now and then glancing up at the screen as well. They were flashing images of Jacqi Garza now, not the jittery thin teenager she'd seen in the cafeteria earlier but pictures from a decade ago.

Wrong picture, Cass thought. Wrong girl. But what did they care? Same with Phelan. All of them chained together in the same basement. Forever.

In the grand scheme of things, she supposed—the economic shipwreck lying dead ahead, for example, except for the hedge fund mafia and their ilk, who'd made off with the lifeboats—something as vain and wispy as love seemed an almost reckless waste of time. And yet she'd thought of little else since that day Phelan showed up again, right here in the ward.

She'd been an ugly duckling, the lanky overfreckled redhead tomboy. Guys liked her okay, she was swell. Good listener. Told great jokes. Pure death with a basketball.

When it got around to sex they turned, well, weird. Like she'd fake them out of their jocks, dunk on them. And so the head games.

I'm into you but, hey, prove to me you're worth it.

Her sister had been no help. Shelly had that magic, damn near tripped over guys in her sleep. If she couldn't come by them honestly, she poached them off her friends, colleagues. Her redheaded sister. One night over cosmos at the Empire in Napa, she'd slung her arm around Cass's neck, smiled and winked and sloppily whispered, "There's only one way to keep a man—confused."

The first long-term relationship? Quinn Chislenko, graduate assistant in organic chem. Weeks of silence punctuated by moody blistering fights, slammed doors, wheedling apologies, kinky makeup sex. Trainer marriage. Training for what?

After that, serial monogamy, one experiment after the next. The male specimen. Don't forget to turn in your lab results.

Over time, like a slow-spreading sickness, she felt it growing, this shame-tinged dread. It just wasn't going to happen. Not her lot in life. She was one of those who never.

Then there was Phelan.

They had that thing, that almost effortless, reassuring thing that any sane woman had to think was a lie. But so far, no, it was good. It had its rough spots, sure, but he got her. He saw her. Not the woman he wanted—or secretly hated—but the big goofy redhead right there: me.

Which was why this bit with Jacqi Garza had her so twisted up. It had her scared. Bad enough she had to compete with the lost wife. Now this.

And that was the irony. Know what bankrupt really is? Being in love. Because you don't earn love, it's a gift. You can never repay what you owe. All you can do is love back, and what if your heart isn't big enough?

Another glance in the TV's direction and there was Teddy again, rooted to his spot, eyes locked on the screen. That same dated photo of the girl. He had his phone out, thumbing in a number, lifting the mouthpiece to his lips.

"LeQuan, yeah, hit me back. Soon. Like now."

44

She was having trouble with the screaming in her head. Thinman lying there, crushed beneath the car, a face not quite human and all that blood—would he live? She saw him hobbling through the streets of time to track her down, make her pay.

How odd then that she'd end up here, and yet how perfect, across the street and down the block from her mother's house—my house, she thought, like she was trying on the idea, checking the fit, so long since she'd worn it—hiding behind the chokecherry tree in the Warburtons' yard, bumping her hip against the tree's grooved bark, feeling the knife-like roughness through her skirt.

Come home. Te amo.

A harsh wind rustled through the jagged green leaves, but it was the throbbing hum of the TV vans that snapped her back.

Three of them camped there, waiting. She could walk right up if she wanted, tell them the story, from Fireman Mike to Thinman. Some kinda day, huh? Sit beside the reporters like they were pals, hanging on every word. Just like old times.

Was it really ten years ago that she'd gone missing, or was it this morning? Was it now?

• • •

She'd been walking the neighborhood that day, thinking of ways not to go home. Ways to stay out of her mother's hair, avoid the latest bitch fit. Ways to avoid Richie. As for Eastwood, well, he hadn't come around in a while.

She wanted to sit on the couch, pillow pressed to her stomach, watch *Smallville*—she was allowed to tape the show on Monday nights, replay it the rest of the week when she got home from school.

She knew the show was wack—how could anyone dreamy as Clark Kent be such a hopeless spaztard?—but she just got caught up in it, like you got caught up in a song.

In fact, she played the opening credits over and over just to hear the theme—Remy Zero, "Save Me"—until Richie barreled in, turned it off, calling her *dundo*.

> I feel my wings have broken in your hands
> I feel the words unspoken inside

Instead, that day, she walked—no sense of where to go, though the playground on Magnolia exerted a kind of gravity. She could sit in the swings and wait—for what? When would this be over? How would she know? What would the next thing look like?

One sneaker slapped the sidewalk after the next and she suffered one of her waking dreams, the one where things dissolved into the background, fitting themselves into the pattern. Everything flattened out, like she wasn't in the world anymore. She was in a movie about the world.

Her throat knotted up. There was nothing to do when this came over her, just ride it through. Nothing felt new or real, it had all been said and done before and would all be said and done again. Like a lost episode of *Smallville* running over and over on some oddball channel and she was trapped inside, everything perfectly predictable and yet scary and strange.

Maybe when she got to the swings. But that would feel same-as-always too. Like she was watching herself watch herself. Like she was the final piece in a puzzle that someone else snapped into place.

And yet—what if she got hurt? If she pushed herself as high in the swing as possible, then let go, sailed through the air, free . . .

Pain would make this go away, wouldn't it? Didn't it have to?

> Somebody save me
> I don't care how you do it

The car pulled up just a little ahead, stopping at the curb, a flare of red taillights. The engine rattled as it died, and a man got out.

He was wearing a shirt with a patch on the pocket in the shape of a badge. He'd combed his hair weirdly, an old man's style, and he had the face of somebody who'd washed all the Me away, his gaze fixed and yet empty, like someone peering through eyeholes in a mask.

They've come looking for me, she figured, at the same time thinking: They've always been coming. This has always been happening.

"You've been crying," the man said. Not an accusation, but not exactly comforting either. An observation. A recognition of the pattern.

She wiped at her face, but her hands came away dry. Her eyes, her cheeks, nothing. What had he seen?

"What's your name?" His voice had that twang.

"Jacquelina." Her official name, the one you gave adults, especially ones in uniform. For reasons she would never understand, she added, "I was going to the park."

"I know," he replied, not like he did. Like he was just saying he did. He squinted at the nearest houses, as though wondering where she belonged, then pointed his keys at the car, thumbed the bob, popped his trunk. He smiled but his eyes didn't change, like this was work, everything was work. And he was tired.

"I was wondering if I could ask a favor. I'm with the animal shelter. Found a kitten a few blocks over, skinny little Manx, got a brown spot on its nose, white paws? I was hoping maybe you could help me figure out who it belongs to. Be a shame if I have to take it in."

Overhead, leaves rustled. Sunlight broke through the shade, blinding her for a second.

He lunged, grabbed her arm, dragged her toward the trunk and half lifted, half shoved her inside. He cut short her scream by stuffing a rag in her mouth, it tasted like vomit and gasoline and she thought of Eastwood, the way he smelled, working at the Citgo, then the man in the uniform punched her hard, once in the stomach, twice to the side of the head. Stars, darkness, retching into the gag as the trunk slammed shut.

Normally there was no way he'd have fooled her so easy. Normally she would have scratched and bit, kicked herself free, run. But it was like she'd been outside her body, watching it unfold—there but not there, a trick she'd master over the next three days with Victor Cope. Meanwhile there was a plan, an elaborate, intricate pattern. She was simply a part of it, the last piece to the puzzle.

And no, there wasn't enough pain in the world to change that.

Snapping back to the present, she reached into her pocket, collected her phone. Time to check for messages. Dragging it out, thumbing the switch—she waited for the display to flicker to life, reminding herself: Three minutes, no more. But what if even that was a trick? What if three minutes was just what they needed to nail you?

She had another text.

Somebody's famous again. Need a place to lie low? Scratch me back: LeQuan.

45

Skellenger shook his wrist, flipped his watch, checked the time: half past six. All in all, given how things had kicked off, the day had turned out stellar. Couple stumbles, sure, a few loose ends. But due to a full-court press across the region, every agency kicking in, plus a little luck, all four meatheads on the front end of the video—still the only part made public yet—had tumbled into custody.

Two right now sat in rooms in the station-house basement—Arian Lomax, Damarlo Melendez—taken from their homes without much fuss and ready for questioning. The other two, Mo Pete Carson and Chepe Salgado, were cuffed in cars and on their way to the station, both tracked to the homes of relatives and apprehended there, one in Hunters Point, one in Boyes Hot Springs.

A coup, really, that things fell together so quick. Even the media, to hear Pendergast tell it, seemed glad for a positive angle. That wouldn't last, of course. The tweets and chat rooms and social sites churned with crackpot theories and wild-ass rumors, not all of them so crackpot or wild-ass. *The Jacqi Garza Show* hadn't gotten beyond previews and speculation, thank God, but that too could change. One way or another there'd be some new spin by the ten-o'clock news, something cheesy or bleak, most likely both.

But he had a few hours to batten things down.

The cages sat in the station basement, four cinder-block rooms arranged in a square, a narrow corridor down the middle lined with one-way glass.

Holmes sat in one room with Damarlo, youngest of the bunch. Kid might get tried as a juvenile, Skellenger thought, if we don't rope him in with the others. All the more reason to turn the Lomax idiot toward the light, show him the way out: Put Damarlo at the center of this, you've got options.

Arian the Unawarian. Man of the hour.

Rosamar leaned into the wall, coffee cup in hand, staring at him through the glass while Skellenger studied his sheet. "What's the story on this bird's second pop?"

"The Special K thing?"

"Where you found him naked in Browner Park, yeah."

Rosamar beamed, took a sip from his cup. "Poor Itchy Homo. So gonna miss him. The sheer entertainment value alone."

"Play by play is kinda what I'm after, Dick. Not color."

"I'm getting there." His eyes narrowed, boring into the kid. "Check out how skinny he is. Got the hips of an eel. Apparently he made some bet, hundred dollars is what we heard, said he could squeeze into one of the kiddie swings at the playground. Well, first he tries with his clothes on. No go. So he strips down to his boxers. Still no. Everybody's mocking him now, telling him to cough up the Franklin. So he goes commando for the final try.

"One of the girls working the park that night has this almond skin lotion with her and he rubs it all over himself, hoping this'll grease him up. Maybe it worked. Anyway, he manages to stuff himself in. Ta-da! Thinks he's a genius, demands his hundred bucks. Just one problem. He can't get out."

Skellenger studied the kid a bit more closely. True, he could fit in a pencil sharpener, but there was a rangy kind of intensity about him too. Howling eyes, caved-in cheeks. Tweaking maybe, wired for sure. And pissed.

Clean him up, lop off the dreads, stuff him in a suit, sit him next to his lawyer—better yet, a pretty little paralegal—maybe a jury would make the connection, maybe not: this kid is a killer. There was always the video, and he was the one who'd played Tyson, swinging first.

His face looked slack, the smokehound eyes heavy-lidded, like he was ready for a nap. One thing you always looked for in a killing, some bug two steps from a snooze.

Rosamar said, "By the way, jaybird naked's not strictly true. He had his kicks and socks on, plus a sweatshirt and peacoat over that. Fucking cold that night. More to the point, the coat's got these monster pockets."

"I'm assuming that's relevant."

"You're paying attention. Cool." Rosamar sloshed his coffee around, stopped short of drinking. The cup's inscription read: Your Life Is Not My Fault. "Anyhoo, Itchy's homies mock the snot out of him, then just leave him there. Take his pants and boxers, wish him luck, hasta la bye-bye. He stays there a couple hours, trying to make like a Pop-Tart. Finally dispatch gets a call, 3 a.m. I think it was. Somebody lives around the corner, they hear an unidentified male yodeling for help."

"We coming to the credits anytime soon?"

"Jordie, relax. You'll love this. Two cruisers roll up, they find poor old Lonesome Lomax stuck there. As if that's not amusing enough, our guys start moseying over—Chuck Tenpenney, Bobby North, those were the guys—and they see Herr Homo here scratching himself raw because he's got some kinda allergic reaction to the almond extract in the lotion he rubbed all over his legs and butt to fit into the swing.

"Well, it finally dawns on him to stop worrying about his skin for a second and pitch the three ten-mil vials of Ketaset he's got in those magical pockets of his. Maybe there were more, but Chuck and Bobby, scrounging around, they found three, and that hurt enough to turn a wobbler into a felony. Possession of ketamine—liquid, injectable— with intent to sell. And since Browner's less than a block away from a detox center . . ."

"Convenient," Skellenger said. Aggravating factor. "How'd they get him out of the swing?"

"They didn't. Had to call the paramedics. Unhooked the thing, took the whole contraption, Itchy still in it, over to RM Gen, cut him out with a bone saw."

"Am I free to assume somebody took pictures?"

Rosamar chuckled. "Mercy, mercy. The grit don't quit. Or, as my dear demented granddad likes to say: 'That's the crackers.'"

"What about the ketamine?"

"Bottles were from some veterinarian. Maybe Arian was going to cook it up into powder, pimp it around the dance scene, or pass it off to someone who could. Regardless, he wouldn't work a deal, hand up his contact, so he took it in the glutes."

"Sheet says he's twenty."

"Nineteen at the time. No juvie juice, though he was still at Stallworth High. Been held back so many years they oughta charge him rent. Practically illiterate."

"Did eighteen months on a two-year stretch."

"For winning a bet. Must've gotten out, I dunno, what's it say?"

"October." Skellenger read, disposition of sentence. Mr. Lomax was still on parole. "We can violate him right now."

"Hello."

"It's leverage." Skellenger folded up the sheets of paper, stuffed them into his jacket pocket. "But I don't want leverage. I want a home run."

"Do your thing." Rosamar pinged a fingernail against the side of his cup. "I'll stay here, learn from the master."

Skellenger hitched up his pants. "Attend to the wind, Grasshopper."

Before heading in, Skellenger glanced in through the glass one last time at Holmes and Damarlo. The kid was touching his face a lot—all that blood rushing to the skin, so many capillaries around the nose, the eyes—which could mean guilt, could mean nerves, could mean nothing. Tough. D-Lo didn't deserve much in the way of pity. Even if he did, it wasn't his day.

Before coming down to the cages, Skellenger had taken a minute to watch the security footage again. Rosamar was right. This Melendez kid went batshit, kicking like a demon, possessed—head region, torso. The throat.

Putting in work. Showing his stuff. *America's Got Talent.*

Put the jacket on him, Skellenger thought, make sure the fit's tight, the Dude Outta Nowhere becomes a nonfactor. And as he goes, so goes Jacqi Garza.

He opened the door to Lomax's room and stepped inside.

46

"How's the skin?"

Arian glanced up slow, as though it was all he could do to lift his dreads. "Yeah." His eyelids fluttered. "Ha-ha."

"I wasn't making a joke." Skellenger pulled back a chair, sat. A tablet and pencil rested on the tabletop. All needs met. "Just wondering if you were comfortable."

He shoved the table against the wall, wanting no barriers between him and the target, nothing to lean on, hide behind. The screech of the table legs against the floor startled the kid and he twitched himself into a less nap like posture, shivering his arms into the sleeves of his hoodie and rolling his long-necked head. Obligatory sniff.

Our children, Skellenger thought. Our future.

"I have to read you something." He took out the Miranda waiver sheet, pulled his chair within two feet of Arian's, then ran through the verbiage calmly, quietly, not too quick, not too slow, like he was reciting the pledge of allegiance. For Latvia. He let Arian use the tabletop to initial every point and sign at the bottom, then sat him back down and tucked the sheet away, mere formality, let's move on. "You know there's a video, right?"

The kid started squirming around in the chair, finally feeling the table's absence. Pretending to get situated. Sit right, think right.

"The service station at the corner has a security camera."

"Uh-huh." Still distracted, looking around him on the floor, like something might've spilled out of his pockets. Except his pockets were empty, everything gone, bagged and itemized, logged on intake.

"You threw the first punch, Arian. Kicked it off. Now somebody's dead."

Finally, the light came on. He blinked. Fussed with his nose. His wrist was heavily bandaged from Verrazzo's snapping it back. "That's, like . . . deflammatory."

Why, Skellenger thought, can't we just shoot them?

"What set it off, Arian? What made you lash out like that?"

"I don't . . . I mean, look. Don't you . . ." He crossed his arms, face knotted up. Whatever thought briefly afflicted him morphed into a shrug.

"One of our guys picked you out, positive ID. Now there's backup from other witnesses. There's no if here. No jiggle. No maybe."

Take heart, Skellenger thought. The kid still wasn't saying it, *I want my* . . . He'd stopped short, flirting with it, sure, almost asking. But asking didn't get you there. The kid was a two-time loser, he knew the drill: you signed the waiver. This point on, you want a lawyer, you don't wonder, you don't whine. You stop the questions and say it. But he was taking his time. He wanted to see what kind of hand he held. Wanted another peek at his hole card.

"You know how this works, Arian. I've got a job to do, you've got a job to do, doesn't mean we can't work together. This is your third strike and that's death. That's checkout. And what are you, twenty? Poof, gone. There's no play here. Unless you step up. You do that, you step up, I can help you."

Count it: One. Two. Wait for it, wait for it . . .

"Let me help you."

The kid did the chair dance, this way, that. "Know what? I don't—"

"That's not gonna walk you out of here, Arian. Look at me."

"I'm just—"

"*Look* at me."

The head tilted back. The drowsy eyes lifted.

"This is heavy, what you're looking at. But it doesn't have to come down all on you. You weren't the only one there."

A murmur, "Damn straight."

"So we can stop the pretend. You were there."

"Whoa whoa, I just—"

"Don't go back, Arian. Go forward. Press ahead. You were there. So were the others. There's video."

"I ain't seen no video."

"It's been all over the news. Trust me. There's video. You're on it. No question. The point: you're not alone."

The kid shrank back into the chair. His own private nature channel: cuttlefish folding into a niche. "The fuck I care."

The fuck you should. "I said go forward, Arian. That's the play here. Listen to what I said: you weren't alone."

"I heards you. Damn."

"Good. Because I'll tell you what else the video shows. Your buddy in the next room, Damarlo? He did one serious *cucaracha* on that fireman. Of all the guys who were there, he stands out. Not you. Him. You know what I'm saying."

The heavy-lidded eyes tracked up again. Houston, we have cognition.

"Let me fill you in on a little secret, Arian. Looks like the thing that did the fireman in was one good shot to the throat. Right here," stroking his Adam's apple, "and Damarlo, he's the one letting the guy have it to the head, the neck."

Arian squinted, thinking it through, assessing angles, calculating. Then: "There was this other guy."

"Hang with me for a minute, Arian."

"White guy."

"Stay focused."

"Yeah, but—"

"Arian?" Skellenger snapped his fingers. "I'm talking about Damarlo. After everybody ran off, when you two were alone—he's your buddy, Arian, I've checked out known associates, yours and his both—when you two had time to talk, what did he say?" He held out his hand toward the next room, as though feeling for some kind of vibration, lowering his voice for the next bit. Their secret. "You saw him connect. Boom, to the throat. You saw what it did. Was he jacked up? Proud? Take credit? 'You see how I nailed that fireman fuck?'"

The kid just sat. Skellenger had to check twice to make sure he was breathing. But ever so subtly, behind the eyes, the dusty clockwork moved.

"Third offense, Arian. For you. Not just any offense. Murder. That's twenty-five minimum no matter what. More likely life, no parole. Given who died, death penalty's not out of the question." You could call Verrazzo a lot of things, fact remained he was a firefighter, which meant PC 190.2 applied, though "in the performance of his duties" was a bit of a stretch. "That what your life, after today, after I leave this room—that what the rest of your life is worth?"

Quiet, almost a whisper: "There was another guy."

"I'll get to that. For now, we're talking about Damarlo."

"I'm just tryin to say—"

"And I'm telling you to listen."

Death stare. Death from within. "Damarlo, like, he's my—"

"I know. He's your friend, your road dog. But there are times—and this is one of those times, Arian—when there is no such thing as a friend. Out there, you weren't alone. In here, you are. He's not going to serve your time. That's on you. Assault's one thing. Murder? He has no right to make you fall that hard, not for something he did.

Not right. He's a man, he's got to take responsibility. Not your job to take it for him."

Skellenger sat back, deciding to let it settle in, let it work. As he waited, the crushing fatigue hazed his brain like smoke, and through that fog he assessed the various layers of damage—this ploy for the pelt of Damarlo Melendez, the rotten in it. There'd come a time to own that but now, like the chief said, this case was political, it was poison, the city teetered on a goddamn riot, and for now the shadow of all that fell across the kid they called D-Lo, parked in the next room, and that was just the way it was. The evidence goes where it goes. Quicker the better.

The kid's gonna hang, he thought—along with the rest of the idiots, sure, but Damarlo would get the loser end. And guess what? I've got no problem with that. I won't lose a minute of sleep over the sorry little fuck, and I couldn't hate him more.

So it goes. Heave the black man.

Arian looked over at the notepad on the table. "Tell me, you know, what it is you want."

It should have felt better. "I can't take dictation from myself, Arian. Has to be in your own words."

The kid nodded, dreads bouncing. "Okay." Squaring up. Eager now. Clear of mind, if not conscience. "Can we, maybe, like, go back over what we kinda just talked about, though? So I get my head right?"

Skellenger smiled. "Sure." Maybe Rosamar was right, the kid was borderline illiterate, but that didn't make him stupid.

"And my end, what's that? You gonna cut me outta this, yeah?"

"I can't make promises, Arian. That's how it works. But I'll talk to the prosecutor they assign to the case. I'll go to bat for you, do my best. That I can promise."

The kid took that in. "And the other guy, white dude, one who jumped in late."

"One thing at a time, Arian."

"But you and me, we're gonna get to that." Not a question. More like a dare.

"Arian, I want to help you. I told you that. But you're gonna have to trust me."

That's the crackers.

47

Parked at the ferry building and weary in every way he could name, Tierney slumped behind the wheel of the Honda, trying to ignore the smell of cold fries and fermenting slaw, remains of a late lunch, rising up from the backseat as he stared through the fogged-up windshield across the strait.

He'd driven around the past hour or two, looking everywhere, no luck. He still felt vaguely jilted, the way she'd run out at the restaurant, leaving him there to fend for himself like a dope. But he also feared the other two, Escalada and Mancinas, had managed to accomplish what he hadn't. Find her.

He pictured the two of them chasing her down, trapping her in some blind alley, grabbing her as she kicked and fought and screamed her lungs out—like putting a headlock on an explosion, wasn't that how the cops described it?—forcing her into the car, hustling her off someplace. To Navarette, or Nefarious Mom. Never to be heard from again. Same movie, different ending. Whatever else might be said for the girl, she had a knack for vanishing.

. . .

Glancing over at his London Fog crumpled up in the passenger seat, he considered making a pillow of it so he might lay down his head and rest awhile—not long, a minor nap in the history of naps—but instead he caught the distinctive murmuring throb of his phone, saw it flashing like some tiny, petulant robot inside the breast pocket.

He dug it out, checked the incoming number, flipped the thing open.

"Mr. Matafeo."

"How soon," Grady said, "can you get down to the pork store?"

The police, Tierney thought, they've picked up Jacqi. "Anytime, I guess."

"Now?"

He glanced at the dash clock. "Sure. What's—"

"You heard about the Verrazzo thing."

A slight deflation. "Sure, who hasn't?"

"Get down there, connect with Cal Katsaros. You two guys've met, right?"

"Yeah. Sure."

"He's been retained by the family of one of the kids caught on the video." The sound of shuffling paper came through the phone. "He wanted me but I'm already booked on this thing—Chepe Salgado? Guy's a one-man employment program, worked his last assault beef, got two witnesses to turn their stories around, lawyer thinks I can fly. The kid Cal caught is named Melendez, Damarlo Melendez. Got any conflicts?"

"Not that I know of." Tierney turned the key in the ignition, revved the trusty four-cylinder. "Except, you know, Jacqi Garza. She's caught up in that mess too."

Grady sighed. "Girl's a fucking tar baby. Let her go. While you can."

"Grady—"

"And you said that was a favor. This is work."

For a fleeting moment he recalled the misbegotten offer he'd made her at the restaurant, bringing in some samurai lawyer, making sure she didn't get ripped to shreds on the altars of law and politics and public pissology. With me, of course, as savvy go-between, investigator if called upon, tutor in the twisted logic of justice. "I didn't say the conflict was professional in nature."

"Remember, bucko, she's a minor. Comes her turn to crap all over this thing, the family'll be driving the bus. Way you told me before, you and the family, there's issues."

Tierney wiped at the fog smearing his windshield. "True dat, as the children say."

"So you'll do this, hook up with Cal? By the way, it's on your license, not mine, bills go through you. May turn out we all line up together—four defendants, kids on the video, mount a joint defense—but for now it's each man for himself. Till we get a little further into it, see what adds up."

Tierney didn't relish the prospect of going head-to-head with Grady, but he liked Katsaros. Most lawyers could hear a dollar bill hitting the snow, and acted like that was their virtue. Calimaco Katsaros still possessed something like a conscience. And with the infamous Mike Verrazzo murdered, this Melendez kid was about to get his own chance to be ripped to shreds.

"Yeah. Sure. I'm on my way."

"Swing by here first, pick up the yearbooks I got. From Stallworth High, St. Catherine's too, just in case. Go back a few years. I'm guessing you'll want to have your boy ID some witnesses, kids who were there."

Tierney smiled. Nice juke, pick and roll. "I thought this wasn't a joint defense."

"It's a favor. You can do me back down the road."

"Understood."

"I figured it was. See ya in a bit, yeah?"

Tierney closed his phone but held it for a second, tapping it against his chin.

That was that then. *As you from crimes would pardon'd be / Let your indulgence set me free.* He could tell Cass when he got home that night. Didn't matter what happened or how he felt about it. From here on out, Jacqi Garza was on her own.

And yet he knew what Cass would say, lying in bed on her side in the lamplight, arm cocked, head in her hand, watching him: Just how *do* you feel about it, bucko?

48

Cass sat alone in a corner of the living room, paper plate on her lap, not hungry, just trying to blend in.

They called themselves the Sonora Hill Light Brigade but most people knew them as the Ho Patrol. Genteel vigilantes. Once a week they donned canary-yellow T-shirts emblazoned with a bright red *interdit* sign and spread out across town to the various corners where the girls worked, hoping at least to scare off johns. They passed out handbills, too, info on HIV testing, child care, diversion programs, treatment centers. Lonnie Bachmann's Winchinchala House.

Before trooping out for the outreach they gathered for an early potluck, meeting here, a hilltop Victorian with Julia Morgan accents, tricked out to resemble a bohemian farmhouse. It belonged to a woman artist named Sam Beery, who'd gained local notoriety not just for opening the most impressive gallery downtown, a rehabilitated storefront renamed Beautiful Wreckage, but for transforming the entire block from a one-stop drug jump and hooker strip to a genuine neighborhood.

Force of nature, people called her. That and bitch on wheels.

Cass recognized several faces from the farmers' market, benefits around town, the local art scene. All women, a tight-knit cadre—the smart, the committed, sprinkled with well-meaning nut jobs. She felt a little like the stepchild at a baptism.

From the lilting crisscross of voices in the room she picked out a vaguely familiar accent—a woman named Katya or Katrina or Karolina, local character, Slovak or Czech, ran a dance studio—arguing with two other women around the coffee table.

"No, no, no, listen to me. You not understand. This is not problem." Ease knot probe limb. "Race I don't care. Affordable housing, I care."

"I meant your comment about welfare."

"No, listen, please. I explain. I have this boy, black boy, beautiful dancer, he come to my studio. I want him teach. Very good with the little kids, this boy. 'I hire you,' I say. 'I pay you, help you open checking account, saving account.' Know what he say? 'My family no want me have checking account. No want me have paycheck. I am have this girl, this girl, this girl. I get them babies. For welfare.'"

To disguise her eavesdropping, Cass glanced up at a nearby collage. Ancient bits of clockwork, ribbon, and plumage seemed in free fall across several singed and smoke-darkened pages of sheet music, with a single line of script along the bottom, wickedly faint: *Without the moral high ground, how am I supposed to look down on you?*

"That was my point," one of the other women said. "The way you talk about this sounds, well, racist."

"No. Cannot be racist. Is true."

Cass thought: What was I thinking? That's it, I'm outta here.

Suddenly, from nowhere, a hand touched her shoulder. She jumped in her chair.

"Sorry." The hostess, the artist. "Didn't mean to spook you. You're the nurse."

Cass rose like a hoisted flag. "I suppose I am," she said. "The nurse, I mean."

The woman's face had a mesmerizing plainness—moonscape complexion, missionary eyes, throat leathered by years of sun. She wore her white hair long.

"Sam," she said. "That's me."

"I know."

"You're shy."

"Not really. Just . . ."

A red wine smile. "Shy?"

"New."

"And very tall." Fanlike laugh lines. Sam Beery held out one of the yellow T-shirts. "Hope this fits."

"Thank you." Taking the shirt, not looking at it. Not sure she wanted it.

The older woman, all wise smile and rude stare, tucked a hand inside Cass's arm. "Come on. Let's head for the kitchen, just you and me. Get away from the intellectuals."

The kitchen smelled of ginger and basil and mildewy sponge. They sat alone at the pinetop table, picking at the last of the lasagna, green beans, flan. Cass felt cornered, not unpleasantly. Sam Beery sat cross-legged, seemingly transfixed.

"So you moved here from Berkeley."

"Couple years after the shipyard closed, yeah. Had a little saved up, wanted to buy, this was pretty much it given what I could put down. Quit my job at Alta Bates, got a position in general medicine here. When I got my OCN, transferred to oncology."

"That must be hard."

"What about you," Cass said, not wanting to get into it. "You came here when?"

"Later than you, '01. Fell in love with the weather—best kept secret in the Bay Area, I thought. Great place to grow roses." A shrug. "Just, you know."

"The crime."

"And the good old boys, the corruption, the inertia. City hall's a cesspool, when it's not a joke."

"Guess we should've done our homework."

"We're doing it now. That's what this is, homework, the new social contract, citizen engagement—hoo rah."

"Sounds vaguely, I dunno, right wing."

"Oh please. Yeah, we've got our cranks and crazies. I try to weed them out but sometimes you just need the bodies. Mostly we're just sick of everything being so hard."

"I was joking," Cass said. Kinda.

"Anyway, back to you—you've lived up here on the hill that long, just a couple blocks away. Never connected, the group here, the gallery."

You, Cass thought, that's where this was going. Never connected with you.

"I kinda keep to myself."

"Not an option anymore, unless you want to kiss your equity good-bye." She reached out, fussed with an egg roll so it lay parallel to the others left behind on the plate. Studied it a second. "So what brought you here tonight?"

Finally, Cass thought. The question. "Been meaning to for a while."

"But why tonight?"

How to say this, Cass thought. Or not say it. "The news, I guess."

A knowing, tight-lipped nod. "The murder over near the school."

"The fireman, yeah."

"Not just a fireman. Head of the union. Ex-head. Mike Verrazzo."

Cass felt pinned by the woman's stare. "I'm not very political."

"So why are you here?"

"Just seemed like the thing to do, given the news."

"No. There's something personal. I don't mean to pry, but you couldn't be more obvious." She reached out again, tidied the same egg roll. "Something's wrong."

"No. Nothing's wrong. I just gathered from the news, you know, if Verrazzo hadn't been where he was, a girl in his car—"

"Not just any girl. Jacquelina Garza. She's famous. And seventeen."

"Yeah."

"You know her story?"

Cass affected a shrug. "Pretty much."

"She got abducted about six months after I bought this house, opened the gallery. Her and Marina Bacay. I'm up to my eyes in debt, then that. I'm thinking: Holy hell."

"Anyway," Cass said, "I just thought if there weren't so many girls working the street here, maybe he'd be alive. Verrazzo."

"Yeah. Lucky him." She leaned back, stretched, eyes never leaving Cass's face. "But that doesn't explain what I'm seeing. The way you interact with people here. Or don't. Way you interact with me."

"Maybe I should go."

"Look, I'm not trying to mess with you. But believe it or not, I try to be careful with who tags along on patrols. We've had a few people, motives were kinda sketchy."

"I'm not racist, or loony, if that's where this is going."

"I'm not talking eccentric. I'm talking violent."

From out in the living room, a voice called out, "Sam? It's almost seven."

"I've got a watch, Lillian. Give me a minute."

Cass said, "You think I'm gonna go out with you folks and cap some hooker?"

"I don't know what I think."

"That's insulting."

"Really? I imagine doing it almost every day."

Toilet flushing upstairs. Scrum of voices in the living room.

What the hell, Cass thought. "The guy I'm seeing, he's been tutoring over at Winchinchala House. In particular he's been working with Jacqi Garza on her GED, but then she left the program and he's been trying to find her, help her, talk her into coming back. Now this. It just feels, I dunno, eerie."

"How romantic," Sam said. "He wanted to help."

Cass swallowed. Nerves. "It wasn't like that."

"No?" She said it wistfully, like she'd been there, a man in her life with a fascination. A father, a brother, an ex.

"Look, we try to let girls know they've got alternatives, they don't need to be out there. Guess how many care? Yeah, they're poor. Yeah, they're not too bright—the schools, Jesus, don't get me started—or they're hooked on meth or they're getting leaned on by a pimp. Not just some chucklehead from the neighborhood, either. We're seeing a lot of Serbians involved, Iranians too, hauling girls here by the vanload, young ones. Granted, the girls are up against a lot. But until something truly awful happens—they OD for the fifth time, their kids get taken away, they hemorrhage during an abortion or get left for dead by some creep—if we get through to one out of fifty, it verges on miraculous. Lonnie Bachmann's a godsend, but a girl's gotta be in truly deep shit to wind up at Winchinchala. How do we help? We scare off the tricks. We turn off the money. It's not romantic. But maybe, just maybe, we're making a difference." She uncrossed her legs, stood up, gestured to someone beyond the door that she was coming. "One thing we're not?

Tour guides. You want to go out, get a good look at Jacqi Garza, what-ever the reason, go home."

49

Jacqi closed her eyes and sighed with relief once the northbound 6 eased out of the transit station and headed toward Homewood, the unincorporated area north of town where LeQuan said he had a place she could crash.

Try not to think about it, she told herself. Yeah, it's LeQuan, your other options being what exactly? It wasn't so much a question anymore of who was looking for her. More like, who wasn't?

Three other passengers already sat on the bus, heads lowered or turned aside, keeping to themselves. She took a seat close to the rear door, a brighter spot than she would've liked, but the smart choice in case she had to bolt.

She pulled the edges of her hood a little tighter and curled up into herself, trying to be small, feeling light-headed and shaky and miserable with cold.

Near the edge of town she ventured a glance out the window. God only knew what jokers were out there, corner commandos, night trade. Slanging in the rain.

To the west the marshy wetlands sprawled into the distance toward the coastal mountains, all that windblown grass, the twisting sloughs.

The slow, relentless river—Napa at one end, the bay the other, San Francisco beyond. Places where things happen: not here. This is where things get stuck.

How quick, she thought, you could end up stuck. In that river.

They roared past the empty bus shelter where Tierney had picked her up a lifetime ago. The streetlamp flashed at the empty intersection and in its pulsing red glow she caught sight of old Mattie—check that, Buttonwillow—wandering the culvert beside the road. She was struggling through the swordlike grass, barefoot, bare-legged, nothing on but that same old scant red dress, a knotted-up stocking on her head, tamping down her nappy-white hair. She seemed to be searching for something—her slippers, that ridiculous wig. Her money.

Not quite left in the river but close. Ben, Hector, Navarette—what did they do?

Quick as that, the bus roared on, the old girl vanished in the darkness behind. The message, though, lingered: *Come home.*

The other passengers got off one by one, and Jacqi rode alone to the end of the line. She almost dozed off but shook herself awake as the bus eased into a turnaround on the edge of a strip mall, jolting to a stop. The door hissed open. Calling out from the front, the driver said, "Gonna need a transfer, you're not getting out."

Jacqi pushed herself up, shuffled forward, and thumped down the steps, landing on gravel. She hadn't once looked at the driver's face and hoped he'd returned the favor.

From behind, he called out, "Sure you know where you're headed out here?"

50

"Why is it I have to hear from Katsaros," Tierney said, speaking quietly into his phone, "what I should've heard from you?"

He stood in the small station house lobby just outside earshot of Damarlo Melendez's grandparents, Winnie Rae and Truman Broyles—soft-spoken, dignified, weathered by life—their hands folded as though at church services as they sat in plastic chairs bolted to the military-green cinder-block wall, right beneath an array of plaques honoring the town's fallen officers.

"Not sure what you mean," Grady said on the other end of the line.

Tierney glanced past the lobby's Plexiglas wall at a half-dozen officers hustling back and forth in a grid of cubicles. "You caught a tip from inside."

There was a pause on the line. "Got me a source on the force," Grady replied finally. "True dat. As the children say."

"And he told you—"

"Who says it's a he?"

"Let's agree upon Officer O'Color then, how's that?"

"Loose lips—"

"Fine. Your source on the force to be named later tipped you off that one of the other suspects, this Lomax kid, laid the killing on my guy."

Another long pause, blurred by static. "I never said it was gonna be simple."

"All that cluck about a joint defense—"

"I said it was unlikely. Which makes that briefcase you're hauling around particularly generous, yeah?"

Tierney glanced down at the giant antique travel bag at his feet, pebbled leather and tarnished brass, stuffed with high school yearbooks he'd just picked up from Grady's office. "You held out on me. We're friends. It's rude. It shows a lack of respect."

"Naw naw naw, don't go there. This thing's perfect for you. The Melendez kid's the only juvie of the bunch, he's musical, he's an orphan, he needs someone like you."

Tierney had covered much of this same ground with the grand-parents—Damarlo's mother barely thirty-four when, on a school-day morning, standing in her robe at the kitchen sink, she rolled back her eyes and shuddered head to foot, then collapsed like a rag right before her only child's eyes. Three hours later she lay dead on a gurney in the ER at RM Gen—heavy drug user in her youth, ten years clean, over-weight, overworked, victimized by high blood pressure and killed by a brain aneurism.

The boy took it hard, his mother more like a stern sister than a parent, and now spent hours and hours alone, in his room mostly, listening to music or making his own. He was gifted that way, Winnie Rae said, had a kind heart, a gentle disposition. But, yes, he'd turned inward since his mother's death. And what he'd found was his anger.

This thing's perfect for you.

"In the future," Tierney said, "I'd prefer you not cherry-pick what you think I deserve to know."

"Way you been moping after the Garza girl? Just give you cause to think twice. Gotta get your head straight. Kid down there at the jail needs you for real, yeah?"

"That's hardly the point."

"Not from where I sit. One last thing—listen up—there's a fifth guy involved, name unknown. You can't see it from the video the cops have released, but my guy's family told me this anonymous dude came up late and took his shot and that's when the thing went off the rails."

"The video I saw," Tierney replied, "seemed plenty off-the-rails as is."

"Yeah well your mission, should you choose to accept it, is to prove that pictures lie. Same as me. We've got leverage is what I'm saying. Let's use it, yeah? Gotta go."

Tierney slapped his phone closed and dropped it in his pocket, turning to offer a good-soldier smile first to Truman Broyles, bearish and white-haired, dressed in his Sunday clothes, then Winnie Rae, clasped hands thumping gently at her breastbone, wearing a crème-colored suit of winter wool, the lenses of her glasses dusty and smeared. Neither smiled back.

Cal Katsaros, leaning down into the receptionist's window, barked, "I'm done being told to wait. I don't get to see my client right now, I'm walking through those doors, understand?" Transplant New Yorker, buzz-saw accent, clockwork mind—his fist drummed on the counter. "I'm gonna plant myself on the station steps in front of all those cameras and microphones and hold an impromptu news conference. Damarlo Melendez is sixteen. He's a minor. His custodial grandparents are here, they're sweet people, good people. They're gonna touch some hearts out there in TV Land."

A frowsy, ample cadet manned the reception window from atop a stool—white blouse, blue epaulettes, moonpie eyes, no badge. She said blankly, "It will just be a matter of minutes. If you'll just—"

"A million years is a matter of minutes." Katsaros picked up his briefcase and straightened to his full lanky height. He wore his wild black hair à la Trotsky sans beard, his horn-rimmed glasses a defiant statement of antistyle. "Tell Detective Skellenger his minutes are down to three."

He turned his back, raised his arm so his cuff cleared his watch, and started his countdown.

Tierney turned to the grandparents. "Looks like we're doing this the hard way. Let Mr. Katsaros make a statement to the media, then he'll probably want you to step forward, say something about your grandson."

The grandparents nodded. The seconds ticked off.

"Showtime." Katsaros gestured everyone out of their chairs and toward the electronic glass doors. "Sorry it has to be this way. Sometimes they cooperate, sometimes no. Let's go out there and put a human face on this, okay?"

51

Katsaros guided them out into the gusty dampness and onto the station house steps, the building's stark façade lit up by spotlights like somebody was praying for a jailbreak. News vans lined the block, some with satellite dishes, others microwave towers, generators thrumming so loud Winnie Rae covered her ears.

Most of the talent remained inside, packed into the press room, but a few reporters loitered out here, chatting up their crews, phoning in updates, grabbing a smoke, or just waiting for the unexpected feature creature to waltz on by for an on-the-spot, man-on-the-street, post-postmodern ironic self-parody, elsewise known as an interview.

The crowd beyond the media crews split into two warring camps, separated by sawhorses patrolled by cops in orange traffic vests. To Tierney's left the crowd seemed made up of firefighters and their supporters hefting signs like "Mike Verrazzo Died for This City's Sins" and "Who Protects Working People?" To the right, minorities predominated, fewer signs, the one catching Tierney's eye reading "Don't Scapegoat Our Kids."

He found himself thinking of *Coriolanus*—he'd seen a production up in Ashland last summer, plus the Ralph Fiennes film—picturing the first moments when Menenius the senator confronts the starving mob, explaining how much they misunderstand power:

> Either you must
> Confess yourselves wondrous malicious,
> Or be accused of folly.

Katsaros, scanning the reporters, spotted a familiar face, a woman with the local ABC affiliate. He discreetly waved her over. She gestured for her cameraman to trail along.

"Cal, you're working on this." Eleven-o'clock smile. Even her gums were blond.

"Charlaine, you look good." His gaze was focused on the cameraman. "Can I walk you through a few things before we go live?"

She leafed through a notepad, bit the cap off her pen. "I'd prefer that, actually."

"I've been hired by the family of one of the kids arrested today."

"One of the kids on the video."

Katsaros gestured the older couple closer. They stared back in fright.

"This is Winnie Rae and Truman Broyles. They're the grandparents of Damarlo Melendez."

"One of the *kids.* On the *video.*" Charlaine, cap of her pen still lodged between her teeth, wrote down the names.

"The boy's sixteen, his mother died this past year. He's a good kid carrying around a lot of bad baggage, okay? Scratch that. Heartache. He's carrying around a lot of heartache." Katsaros splayed his hand across his chest. "They've come down here to make sure he's okay. Cops won't let them in to see him."

"They don't have to, do they?"

"We're talking about what's right here. He's a juvenile."

"Mike Verrazzo's dead, what's right about that?"

"That Bonnie Ferro from Pacifica over there?"

"Cute. Okay, let's start with . . ." She glanced past Katsaros toward the lobby's glass doors. "Who's that?"

Tierney and Katsaros turned in unison. Skellenger glared at them through the tinted glass.

Katsaros turned back and said, "Charlaine? Change of plans." He eased the grandparents toward the reporter and cocked his head toward the door, a cue to Tierney. "Mr. and Mrs. Broyles can fill you in on their grandson."

Winnie Rae trembled. Truman coughed. Katsaros leaned closer to the couple, lifting a cautionary finger. "Just the things we discussed. Background. No more."

The glass doors slid open. Skellenger didn't move.

Tierney had been anticipating this moment ever since he'd first learned who was steering the ship on this little disaster. The man, he thought, who came to Jacqi Garza's rescue, took down Victor Cope—one of them, anyway, a limelight name. More to the point, the man who, only a matter of hours ago, threatened to put you in jail.

I know what stalking is.

Wondrous malicious.

"Detective!" Katsaros stuck out his hand. "We're here to see Damar—"

"We?"

"This is Phelan Tierney, my investigator."

Almost imperceptibly Skellenger stiffened. "I know who he is. We've met. I've got no go-ahead for an investigator."

Games, Tierney thought. Nobody was in the dark about why he was here. In the event Damarlo vanished, died, or changed his story,

Tierney could testify. Katsaros, his lawyer, couldn't. Nothing unusual. Nothing unexpected.

Katsaros pointed a thumb over his shoulder. "I can always go back out there."

Folly.

Skellenger glanced from one man to the other, like he was trying to determine which of them he loathed the least, then turned toward the door that led beyond the lobby and gestured for the plump woman cadet to buzz them through.

Katsaros and Tierney followed him down a narrow line of cubicles to a brightly lit, low-ceilinged corridor boiling with thickset men in uniforms—the press room one direction, a stairway down to the holding cells and interview rooms the other.

"You've been here before." Skellenger positioned himself like a defensive end with weak-side contain, sealing off the reporters. A special wariness in his eyes for Tierney. "Sergeant Rosamar's down there. He'll show you which room."

52

The Homewood streets—edged with gravel, no curbs—went from dark to darker, streetlights a rumor this far out. The rain had stopped, just the same damp wind, but the cloud cover blacked out the moon.

The occasional table lamp glowed solo in a curtained window, a porch light here and there, the houses resting farther apart and deeper into their lots than back in town, the rough yards swaled and marshy and littered with junk. Some contained pens for chickens or goats, even the occasional hog parlor, ripe with slop. Almost all had dog runs.

The barking tracked Jacqi's every turn, and she had to check the stamped-tin street signs twice to make sure she'd gone the right way, only feeling confident she'd reached the right place when she detected in the near distance the outline of some guy standing on the hood of an F-150 pickup, taking a piss on the windshield.

Once she was close enough to speak quietly, she said, "I'm looking for LeQuan," wanting to back up from the beery stench.

The guy shook his pecker, hopping a little on the balls of his feet, the pickup's hood buckling. "Next house down"—zipping up, pointing with his chin—"cross the street." He flipped off the nearest house, the one the truck seemed to belong to, down a muddy grade littered with car parts. "Thanks for the suggestion box, asshole!"

A door flew open, but not there. The house he'd pointed to: LeQuan's.

Jacqi recognized the silhouette instantly, framed by the hazy light, and suffered a sudden impulse to turn around. Run.

As in where?

LeQuan stormed from his doorstep across his yard and into the street, loose shirt billowing, reaching the pickup as Mr. Whizzler jumped down. The pistol came out of nowhere. LeQuan lashed it across the other guy's face, knocking him to his knees.

Hissing: "The fuck I tell you. Don't need no vigilante shit from the hillbillies."

LeQuan glanced down at the dark house, tensing. Waiting. Finger hooked on the pistol's trigger now. The other guy tottered, trying to regain his feet. LeQuan kicked him hard in the ribs.

"You move when I tell you to move, numbnuts. I gotta live out here, unnerstan? Just 'cause you white don't make you right, you feel me?"

The guy knelt there, palming the side of his face. Whimper in his exhale.

"I asked you a fucking question. Do. You—"

"All *right*. Yeah." He checked his face. His fingers came away bloody.

Not like LeQuan, Jacqi thought, to leave marks. He had technique, pointers learned from a twisted cop, worked riot squad, or so he said. You go for the groin, the armpit. Soft flesh—minimum pressure, maximum pain. His favorite was the eye gouge. No pain like it, and the redness went away in just a few.

She stood there, barely breathing. I'm invisible, she thought. Here but not here.

The magic failed. LeQuan glanced up, pirate eyes. Big gold tooth in his smile.

"Hey, girl."

He lifted his shirttail, tucked the gun in his pants, nudged the kneeling whiteboy one more time with his shoe. That eerie gentle voice she remembered, almost forgiving: "Get back in the goddamn house."

The guy struggled up from his knees, staggered toward the waiting doorway, a slice of light in the darkness.

LeQuan turned back to Jacqi. He seemed thinner, all muscle and jump, his face reduced to angles. The big shirt draped from his shoulders like a billowing flag. Hair no longer conked, a close-cut natural instead. Same eyes, though.

"Knew you'd come back, girl. Just had to leave the door open long enuff."

53

The three of them sat before a large-screen TV—LeQuan and the whiteboy on the ends, Jacqi in the middle, repeatedly declining as they passed a bong and a bag of Takis, Nitro flavor, back and forth, nipping off a bottle of Gilbey's Gin. No crank, no pipe, not yet. But if she knew LeQuan, they'd come.

They'd downloaded videos off the net, routing them through the Blu-ray, the seeming favorite a YouTube clip titled *Hitler's Kids*. An actor made up like the Fun-Loving Führer invited all his favorite tykes down to Camp Treblinka: swimming, camping, fireside songs. "It's not what you think," he said, standing outside a shack marked "Smokehouse."

Every few minutes, LeQuan rousted himself from the sofa, waved his way through the beaded curtain separating the den from the front room, and shuffled to the window looking out on the street.

Edging the curtains aside, he'd study the pissed-on pickup and the house beyond, looking for phantoms in the darkness, paranoid the Ku Klux neighbors were ready to launch some unspeakable revenge. Two minutes, five, sometimes ten he'd stand there watching, then come back, swimming through the beaded curtain again, letting it rattle behind him, the strands swaying for a moment, then still.

Jacqi teased out the whiteboy's name—LeQuan called him Fishbelly, because his skin had a speckled whiteness—and he had a chastened meekness about him now, his cheek shiny with Bactine.

LeQuan, taking Jacqi into the kitchen at one point to microwave a cup of tea, said, "You probably wonderin what I'm doin out here in the Land of Cracker."

"To be honest," she said, lifting the microwaved cup to her lips, "My head's been kinda elsewhere."

He looked at her as though wondering whether he should take offense. "Yeah, well, thing of it is, got me a whole new situation."

He told her he'd teamed up with Fishbelly—who, it turned out, had a master's in botany, UC Davis—and together with a few other partners, more silent in kind, they were maintaining grow houses tucked away inside absentee rentals and foreclosures all around the area, feeding quality dank to the medical pot dispensaries.

Ridiculous money, LeQuan said. Like stealing from a blind girl.

"I've known a few blind girls," Jacqi said, "I wouldn't try to rip off."

They returned to the den as Fishbelly downloaded some vintage porn. *Kaptain Kornhole and the Kinky Kandystripers.* "Lemme fast-forward to the good part," he said, aiming the remote. He held up the Nitro Takis, shook the bag.

Jacqi said, "LeQuan, there any way I might lie down somewhere for a while?"

The room had an honest-to-god bed, queen-size, and Jacqi couldn't flop down fast enough, curling up on her side, jamming one pillow beneath her head, gripping the other like a big stuffed panda. LeQuan closed the door and eased on up behind her, pressing himself against her back, a hand on her hip.

"You smell like rain," he said.

She'd left her shoes on, lucky accident. Make sure they stay on, she thought. That was another pressure point, the soles of the feet. Soft flesh.

"Heard about the reward. Hundred thousand dollars. That ain't no joke."

So, she thought. Scratch me back.

"Seems to me, you should check out your options. I'm not saying turn snitch. That's the stupid move. Too long a wait, no guarantees. They don't convict, you get squat. Might have to share regardless, no telling what you'd get in the end. But may be there's somebody willing to pony up for you to keep quiet." He leaned in closer. "Like Mo Pete. Like Chepe. Maybe—"

"LeQuan, listen. I got nothing to say about Mo Pete or Chepe or anybody else on the video that the picture doesn't say."

"Video ain't gonna do it. You seen that thing?"

"I already talked to a cop, LeQuan, one of the detectives."

She felt his coiled body tense up behind her. "Did what?"

"I knew him from, you know, before. Just bumped into him at the hospital, I didn't say anything. Trust me, he wants me a million miles away from this. Told me straight up: get outta town. They fucking hate me, LeQuan. Believe it."

The hand on her hip tapped out a mindless code. "That don't mean you don't have value. And cops don't run your business."

"LeQuan—"

"You keep that shit under your hat, understand? You got value, bitch. Use it."

He dropped onto his back, as though spent from sex. Or failing at sex. Jacqi had to remind herself to breathe.

"I'm gonna tell you something, and you gonna listen. You walked out. I coulda come looking, found your ass, collected on what you owe—and make no mistake, girl, you owe—but I decided, Hey, let it be. I know what you been through. I ain't some slightweight don't unnerstan. But now you come running back, all *help me* and shit, put me in a position. And you think you're not gonna set this right?"

For just a second, in a kind of get-me-outta-here daydream, she imagined herself standing in a long dim hallway, flickering lightbulbs overhead, grimy psycho carpet beneath her feet. Otherwise, nothing but doors, hundreds of them, and a queasy sense they were all locked shut.

"So here's what's gonna happen. Got this friend, does the build-outs for the grow houses. Hooks up the filtration systems, air conditioning, circulation fans—average nigger got no *clue* the shit goes into his high—jacks the wiring and hangs the grow lamps so they don't max out the breakers, burn the place down. Works the bypass so PG&E don't get wise to the big bump in juice. Couple pinheads tried the do-it-yourself route back last fall, damn near burnt off their arms. And you leave a trunk line exposed, some fool's gonna get fried—could be just a cat or a raccoon, but that tips people off. Cops come poking around. And if some kid stumbles onto it, Jesus. This friend, he looks after all that. Smart man, useful dude, call him Teddy Toolbelt. Got a call from him earlier, right about the time they start barking your name around the news. He asked about you. Knew you and me used to be hooked up—think I didn't brag? Miss you, girl. We made us some money. But he asked about you, said he wanted to meet up. Said it was important."

Jacqi tried to get to her feet but he caught her, dragged her back down.

"Where you think you going?"

"I need to pee."

"You can hold it."

"LeQuan—"

In a flash he was straddling her, knees gripping her hips, one hand pinning her shoulder to the bed. The other hand clamped down on her throat.

"This how it is? Gonna make me do this?"

She felt his thumb press down and that brought Fireman Mike to mind, the hideous bruise on his throat. I'm gonna die just like him, she thought. How romantic.

"I told you. You got value. And I don't know just what it is ol' Teddy Toolbelt thinks is so damn important, but I got a notion. Could hear it in his voice. You saw something. You saw him. And he can't have that. He ain't in no position to be seen. Too much exposure, too many questions. Too much at risk. Well, that's worth something."

His lips were gummed with sticky whiteness, his breath stank. A stare like he wanted to dig out her brain. Then, ever so slightly, the pressure eased up on her throat.

"Real name's Teddy Buker, unnerstan? Say it."

She coughed, needing air. "Please—"

"Fuckin say it!"

"Teddy. Teddy . . ."

"Buker."

"Teddy Buker."

"Again."

"Teddy Buker."

"That's good. That's real good. You keep saying it. You memorize it. You put it away someplace in your mind where you can't never lose it. Because I got a feeling, girl, that's your ticket. Yours and mine."

54

The interview room was blindingly lit and walled in cinder block painted a brown found nowhere in nature, the air smelling of funky sweat with just a righteous hint of ammonia. And there were ghosts: rough men broken down into easy liars, drunks blubbering into their fists, mouthy girls turned mute.

For this round, Katsaros asked the questions, Tierney jotted notes. Damarlo resisted at first, all toughness and sulk, but Cal produced a letter from Winnie Rae, telling her grandson to trust these men, and just the sight of her shaky handwriting uncoiled the boy a little. From there it was peck, peck, peck.

"So you were just a tagalong," Katsaros said, cleaning his glasses with his tie.

"Arian, he the one had business with them all. I just kinda saw an opportunity."

Damarlo sprawled forward in his chair, elbows on the table, clutching his head. His mumble sounded sleepy, but his eyes bulged like saucers.

"Opportunity with who?"

"Mo Pete. He the one got the connection. Thuggy Fresh and Strange Mobb."

"The music producers."

"Had me a demo, thought I'd slip it to him. Jams is the slap, ya know? Wanted him to check 'em out."

Katsaros slipped the horn-rims back on. He fooled a lot of people with the geek bit. A micrometer beneath the surface, he was the scrappiest fighter Tierney knew.

"You were there to talk music."

"Thought he might front me up, let me lay down some tracks at the studio."

Spends a lot of time alone, Tierney thought, in his room with his music. If you looked you could see Winnie Rae and Truman in the boy. But you had to know that, had to look. Katsaros said, "And Arian figures in this how?"

"Arian knows Mo Pete, least a little. Better than me."

"And why meet at this particular spot?"

Damarlo scratched at his nose, using his sweatshirt sleeve. "Can't tell you. All I's know is Mo Pete wanted to meet up with the *cholo*, guy called Chepe. Mo Pete was gonna let 'em know he'd back their play. Something to do with who gets what now that, you know, some baller left town and everybody's scrambling for his action, wanna post up on his corner, something like that. Honestly? Wasn't paying much attention. But Arian, he wanted Mo Pete to feel it. Like: Hey, I'm wit' you. Show the flag, ya know?"

"You had nothing to do with that."

"No, man. I'm just thinkin, hey, this the guy knew Hookie personal, knows the dudes who mix Thuggy and Nation of Thizzlam. Be cool if I could hang wit' that."

Katsaros clasped his hands behind his back, arching his neck in a catlike stretch. "Back to the place," he said, "nobody said why they were meeting up there?"

Damarlo shook his head. "Mo Pete started walkin, Arian and me started followin. Figure cuz it's close to school and yet kinda like, ya know, nowhere. That's just a guess. Never even noticed that street before. But we all get there and this red car, fire car, whatever, it's parked midblock. And they see the girl, you know—"

"Jacqi Garza."

"Who did?" Tierney glanced up from his notes. "Who saw her?"

Damarlo's brow knitted, eyes hazed. "Can't remember. Maybe the Mex dude."

"You mean see her, or recognize her?"

"Yeah, that's what I meant: recognize. Arian's the one pointed out the car and, like, there wasn't just the guy inside."

Katsaros, stepping back in, "So he sees her in the car."

"It's like, no secret what's going on. Mo Pete and this Chepe, the Mex, start laughing. Arian, thinkin he's gonna show he's a soldier or some shit, picks up this big-ass rock and heaves the thing. Nails the damn windshield, *boom*, I mean serious. Guy in the car, the fireman, he busts out and just, like, freaks. You know, calling us names—"

"What names?"

"All sorts of shit." Damarlo puffed his cheeks. "Called us girls."

"Nigger?"

"Naw, not like, specific." Damarlo winced, scratching the back of his head. "Porch punks, said that. Corner jockeys."

"But it was racial, sexual, the insults."

"Yeah." Damarlo sighed, like all this remembering wore him out. "Turd burglar, that's what set Arian off. He got, like, faggot phobia or some shit."

"Okay."

"Was like somebody pulled a damn trigger. Arian, he just wound up and wailed. Fireman caught it, the punch, like it was nothing— dude was tough, give him that. Bent back Arian's wrist, some kinda jujitsu street-fight shitkicker move, fucked Arian up for real. That's when the rest of us jumped in."

"Weapons?"

"Naw, man. Just kicks and fists. Wanted to mess him up, not do him."

The last words landed with a put-upon thud, and Tierney wondered whether it had really sunk in. The man was dead.

Tierney reached over to touch Katsaros's sleeve, a bit of tag team. "Damarlo," he said, "it's pretty clear from the video you went at him hard. Verrazzo, the fireman. Especially once he was down. Why was that?"

Almost imperceptibly a twitch compressed the bridge of the boy's nose, the merest tic, except the compression spread to around the eyes, a wincing tightness, and then his whole body gave in, as though some invisible hand was dragging him away from the question, his body going with it. He eased back from the table, dragging his hands until they dropped into his lap and he slouched into his chair, saying nothing.

"Did you know him? Did he say anything specifically to you that set you off?"

The kid blinked. The edges of his mouth quivered.

"Was it about the girl in the car?"

"*Hell* no." He reached up and, using the heels of his hands, rubbed his eyes. "Don't even *know* her, not like that."

"Then what?"

"I dunno, man, it just, you know, felt like it had to get *out*."

"What had to get out?"

The boy's eyes began to glisten. He made no move to wipe at them.

"Just making sure I understand, Damarlo. This is important. What had to get out?"

If there was a way to be sitting right there while also sauntering the face of the moon, Damarlo had figured it out.

"It's okay to miss your mom."

The boy shot up, kicked his chair away, turned his back, took a few steps. Just standing there, breath quick and ragged. Mopping his face with his sleeve. As though, if he waited long enough, the opposite wall might just open up.

A minor eternity passed, then Tierney rose from his chair, approached the boy, stopping just beyond arm's reach.

"Nothing hurts worse, losing someone like that. Nothing prepares you for it. All the things you thought you understood feel like a lie. All the things you used to want to do, they seem pointless. People talk to you but it's like you're underwater, you can't hear. Or if you can, the words sound familiar but all the meanings have changed. For you, anyway." He inched closer, ready to put his hand on the boy's shoulder, wondering if that was wise. "The anger just comes."

The kid rolled his neck, mumbled something. He was trembling.

"I'm sorry, Damarlo, I couldn't hear—"

"I didn't *say* I was *angry*." His voice, for the first time loud, pinged off the walls.

"Okay. I don't mean to put words in your mouth."

"Then *don't*."

"All right."

"Don't *know* what happened, understand? Just remember the dude's voice and him calling us out and Arian taking a swing and the guy fucking him up and then it started, ya know? There was just—I don't know what to call it—just this thing, like it wasn't me or the fireman or Mo Pete or nobody, it was something, like, outside us but it was in us too. Everywhere. All at once."

Blame the eerie, mysterious, enveloping thing, Tierney thought. If only we could.

"What do you remember thinking?"

"I don't remember much of nuthin. That's just it."

"Can you tell me what you do remember?"

"I remember kickin him in the nuts."

"Okay."

"He was just, you know, wide open. Saw the shot, took it."

Sports as life, Tierney thought. For just an instant, he wondered what Cass would make of that. "Okay, then what?"

"It's all just kinda, I dunno, blurry and shit."

"Okay. That's not unusual, actually. But I have to ask you one specific thing, okay? Do you remember kicking the fireman in the head, the throat, the chest . . ."

The boy said nothing, hunched forward a little, shoulders tensed, as though expecting a smack. It was one of those things hard to get across to a jury—mom on the pipe seven years before she got clean, parade of strangers through the home. The secret beatings a kid took. Tierney wished he could turn him around, see his face.

"I'm not blaming you, Damarlo. I just need to know."

"Don't remember," he said, murmuring into his shoulder.

"Nothing?"

Damarlo shook his head. Too bad, Tierney thought. Because there's been a break in the case. Just not for you.

"The problem, Damarlo, is that your buddy, Arian? He remembers clear as a bell. Or at least that's what he told the detectives."

55

Damarlo turned, not all the way, but eyes bulging again. He swallowed like he was trying to get a peach pit down.

"Arian handed you up, Damarlo. He gave the police a statement saying you kicked the fireman in the throat—because that's what killed him, so far as anyone knows just yet. A crushed windpipe."

It was like watching a time-lapse sequence of storm clouds—shadow and speed and threatening silence—the emotions whisking across his face. That tightness coiling around the eyes again, sinking into himself, the helpless twitch of his mouth as though words were whispering through his head but he couldn't quite catch them fast enough.

"He also says you bragged about it later, when you two were alone together."

"We wasn't together." The voice, like it was coming out of a different kid. No more put-upon thug—that vanished. This, finally, was somebody's grandson, and scared.

"Who were you with?"

"Nobody. Mo Pete was like, you know, Scoot LeBoot, and Arian just kinda slinked off too. I went home."

"Remember what you did? If you watched TV, what program?"

Another circus of facial tics. More silence. Tierney gestured him close. The boy leaned in, using his hand to shield his mouth from view through the one-way glass. "Had me some lean." Like that was more damning than the fight.

Fabulous, Tierney thought, a robotripper, picturing the kid stoned stupid, cradling a bottle of Purple Drank, Sprite turned the color of grape jelly from a spike of high-octane cough syrup: promethazine, codeine. "You high at the time of the fight?"

"No."

"Was anybody with you at home?"

A headshake.

Jesus. Give me something, anything. "Did anybody *see* you go home."

"I don't know."

Tierney turned toward Katsaros, they shared a hopeless glance. "I'll check with the neighbors. Did you chat with anybody on the phone—where's your cell?"

"Cops took it."

Perfect, Tierney thought. Either they've already logged the kid's calls or they're just waiting for the warrant. It'd be days, longer, before he got a look. "Okay. But did you talk to anybody, a friend, classmate—"

"I don't know, I can't . . ." For the first time, he sounded genuinely ashamed.

Tierney rested one hand gently on the young man's shoulder. "I need you to sit back down, Damarlo. Okay? I need you to think hard and write out the names of the people you may have called, or who called you. Even if you're wrong, that's okay, I'll check it out. If you can remember numbers too, that'd be great." Fat chance, Tierney thought—who remembers numbers anymore with speed dial?

Damarlo nodded, still only half there. They returned to the table and sat back down. Tierney tore a sheet off his notepad, handed the kid a pen, and Damarlo bent down to his task, encircling the paper with his arms, holding the pen like he was a little scared of it, his handwriting boxy, the letters large.

As he finished writing, he said, "What about the guy who came up late?"

"Don't worry. I was getting to that."

"Cuz I didn't see nobody die."

Trust me on this one, Tierney thought. That's not the issue.

"I mean, I know he's dead, I'm sayin he was alive when I ran."

"Why did you run?"

"Everybody else was takin off, thought somebody'd seen somethin."

"What did *you* see, Damarlo?"

"What you mean?"

"When everybody took off, did you look around, notice anything?"

"You mean as I was runnin?"

"Before you ran."

"I told you, things was crazy, I wasn't payin much—"

"I need you to focus on this for me, Damarlo. I need detail. The police, they're only showing the front end of the video, the first ten seconds or so."

"We won't get our hands on the full video for weeks," Katsaros said. "And that'll be way too late. The police will have locked in everybody's story by then, true or not so true. They're gonna try to lay this all on you. We've gotta get there first."

"I need you to tell me exactly what happened after the fireman hit the ground."

The kid tensed up again. "Look, I'm not tryin to be a bitch about this, but I'm sayin, it's all, like, a blur, okay?" He put his hands to his temples, like his fingers were electrodes. "There's, like, just craziness."

"Start from the end and work back. This guy came up . . ."

Damarlo shrugged. "Don't know him, don't know where he came from."

"Was he white?"

"Yeah. Think so." Damarlo dug into his shoulder, scratched. "Didn't get much of a look, t'be honest. But yeah, white."

"Could you pick him out from a photograph?"

Tierney glanced down at the travel bag full of the yearbooks, the defense version of a photo lineup. Poor man's eight pack.

"Look, I was kinda off at that point, okay? I mean, I saw somebody come up, figured it was just some fool from the crowd, wanted to get in one last lick. Snatch a little boast wit' his boys. At that point I was hangin back, felt wore out. Felt dizzy. All this screamin and shit, and I was breathin *hard*, ya know? There were these girls creepin in close, tellin us to fuck him up. And so this guy drifts in, it's just part of the flow."

"What did he do?"

"Hammered the dude on the ground."

"You saw it."

"I musta, but I don't have, like, a picture in my head. I mean, I remember, but it's all mixed up. I just remember Mo Pete takin off. Big dude, you notice when he's movin. Kinda remember Arian draggin me by the arm or some shit and everybody's goin off, like, all sudden, and I'm still just thinkin, 'Take *that*, loudmouth motherfucker.' I got no idea he's, like, dyin."

56

LeQuan let Jacqi catnap. Screwed though the situation was, she cherished the time alone, the chance to curl up on her side, back to the door, turn the light out, be still. Let her thoughts swim around. Swim away.

Still, she didn't take her shoes off.

Maybe later she'd shower, throw her clothes in the washer—LeQuan with a washing machine, there's a trip—try to stitch back together some sense of being human. Maybe even eat, if she could keep it down.

Hard to believe, she thought, just twelve hours ago life felt okay. Not yet up and dressed, lying with Snickers in the back of Bettye's, waiting to head off for her hookup with Fireman Mike. Still had her $193—Christ, still had her clothes—and the future had a plan tucked inside it. Now the future, if you could call it that, meant just two things: where she could hide, and what she'd have to put up with to stay there.

She didn't know how long he'd been standing in the doorway, but finally she sensed it, someone there. LeQuan, she figured, eyeing her like a Lotto Scratcher, laying claim. And it would come to that, she knew. One of those things she'd have to put up with. She made him wait, pretending to sleep, until she couldn't.

She rose up on one elbow, looked over her shoulder.

Not LeQuan.

Strange how the body knows so much quicker than the mind. Before she placed him her stomach knotted up, her skin felt cold—the long, bag-eyed face, older than the rest of him. The lonely angry nothing in those eyes.

Say it. Put it away someplace in your mind where you can't never lose it.

"Hey," he said. Timid smile. "Mind if I sit?"

He didn't wait, just stepped inside the room, closed the door. No chair to be had, just the bed, so he perched on the corner, far enough to show respect, close enough to touch her. He'd tossed the hoodie, wearing a leather jacket instead, a T-shirt underneath bearing the logo for a band—the Pretty Things, a concert tour called Rage Before Beauty. Made him look different, vaguely more normal, reminding her of someone, the name just out of reach.

Teddy Buker shook his head, laughed softly. "Some kinda day."

Her neck hurt, a needlelike ache in the muscle, then a flare of real pain. She hadn't moved, her body all locked tight, ready for a blow. Or worse.

"Yeah," she said, looking closer at him, wondering, hoping she'd been wrong. The eyes weren't truly empty. Someone was there. Someone she could bargain with. Maybe the emptiness was inside her.

"Fucked up, how it turned out."

"Yeah." Stop saying that, she thought.

"You knew him. Mike Verrazzo, I mean."

"No," she said.

He seemed to find that amusing. "You were in the car."

"I didn't know him."

"I saw you with him before. After the city council meeting, at the hotel."

That settled that—it was him after all, that eerie presence just beyond the door. "You're wrong."

"Few times before that, too."

"What are you, a cop?" She pushed herself upright, swung her feet to the floor. "Need to get LeQuan in here."

"I'm no cop," he said, like he still found her comical. "LeQuan knows it."

"Some undercover ass-toad then." On her feet, her head swam.

"Sit down."

"You follow me around?" She felt sick, felt shaky. "You're somebody's bitch."

"Not you," he said, unfazed. Reaching out a hand. To steady her. "Him. I was following Verrazzo. And I'm nobody's bitch."

She dropped back onto the mattress like it was all she could do, chafing her arms for warmth. But the chill wasn't coming from the air. "No reason to follow him around except to nark him out to *some*body."

"True."

"So who then?"

"Not important. What's important is what you think you saw today."

57

Tierney checked downtown first, corners outside camera range, the ones the girls often worked, then the bars. He even returned to Los Guanacos, hoping maybe she'd circled back, ordered a second round of *pupusas con loroco*, actually finishing this one instead of leaving it behind like a piece of performance art, something for him to contemplate as he reintroduced himself to Navarette's goon squad.

Widening the circle, he moved on to the more notorious motels, both those along the interstate and the ones near the White Slough interchange, where the Napa Highway intersected Blood Alley heading west.

He scanned the nearby sidewalks first, and if a girl stood there in a sheltering doorway just outside a drizzly patch of lamplight, he'd roll down the window, mention Jacqi by name, ask if she'd been around. One after the next, bending down into the window, fingering back the curtain of wet hair, the girls offered variations on a theme: "Forget her, baby. I'm standin right here, right now."

He'd apologize for the waste of time, then head for the nearby motel serving as mother ship, ease into the parking lot, get out, scan the catwalks and doorways before heading in to chat up the desk clerk.

Most cases, the guy was Pakistani, exile from the land of hoteliers, otherwise an occasional Sikh, one dour Filipina—the lone female—one slyly agreeable young buck brother in a jumpsuit, spangled with bling.

A couple times a girl sat slumped in one of the office chairs, legs crossed, skirt hiked high, nosebleed heels, thumbing her phone or slathering on a fresh coat of eau de Walgreens. Some of them lived there, coordinating with tricks over the net, only venturing out on the street when business turned slow.

He gave out Jacqi's name, provided a description, asked if she'd come around. In return—speaking of performance art—he earned himself a monotony of calculating stares, dark chuckles, easy shrugs.

Never say die, he thought. Chisel that on my headstone.

As he widened the circle farther, sometimes driving at the mercy of whim—glimmering streetlights mirrored in lakes of rain, neon storefronts hazed with mist—he'd mentally assess the new state of things.

Damarlo had been worthless with the yearbooks, tentatively naming a mere five kids beyond the perps—didn't hang much at school, he'd said, and kept to himself when he did—and no ID at all on the last guy there, the mysterious walkup.

And so, with a level of irony worthy of Kierkegaard, it all came down to the girl with a knack for vanishing who somehow never vanished. Quite possibly her alone.

No need to save her anymore, he thought, no more stumbling over my own sincerity. She'll appreciate that. Or not.

Time to save someone else. You were there, Jacqi, no pretending you weren't. And fate's put a young man's freedom in your hands, maybe his life. You can step up, be the plucky heroine again, redeem the past ten years. Or you can double down on life as you know it. And if that's your choice, just remember, Damarlo Melendez—with his young dead mother, his withering sorrow and fathomless rage, his fondness for lean, his unheard demo, his mercurial thugstar dreams—gets sent away for a long, long time.

Maybe that's something you can live with. But I think you're bigger than that.

Every now and then he thought he spotted her in the corner of his eye, practically gave himself whiplash braking, craning to look. Each time he turned: nothing.

Sometimes it almost felt as though the girl was right there, sitting in the passenger seat—crayon eyeliner, sparkly lipstick, knuckle of gum—like it was yesterday morning all over again, always had been, always would be, now and forever. The sense of her, like a hologram, near enough to touch but untouchable.

He realized then that he wasn't just obsessed. He'd become the obsession itself. If she didn't exist, neither did he. He had no idea why, any more than he knew the honest why of anything. But every time he thought of packing it in, realizing he might never find her, she was gone, spirited off by the family, never to be seen again, he remembered that last real conversation with Roni, when he had to tell her the cancer had won—it was time to stop fighting and start dying—then his throat would clench, his stomach would pitch, and he told himself he hadn't given up at all, never, he was still fighting.

Chisel that on my headstone.

58

"Little-known fact, guys my age had better luck finding a job back in the Depression. No lie. Think college makes a difference? Fifty percent, recent grads, unemployed. Yeah, give me a shot at that. Think I wanna be tricking out grow houses? Work's work. Union's got nothing. Under forty, no seniority? Sorry, bub. Know why? Fucking Mike Verrazzo."

He'd been rattling on like that, knee bouncing like a jackhammer, muscles in his neck all corded and tense. Voice a murmur, angry and jagged. *Little-known fact*—he said that a lot, a kind of mantra, like he was the only one who *knew*.

But there was something else too, a fierce, almost defiant loneliness, like the truth was a vantage point no one could share. Nobody wants to hang with the hangman.

"Too bad he's dead, you know? Too fucking bad. Then again, he had it coming."

Half listening, she tried to think up some way out. LeQuan would be watching the door. And this guy—Teddy Toolbelt, Teddy Buker, the name tattooed to her memory now—no chance he'd let her just slip out the window.

"Amazing how you still hear these ass-clowns propping him up like some kinda hero. Yeah, sure, he was good to his pals, plenty of perks for his buddies, laughing all the way to the goddamn bank. Now it's all, Oh boo hoo, we want justice. Sick greedy fucks."

He shot a glance her way, and it lingered. He seemed so caught up in his own bitterness—entranced with it, in love with it—and yet he seemed almost shy, too, like the issue wasn't what happened or what he thought about it or even what she thought about it. It was how she felt about him. He needed her approval, her say-so. She had the magic power. The female always does. It's her curse.

"Bet Verrazzo was nice to you too," he said.

The tiny gold hummingbird around her neck suddenly felt like an anchor. What, she thought, I'm supposed to feel bad a guy treats me okay? Offers to take me outta here? She missed him, or the idea of him. Fireman Mike to the rescue. Wouldn't that have been pretty?

"It's what he did, he bought people. Only reason I was following him around? Keep tabs on him, see who he met, report back if money changed hands. Found out pretty quick, guy was a total muffhound. Banged you what, six times in two weeks?"

"Don't talk to me like that," she said.

"I'm sorry." He shrank a little, turned away. "What you want me to call it?"

"Don't call it anything. It's none of your business."

"You made it my business."

The way he thought, it was crazy making. "I didn't do anything to you."

"It doesn't matter. Look, all I was trying to say, what Verrazzo did to this city is kinda like what happened to you. The city got taken hostage. It got raped. The guy's no more a fucking hero than the piece of shit you sent away."

What do you know about it, she thought. What does anybody know about it? "Can we talk about something else?"

"Except Verrazzo was gonna get away with it. Walk away clean. That's what drove Bauserman nuts. And so he had me taking pictures, of him and you—"

"You've got pictures of me?"

"Him and his other hookers, too." He gave her a cagey look. "He was cheating on you, know that?"

Little-known fact, she thought. Men are like dogs: if you can't eat it or screw it, piss on it. "How many pictures?"

"Not just pictures. Video. That's what I was doing there on Goldenrod. Which kinda brings up what I really need to talk to you about. What happened there at the end of the fight."

The fight, she thought. Not the beatdown. Not the murder.

"I'm watching the thing from the corner, you know? And as bad as I hate the guy, as much as I enjoy watching him suffer, I get that enough's enough. I figure somebody's gotta stop this. And Bauserman, guy who has me tailing him, he can't get his revenge, not the kind he wants, if the guy's dead. So I walk up, and it's obvious, I start mouthing off to those guys wailing on him? They'll just turn on me. But I figure if I can just act like the ref, call the fight, let everybody know who won and get him up, drag him to his feet, maybe I can hustle him outta there, you know? But I crouch down, roll him over, and there's like this look in his eyes, this weird kinda far-off nothing, and he's pale, I mean for real. He's all tensed up, not just from getting hammered. It's cuz he can't breathe. He's making this noise, wheezing, trying to suck in air, but he can't."

No, she thought, you hit him, three good cracks at least, I saw you. Or did I?

What he'd just said, it wasn't so far off from what she thought might've happened, could've happened. Eerie, hearing it from him.

Maybe her mind was playing tricks, she'd gotten it wrong. He hadn't delivered the final blow, the others had already seen to that.

Rendered their verdict. If so, she and Teddy Buker weren't so different after all. Both just there, wrapped up in the same bad luck. In this.

"The other guys can tell they fucked up, took it too far, he's dying, you know? So everybody bails. And I'm stuck there, wondering what the hell to do. I kinda freeze for a second, I'm not proud of that. Then I think: Go to the car, create some distance before you fire up 911. So I turn around, start humping back. That's when I saw you."

He wasn't glancing at her now. He was staring. And his eyes had this hard, feral want. He needed her, needed her to understand. The truth is never what it seems. The truth is complicated. The truth has a life of its own.

"I don't know what you think you saw, but you went off on me like I was one of them, like I was no different. I didn't have time to get into it with you."

The room seemed to shrink, drawing him closer. She wished for the courage to reach out, lean over, touch him, reassure him somehow. Tell him: I do, I understand. But she couldn't bring herself to touch him, couldn't bridge that gap, not yet.

They both knew what it felt like, being used and angry, young in America, Land of the Gone, but they were different too and right now she needed to cling to that difference because it felt like everything, even if everything was a lie.

"Look," she said, "I don't know why you're telling me this, what you—"

"I'm telling you what happened."

"Nothing more unreliable than an eye witness—that's what they say, right?"

"You're not listening," Teddy Buker said. "I'm telling you what—"

"Look, I already spoke to one of the detectives, he wants nothing—"

The guy reached across the bed, snatched her arm. "You spoke to the cops?" His voice like a saw biting wood. "What did you tell them?"

"I didn't tell them anything, that's the point."

"I just told you what happened. You tell them anything, you tell them that."

"Now you're the one not listening, I'm—"

"I was trying to help the guy."

"Okay. I get it, I heard you."

"Then say it back to me. Tell me what happened."

She almost wanted to scream. *Nobody wants me on a fucking witness stand. They'd rather see me dead.*

"I'll say whatever you want me to say."

"I want you to tell the truth."

"Okay."

"So say it back to me."

She swallowed from fear, her mouth stone dry, and fussed with her hair just for something to do. Trying to look past the angry mask and the feral need to that deeper thing she'd sensed just a moment ago, the hunger for approval. *Her* approval. And yet she knew if she joined in his lie he'd hate her even more, hate her forever. Not a lick of safety there. *I want you to tell the truth—yeah, sure. So what to tell him?*

"I know what it feels like to want to kill the person who ruined your life."

His eyes tightened and his gaze seemed to back away as the rest of him tensed. "I didn't say I killed him. I said just the opposite."

"I know. I'm just saying, I'd understand."

He took in a short rough breath. "Understand for somebody else."

"Okay. If I have to."

And she finally had it in her to reach out, bridge the divide, touch his arm gently. Because she did understand. How many thousands of times had she wished she'd done exactly what he'd done, put an end to it, the big sick bullying thing, the face that wakes you up in the middle of your nightmare, then lingers, like it knows you better than you know yourself.

And then it came to her, the person he reminded her of.

She started rubbing his shoulder, stroking his back, a metronome: I care, I understand, I'm right here.

He sat there, accepting her touch, the tension dissolving a little in his body. His head sagged an inch, then an inch more. He whispered, "Thanks, okay?" Eyes shut tight. Rain pattering the roof in windy bursts.

He cleared his throat, shook off some shuddering thought. "It just, you know, happened fast. Turning him over and seeing his fat, scared face and not thinking, you know? Not till after. That wheezing sound I told you about. Trying to suck in a breath. Felt righteous for a second, then it felt wrong. Then, I dunno, just felt done."

Something inside him weakened as he spoke, withered, she could feel it beneath her hand, like sand giving way. "Yeah," she said quietly.

He looked at her—not long, just a second—and from somewhere, not in the room but in her mind, she detected the faint scent of plums.

The door cracked open. It was LeQuan. He took a moment, studied them, sitting close on the bed, touching. "You two cool?"

"Yeah." Teddy Buker straightened, shook off her hand, then stretched like he'd just woken up. "Everything's copacetic."

LeQuan gestured with two fingers, like he was summoning a pet. "Give me a minute, my man. Something I need to tell you."

59

Teddy couldn't quite believe just yet he'd said what he'd said. The beginnings of regret fished around inside him and yet the girl seemed okay, she got it, she understood. At least that's what she said. But women do that, it's why they exist—to fuck you up, fool you. *I'll say whatever you want.* Next thing you know . . .

Jacquelina, he thought, pretty name. How come she didn't call herself that?

Fishbelly, the botany bum, had left, just LeQuan and him and the girl in the house now, the lingering smell of dank and gin and Nitro Takis, XFO cage fight on the big screen, sound muted. Chrome S&W .44 on the coffee table, whomping big and deadly.

LeQuan went to the front window, peeked out the curtain, came back, his nerves electric, a sheen of sweat on his coffee-dark skin. The beaded curtain rattled behind him.

"Listen, my man, need to ask a favor. Ever hear of a dude named Pete Navarette?"

Teddy felt a vague hint of recollection, nothing specific. "Can't say. Why?"

"Not the kind of guy you cross in this town. Can bring the hammer down, anybody he wants to, anytime, you feel me?"

On-screen, some tatted-up Serbian monster in red board shorts had a Latino cat down, pounding him hard, the spic's legs twined around the Serb's waist. Strange, Teddy thought, how often X-treme fighting looked like rough sex.

Then it was him in the red shorts, Verrazzo on the ground.

"Okay. So . . ."

"Just got a call from one of his guys," LeQuan said, "motherfucker named Escalada. Seems they're lookin for our girl in there, just like you were. They found out she used to be in my pen. Him and this meathead, Hector—you do *not* mess with this hook, trust me—they wannna drop by, have a conversation. See what I know, get me involved in the hunt. Make an impression."

He dragged the back of his hand across his mouth, eyes darting toward the window again, past the hypnotic beads.

"Now I got no business with them direckly, not like I got with you, so I don't owe 'em nothing, right? Except respect. I don't show respect, I'm in a goddamn world of pain, ya know?"

"LeQuan—"

"They're on their way. Like, now."

On-screen, a reversal, the Latino fighter on top now, the Serbian looking like the one getting his ass tapped.

Teddy said, "You're gonna hand her over?"

"No, man, I want you to get her outta here for a while, so there's no possibility of a fuckup on that front. She can't come hard-charging out of that room, slinging her banshee bullshit."

Teddy hardly knew LeQuan well, fist bumps and money, but he knew enough to recognize there were angles to this, and more angles tucked inside those.

"And once we're gone, what if these guys press? What's to stop you from telling them where she's off to, who she's with? Then who's in a world of pain?"

LeQuan's eyes narrowed for just an instant, like his brain had an itch, then he reached out, put a hand on each of Teddy's shoulders. "I said I owe them respect. No more. I know where the money comes from." Then the weirdest thing—he patted Teddy's cheek, a Brando move. *The Godfather.* "You ain't gotta lot of time. Get her up and outta here."

60

Tierney, having exhausted all the likely haunts inside the city limits, headed out to the river road, the spot where he'd found her the day before. Last stop before heading home, he supposed. Then again, given the jangle of his mood, he might just retrace his steps, drive around all night. Never say die.

His heart sank as he drew close, spotting the telltale T-shirts. Ho Patrol. He'd seen a few other gatherings during the night, the do-gooders clustered together like corner choirs, trying to scare off johns, pamphlet the girls, stare down the pimps. Noble cause, largely futile, but how many noble causes weren't?

There were four of them here, huddled inside the bus shelter, staying dry. Fat chance of finding her now, he thought, only spotting the wild red hair after a second, then recognizing the proud height, the lanky build.

He would have felt less stunned seeing a gryphon.

He threw the car into park, left the lights and wipers on, got out. As he headed for the shelter, a nimble little biddy—wearing, of all things, a sombrero—stepped out into the rain and aimed a camera, thumbed the shutter button—ticking delay, then *flash*.

"You use that image without my permission," he said, "I'll sue you into ruin."

"There's no one for you here," she began, her voice warbly and brave. She reached into a satchel for a flyer.

He eased past her. "Don't jump to conclusions."

Cass stood waiting inside the shelter, wearing perhaps the blankest expression he'd ever seen. Two other women lingered behind her, one with her chin out, the other just sad. In their dayglow shirts they looked like a highway cleanup crew.

He was about to ask what she was doing there but she beat him to the mark.

"You're not the only one looking for her," she said.

He instantly thought of Navarette's men, then realized that wasn't what she meant. Not exactly.

"Let's go home," he said. "Talk about it."

61

Jacqi had the window up and one leg over the sill, ready to head off into the dark, when Teddy Toolbelt slipped back into the room.

He shut the door and just stood there for a second, staring at her, puzzled, like she'd broken something. For some reason, rather than duck out, drop to the ground, she stopped, staring back the same way. Like they had something to discuss.

Shouldn't have turned out this way. It's me, not you.

He lunged across the room just as she got all but the second leg out, his hands clamping down, one on the straggling leg, the other snatching her arm—his grip so strong, like a winch was dragging her back inside.

Too tired to fight, a few listless kicks just for show. He pushed her down onto the floor, straddled her, pinning her arms with his knees.

His eyes blazed. "The fuck were you thinking?"

"I need to get out of here."

"Dumb cunt, I'm gonna *get* you out."

"Let me go."

"Settle down."

She waited for him to hit her but the blow didn't come. He leaned down, gripped her head in his hands, forcing her to look straight up into his face.

"Listen to me. Calm down. Nothing's gonna happen if you do like I say."

Yeah, right, never heard that before. That basset hound howl in his eyes, the dark folds of oyster flesh, the long grim undertaker face. He loomed so close, like he meant to kiss her. Or bite out her eye.

"Okay, Teddy. I'll listen."

A mystified look, confused, scared. Eyes narrowing.

"Your name's Teddy Buker." Her hands had gone all pins-and-needles—his knees, nailing her arms to the floor, cutting off the blood. "Wanna guess how I know? LeQuan told me. Made me memorize it. He's setting you up. Either I nail you and claim the reward or he shakes you down to keep me from talking."

A pained expression, like his thoughts were too loud. "He just told me to get you outta here."

"He's gonna shake you down."

His grip tightened. "I told you, I didn't *do* anything."

So we're back to that, she thought. Like a curse. Keeping other people's secrets was her reason for being.

"Your turn to listen to me. He's *going* to *set*—"

The door banged open—LeQuan, thundering across the hardwood, shoving Teddy aside with one hand, the other gripping the chrome-plated pistol, raised like a hatchet.

The gun slammed into her skull so hard the room exploded. She could smell the stench of his sweat, feel the scrawny meanness of him, the cold jagged metal slamming down two more times, cutting her face open, then Teddy Buker dragged him off, the two of them spinning away like a Siamese dervish.

In the dizzy blur, trying to sit upright, trying not to puke, feeling the stream of blood down her jaw, she saw them scrumming, heard their clenching grunts and their bodies slamming into walls and then the hellish, deafening boom of the gun, the devil's welcome, the hiss of falling plaster, and she told herself: Get ready. Get ready to die.

She got as far as up on one elbow, arm cocked beneath her, eyes floating toward the two of them locked together, waiting out the next gunshot, but then Teddy pulled some deft move, a twist and a whirl of punches, a kick—the gun fell, clattered, spun.

Grab it, she thought, unable.

LeQuan's legs vanished beneath him, he dropped to the floor, Teddy jumped on top of him, pinning him like he'd pinned her, but now the arm raised up, hand knotted in a fist, and down it came, three hammering blows, all to the throat.

Jacqi grabbed the mattress, dragging herself to her knees, saw her blood dripping on the sheet like dark rain. Only a few feet away, that terrible desperate hiss, a sound she remembered. Not Verrazzo this time. LeQuan, scraping the air for oxygen.

She sensed Teddy somewhere in the room, a mere reach away but lost in a trippy haze, like everything had turned to a kind of smoky shimmer.

"I gotta," she said, "leave," a whisper lost inside another whisper.

Not lost. Trapped.

Then his arms wrapped around her waist, he was hoisting her to her feet. "Come on," he said. "Up."

She couldn't stop blinking. It was the blood—dripping fast and steady now, into her eyes—and she lifted her hand, clumsily tried to wipe it away as he dragged her toward the door, her legs scissoring beneath her, the weight and bulk of her body sloshing left and right, until it came again, that freakish earsplitting *boom*.

The gun. LeQuan.

The sound like a shock wave, a rippling pulse of noise, as Teddy staggered with a back-bending jolt, his hold weakening around her waist, then clenching tighter, a shudder in his legs. He hit the floor hard, both knees, just toppling, dragging her with him.

She lay there, unaware of time, feeling the crippling throb of pain in her head, exploring with shaky fingers the sticky coppery paste tangled in her eyebrow, clinging to her cheek, her lips, her chin. She could hear LeQuan's scratch-like wheezing and feel Teddy trembling from shock.

No voices, not from them, but soon there were footsteps, quick at first, then hesitant, a faint whiff of men's cologne and someone murmuring, *"Puta madre."*

62

Someone trying to drag her up, onto her feet—instinctively, she fought back, squirming, windmilling, the effort comical—butterfly elbows, katydid kicks. So weak it was cruel.

"Jacquelina." A man, a hiss. "Knock it off. We gotta get you the fuck outta here."

Vague recognition, the voice. Ben Escalada. Navarette's *recadero*. His *sicario*. But it wasn't his arms around her. Those belonged to the bear, Hector.

"We're taking you home."

She struggled. "No, no . . ."

Hector, whispering through his teeth, *"Pinche chicabonchia."*

Escalada again: "Your family is worried."

"Fuck my family. You can't leave him here." She pointed at Teddy, bleeding out.

"He's not your problem."

The room swam, her legs swam with it, the world muddy with color, plus this throbbing hum, a soundtrack in her blood.

Hector, arms locked around her waist, dragged her down the hallway in windmilling hops, finally entering the living room, where the Blu-ray flickered, some kind of televised fight.

Escalada came around, grabbed her jaw and squeezed, pooching out her lips to get her attention, his own mouth curled in a pending insult, but before he could get out a word the first window shattered.

The crash came from the front, work of a ball bat or crowbar, jagged glass shards flying so hard and fast they tagged the beaded curtain ten feet away. The clicking tendrils began to sway as Hector let go—she dropped to the rug, he reached inside his jacket for a weapon. Escalada drew as well as the next two windows exploded—the two men crouching, shielding their heads—while from the rear of the house Jacqi heard other windows breaking, the thumping crack of impact, the clang of splintering glass, every pane bashed in like some kind of ritual blinding.

Whoever it was, they had the house surrounded. The neighbors, she thought, recalling Fishbelly pissing on the pickup's windshield, LeQuan and his redneck paranoia.

No sooner did this idea form in her mind than a squarish bottle with a lit rag stopper, tossed in through a broken window, clunked across the floor, careening off the far wall, bouncing back in ricochet, not breaking. She could make no sense of it at first, like it was a flaming toy.

Escalada chased it, picked it up, cocked his arm to pitch it back out, only to see it followed by a second through a different window, a third through another. These hit and shattered and the flames spread fast, thick black smoke erupting in boiling clouds, the sickening smell of burning kerosene.

She scrambled onto her knees. Not toward the front, she thought. They've got the place surrounded, fine, take your chances out back. If you can just get your legs to work.

Through terror or madness or animal will she managed it, got herself upright, staggering out of the room, pinballing down the shotgun hallway, arms stretched out, pushing off against one wall then the other as she stumbled forward, glancing just once into the bedroom, seeing the two bodies—Teddy curled up in a lake of blood, LeQuan corkscrewed across the room, half on his back, fish-mouthed, eyes bulging.

She found the back door, unlatched the bolt, threw it open and tumbled out onto the rain-slick deck, almost losing her feet just as Hector and Escalada caught up, barging out blind, hacking up toxic phlegm. On cue, one after the other, they skidded and slipped and dropped like sacks.

She blinked at the darkness, making out a patch of yard, shallow and rimmed with a ragged hedge, and beyond that, towering evergreens.

She stepped off the deck onto wood chips and sawdust and fumbled her way ahead, reaching the hedge and searching for a gap just as an arm reached out, a fist gripped her sleeve.

Someone ripped her through the bushes. A blinding light flashed on, straight in her face.

"The girl."

"Jesus—"

"Careful now. Don't touch that blood."

Rough voices, muffled by bandannas, a touch of Arkie twang. The hand gripping her sleeve dragged her farther beneath the evergreens and shoved her toward someone else, the figure coming clear for just a second in the flashlight glare—just as stocky as the others but shorter, a woman.

Jacqi's eyes adjusted. She could make out a hat tugged down tight on a pigtailed head, the face, like the men's, masked.

Back near the house, Hector and Ben kept coughing up their lungs.

"Well well, look at you." The woman's voice, throaty and even more thickly accented than the men's. Older, too. "I'm guessing you deserved what you got."

Now Jacqi started coughing and couldn't stop. It felt like her lungs had turned to paper and something intended to rip them to shreds.

The woman waited her out, then: "Ain't no more reason for you to come around here, little girl. Nowhere to come to. Closest station house? Twenty minutes away, ever since they closed the one in north-town. Time the fire crews get here place'll be a total loss. Too bad. But you live like an animal, got nothing to cry about you die like one."

A small scrape of a voice. "I didn't live here."

"Like that's the goddamn point." The woman turned her head, lifted the edge of the kerchief, and spat. "Don't come out here no more. And you tell the police or anybody you were here, you say anything at all, we'll find you. You can bet your cheap little life on that. Now git."

She gripped Jacqi's shoulder and dragged her down a cramped path of well-trod mud bristling with pine needles and steepled with dripping trees, the smell of the fire mingling with a heavy scent of resin, freshened by the rain.

Stumbling, her skin feeling raw and hot: "There's four people back there, at least two of them alive, maybe three."

"I told you once, girl. Get gone. Don't test me."

63

At the crest of Holcombe Hill, Cass asked him to stop the car—"Just for a minute"—facing away, a whisper against the glass.

They'd driven in silence from the river road bus shelter—tacit agreement, mutually reached. Best to wait, let the surroundings of home buffer what was to come.

The storm had broken; through islands of cloud you could make out stars. The rain had scrubbed the landscape clean, streets etched with pinpoint lights, downtown a display case of window-lit high-rises with the incandescent transit center at the western end. The river drew a glimmering, sinuous curve in the dark, city on the nearside, the black sprawling marshlands beyond. Further still, sawtooth mountains lay shrouded in haze.

"This is where I stop when I'm walking Noble," she said, looking out. "Reminds me why I live here."

Day like this, he thought, some reminding can't hurt.

He shuddered at the thought of the nightly news. But he understood what she meant. Those who stayed here, who stuck it out, hanging in there—stone masons and jazz guitarists, yogaphiles and Harley freaks, the sleep-deprived hoi polloi: dental techs, vet techs, taco techs—all of them trying to eke out some kind of American life, all of them nailed to one question: Why?

You bought yourself a fixer-upper in a neighborhood on the edge, settled in and found a few like minds, made a few friends, dealt with the hassles and discovered, sooner or later, that you genuinely liked the town, the boondock pace, the funky charm, liked the ease of ferrying into San Francisco or day-tripping up into the wine country on weekends.

Now? Some couldn't afford to leave, hopelessly underwater on their mortgages. Some had stubbornly put down roots and refused to budge. Some had grand ideas the place might change.

But sooner or later, in a quieter moment, you'd hear them admit that there were nights like this, looking out across the town and the river and the wetlands, stars or storm clouds overhead, spray of lights below, the scent of orange and lemon trees in the background, heavy with winter fruit, or the fragrance of gardens thick with rosemary and lavender and jasmine. If home wasn't here, then where?

Trick question. Sitting there, watching Cass gaze out across the city, he reminded himself that home, now, was her.

Finally she broke the silence, saying quietly, "I don't need any more apologies, okay? What I need is a decision."

She turned away from the view. The yellow T-shirt with its red *interdit* sign lent an air of the absurd. Her eyes, though, canceled that.

"I always thought," she said, "the problem would be that I'd never measure up. Measure up to Roni, to what the two of you had. What the two of you went through."

"Cass?"

"I'm scared, Phelan. I'm not smart the way she was, I don't understand the books and movies and other stuff you talk about like she did. How am I supposed to compete with a ghost?" She looked at his face as though hoping to find the thing she'd lost. "Ghosts are perfect. Ghosts can't let you down."

"Trust me," Phelan said. "Ghosts let you down."

She turned away, taking a sad tight smile with her. Outside, the wind shook the branches of an ancient magnolia, ripe with waxy blossoms, towering over its white-fenced yard.

"Know when I fell for you? I mean, I'd kinda had my eye on you for a while but that happens. Flirting, I mean. Weird, I know. But cancer gets real fucking tedious."

"Hon, you don't need to go into this."

"But when I *fell* for you," she said, "was after the clinical trial failed and you met with the doctors and they said, That's it. That was your last best shot."

"Her last best shot."

"Phelan, stop interrupting, okay?"

"Sorry."

She fussed with a thread working loose from her turtleneck's sleeve. "And you had to make the decision, end all treatment, just nourishment and morphine. You had to let her go, watch her die." She broke the thread off, whisked it off her fingers. "And I remember the look on your face, wandering the halls the next few hours, and I wanted so bad to hold you, make you feel better, but when you finally broke down it was Agnes standing there, holding you—I mean, come on. Agnes?"

He hadn't thought of the woman in ages: slender, tiny, Taiwanese, a gunnery sergeant among nurses. "She could be strangely maternal in her way."

"If Agnes had babies, they'd hatch. And I asked you not to interrupt."

"Sorry. Again." He lifted a hand. Surrender.

"Make matters worse, I can't remember who it was now but somebody ordered the morphine recalibrated, and we had to back it down, then build it up again, like there was some sweet spot to find instead of just knocking her out. You know how that went."

He did. So much for fabled comfort care.

The pain team, as they called themselves, had told him, well before the decision to end treatment, that Roni's suffering baffled them. "If the six of us," the team leader said, "were hit with the same dose she's on we'd all be asleep." Which meant, no question, the pain was real. Roni, anxious and restless and demented, refused to lie still. But some genius decided to reinvent the wheel, drop down the painkiller to see what level she *really* needed. They turned the love of his life into an exercise.

"There was nothing the nurses could do, we had to follow the protocol, only her oncologist could change it and he never got back to us—calls, pages, nothing. What was it, about five hours went by."

Four, he thought, keeping quiet this time. Four hours watching Roni writhe in her bed, neither asleep nor quite awake, wincing, turning, like she was trying to claw her way out of the grave.

"And you'd had it. You went out into the hallway—I'll never forget this—you went out into the hallway and bellowed like you'd just escaped from a cage: 'Who the fuck do I have to kill to get my wife out of pain?'"

Strange, he thought, how blurry his own memory of that moment felt now. And he couldn't decide whether it made him feel heroic, romantic, or pathetic.

"You spotted Goerling over by the nurse's station, writing something up in a chart. Sitting there like nothing was happening, oh la-di-da, ignore it and it goes away. Narcissistic dork. But most of them are, the men anyway."

For whatever reason, the doctor came through crystal clear: young guy, hip little beard, chichi glasses, tennis player from the look of him, maybe a cyclist, trim and fit. Probably a lady-killer, ho ho.

"And you went over and asked him to check Roni's morphine level. He gave the door to her room the over-the-shoulder bit, then said, 'She's not my patient.'"

I would've been a hero in prison, he thought, if I'd strangled him to death right there just for saying that.

"The rest went by pretty quick. I remember him screaming, 'Call security!' I hurried over and grabbed your arm, stuffed you in the visiting room."

He remembered that part well. He'd felt cared for in a way he hadn't in a very long while. The preceding few seconds, though, remained a mystery. The doctor, Goerling, would claim he was attacked. "The man lunged at me." Phelan, in contrast, remembered the guy getting up to leave and he just naturally followed. They were probably both right.

"The other nurses and aides and me, we got together, and when security showed up we told them: Look, he's not some kind of loon. He's not a menace. We'd all seen you there, day and night, no sleep, no food."

"I had no right to go off the way I did."

"Oh, please." She raked back her hair with her fingers. "At least you didn't break his jaw." Something seemed to unlock inside her, letting a little of the anger out. "To be honest? I was kinda sorry you didn't kill the twerp."

"You'd come visit me on death row?"

A dry, sad chuckle. Still not looking at him. "Well, I'm kinda engaged to the Night Stalker, but I could probably fit you in."

"So hard, being popular."

"My point is, what I saw in you that day—I dunno, it's complicated. It wasn't just that you loved her—I mean, duh—it was that you were still trying to save her and you couldn't and you'd never forgive yourself, so you started howling at the moon, wanted to kill some-body—to protect her, sure, but to get even too. You're bitter, you're lonely, you're wicked sad and you know it's only gonna get worse. All of that, all at once, like you were utterly crazy and stone sane. I'd seen a lot in that ward, but never that. Not until then. Until you."

"No offense, but I find that hard to believe."

"Maybe I just didn't see it till then. Maybe you showed me."

The warmth of their breath as they spoke had begun to fog the windows, the cityscape now gauzed in a beaded haze.

"I wasn't half the noble mess you're making me out to be. Secretly, I felt relieved. Finally we had an answer. It sucked, but it was an answer."

She looked at him as though, if she saw him just right, things might change. "That's nothing to feel guilty about. We all get there. You deal with death enough, day in, day out, sometimes it can't come too quick." Tucking two fingers inside her mock turtleneck, she tugged the clinging fabric away from her throat, as though suddenly too warm, or bothered by how close it felt. "My point is, when the time came, it was like your golden moment and your worst nightmare were all wrapped up together. You were never better, never stronger or more true than you were with her at the end. I know. I saw. But you never failed so bad, either. And you're stuck there, Phelan. I didn't see it till this thing with Jacqi Garza, but you are. Stuck, trapped . . ."

The magnolia groaned and rustled in another burst of wind.

"I mean, it's not like I'm blameless here," she said. "I know that. I was jealous of a dying woman—how sick is that? Still am jealous—Christ, if anything it's worse. Maybe you feel guilt for letting her go and you think you have to atone—that happens a lot—but people die, Phelan. We all do. But you just won't accept that, not down deep. It's like you're still back in that room with Roni, trying one more time to get it right. Save her. Except now it's this Garza kid. After her it'll be somebody else, a married woman in a lousy marriage, another woman with cancer—"

"No—"

"I feel so fucking beside the point. What am I supposed to do? I don't need you to rescue me, Phelan. I need you to love me. And if you can't—I need you to leave."

For just an instant he pictured Roni rising from her hospital bed right after he'd told her the treatments had failed, shuffling in her gown and her treaded slipper socks toward the bathroom, opening the door as though it might lead somewhere else, somewhere better, a place where you get to live.

"Cass—"

"You're always saying I'm the best thing to happen since Roni died. Well you're the best thing to happen to me, period. I don't want to lose you." One shoulder nudged up, a guarded shrug. "I dunno, maybe I already have." She met his eye. "I miss you."

"I'm right here."

"Actually, you're not. That's the problem."

He tried to think of a time when he'd felt more ashamed. He was a drunk and the bottle was filled with his beautiful misery. No one's ever suffered like me, the very definition of asshole.

"Is this it then? No more chances. Pack up. I'm out."

"Is that what you want?"

"Christ, no."

She puffed her cheeks for a sigh. "To be honest? I'm tired. Maybe I'm just not cut out for this. It's too hard, wanting you so bad, not getting it back. Regardless, I've had it. Stick a fork in me and call me Dunn." A small, distant laugh. "My mom says that. Dunn's her maiden name."

Finally he got the nerve, reached out, took her hand, laced his fingers in hers. The skin felt hot and strangely dry. He squeezed. The hand just lay there in his grip.

She said, "Know what my plan was? You'll laugh at this." She sniffed, wiped at her nose with her free hand. "I thought, if I could talk to her, this Garza kid I mean, I could get through. Because you're so on the wrong track." She chuckled, like everybody but him knew the joke. "You keep thinking there's a way out, a happy ending, you can fix it, and she's like miles ahead of you there. You can help her, maybe, a little bit. But that's gonna be a long hard slog, and honestly? I don't want her in our lives that long. So I came up with my stroke of genius. I figured if I could just talk to her for a second face-to-face, fill her in on the background, get her to realize you haven't got some secret weird agenda, she might give in, talk to you. Let you be the swell guy you need to be so bad. And refuse to realize you already are. And the thing would be over and we could all move on."

He gave her hand another squeeze. Like trying to revive a trout. "I gave her the background, actually," he said. "She was unimpressed."

She lifted her chin, shook the hair off her face. "Then fuck her."

"You mean figuratively, I assume."

She turned his direction. A wounded smile. "You ever so much as check out that girl's shoes and there won't be a surgeon in the world who can stitch you back together."

64

Back at the house they let Noble out and watched him fussily sniff the yard, the ground heady with scent from the storms.

In a moment of exhaustion-cranked fantasy, Tierney imagined following suit, pushing his face into the mulchy leaves, the soggy clover and woody moss, the earth not just soft but loamy, the air almost busting with the rainy tang of rot. To be a dog. Better yet, to be Cass's dog.

Easing up behind, he wrapped his arms around her, nuzzled her. It took a second but she eased her weight back into him, pulling her hair away so he could kiss her neck as Noble ticktocked back up the porch steps, a collar-rattling shake, nudging past them and making a bead for his water bowl.

As though forgiveness were gravity, they drifted toward bed. Beginning in a kind of tentative trance, they made an awkward ritual of it, him kneeling to unlace her shoes, tug them off, strip away her socks, her lifting her arms so he could pull the awful yellow T-shirt over her head, then the mock turtle underneath, her red hair crackling with static.

They kissed and the stale scent of her breath became one more reminder she was real, she was flesh, she was here. Sitting in just her jeans and bra, she let his fingers search out the scars and moles on her arms, her shoulders—his touchstones, like he needed to convince himself of something, rediscover her.

Standing up, he shuddered out of his sport coat, nudged off his shoes, and her hands went to work on his shirt buttons, belt buckle, zipper, the teeth unlocking with a tight little whisper. He stood so she could tug his slacks down his hips, and he stepped out—one leg, the other—as she reached inside his briefs, pulled out what she wanted and kissed it, licked it, slipped it into her mouth and let it grow hard there.

The rest of the clothes came off in blind tugs and tosses, and once in bed he wrapped his legs around hers and pressed hard into her body, as though if he didn't she might get away. He cupped her breast in his hand and she arched her back, eyes closed, pounding a soft fist against his arm until she slipped beneath him, pulled him on top, locking her legs around his hips and guiding him in.

Her eyelids floated open and closed as his rhythm stuttered, then found itself. His strokes grew angry, he was punishing himself, hating himself, maybe hating her a little, too, and with the punch-like retort of her hips she answered: I get it, I do, I know.

She bit her lip against the trembling and her eyes clenched shut, she was slapping him now, his arm, his chest, whipping her animal, and when she finally bowed her back, head thrown to one side, she emitted a moan so wounded, so strange, Noble reared up from the braided rug and barked.

She lay there a moment, shuddering in little aftershocks, saying in breathy jolts: "Good boy . . . It's okay . . . Good boy . . ." Reaching out her hand toward the edge of the bed, she held it there as the dog slinked forward to lick her fingertips while, with the other hand, she covered her face. Please, Tierney thought, look at me.

She cried like she was trying not to, almost ashamed. He settled down beside her, wrapped her up, tucking her face into the hollow of his shoulder as he stroked her mad red hair.

"It's okay, it's okay, it's okay." Empty words. Lucky for him, not empty enough.

The old house settled into its nighttime whimpers and moans, winter wind thrashing the trees outside. Cass lay beside him, fetal in sleep, the dog snoring off in a corner.

The conversation from earlier just kept playing over and over in his head, and the more it repeated, the more frightened he felt, wondering if everything he thought he knew—about himself, his life—wasn't spectacularly wrong.

Cass had put her finger on a disturbing truth. Without realizing it consciously, he'd somehow convinced himself that Jacqi Garza remained trapped in her past, holed away in that terrifying cellar, mentally at least, incapable of getting out, moving on, living her life. He was the one, the only one, who could help her. Free her.

He was the expert, after all, on ruin and reclamation. A handyman of the heart. Wonder Widower.

Such a crock. He'd unconsciously rigged the whole thing, this elaborate trick of the mind, so he could ignore his own situation. His own prison.

An eerie, Jekyll-and-Hyde unease descended. He had a doppelgänger, or rather the doppelgänger had him.

This person out here in the world, this Otherwise-Known-as-Me, bothering with things, answering phones and asking questions, rescuing runaways and romancing redheads, lying awake in this bed—*that* was the shadow. The actual body lay elsewhere, parked in that hospital room outside time, invisible but strangely all the more real because of that—waiting out the miracle that never comes around, unable to leave, trapped in *Phelan Tierney's Finest Hour*, his Hallmark tearjerker, his defining tragedy.

For all he knew his life was just an elaborate hallucination, concocted by a brain in a jar, tucked away on some laboratory shelf. He was Neo in *The Matrix*, waiting for Morpheus to come along and flush him into the world.

He recognized such imaginings as the stuff of adolescence, overheated riffs on H. P. Lovecraft and *Twilight Zone*, freshman misreadings of Plato and Berkeley and Derrida. He was also aware they couldn't be proved false.

For some reason, in the thick of all this he recalled a favorite saying of his mother's: *A lone wolf is a lost wolf.* She wasn't referring to lupine sociobiology. She was expressing her understanding of love as a mirror. Her belief that, though we die alone, we build a life among others.

True, both he and Jacqi Garza had locked themselves away somewhere else, and that was the secret of their connection. Except, there was Cass.

She wasn't just the next woman in line. She saw him more honestly than any woman he'd ever known, more so even than Roni if he himself was honest.

Roni, the artist, bravely romanticized life, which made her death all the more cruel. Cass was an entirely different creature. He'd watched her back a thoracic surgeon into a corner at a cocktail party, tongue-lash him like the arrogant ass-hat he was. For her the heart was a muscle, love a cure for the disease called loneliness. That kind of pragmatism might just save him from his bullshit if he let it.

A perfect match? Perfection was for suckers and zealots. Perfection was for the dead. And for the first time in a very long while he allowed himself the stark white fear of once again wanting to live his vastly imperfect life.

Lose her, he thought, and you'll spend the rest of your sorry life chasing the next bright lie. Wrapped in a fool's cocoon. Because the truth doesn't lie in a book or an axiom or the mind of God. The truth lies between people, if they're up to the task. His truth, in particular, lay with Cass, if he was man enough to hear it.

In time he managed to drift into a kind of half sleep, then from somewhere on the floor, inside his tangled sport coat, his cell phone emitted its nagging, muffled hum.

"I know you need to get that," she said—suddenly wide-awake.

He murmured into his pillow: "Voice mail."

"They never call this late unless it's important."

"Depends"—he lifted his head just a little—"on who, exactly, 'they' might be."

"That's why you're supposed to answer. To find out."

He couldn't help but think that was a spectacularly bad idea.

She said, "What if it's her?"

He rose up on his elbow so he could see her face. The room was dark, he let his eyes adjust. Somewhere in the scrambled mass of shadowy hair, her eyes and mouth and freckles lay waiting.

"I know what it feels like," he said, "to lose everything. I'd rather not go through that twice."

She lay there perfectly still. "Then don't."

Part VI

65

From what she could tell, the bleeding had stopped.

Stop touching it, she thought, and yet, at that moment, the stiffening tacky feel of it, the clumps of matted hair, offered what small consolation she could wring from the situation—she wasn't dead yet.

Tierney was on his way, fine, but he'd sounded pretty put out about it. Couldn't chase her enough before, now he's all, like, *You want what?*

Fuck him. Fuck everybody. Fuck Jesus.

She sat in a dark clump of hawthorn just beyond the plaza of a gas station, lit up for the nighthawks, its nozzle-armed pumps like robot soldiers in the buzzing stillness. She still felt unclear as to how exactly she'd gotten there.

She'd been unable to return to the bus stop the way she'd come—Mama Cracker and her arson army had blocked the way. Them and the fire.

She'd stumbled, coatless, beneath the evergreens instead, the Homewood hills a pathless maze of darkness and blackberry brambles, tendrils coiled like barbed wire, thorns like razors, getting snarled up and cut and then turned around in the wind-whipped night even as she heard the fire crews arrive, saw their whirling lights beyond the crosshatched pine branches and the haze of smoke. They seemed to come to a dead stop several times before reaching the fire. Somebody'd thrown up barriers in the winding street, another vigilante trick. Delay all rescue, burn that shithole to the ground.

She found her way to pavement finally only to discover she'd trudged the wrong way down a long cul-de-sac—that happened twice—then needing to retrace her steps, try a new direction as rain came and went and the wind slapped her around.

The coyote damn near did her in. She stumbled into a small clearing and saw nothing at first, just heard the low whimpering yip, then a growl. Turning slow toward the sound, she saw in the darkness of the nearest brush the narrow-set yellow-gray eyes. She could smell something too, rank with decay—the coyote was feeding. She'd heard they'd been coming down from the hills, preying on house pets or their scat. A meter reader had come across one curled up in a lawn chair, gutting a rabbit snatched from its hutch. But those were stories. This was here.

Not knowing where the impulse came from, she crouched and uttered a menacing, bare-tooth hiss, then began edging back, retracing her steps, wondering if there were others around, a den. Her heartbeat hammered in her chest for ten minutes as she tried another way down the hill.

Despite the adrenaline, she'd felt exhausted, still did. Scared to close her eyes, because every time she did there they were—Teddy Buker, LeQuan, Ben and Hector, the fire—each image like a diamond in her mind. Not just the images. Fires, she thought, they don't sound the way you imagine. They're quieter than you expect, even as they cackle and hiss and groan, eating away, the wood, the cloth. Flesh.

By the time she'd found her way to the strip mall turnaround, the buses had stopped running. She saw lights a couple hundred yards off, hoped for an all-night service station, got lucky. She got change from the curry-scented night clerk, ignored his stare, made the call from a nearby pay phone, squinting to see the number clear enough to recite it on the voice mail recording, fearing the overhead light, wondering who else might be sharking around, looking for her.

It took a while, but Tierney rang back, the trill of the phone like the starting bell at a dog track, and at the sound of his deep, raspy, egghead voice her heartbeat started racing, ecstatic and resentful and scared all at once.

It wasn't till after she hung up the phone—having provided her location and a brief account of the mess she was in, with a promise she'd actually stay put till he got there—that the eerie circularity of it all hit home.

The escape through the forest, the barbed-wire blackberries, even the goddamn coyotes—not just a threat this time but real—like everything fit into a pattern, an elaborate moving jigsaw, and except for this little twist or that random change it would all just keep happening over and over forever.

The clincher: once again she was waiting for a car to appear, someone to show up and save the day. And just like last time, rescue wouldn't come free. The man would have his own agenda.

He didn't come alone, and it wasn't him who got out first. It was a woman, Amazon tall with legs to prove it, topped with a mane of wild hair. The nurse, she thought. He brought his girlfriend along. What was up with that?

For a moment she considered staying hidden, pretending she hadn't stuck around. But the cold, the pain, the blood—she just wanted to lie down somewhere, if only for a little while, even the backseat of Tierney's sad little beater.

Turned out it didn't matter, the nurse picked out her hiding place like it was flashing a signal.

"It's okay," she said, pulling out a tiny flashlight. Crouching down, she clicked it on and aimed the beam at an angle, a little up, a little to the side. Jacqi winced, even as she felt the fear and anger inside her subside, like the embers of a fire growing dim.

Tierney came up behind the nurse like an umpire, hands on his knees, face masked by the flashlight glare.

"Good God . . ."

66

After her run-in with the coyote, the dog scared her at first, but he seemed old and slow and harmless. His tail wagged sleepily as he nosed up, sniffed her knee.

The nurse said, "Noble, don't bug her," as Tierney locked the door. He'd been weirdly quiet the whole trip here, sitting up front alone, glancing in his rearview as his nurse girlfriend did her bit—tracking Jacqi's response to the flashlight, looking for fluid trickling from her ears or nose, asking if she had a sweet taste in her mouth.

The routine conjured Polly Bell, the tattooed nurse in Santa Cruz. One more piece in the looping puzzle. And just like back then she let herself feel, though never longer than an instant, that all this concern wasn't just a chore. For the first time in a decade it didn't feel dirty, being looked at, being touched.

Dishes lay racked beside the sink, pictures and knickknacks cluttered the nearby shelves, the kitchen table piled with papers and mail and magazines. It's her house, Jacqi thought, not his, not Tierney's, just like he'd said, though clearly he felt at home, kicking off his shoes, slipping off his jacket, draping it on a chair back as the nurse wrung out a hot towel, filled a bowl with soapy warm water.

"Have a seat," she said, nodding toward the table.

"Don't make me go to the ER, okay?"

"I'm not going to make you do anything." She started dabbing at the blood with the towel. "But I need to take a look at that wound."

Jacqi sat still and let the nurse go at it, but after only a moment of trying to stay quiet a fidgety restlessness made her feel naked.

"You said your name was Cass. That short for anything? Cassandra, right?"

"Cassidy."

"Wow. Cool. Great name. Can I have it?"

The nurse shot Tierney a look. "You can't afford it."

Tierney said nothing, just leaned back against the counter, arms crossed, looking like he couldn't make up his mind about something.

"You're different," Jacqi said as her chin and cheek got washed. "You're, like, quiet."

He chuckled like that was funny, not wack. "Been a bit of a day."

"Yeah. Say that again—ow!" She backed away from the towel, which now was stained pink with her blood, same as the water in the bowl.

"I've got my mind on a few other things now," he said. "Maybe that's the change you're noticing." He leaned down to scratch the dog's ear. The dog leaned into it, panting quietly. "For example, I've been retained in the Verrazzo matter. On behalf of someone you may know. Young man named Damarlo Melendez."

Jacqi shrank a little in the wooden chair. Felt sick. "D-Lo, huh. Imagine that."

The nurse stopped, studied Jacqi's face for a sec, the eyes in particular, like they'd just gone wrong, then turned toward Tierney. "Phelan? I need to ask a big favor. I need you to leave us alone for a minute, okay? I'd like to ask Jacqi here a couple questions and I need her to give me honest answers. I think that'll go a lot easier if you're not in the room.

Sorry. Before you leave, though, how about wrapping some ice in a dish towel?"

The nurse, Cass, knotted the towel with its clatter of ice cubes inside and stuck it in Jacqi's hand. "Put that where the pain is. You've already got a nasty knot. This should help bring it down."

Jacqi did as she was told. Weirdly, she enjoyed it.

"This is a mean cut. You're lucky you don't need stitches. What did he hit you with?"

"A gun." She felt trashy saying it.

"How many times?"

"I dunno, two, three maybe. Only the first one landed hard."

"Not from where I sit. The others made their point. Not to mention you've been scratched to hell—blackberries?"

Jacqi nodded.

"Okay. What else happened? I'm not trying to be nosy. I'm trying to make sure I haven't overlooked something."

Jacqi nodded and picked a place in her recollection, Fishbelly pissing on the hillbilly pickup, started from there, and bit by bit the rest just tumbled out, even the part about Buker nailing LeQuan, three fierce punches straight to the throat, just like he'd done to Fireman Mike. Of that, she thought, there's no longer any doubt.

It felt less lonely, talking, despite how ashamed she felt. That was new. She readjusted the ice on her head.

"Your old man's lucky, having a nurse in his life. Wish I had one."

Cass fussed inside her first aid kit, picking through ointment tubes, cotton balls, gauze. "You do have one, at least for the moment."

"I was thinking more, like, you know."

Cass looked up from the kit box, eyes like her touch, all business, but not rough. "This LeQuan, the guy who hit you, or the other guy, Teddy, either one rape you?"

It wasn't an accusation, not really. "Didn't get to that." Again, she thought of Polly Bell, the swabs, the speculum, the special lamp. Maybe kindness was just a cover for scrutiny. *Who are you?* Melting ice began to drip into her hair. "There's something going on between you and your old man. Tierney. You guys have a fight?"

Sister Nurse stiffened, then sighed. She tried to hide it with more fishing around in the white tin box. "If we did, what makes that your business?"

"Nothing. Unless it's about me."

"This might be a good time for me to turn you back over to Phelan."

"Might be a good time to get me out of your hair. Yours and his both."

"You're not in our hair."

"So you say. I see different. I grew up around angry people. I know the vibe."

"If you leave I want Phelan to take you down to Kaiser, or Rio Mirada General."

"That a threat?"

"You've had a concussion. You shouldn't be alone."

"Yeah, well, that's not really your problem."

"You're right. Absolutely."

Like that, no more Sister Nurse. She got up and went to the swinging door that opened onto the dining room, nudged it open. "Phelan? She wants to head out. Maybe you can give her a lift someplace?"

Suddenly, the dog, who'd been snoozing in the corner, got up, shook himself, padded over across the linoleum, and stuck his nose under Jacqi's hand, hitting her up for one last pet. You whore, she thought. You stinking, blind, needy creature. You thing.

How she got there, she wasn't quite sure, but there she was, on her knees in the kitchen, arms wrapped tight around the old dog's neck as this pulse, this pressure, built up inside her—not tears, deeper than that, the thing beneath tears, a growl in the dark, a coyote rank with blood—and she thought that something might break in her head or in her chest and she buried her face in the wiry fur, taking in the musky stench and wishing it were hers, wishing she could take it with her, that and his terrible breath, the old dim eyes. You whore of a slut dog monster. I would give anything. If.

Tierney and Sister Nurse, the two of them stood there near the door, staring, she could feel it like a burn. Could hear them thinking: Get her out. Get her out of this house, out of our lives. She couldn't get up. Couldn't move.

"Here's an idea." It was Tierney. "Cold as hell out there, probably more rain on the way. Lousy night for going out. And given the whole concussion thing, be a good idea to stay awake for the next few hours. How about you wash up, change into some dry clothes, grab a bite if you're hungry, then some TV. Maybe watch a movie."

67

A shower not a bath, the nurse said. "I don't want you falling asleep in the tub. And be gentle when you wash your hair, don't open up that cut again."

Sister Strict now, but who could blame her.

It was a giant white claw-foot thing with plastic curtains all around, tropical fish pattern, hung by rings from an oval chrome rod. Creaking ivory handles on the faucets and it took a while for the hot to get going. She knelt there a moment, leaning over the porcelain rim, chin resting on her arm, hand stuck beneath the warmth and the tumbling wet roar, enjoying the simple do-nothingness, the blank state of mind.

Standing up again, she stripped off her filthy clothes, kicked them away like rags. Caught sight of herself in the mirror—skinny and bruised and in a strange place. Same as it ever was, except for the little hummingbird hanging from its cheap gold chain.

How long had it been since she'd knelt there in the wet street, watching Verrazzo die? How long since the last time she'd really thought about him, not just the hundreds of problems his getting killed created?

Sorry, Mike. You deserve better. But I'm up to my neck right now and I kinda get the feeling you'd understand. Thanks for offering to take me away. Not quite Mexico, but hey. You were willing to take me in. I know I woulda paid in trade but still, I'm grateful.

Her makeup looked like she'd put it on with a spoon and she searched the drawers for cotton balls, discovered some, found a bottle of lotion too. Leaning over the sink, face inches from the mirror, she carefully smudged the mess away, eye shadow, mascara, gone. Blinking, she checked out her naked face.

By the time she stepped under the spray, the steam had risen thick and soft and hot and she tried not to think of smoke. The nurse's shampoo smelled like lavender, her soap like oranges, both stung. It felt good though, minor miracle, getting clean.

As she lingered under the water, wrapped up in its warmth, a knock came, the door clicked open, and Cass slipped in to deliver a fresh towel and a pile of clean clothes—sweats and socks.

She toweled herself dry and brushed out her wet black hair and tried not to look anymore at the mirror. The sweatpants were huge and she cinched the waist just under her breasts like a clown, then still had to cuff the bottoms. The sweatshirt, hooded with a pouch, engulfed her, while the socks were thick white cotton, cool and clean and smelling like cedar and bleach.

No longer naked, she ventured one last glance at the mirror. You look like a punching bag, she thought, all dressed up in her mom's clothes—and deep within, like distant lightning, something crackled silently across the sky of her soul.

• • •

The kitchen smelled like popcorn and there was Melba toast laid out too, plus a glass of 7-Up. "If you can keep that down," Cass said, "we'll try some soup or something."

Tierney stared. An impish smile. "We're going to get indicted. For shrinking a minor."

Cass said, "It's the smallest stuff I had. Grab a bowl."

"It's fine," Jacqi said. "Thank you."

They moved into a den lined in bookshelves, with armchairs and a couch and a TV, everyone but the dog with popcorn. Tierney, the guy, worked the remotes.

"There's this French thing I've been meaning to watch," he said as the screen flickered to life. "If it's boring we'll try something else."

He didn't say it like he expected anyone to object. Cass curled up on one end of the couch, legs tucked up beneath her, looking like her thoughts had her all knotted up. Tierney took the other end of the sofa, letting Jacqi sit in between. The better to watch her, she supposed, sipping her drink. Or maybe they'd had another tiff.

The movie was black and white, subtitled, the intro music circus-like and hokey. She thought at first she might drift off—not exactly the plan—but the title grabbed her, *Eyes Without a Face*, and almost instantly the thing turned scary.

A woman wearing a slicker and a thick choker of pearls was driving a small car far out into the country at night. A figure in a large man's coat, face obscured by a downturned hat, sat huddled in the backseat.

The woman in pearls stopped along a night-black river, checked to be sure she wasn't spotted, then dragged the figure out of the car—a woman, naked under the big coat—and dropped the body into the water.

Next scene: a renowned plastic surgeon (actually, he kinda looked like a magician) got told a body washed up in a river outside the city—a dead young woman matching the description of his missing daughter. The daughter was in a terrible, disfiguring car accident, and the body they found is missing a face. But it's odd—the wound has edges so precise they almost suggest a scalpel.

Jacqi almost forgot her throbbing head. Fucking magician killed his own daughter—worse, he was experimenting on her.

Crossing her legs like an Indian, bowl in her lap, she started in on her popcorn.

The surgeon identified the body as his daughter, a funeral was held—and the woman in pearls was there. The surgeon's sad, beautiful assistant. They went home to this eerie humongous mansion with a kennel in the basement full of barking dogs—Noble, not lifting his head, growled sleepily at that part—and on the top floor in a hidden room, a room full of caged doves but without mirrors, a young woman sobbed on her bed. A young woman with perfect eyes. But no face.

The girl at the morgue wasn't the surgeon's daughter after all—it was a girl who looked like his daughter. They'd abducted her and he'd operated, slicing away her face to see if he could graft it onto his daughter. But it didn't work. They'd have to try again.

The daughter said no, the father insisted, and he told her for the sake of preserving her tissue she had to wear her mask: this eerie blank mannequin thing with eyeholes.

"My face frightens me," the girl said, "but my mask terrifies me even more."

The rest of the movie just got spookier, and time vanished. Jacqi sat there mesmerized, even as she realized Tierney, crafty bastard, had no doubt planned it all, choosing this movie precisely because he knew she'd dig it, knew she'd see herself in it. She was the girl forced to wear a mask—not for herself, for everyone else, though nobody copped to that. And she gave in, she tried, one face transplant worked—but just for three days. Then the tissue blackened and shrank and decayed, she was even more hideous than before. Back on with the mask. Another girl is abducted—but finally the daughter rebels: no more surgeries, no more cruelty and lying, no more killing. She can live with her face but not the guilt.

Using a scalpel, she cuts away the captive girl's bonds, stabs the woman in pearls, then runs to the kennel—the dogs were also prisoners, raw flesh for her father's experiments—and opens all the cages. The dogs lunge for her father and maul him to shreds as she liberates her doves. The cooing white birds flutter on her arms and shoulders as she walks out with them into the woods, free.

For the first time since the terrible, horrible thing: free.

"You okay?"

It was Tierney. He was holding out a Kleenex.

Jacqi shook her head, whispered, "No thank you," and wiped at her face with her hands. She turned toward Cass, who was watching her with those nurse eyes, and instantly felt small in the bulky clothes, like she had in the giant sweater the waitress named Dawn had provided that night at Bernadette's, the diner outside Santa Cruz.

The night, she thought, everyone keeps saying I got away.

The pattern started closing in again—she felt the tightening of its screws, heard the snapping into place of the final puzzle piece. All of this had happened before and would happen again for all of time, it was part of an endless loop, an episode that would never stop repeating, never. Assume your mask. You're here, but you're not here.

Then the nurse, Cass, reached out, touched her hand, fingers as weightless on her skin as a moth. Tierney stayed put. She glanced at one then the other and saw in their eyes something she barely recognized, an absence of demand, a lack of claim—or less of a claim or demand than she'd known in a long, long time. This is where the pattern ends, she thought. Trust these people, these strangers, or the nothingness wins for good. Whatever they want, you can live with.

Ever so slightly, the spell broke. The haunting, awful, repetitive eeriness in everything gave way to a dizzying sense of openness, like a door had opened and she saw, for the first time in forever, her frightening face.

Staring at a spot on the floor, she wiped at her eyes again, gathered up some strength and said, "I guess it's time to tell you what really happened."

68

His name was Clint, so kids called him Eastwood. His hair was rusty and his face was freckled and cockeyed, one ear way smaller than the other and his mouth slanting down on one side. He walked kinda funny, with this hunch, leaning kinda forward, like whatever was coming, he was ready to jump in.

He hung out with my brother, not at school so much. Eastwood didn't go to school. His foster parents, they just cashed the checks, didn't care what he did.

I was eight. He was twelve.

He came over a couple times and he seemed so cool, just kinda reckless and not scared. I told you he brought these plums from a tree where he worked and he always offered me a couple. I had this monster crush on him, no lie. He was nice. He talked to me like I wasn't stupid, which Richie thought was hilarious.

It irked the hell out of Richie, the fact his buddy didn't think I was wack. Boys always think girls have it made. It's why they hate us.

Richie comes into my room one day, all weird and serious and kinda mad. He says Eastwood likes me, he talks about me all the time, wants to come over and visit.

Be nice to him, Richie says. He's like grabbing onto my arm, it hurts. Don't bitch, don't whine, don't act stupid. Be nice.

Couple days go by. Mom's at work. Richie and Eastwood show up, but then Richie makes himself scarce, and it's me alone with Eastwood in my room.

He's nice again, but nervous. He starts by digging into the paper bag he brought and offers me a plum, he takes one too and we stand there, like neither of us knows how to dance, then he takes a bite and so I do too, they're not quite ripe and a little tart but still, I get juice on my chin and so does he and we're slurping and giggling. I get a washcloth from the bathroom and we wipe off our hands and faces and he starts telling me how pretty I am.

Bet you hear that all the time, he says, like I should be proud, but ashamed too. Bet you hear that all the time.

Then he sat me down and kissed me. Not much of a kiss, really. A bump on the mouth. He smelled like the gas station he hung out at and his fingernails were grimy and he had these wispy, like, whiskers here and there—his sideburns, his chin, upper lip.

He leaned me back onto the bed and ran his fingertips across my face, real gentle. It felt funny, but good. I got goose bumps. Then he did the same thing along my arms, my neck. His hand moved down and across my shirt—nothing there to stop for, but he did anyway—then down to my belt. I flinched, scared, grabbed his hand. He liked that. Leaned down, kissed my fingers, looked at me. It's hard to explain. He just seemed like he cared about me.

He said the thing, like, every guy since one way or another's said: I'm not gonna hurt you. And I told myself it was okay. Because I wanted it to be. So we were both lying.

He put his hand on me down there, just cupping my crotch, looking at my face. How's that feel, he asked. That feel good? I couldn't talk, like somebody'd snipped the connection, my mind, my mouth, so I just nodded, thinking: Be nice. Visit.

And we just kinda stayed like that for a while, him touching me down there with one hand, stroking my hair with the other, looking into my eyes and smiling. I could tell he was nervous too and it's funny but that's what calmed me down. He liked me. That part wasn't made up, he really did. I felt it.

That's all that went on that day. He asked if he could come over again, just me and him, and I nodded, still tongue-tied. My heart was banging like a monkey on a drum and when he left with Richie I felt so lonely. And yet kinda relieved, too, like I'd dodged a bullet, but not sure how exactly.

He didn't come back for a week. When he did it was during the day again, Mom at work. Richie disappeared real quick, like before. Always wondered how much they talked about it. Never did find out.

I was glad to see him, though nervous still too. That probably gave off a signal, like I was eager. I didn't know any of that then. I'd like to say I was innocent but I was just dumb.

I'd put on a dress for him—what's that tell you?

I still don't know how to describe it all. Again, he acted nice to me and I know he liked me, he talked to me and said nice things, but he was impatient this time. No kisses, no touchy-touchy spider hands. He reached up under my dress and I wanted him to, but then I got scared and he pulled away. You like this, you know you do, you said so.

He sounded mad, didn't occur to me it might be guilt. And in my family, when people get mad, you do what they want. It's like the code. Angriest person wins.

And so I lay back down and let him do what he came for. He was smart enough to put a towel underneath me, probably picked that one up in *Penthouse* or something. I was so scared I barely felt it, though I knew it hurt and I was grateful it went quick.

He couldn't look at me after. Just sat on the edge of the bed, hunched over, back turned. I wasn't so pretty anymore.

Then—this is kinda strange—he started to cry. And I went over to him and put my hand on his arm. He flinched like I'd shocked him but didn't get up, just sat there, one hand covering his face, the other reaching blind for mine. He took it, held it.

We sat like that for, I dunno, five minutes, ten. Then he let go of my hand and got up off the bed, turning to look at me finally. Way he smiled—all sad but kind, too, and, you know, ashamed—I knew he wouldn't be coming over anymore.

He left and I threw the towel out, stuffed it way down at the bottom of the trash, and when Richie came back he was furious. I don't know what Eastwood said exactly but Richie wanted to strangle me. Not because of what I'd done, or what I'd let happen, but because Eastwood seemed bent out of shape or unhappy or something.

Richie grabbed my arm and shook me. What the hell did you do? I did what you told me to, I was nice, but I didn't tell him that. I figured I'd messed everything up but I didn't know how so I didn't want to say anything.

Richie said if I ever told anyone about what went on, Mom especially, he'd tie me up in a sack with stones in it and throw me in the river. And I could tell by his face and his voice he wasn't just making that up. He'd thought about it.

I hated going home after that. Mom was always angry, or disappointed, nothing new in that. Now Richie was too, more than before, and even though I kinda hoped Eastwood might come back I thought maybe that wasn't the best thing in the world. In fact, maybe it was the worst thing.

I was wrong about that, obviously.

It wasn't all that long between Eastwood and the Cope thing, but I don't remember much about it. That whole period of time is kind of a blur. You know a lot about what happened after that, all the stuff you read, but here's what you don't know.

At one point, when he's doing what he did to me—Cope, I mean—I could tell he'd figured it out. He wasn't the first guy I'd had. That was his trip, or part of it, but now I've spoiled it for him, and everything stopped. His eyes went steely and I was so damn scared he was going to kill me right there. So I just started talking. Didn't know what else to do. I told him all about Richie and Eastwood and how I wasn't worth anything anymore. I thought if I disgusted him, he wouldn't want me, and he'd let me go.

I wasn't all that wrong. He did leave me there. Went off to get what he'd need to kill me and bury me and make sure I stayed buried. Maybe he found out who my dad was, too, caught it off the news, and that just made him want to ditch me quicker. He wasn't just dealing with an eight-year-old now. He was dealing with a man who could call out a hit from inside, and that meant life on the run. Forever.

Whatever the reason, he stayed away long enough for me to chew through the leather on my wrist cuffs and pull the ankle chain out of the wall. I didn't know what time was until that day. Hour after hour after hour, every second feeling like a bomb going off. But I did it. I was free. For a couple hours.

Ran through the woods to the road and some guy picked me up—I lied about who, nice guy, didn't want to come forward, I'll tell you about that later, it's not important. Except the lying part. Seemed like everybody needed me to lie about something. But I wound up at the hospital, and the nurse is in the middle of the rape kit when two detectives from here show up.

Older one's name was Daddeo. Young one, Skellenger. Guy you talked to today. I saw him too. Told me the best thing for everybody would be if I just skipped town.

I tried. Here I am.

They told the nurse to take a break and she argued but they wouldn't leave, so she did. I really wish she hadn't, but I understand. Daddeo sits down next to me, one-cheeking the examination table, that thin waxy paper crackling under his butt, and he looks at me like I'm the cause of all his headaches but he forgives me. Maybe.

He says they don't have much time. If Marina Bacay is still alive, they need to act quick. So start at the beginning, tell us everything. Now.

I did. And when I got to the part about Cope taking off, what had happened just before, what I told him about Richie and Eastwood, the two of them looked at each other like I'd just pissed on the floor, then Daddeo lifts his hand. Okay, he says, that's good. That gives us something to go on. If you can backtrack to the house where he had you hid, that'd be good, we'll send some people up there quick.

But I want you to do something for us, he said. I want you to wait for your mother to show up before discussing this with anyone else but us. Can you do that? Talk to no one. Not the nurse, not the doctors, nobody. Not till you've talked it out with your mom.

My mom shows up not long after that. She talks with Daddeo and Skellenger first, then comes in to deal with me.

I said she was mad a lot back then. She was never madder than she was with me in that room. Locked the door. Said: You listen and you listen good. All this nonsense about Richie, about his friend. You forget about it. You say nothing about it ever again. Never. Anything that happened there, it's nobody's business but the family's. And the family will take care of it. But to the police, to the doctors, to anybody else who ever asks, there is only one man who ever touched you and it's that piece of shit who took you off the street—do I make myself clear? He's the one who deserves to suffer. And if the police or anyone else ever asks you about Richie or any of his friends, you pretend you made it up. You were confused, you were scared. That sick freak, that animal, he scared you. You were afraid if you told the truth he'd come back and find you and finish what he started.

And hear me good: You'll wish he had if you ever bring up your brother's name again.

And so I changed my story. There was no Eastwood. There was only Victor Cope. I told that lie at the prelim, told it at trial, told it to the press. Recited it so often I kinda believed it myself. I described in sick, twisted detail just what Cope did to me, except he didn't, not all of it. He did plenty, don't get me wrong, and I hope he rots in hell for it. I didn't lie about that. But the part about him raping me and using a condom so he didn't leave any stuff behind, my mom coached me on that part. And then everyone said what a brave girl I was, how courageous I was to tell the ugly truth about this horrible man. And I told myself that this is what the world is like. Truth is no match for evil. Only children believe such things.

And I wasn't a kid anymore. That part of my life was over.

Cope sat there during trial staring at me, knowing I was lying—smiling, like he'd get the last laugh. But he didn't. The DA made sure the public defender couldn't go into anything outside my direct testimony, and he didn't have much stomach for even that. No way Cope was gonna take the stand himself. Nobody'd believe him. They believed the brave little girl.

Cope went away, everyone said justice was done. Secretly, though, I could feel it. Everybody wondering if there wasn't something else, something I wasn't saying. I didn't know Cope wrote the judge till you showed me that letter, but I had this sense the whole time that it'd leaked out somehow anyway. Or people just made it up. Because when all was said and done it wasn't supposed to be me who escaped.

Here comes the worst part.

Somewhere in all that, Eastwood disappeared. Nobody knew at first, his foster parents just kept pretending he was around so that the county would keep sending money, but finally a teacher spoke up, I guess, and CPS asked some questions but everybody figured he just ran away. Thirteen, he woulda been at that point. Didn't even make the news, his disappearing.

I knew he didn't just leave. Richie wouldn't talk to me anymore, wouldn't look at me. But he didn't bother me, either. I just stopped existing.

Mom said I should be grateful there were people in my life willing to look after my best interests. And Pete Navarette started spending a lot more time at the house, paying more attention to my mom.

Burkhead was his last name. Clint Burkhead. I don't know for a fact they killed him. I don't know if Richie was involved, if they made him do it or just made him watch or if none of that happened. But I think about it almost every day, even though I try not to. I'm supposed to be grateful but I'm not, I hate them for making me part of it and I want to know what happened to him.

If you help me with that, if you help my brother because he's the key in all this, you help him with Eastwood and you help me come clean about Cope—because I'm sick of carrying that around, I'm sick of living a lie, being a lie, I'm tired of being angry and scared all the time, and I know he'll file papers for a new trial and everybody—absolutely everybody—will hate me. I'm going to need you. I'm going to need somebody to be on my side. I need at least one person to believe me.

You do that, I'll help with Damarlo. I'll come forward and tell what I saw and what Teddy Buker told me. I mean, it's not like D-Lo's innocent, but I can let them know what I know. Maybe that'll help. You know better than me.

But if you want no part of all that, no part of me, I'll understand. Trust me. I'll get my clothes, make like a baby and head out.

What time is it? Jesus, three o'clock. *La hora de los fantasmas.* My *abuela* used to call it that. The hour of ghosts. Or dead time—that's what they called it on *Paranormal State.* Kinda weird when you think about it.

69

Summoned from bed after three hours' sleep, Skellenger stood outside the fire-gutted house, the air still reeking of smoke and unspent gas tinged faintly with chlorine from so much water. Hoses snaked from the hydrants to the scene, the house a total loss, just a blackened husk, fire crews still checking for reflash as they went in with their axes and rakes and Halligan tools to start the overhaul.

A handful of news vans had shown up—they were putting in some real work the past eighteen hours—and he could imagine the beguiling simplicity of the angle: a fireman is murdered, followed by a deadly fire. Possible connection? We'll have the details after these messages.

Which was good, he supposed. It meant they were no longer hanging out at Nina Garza's house, but that would change. One of the two charred bodies inside the wreckage belonged to LeQuan Joiner, if their anonymous phone tip proved true.

A second body, found in back, belonged to a hulk in a nice suit, a guy named Hector Mancinas, one of Pete Navarette's men—he'd been polite enough to have his wallet in his pocket when someone altered his face with close-range buckshot.

The third body, found nearby, remained as yet unidentified, but one of the pickups parked on the street belonged to a Theodore Buker, and the address on the registration was back in town, not here. Time would tell what that meant, he supposed.

As for suspects?

He'd just spent twenty minutes across the street in the home of Rose Bolander—tartan robe, blue-veined feet tucked into sheepskin slippers, gray hair coiled into wiry pigtails—the mother of Skip Hoskins and Derek Short, Irish twins from different fathers.

Skip was on parole for sale of stolen car parts—catalytic converters, valued for the platinum: "harvesting cats" it was called. Derek had recently posted bond for possession of piperidine and cyclohexanone, precursor chemicals for the manufacture of phencyclidine: PCP, Angel Dust, Ozone, Hog. Yes, there were those who still made it. Used it. And they had mothers.

From the corduroy armchair in her knotty pine den, the paneling stained from years of nicotine, Rose had stubbed out her cigarette into a beanbag ashtray and said, "All I heard was smashed glass. That and some shouting—jibber jabber, couldn't make none of it out, Mex'can, Ebonics, whatever. By the time I got outta bed, found my specs, got myself decent, and went to the front, whole damn house over there was on fire. Pretty quick I heard gunshots and so I killed the lights and hunkered down."

"What about the cars parked in the middle of the street," Skellenger said, "blocking the way in?" There'd been two, both stolen, the interiors getting printed now.

She lipped a Kent from its crumpled pack and lit up with a flip-top lighter, the flame brightening her face, all pockmarks and crow's-feet and roughshod flesh.

"Why not admit that you guys are as much at fault for that fire and whatever else happened over there as anybody? You and the firefighters hadn't held tight for your pay, city wouldn'ta gone belly-up and the northtown firehouse would still be open. You guys hadn't decided to trade staffing for your goddamn wage rate, force wouldn't be cut down to squat. That gave the green light to every asshole this end of the state. Set up here knowing they could do as they goddamn please."

She tapped away a crumble of ash. Hand spotted with age, arthritic knuckles.

"We tried to contact the owner, fill him in on what was going on, tell him they'd turned the place into a magnet for fuckheads, but he was nowhere to be found. Called the bank that foreclosed, they said it's not their problem, contact the owner. Round and round. Merry-go-fuck-yourself. Called the sheriff, you guys, anybody else we could think of. Same deal. Jig who answered the door waved a phony lease and that was that. Whole damn situation out here is screwed. So tonight one bunch of monkeys shows up to teach another bunch a lesson. Big surprise. But hear me out: comes time to point the finger at who's to blame for that fire, don't forget to check the goddamn mirror."

Thank you, Rose, for your candor.

Yes, Derek and Skip would get a visit, and he could imagine the wisecracks. *You telling us a soul brother burned up in the fire? We call that a coonflagration.* But that wasn't what weighed on him at that moment. That privilege belonged to Jacqi Garza.

The girl had a strange black genius for returning to relevance. A simpleton could connect the dots. Why couldn't she listen and just leave town? Why couldn't the mother do what she promised, find the kid and get her the fuck outta Dodge?

With his luck he suspected they'd find the phone buried some-where in the ashes, damaged but not destroyed, and for a moment he indulged the fantasy that a fourth body would get found right there along with it. A girl's.

Pissy little notion. Cheap and chickenshit and creepily pragmatic.

Don't, he thought. Just don't.

70

They finally tucked her up in blankets so she could sofa up and get some sleep. Sister Strict had given way to Sister Nurse again and she said she'd come in after two hours and wake her, make sure she hadn't blacked out—that was the danger, she said, with concussions—but Jacqi doubted she'd ever drift off. Every time she closed her eyes, five seconds max, they popped back open, her thoughts sparking around inside her brain and this invisible hippo on her chest.

With all the kicking and flipping under the blankets, she woke the dog. He whimpered and rose and shook, then came over and nosed her hand, so she scruffed his spiky ears and smiled into the hazed white eyes, shrinking from the hot stench of his panting breath but thinking: Let's run away, Noble.

But he was exactly where he belonged. Old dog. Lucky dog.

"I'm scared," she whispered.

The dog stopped panting for a second, rested his chin on the edge of the couch. His tail wagged once, just once, and slow.

"I'm scared but it's different. I don't know what this is. I don't know who I am."

She ran the backs of her fingers across the stiff bristly fur of his jowls, scratched a spot between his ear and the hinge of his jaw. How wonderful, she thought, to be old and stinky and lucky and blind and loved.

In the dim glow cast by the light over the sink, Tierney attacked the clutter on the kitchen table, collecting the dusty papers and magazines, delivering them in piles to the floor. It was just before dawn.

Cass said, "You're not really going to make her testify, are you?"

Barefoot, robe cinched tight, she stood framed by the cabinets with their frosted glass panels, one arm folded across her midriff, the other hoisting her mug of tea.

He squeezed out a wet sponge at the sink, then went back to the table, wiped away the cup rings, the sprinklings of pepper and salt, the hardened beads of spilled jam. "You should try to catch some sleep."

"Maybe later. Answer my question."

He toweled the tabletop dry. "I'm trying to think of a way for her not to. Testify, I mean." Reaching into the travel case, he hefted the yearbooks out and plopped them down on the table, organizing them by school.

"She's been through enough. Make her testify, she has to go through it all over again. And more."

"I get that." He offered a grateful smile. "I appreciate this. What you're doing."

"What am I doing?"

"Looking out. For her."

"It's you I'm concerned about."

"Liar."

"Oh go to hell."

He chuckled. "I stand by what I said. I appreciate what you're doing."

She pushed off from the corner and padded across the linoleum floor, flipped on the overhead light, then pulled out a chair and dropped down into it, terrycloth tush connecting to the tapered wood with a muffled thump. "You told me what I needed to hear. Showed me what I needed to see. And I've had my chance to see her up close and personal, more so than I bargained for. I'm not scared of her anymore."

"I'm glad."

"You're welcome."

She reached out and grabbed the hair at his nape and pulled him toward her. The kiss was long and warm and greedy and she bit him twice and never let go of his hair until the end. "I'd kill you if I didn't love you so much."

Sitting back in her chair again, Cass studied him, like a drawing she wasn't quite sure was finished. "So what's your big idea?"

"These." He nodded toward the yearbooks. "Forty to fifty kids were there when Verrazzo got killed. I figure if she can give me ten, twenty, however many names, I can make somebody else step up."

"None of them have. Not one. Listen to the news."

"I'll go find them." He reached across to tuck a curlicue of hair behind her ear and she nuzzled her cheek into his palm. "I'm good with people," he said. "Remember?"

"You guys are talking about me."

She stood in the doorway, still miniaturized in the gargantuan sweats. Noble, tail swaying lazily, trooped up behind.

"You're supposed to be sleeping," Cass said.

"Like you?"

"Come on." Tierney dragged a chair away from the table. "Have a seat."

Skidding a little in the thick white socks, she made way to the chair and scooted into it. Noble nudged his way beneath the table, found a spot between the two women, and thudded to the floor.

Jacqi, glancing under the table's edge, reached out with her foot and nudged his hip. "Really like your dog."

Cass smiled appreciatively and reached out with her own foot. "If California would let me, I'd marry Mr. Noble."

"Make an honest animal out of him," Tierney said. To Jacqi: "You want anything? Tea, juice, some cereal?"

"I'm good, thanks." She couldn't take her eyes off the dog. "So what were you guys talking about? I just kinda caught the last part."

Tierney and Cass glanced at each other.

"Phelan here's thinking of ways you won't have to hassle with court."

"I'm okay with court."

"Cass thinks you've been through enough. I tend to agree. Like I told you at the restaurant, I can find you a lawyer who will keep you out of all this. That said, I've got a duty to Damarlo."

"I get it." Jacqi flipped open one of the yearbooks. "That what these are for?"

"I was hoping you could maybe pick out some of the kids who were at the scene. Saw what happened. In particular, watched this Teddy Buker character walk up."

For the merest instant, Jacqi stopped. Her eyes drifted.

"You don't have to," Tierney said. "If—"

"Sure," she said, snapping back. "This is St. Cat's, though. The kids at the scene were all from Stallworth. From what I could tell anyway."

"I've got those here." He slid the yearbooks toward her. "Most recent on top."

The tip of her tongue appeared and she absently stroked it against her upper lip as she flipped open the topmost yearbook. "By the way, I gave a few names to Skellenger. At the hospital, when he told me to take off."

"Yeah. I need to hear more about that. His telling you to leave town."

"Two of the names I gave him were made up."

Tierney cocked his head. "They weren't really there?"

"They don't exist. I just kinda pulled the names outta my sweet spot."

"Okay." Tierney nodded, taking that in. "Try not to do that with me, okay?"

"Gotcha."

She turned back to the yearbook. Tierney reached into his brief-case for a tablet and pen. Cass stuck out her hand.

"Whoa. Stop. I've got a real problem with this." She looked across the table at Jacqi. "I think it's way too soon for you to be doing this. All you've been through, not just the past ten years and not even yesterday but here, tonight, what you said. My God. Broke my heart to hear it, made me furious, made me want to kill somebody—your mother'd be a good start, the cops, Cope, everybody—and I can only imagine what's going on with you right now. You need some time to get your head around it. Need to think through the consequences, all of them, need to be honest with yourself about what you can handle and what you can't. What you want. What you want no part of." She waved a hand at the yearbooks. "All this, it just feels, I dunno, wrong. You need to know you've got a choice. You've been boxed in to way too much already. You need time."

No one spoke. No one looked at each other. Then Tierney cleared his throat. "She's right. And yet—"

"I don't want Damarlo to suffer," Jacqi said, "because I punked out."

"You let Phelan worry about Damarlo," Cass said. "You let *Damarlo* worry about Damarlo."

"That's all I've ever done." Jacqi picked at the nail polish on her thumb. "Past ten years anyway. Me, me, and hey, while we're at it: me."

"From what I heard," Cass said, "it's exactly the opposite. You've been hauling everybody else's burden, on top of your own."

"Honestly? I feel like I just got outta jail. I wanna help somebody, help Damarlo."

"You can," Tierney said. "You will, it's just—"

"The point?" Cass tapped a fingernail against the tabletop. "You don't *have* to do it at all. Sure as hell not *now*. You need to know that. Feel that. Own that."

"I do. You're right, I'm kinda confused. And scared." Faintly, her chest shook, a pent-up jolt of old business. She closed her eyes. Bit her lip. In the tiniest voice: "I don't want to die."

Cass reached across the table, took Jacqi's hand. They sat like that for a moment, leaning toward each other, then Cass said, "You're in luck. We don't want to kill you."

Jacqi—sputtering, sniffing—laughed. Her free hand rose to her face and she wiped at her eyes, using the big cuffed sweatshirt sleeve. "This is gonna sound dumb, but I always kinda wondered what it might be like. You know, a sister. Big sister."

Cass cocked an eyebrow. "I have a sister. Take it from me. As experiences go, it's vastly overrated."

Tierney reached for the yearbook under Jacqi's hand and gently tugged. "I think we've agreed this can wait."

"No." Jacqi clapped her hand down on the open page. "I meant what I said. I don't know how to say it, really, but I've gotta get out of my own head. It's driving me a little nuts. And yeah, not later. Now. I'm tired of disappearing, I want to help somebody. For the right reason. I want to help Damarlo, help Richie, help Eastwood maybe. Christ, help ol' Fireman Mike, not that he needs it at this point. Tell the truth about what happened to him. Including me, what I was doing there, why." She reached up with her free hand and stroked her breastbone gently with her fingertips. A dull gaze and a shrug.

"I'm, I dunno, ready."

Part VII

71

Daddeo's son answered the door, dressed in jeans and an old ragged T-shirt from his D-line days at Santa Rosa CC: "Play Physical—Play Hard—Play with Violent Hands."

"Hey," Skellenger said. "Old man around?"

Vince Jr.—what was he, twenty-four or something? Stocky in the chest and arms like his dad. One tour in Iraq, a second in Kandahar, he had that Klonopin stare.

Licking his lips, dry mouth. Finally: "Yeah. Sure. Come on in."

The back of the T-shirt read "You Can't Play Scared." Skellenger followed it through the tricked-out two-story Craftsman—living room, dining room, all original maple and leaded glass—to the remodeled breakfast nook just off the sunroom.

Daddeo, with a better nose for such things than most other guys on the force, had opted for retirement as the bankruptcy loomed—making sure first he'd bulletproofed his exit package. Worked for Nordstrom now, battling "shrinkage"—shoplifting, employee theft, embezzlement—the house his monument to getting out smart.

Junior stopped at the kitchen doorway, offering a stalwart nod—"Nice seeing you again," his voice a ghost of what Skellenger remembered— then drifted off toward the rumbling TV in the den.

Daddeo wore black-and-red plaid, a hunting shirt, and sat at the corner banquette in the breakfast nook, scooping up the last of a bacon scramble with a wedge of rye toast, reading glasses perched on his nose, newspaper folded beside his plate. Once upon a time the greasy aroma from the frying pan, still on the stove, would've made Skellenger want to pick the thing up and lick it. Now he felt like a dozen fists were strangling his colon.

"Jordie. Surprise, surprise." Over the rim of his reading glasses, Daddeo eyed him warily, but smiled. "Snag a cup from the cabinet, you want coffee."

"Thanks, but I gotta make this quick." He slid in across the table. The backyard looked like a putting green rimmed with thorn stalks— roses cut back for the winter. "Not too early?"

"You kidding? We're the dogs of dawn around here."

The last time they'd spoken, months ago, Daddeo had described Junior's homecoming horrors. They'd pumped the marines full of Adderall at the forward bases, all those sleepless stretches of unmarked time—hunter-killer patrols, perimeter probes, recon, roadblocks—and the drug's after-traces made memory viciously clear, creating night-mares so hi-def that sleep became torture. Better to ride out the darkness with the wide-screen, watching ex-jocks and wannabes belabor minutiae on ESPN, then catnap during the day. His old man looked no less ragged, a big man going heavy, private-sector paunch, with tea-bag eyes, desk-jockey jowls.

"A situation's come up," Skellenger began.

"Lemme guess." Daddeo reached for his coffee. "Verrazzo."

"You've seen the news."

"You're primary, right?"

"Jacqi Garza's in the middle of this thing."

Daddeo nodded, plucked off his readers, dropped them gently onto his paper. "Lucky her."

Skellenger ran it down, all the way to the fire out in Homewood early that morning that killed three men, two clearly connected to her, the third wait-and-see.

"Bottom line is I was hoping to keep her out of this—Christ, even the chief was on board with that—but this thing just keeps eating its tail. I don't know where she is and I don't know what she'll say, but she's bitter as ever and no less loose on deck. I thought I should plug you in."

Daddeo sat back in his seat, brow creased with thought, then he folded his thick arms across his chest with a look of studied confusion. "I'm not following."

It took a second for Skellenger to register the voice. Like a stranger's. "Vince—"

"She was stellar in the Cope thing, on the stand two full days, weathered cross like a pro—what was she, eight, nine?—and we put that shitbag away. Couldn't nail him for murder on Marina Bacay but he's not coming out again. A predator, Jordie. Raping kids. Killing kids. He's gone, because of us." He reached for his coffee, drained the cup, then set it back down slowly, like he was rooking his king. "But yeah, the Garza kid, she's been skiing straight downhill ever since. Pissy little witch—can't blame her, given what she's been through—but why bring that here?"

"Like I said, I had some face time with her. She's got an ax to grind. Thinks there's an angle in how we handled her down at the hospital in Santa Cruz."

"Jordie, again, not to seem dense, but—"

"Don't do this, Vince. She's gonna say we suborned perjury."

Daddeo stood up, collected his plate. "Sure you don't want some coffee?" Not waiting for an answer, he went to the sink, rinsed off the plate and silverware, racked them in the dishwasher, then freshened his coffee and ambled back, dropping down into his seat again with all that neglected muscle, the contented girth.

"Look, Jordie, I don't mean to make things difficult, but I've got no fucking clue what you're talking about. I'll admit, I'm getting old, memory's not what it used to be. I destroyed all my notes so I'll have to rely on my reports, but I gotta tell ya, perjury?"

Skellenger glanced out again at the immaculate yard, the stubby, dismembered roses. He leaned in over the table. "Vince, you prick, you think I'm wearing a wire?"

Daddeo lifted his cup. "Why would I think that, Jordie? By the way, are you?"

"I came here as a goddamn favor."

"Jesus. What's got you wound so fucking tight?"

"She goes off half-cocked, Cope files a motion for a retrial, how's retirement gonna look then?"

"Okay." Daddeo put the cup down, leaned forward, bracing his elbows on the table. "I'm gonna say this just once more. I don't know what you're talking about. If the Garza kid wants to change her story now, that means she's a liar. Either she was lying then or she's lying now. Same with you. You got any problem with how things went down, you want to go back and revise your testimony, I gotta ask—and I won't be alone—why didn't you bring it up back then? Memory makes liars of us all, Jordie, that's why I'm sticking to what I said back then. Not because it's convenient. Because it's true. Most recent recollection, best recollection."

"I can't afford this, Vince. I can't afford the risk, can't afford the lawyers."

"You're still on the force. City has a duty to defend. Other than that, if money's tight, don't say I didn't warn you."

"She's gonna be the centerpiece wit again, Vince. I can't help it, and she's not the kind that can handle that. Not even the mother— you remember her, no doubt, Christ, eats tarantulas for breakfast—not even she's got a grip on the kid anymore. Pete Navarette's apparently got his mutts hunting her down and now one of them's dead too, same fire as the pimp up in Homewood, all of which just makes for more drama and she's loving it is my guess. She'll think it's her shot at stardom. *American Idol, Special Victims Unit.*"

"Jesus, Jordie, whoa—"

"She'll play the fucking pity card, Vince, play it for all it's worth and you know the media, they'll jump on that like cats on a cricket. She'll milk it. She'll screw us."

Daddeo leaned back in his seat again, as though trying to discern who this was, this supposed ex-partner, this cop with the face of a man he once knew. "I hear what you're trying to say. I can tell you're upset. But I just don't see the problem. Not just because I've got nothing to hide." He nodded toward the den. "When it comes to kids worth giving a shit about, I've kinda got my hands full already. Jane's out of her mind with worry but she doesn't know what to do, so it falls on me, and that's fine. He's my son. But you think I'm gonna waste two seconds worrying about what Jacqi Garza feels or what she thinks or what she might say, you clearly don't know where my head is at. You ought to hear his stories, ought to hear about the guys with their legs ripped off from IEDs and Vince holding an artery in his bare hands so his buddy doesn't bleed out. You ought to hear about the kids the ragheads used as bombers and the women buried up to their necks and stoned to death—that's how they'd find them in the villages after the sick fucks fled. You ought to hear the howl, like a gut-shot dog, when he wakes up at night. Forget about a job. Other day, I'm watching one of those morning shows, and this pencil neck in hair gel says, 'Why have all the jobs gone to China? The Chinese worker is more flexible, more dedicated, better trained.' Kid puts his life on the line in the middle of hell for four fucking years but he's not flexible, he's not dedicated, he can't be trained. You following me here, Jordie? But I'm supposed to wring my hands over Jacqi Fucking Garza? I put in my twenty, and think what you want but I never, not once, had to back up to the pay window. That skank wants to change her story, she's the one looking at perjury, not me. I've got an imperfect memory but a clear conscience. Understand?"

72

Skellenger came in through the garage and hooked his keys on the pegboard, hoping he might grab an hour of sleep before heading back into the meat grinder.

Taking a second, glancing around the kitchen, he felt the full impact of the contrast—Daddeo's house, this house—like the final insult. Countertop tiles cracked or loose, grouting dark with mildew, curtains an afterthought, linoleum older than the kids. Faucet dripping like depression's metronome. *Don't say I didn't warn you.* One of those moments when the gun on his hip felt less like a weapon than a way out.

The folder lay waiting for him on the dining room table, a note pinned to it, Rosellen's script. *You need to look at this. You need to deal with it.*

He took a chair, opened the folder. On top was a letter from the principal at St. Catherine's Academy, two pages, single-spaced, his eye catching briefly on case citations, but even so he put it aside for the moment. Consider the evidence, he thought, before the argument.

Beneath the letter were about a dozen pages of coarse white paper ripped from a sketch pad, six inches by four. Each page featured pencil sketches of kids about Ethan's age, two girls and a boy, classmates maybe. The unsettling nudes.

Erasure marks smeared a couple, the others were disarmingly clear and, to Skellenger's mind, not half bad. Simple stuff—one girl on a sofa, ankles crossed. The boy arching his back, looking up, with quite a package. The other girl, chubbier than the first, holding up her hair, full frontal, nice rack. More clinical than erotic, to his eye at least, which made them no less disturbing. And yet that could work in the boy's defense. They were studies, meant for practice, not passing around.

Putting aside for a moment the subject matter, the kid had talent. Skellenger wondered if the models had willingly posed or if Ethan had simply relied on his hormone-addled imagination—and which would be more disconcerting to the prudes and paranoids? Or the lawyers.

Time for the letter.

He skimmed most of it, lingering on the citations—*Tinker v. Des Moines Indep. Cmty. Sch. Dist., Bethel School District No. 403 v. Fraser*—and the operative language the school's legal counsel applied—"creates or threatens a substantial disruption or interferes with the rights of students to be secure . . . offensive or lewd or runs counter with the school's educational mission to inculcate values . . ."

"They're treating it like sexting." Rosellen, having slipped down quietly from upstairs, stood in the doorway, arms crossed, dressed in a V-neck and drawstring pants. "Like he took naked pictures of these kids on his phone and shared them with everybody in school."

"Where's the rest of the sketch pad?"

"I don't know, they gave it back I guess, why—"

He held up the drawings. "They make copies of these?"

"They didn't say."

"They did, that's possession of child pornography."

She cocked her head slightly. "You're not serious."

"If he wasn't showing them around, they've got no basis—"

"Is that really the point?"

"How'd they find out he drew these?"

She leaned against the doorframe, eyelids fluttering, like he was troubling her. "Some other student caught him sketching, I think, glanced over his shoulder or maybe grabbed the pad, I'm not sure, but a couple kids found out and you know how they talk. Then one of his teachers asked for the sketch pad or searched his backpack and he got called down to the office."

"He give them his consent?"

"Them. Who?"

"The principal, teacher—"

"You'll have to ask him."

"Did he think he had a choice?"

She started to say something, checked herself. "Jordie, that's not what I'm worried about."

"Do the kids in these pictures know he drew them? Do the parents know?"

"Jordie, what are you so angry about?"

"If these kids posed he can be accused of lewd conduct."

"He's a minor."

"So are they. All it takes is one parent."

"I don't know if they posed. I don't know who they are. One I recognize, I think, the McPartland girl. But I don't know what happened, I was waiting for you."

"Say one of these girls—better yet, the guy—starts getting the business. 'Hey, faggot, wanna pose for me? Wanna sharpen my pencil?' What if he gets depressed, starts talking suicide? What if he follows through?"

She moved from the doorway, drew up a chair, and sat. Hands flat on the table, like she was joining a séance: "Jordie, calm down, okay? Let's not get ahead of ourselves."

He picked up the letter, shook it. "You know why they're doing this, right? He's the son of a cop. Yesterday morning, Mike Verrazzo gets caught with a seventeen-year-old hooker in his car, four guys not much older than Ethan beat him to death with fifty other kids watching. Not one steps up. *Not one.* Hear a single school official pipe up on that?" He pitched the letter back down and it sailed across the table, spinning to a stop as it hit the pepper mill. "Inculcate values. Fucking farce."

"Jordie, I'm not following, I'm sorry, but—"

"Schools are an open sewer but it's our fault, not theirs."

"Our fault—what, you mean me and you?"

"I *told* you—this is because he's the kid of *a cop*."

"You think this is about you?"

"Where is he?"

"He's still in his room."

"Get him down here."

"He may still be asleep."

"Wake him up."

73

Tierney left with his notes and yearbooks. Jacqi and Cass drifted from the kitchen to the TV room, parking on the sofa and sipping tea, trying to avoid the morning news shows. A welcome sense of normalcy crept in, like sunlight warming the room. Noble started barking near the back of the house.

Jacqi said, "He okay?"

"He gets restless when he needs to go," Cass said. "And he hates squirrels." She put down her cup, rose to her feet. "I should take him out."

"You gonna walk him?"

"Wouldn't be a bad idea."

"Can I come?"

Like it was the coolest thing imaginable. "Not like that." Cass twiddled her fingers at the oversized sweats. "Your clothes should be done, go get them out of the dryer. I'll put on some shoes and leash up the boy."

• • •

Her things were still warm as she tugged them on, everything feeling too snug now, the tights especially, like she was a teenage mummy. But clean.

Where the hell were her shoes?

She padded up the wood plank steps from the cellar with its smells of bleach and wood and stone, Noble going nuts now at the door to the back, sounding a little unhinged, his bark high-pitched and sharp like a punch, nails clicking against the glass.

At the top of the stairs she caught sight of Cass near the sink, gripping the phone, looking pissed—gesturing: *Wait. Stop. Don't come out.*

And Jacqi knew. Like a nervy little gong inside her mind, she knew what and who and as she stood there, no shoes, toasty in her fresh-smelling clothes, she made peace with it. I had these few hours, she thought. I felt cared for and listened to and seen. For a couple hours at least I got to be the girl they were glad was alive.

"It's all right," she said, and came out into the kitchen and walked back to the sliding glass door where Noble was still going batshit at Richie and Ben Escalada on the porch. Richie looked haggard and, guess what, mad. Escalada looked like he'd been dragged behind a car for a couple of blocks and was ready to get even—hands bandaged, cuts and splotches of harsh red skin on his face. You need a nurse, she thought, then watched as one gauzed hand reached inside his jacket and she knew she had to be quick.

"I'm coming," she said through the glass, trying to calm the dog. "Don't hurt anybody, okay?"

She spotted her shoes in the kitchen and sat down to tug them on, trying not to look at Cass, who was gripping the phone like a rock she wanted to pitch at whoever was on the other end.

"What do you . . . Look, I get it, I hear you, you're backed up on calls, but I've got two men at my back door, trying to break in, okay? They've come to . . . I told you, Jacqi Garza, you know who I'm talking about, she's here, she's staying with me and these two men are here to take her, they're going to hurt her, I can't wait in line for the next—"

"It's okay," Jacqi said, getting up.

Cass shouldered the phone. "No. You stay here. Don't go out there. Don't—"

"I had no right to come here, bring this. I shouldn't have."

"Stop talking like that, all this I'm-not-worth-it fucked-up loser horseshit. You're not that girl, okay? Just sit tight, we'll—" The voice on the other end of the line squawked into her shoulder and she pressed the phone to her ear again. "Yes. I told you. Two. *I don't know*—"

Jacqi went over and took Cass's free hand. "Thank you," she whispered. "It's okay, I promise. Don't come out, okay? They've got a gun. If anything happened to you or Noble I'd never forgive myself. Whatever this is, I can handle it. I have to."

Cass tried to lock their hands together but Jacqi broke free and crossed the kitchen and unlocked the door, holding the dog back with her leg—"It's okay, Noble, good boy"—wanting to kneel down, bury her face in his fur one last time, then squeezing through the opening and sliding the glass door shut behind her.

She turned and hurried down the steps into the yard, scared if she didn't move quick she'd lose her nerve or Cass might come charging after her. The trees dripped, the soft wet ground gave beneath her feet. The garden smelled like morning.

Beyond the wood gate Richie's Impala idled at the curb. Someone was sitting in the passenger seat, a man, his back turned.

"How'd you two numbnuts find me?"

Escalada spun fast and his gauzed backhand came with it, catching her hard across the face. She almost went down.

"You don't open your mouth," he said. "Get in the car."

Richie just stood there, gray hooded sweatshirt beneath his old letter jacket, hair wicking up in the breeze off the river. Finally, he said, "Don't make this hard. Mom's worried half out of her skull."

"You don't have to do this, Richie. You don't have to be this *huevón*'s bitch."

Escalada grabbed her hair, gripped it tight in his fist and he dragged her to the car like that, slamming her face against the roof just once for punctuation.

"Oops, clumsy."

It felt strangely good and right, the pain. She hoped she was bleeding. She never should have come here, bothered these people, invaded their home with her Jacqiness. She should have stayed in the hills. Give the coyotes a nosh.

The car door opened, Escalada shoved her into the backseat and then slid in beside her. The interior reeked of leather conditioner and rug shampoo. Richie got behind the wheel and lodged the tranny into drive and they roared off as the man in the passenger seat finally turned back to look at her.

"You may be wondering," he said, "where Hector is." As always the voice was calm. Quiet as a flame. The Impala's V-8 almost drowned him out. "Hector, unfortunately, was unable to make it."

Escalada tensed beside her, and she wondered how many seconds would pass before he took another shot. In the front seat, Pete Navarette just sat there, bulky and still.

"You've made things difficult and dangerous for a great many people. That's over, you understand? You're now going to make life simple and safe and easy. For everybody."

74

Girls, he thought, waiting for Rosellen to bring Ethan down, they're so much easier than boys. No matter how much they scream and stamp their feet and call you every godless name they know, in some deep recess of their being, they get it: you're trying to protect them. No matter what else fails, there's always that between you.

Couple months back, the new manboy came over to pick Emily up in his tricked-out Mustang—blue flake finish, monoblock chrome lip wheels, cherry-bomb glass pack dual exhaust.

Skellenger, never one to sit and wait for disaster, saw an opportunity—Em still upstairs, teasing and spraying, locked on the mirror—so he barged out the door and down the porch steps and plowed toward the car with his hand outstretched, catching the guy— Trent, the clown's name—before the kid could even plant the first foot on the driveway.

"Whoa, that's like a gearhead's wet dream. How much this set you back?"

Barely waited for the answer, didn't hear it when it came.

"Okay if I sit in it?"

Tooled around to the passenger side, dropped down into the deep bucket seat—vinyl, not leather. Chucklehead.

"Man, this is sweet. Mind if I push the seat back?"

It's some kind of universal law. Always the passenger side. Sure enough, seat pushed back, there it was—the pipe, the plastic bag. Dirt weed from the looks of it.

"Gee, Trent. What's this?"

Sure, Em threw a fit when the Mustang drove off but it was theater. She knew she was slumming, the guy a hunk but a half-wit, and she knew as well that word would get around, about Emily Skellenger's cop old man. It meant she was safe. Because things happen. And sometimes you never see it coming.

Rosellen's slippered feet slapped down the wooden stairs. For whatever reason—because he sensed she had the more honest handle on this, because that's what mothers did, it was their privilege, seeing the kids clearly, so much more hands-on, because he resented her for that, because they hadn't made love or even talked about it in how many months or was it millennia, because she'd set the terms when he gave up drinking—he couldn't look up when she entered the dining room.

Pulling out a chair, a ragged sigh. "He'll be down in a minute."

"He's still in bed?"

"Kids need their sleep." She waited till, finally, he met her eye. "So do you." Pushing back her tinted hair. "You look like hell, Jordie. You're pale, you've got coal-miner eyes. Your hand's got the shakes."

Should he tell her? A kid was about to ruin their lives and it wasn't their son, though he sure as hell wasn't helping. Jacqi Garza, God bless her pitch-black soul, maybe not today, maybe not tomorrow, but someday soon was going to get her second fifteen minutes of fucked-up fame. At risk was his tin and all that went with it, the income, the health care, the pension. This house. This life.

Should he tell her?

. The slow mindless thump of bare feet on the stairs, the boy coming down. Skellenger told himself: Take a deep breath. Feeling the piece on his hip and thinking: There are days.

75

Tierney sat at his desk wrapping up the list, the names of the kids Jacqi'd identified, kids at the scene, kids who'd watched a man get murdered like it was entertainment. Alphabetical order, Patrick Valdez the last, and he chuckled, remembering the girl's surprise. "Only name I ever heard him go by was El Palillo." Toothpick.

His cell lit up and shuddered atop a stack of bills—incoming call, Cass. He thumbed the sliding lock. "Everything okay?"

"They came and took her." Voice tight in her throat. "Two men, they were at the back door."

Processing that. "They break in?"

"No, no—I tried to stop her but she said one of them had a gun." Breathless pause. "I'm feeling sick about this."

"You called 911."

"Don't get me started, but yeah."

"Was there a car, did you see it?"

"An old Chevy sedan, I told the police all this."

"And?"

"I fucked up, said she left with them. The dispatcher's like: So what's the problem? I'm almost screaming: *She had no choice*. And the woman, swear to God, she actually says this: 'Well, we don't know that for a fact, do we?'"

He patted his pockets, wallet, keys. "Sure you're okay?"

"Phelan?" A crack in her voice, but just a crack, then a breath. "I'm sorry."

"Don't be. Sit tight. Lock the doors. I'll call back when I know something."

He went out to his car and felt through the grit beneath the bumper and sure enough, there it was, exact same place, just like the first one, tucked inside a magnetic box. Probably put there at the restaurant, he thought, Los Guanacos, when they drove up and saw the Honda in the lot. *God, they must think I'm dumb.* And they were right.

76

Richie closed the bedroom door behind him and threw a suitcase onto her bed. "I'm driving you to Chico. Pack your shit."

Jacqi stared at the bag, pink shiny vinyl trimmed with yellow, a girl's bag. It was old and scuffed and dusty. Inside, no doubt, it smelled. Not the kind of thing you used for stuff you actually wanted. Just stuff you intended to throw away. Your shit.

"What's in Chico?"

"What's the difference?"

He went to the window, slumped against the wall, and began gnawing on his thumbnail as he stared out through the blinds at the tiny backyard.

"There's nothing in Chico," she said. "You know it, I know it. I'm never gonna make it there."

"Will you just shut up?" Closing his eyes, he leaned more heavily into the wall, as though hoping he might sink into it, merge with its solidity. "Sick of your mouth."

She ran her hand across the comforter, so cool and smooth, like she never expected to touch it again. "What happened to Eastwood, Richie?"

He opened his eyes and stopped breathing for a second, like she'd somehow managed to peel away a bit of his shadow, and it hurt. Then he shoved off from the wall and came toward the bed, clicked the latches on the suitcase, ripped the thing open—sure enough, musty and rank—and he turned toward her bureau, jerked open a drawer, started grabbing things.

"Richie, I need to know, okay? I need to know what—"

"He took off for Texas." Richie threw two fistfuls of blouses into the bag. "Said he knew a guy."

"How the hell could he know a guy in Texas?"

"I don't know, it doesn't matter, fucking drop it." He turned back to the bureau.

"They killed him, didn't they."

He stopped, back still turned. "I told you already, he left. Let it go."

"They made you watch."

"You always think you're so damn smart, everybody else is stupid."

"They made you do it, made you kill him. So you'd be stuck."

He yanked open another drawer. "You don't know what you're talking about."

"I can't live like this anymore, Richie."

"Then don't."

"They're going to kill me."

"Will you shut . . . the fuck . . . *up!*" He rested his elbows on the top of the bureau and clutched his head. "You're going away to school. You had any sense, you'd realize you got the best hand of anybody. Play it."

"I don't wanna go."

"Then fuck yourself."

"Richie, please, look at me. I'm not some crazy bitch—"

"Swear to god, you don't shut up—"

"I care about you. I know some people, they can help us, help you."

His head started shaking slowly, hypnotically, back and forth in his hands. "Not telling you again . . ."

"It doesn't have to be like this. It can—"

He pivoted, came at her, looming there at the edge of the bed, breathing raggedly in and out and staring down like the backs of his eyes were on fire.

She lowered her head and readied herself. "I get it, Richie, I do. It's okay."

The blow didn't come. Instead he turned away and when she looked up again she saw him standing there, stock-still, like he'd walked into some invisible hook and it was lodged in his chest, ready to hoist him up.

"The shit you make me do," he said quietly. "The shit they make me do because of you. I'm fucking sick of it but that's how it is and I'm not going to listen to you, I'm not going to have your craziness in my head, understand?"

Looking at his back, seeing the tension in his neck, the locked-up shoulders, she felt a strange calm silence inside her. Strange and yet familiar, like she'd misplaced it, forgotten about it, given it up for lost, but then suddenly, hey, there it was.

The sad unfriendly answer.

"That's not good enough, Richie. I'm a skanky selfish bitch. I use everybody I can, every way I can think of. But you're a coward. You killed your own friend because you were scared. Scared of *your mother*."

He spun around, charged toward her, and pushed her down on the bed and climbed on top, pinning her with his knees, clutching her face in his hand.

She closed her eyes, swallowed hard, almost hoping he had the hate to finish it.

He didn't. His body went lax and he began to shake. Opening her eyes she saw him cover his face to hide from her, then he dragged himself off, got up from the bed, only to drop straight to the floor with a whimpering keen, a boy's sob, and turning this way, that way, like there was someplace to hide, someplace he could crawl to and disappear if only he could think of it, find it.

After a moment she got up and went to him, knelt, wrapped her arms around him gently, pressing against his back, resting her cheek on his shoulder.

"It's my fault too," she whispered. "You're not alone, okay? Not alone. Let's not live like this. We can go somewhere, not Chico, anywhere. We don't have to be who they say we have to be."

77

Pillow-head hair sticking up like tussocks—his father's bones, his mother's soft eyes—the boy shambled to the table and sat.

"So nice you could join us." Skellenger glanced at his watch. "I'm due in."

Ethan looked up, a quick helpless glance, not at his father.

Skellenger had been scavenging his brain, trying to think of how to go about this. They needed options, needed not to get cornered, forced into playing defense. There were ways to go on the attack, if he could just get Rosellen on board. If the kid was up to it.

He remembered Nina Garza arriving at the hospital in Santa Cruz, Daddeo telling her what Jacqi had told them—the brother, Richie, basically pimping out his kid sister to his *clica's* knockarounds. If hate had a face, Nina Garza slapped it on before heading into that room to put the kid right.

Now it's my turn, he thought, to put my kid right. Hoping hate had nothing to do with it. Knowing better.

"Been sitting here trying to imagine how many ways people are gonna think about this," he said, "talk about it. You don't owe anybody an explanation, not yet, but that creates a vacuum. And people, they can't help themselves." He lifted one hand, gestured: yack yack.

He glanced across the table at Rosellen, checking in on how this was landing. She looked puzzled but not upset, not yet. Above the table, the gilded chandelier with its dusty glass pendants hovered and glowed like a miniature spacecraft from Home Depot.

"I mean, I look at these"—he slid the folder closer, flipped it open, pretended to look inside—"and I think, Internet's crawling with images like this. You wanted to sketch one out for practice, be easy enough. Find it in a heartbeat. And there's plenty of places to get pictures of your classmates. Maybe you have some on your phone. Or somebody you know does. You stick a face you know on a body you've never seen in your life."

"Jordie?" Rosellen folded her arms across her plump chest, head tilted a little. "That's not, I think, quite what happened. At least—"

"Just bear with me a minute." Skellenger checked the boy's expression—that dazed, vaguely put-upon look, badge of youth. "I'm not talking about what happened so much as all the ways people might view this thing. The situation. How they might react."

"I'm not sure—"

"Because one of the biggest problems in something like this—something that upsets people, something that gets them talking—is they make up their minds quick. Doesn't matter what the truth is, they make up their own truth and just run with it. That's what makes this so difficult. So complex. But I think that also provides opportunities." He spread his hands. "There are options we may not be seeing."

She nodded like she was thinking that through, like it made sense. "Jordie," she said, her voice delicate, testing eggshells, "I think we should be talking about what steps the school will probably take. This isn't Stallworth, it's St. Cat's."

"I get that. I'm not disputing that. I'm saying we shouldn't overre-act just yet. Don't prejudge the situation. It depends on a lot of factors. It's not set in stone."

"Maybe so, but however we look at it, Ethan's in a spot. I'm not just worried about how the school will react. I'm concerned what some of the kids might do."

"I'm right here." The boy reached under his armpit, scratched, glanced at both of them, looked down again. "You don't need to talk about me like I'm not in the room."

"I'm sorry, hon. You're right. Look, why don't we let you—"

"I was trying to make a point about taking a broader perspective—"

"Jordie, no offense, but I feel like we're wandering off topic—"

"They're not mine."

All eyes turned toward the boy.

"What do you mean," Rosellen said, "they're not—"

"Just what I said, they're not mine, I didn't draw them."

Rosellen sat back, tightened the cross of her arms. "Ethan, that's not what—"

"I don't know who they belong to. There was a sketch pad, the kids in class were passing it around, it was pretty, you know, weird. When it got to me I did what everybody else did, I checked out the drawings, thought like, you know, Jesus, then I flipped to a blank page and started drawing one of my own. Just a joke. Then Mr. Stalter, I dunno, noticed or something and he came down the aisle. Said, 'Give me that.'"

The delivery was soft, a drone. Skellenger felt uneasy and yet relieved and vaguely proud. The kid understood. Don't admit to any-thing they can't prove.

Rosellen sat there stunned. "Ethan, don't lie."

"I'm not *lying*."

"You told me earlier—"

"Well, I'm telling you this now."

"There's no crime in getting your facts a little cockeyed." Skellenger waved his hand back and forth. "These kinds of things are upsetting. They're confusing."

"You're making things worse, Jordie."

"Rose, let the boy speak for himself."

"And when his teacher says it didn't happen like that, what then?"

"Will that happen, Ethan? Will this Mr. Walker—"

"Stalter."

"Will he have a different version of events?"

The boy swallowed. Like a jawbreaker squeezing down his throat. "How am I supposed to know what he'll say?"

"Give it a shot: What do you *think* he's going to say?"

That look again, like he'd taken a slap. "He had no right to look in my backpack."

Rosellen uncrossed her arms and folded her hands, tapping her thumbs against her lips, pensive, helpless, and it aged her, the last few years doubling up around her mouth and eyes. "Ethan, listen to me. The situation won't get easier if you change your story."

Skellenger said, "That's not necessarily—"

"Jesus, Jordie, please."

"Stories change for a thousand reasons." Memory makes liars of us all. "Even under oath."

She pushed her hands up into her hair. "I can't believe I'm hearing this."

"Look, let Ethan finish. There was this sketch pad, the kids were passing it around, everybody's giggling and pointing and all, Oh My God, then it gets to you."

"Jordie, for chrissake, please."

"You started drawing something yourself—which, by the way, was stupid—you noticed Mr. What's His Name—"

"Stalter."

"He was paying attention, getting interested. You stuffed it in your knapsack."

"I won't sit here and let you teach him how to lie."

"I'm not *lying*."

"He came up—maybe then, maybe later, whenever—and demanded to see what was inside your backpack. He took it from you, rummaged around inside. You didn't give your consent. That a fair summation of what happened?"

The boy stared at a pocket of air six inches from his eyes. His right hand rose as if of its own accord, reaching up to scratch again, this time his shoulder. "I guess."

"Okay. Great." Skellenger sat back. "It's a story I can live with. A story you can live with. I wouldn't be surprised if it's even a story your mother—give her some time—can live with. Who knows if Mr. Stalter can live with it, but let's put that aside for the moment. And if the kids who were sitting around you in class don't back you up, then yeah, we may have a problem. If it gets that far. Hard to tell right now. Then again, if those pictures are drawings of real kids, kids you know, kids who sat there naked in front of you and they have their own stories to tell, well, yeah, things get complicated. They get messy. Because everybody else is gonna find a story he can live with, or she can live with, and there'll be a big nasty fight over which one wins. Let's hope it doesn't get to that. Let's hope those kids, assuming just for the sake of argument they even exist, let's hope they don't want this out in the open any more than you do. Let's hope their parents feel the same way, which is kind of a stretch, but hey. Regardless, for now, we've got our story. That's half the battle. Now here comes the other half. Tell your mother and me what actually happened."

78

Richie came out of his mother's house like a thief, hefting an old pink patent leather suitcase, the thing heavy from the look of the young man's walk, tacking to the opposite side, using his hip and thigh to manage the weight.

Tierney got out from behind the wheel of the Honda, closed the door quietly, and headed up the drive as the kid popped the trunk of his immaculate vintage Impala and threw the bag inside.

"Somebody going somewhere?"

Richie froze, clutching the bag by the handle, the other hand gripping the rim of the trunk.

"Remember me? Yesterday, the Wall of Weirdness, we talked a little while."

Not turning, just an over-the-shoulder glance. "Yeah." The word muffled by his shoulder. "I remember."

"What's in the bag, Richie? Who's going away?"

The same dark shagginess as before, the lost haunted lonesome look.

"Sister inside the house? I need to talk with her."

"You really don't get that no one wants you around."

"Really? Your sister almost gets killed in the middle of the night, nasty head wound. Who's she call for help—you? Or some guy she doesn't want around."

Richie finally let go of the bag and quietly shut the trunk. "I don't know what you're talking about."

"I got a description of the car, Richie, this car, I know it was you. You came to my house and snatched your sister."

"She walked on her own two legs, nobody—"

"You stuff her in the trunk like Cope did?"

That got him to turn around. His face seemed even more haunted than the rest of him, if that was possible, the eyes heavy-lidded and red, like he'd just had a beast of a workout, or wept.

"She's my sister, I came by—"

"Not you. You wouldn't know where to find me. You needed help for that." He dug the tracking device out of his pocket, held it up like a badge, then tossed it—gently, so the kid could catch it. "Don't leave that part out."

Richie stood there for a second, studying the Ranger like it had him in a spell. "Look." His voice quiet, almost intimate. He swallowed. "Things have changed."

"Absolutely. Couldn't agree more."

"Shut up for a second. I need you to hear this." He pitched the tracker across the yard, then shoved his hands in his pockets. "I need you to listen to me. It's gonna be okay, understand?"

His voice, like the words were torture.

"What's going to be okay?"

"What you're worried about."

Tierney studied his face, looking for something to trust. "No offense. But I need to hear that from Jacqi."

"If you'd just leave things alone, everything—"

"Leave them alone. That's priceless. You mean how they've been the past ten years?"

Like somebody turned a screw—Richie clenched, his eyes tightened.

"Either I talk to her or I call 911 and you can explain it all to the police. And by 'all,' I mean all—following me here?"

A tremor fluttered in his neck. Down the street, a UPS truck rumbled to a stop. "Just what is it you think you know?"

"I don't have time for this, Richie."

"What'd she say?"

"I want to talk to her. Bring her out, or this whole thing blows up. You know what I mean."

The kid lowered his eyes and nodded, like he'd been turning something over in his mind, this way, that way, hoping this, fearing that. Finally, now, it made sense.

"Know what?" He nudged some hair behind his ear. "Congratulations. You just fucked her last good chance. All because you don't know when to let it go. You don't know how to shut up. Remember that."

79

"We were over at Jen McPartland's house," Ethan said, "down in her basement, and you know, stoned."

His eyes darted up then away as he shrugged, dragged his hand through his hair, each movement disconnected from the next. Skellenger had to remind himself the kid was fifteen. The jitters made him seem younger. Maybe it was an act.

Meanwhile, across the table, Rosellen sat there in maternal agony.

"I'm showing Sophie Bensing my sketchbook. There was just, you know, art class stuff in it, faces and hands, still lifes—"

"None of this," Skellenger said, gesturing to the folder on the tabletop.

"No. But Chris Kelechava, he's like got a case of cancer for Sophie."

"Excuse me?"

"He's, you know, into her."

"Ah."

"And she's talking to me not him and he's getting steamed or jealous or whatever and he sits down and says, like, 'Hey, check this.' And he takes off his shirt. Sitting there, like: Come on, artisto. Draw me."

Skellenger said, "The parents were where?"

"I dunno." Ethan scratched his ribs. "Not home."

Rosellen, gently: "What day was this, Ethan?"

"Wednesday."

"This week." Her voice wistful. "Two days ago."

Ethan nodded.

"Okay," Skellenger said. "So this kid—"

"Chris," Ethan said. "Kelechava."

"He takes off his shirt."

"And Sophie's kinda like, whoa, you know, put off, but also sorta into it, maybe a little scared not to be. And Jen says: 'Yeah, Ethan. Do it. Draw him.'"

"Jen McPartland," Skellenger said. "She and this Kelechava kid, they kicked it off. They goaded you on."

"I dunno about *goaded*."

"They encouraged you."

"Yeah. Whatever. I'm kinda boxed in at that point, or else things get tense. I'm not sure how to put it—I just got this feeling I could change the mood, chill Chris out, if I just, you know, made him look good. He plays lacrosse and he's kinda, you know—"

"A dick," Skellenger said.

"Vain," Rosellen offered.

"I figured, let him be the hotshot, we can all relax. So I tell him how to stand to show off his chest, his arms. He's, like, into it. Seriously. Stands real still like that's, you know, hard. When I'm done, I pass it around, everybody's like, wow, that's cool. That's good. And he turns to Sophie, all smug now, and says, 'Your turn.'"

"He told her to take off her shirt."

"Not like, *told* her, but yeah. She knew what he meant. And she and Jen look at each other all like, you know, it's a dare or something and Sophie blushes up big-time, I mean all the way down to her neck, like she's got an allergy or something. Maybe Jen figures she'll let her off the hook, I dunno, but she's the one takes her shirt off."

"Jen."

"Yeah."

"Just her shirt?"

"She keeps her bra on at first but Chris is like, come on, don't be that way, we're all friends."

"He said that? We're all 'friends'?"

"Something like that. Yeah. Pretty sure."

"That's important," Skellenger said.

"Okay." Ethan nodded, like he was lodging that somewhere. "He also said, like, don't be a pruda cuda."

Despite himself, Skellenger grinned. "Never heard that before."

"It means prude."

"Yeah, I caught that."

"Anyway, Jen unhooks her bra and everybody's like, nervous, giggling, and I think: Just draw, you know? Just draw. I like Jen, she sits next to me in homeroom, doesn't treat me like I'm a Hobbit or something. Asks me questions and actually listens to the answers. So I take my time. She's got this kinda flat nose, it sorta spreads her face out, but I make her look pretty."

Silently, Skellenger noted that. The boy talked about her face.

"And everybody's real quiet now, waiting. When I'm done I show her and she looks so proud, and I just feel like, you know, I did good. Chris and Sophie like it too and then Sophie, I dunno, maybe that's what it took, but she's finally cool with it. She takes off her sweater and says, 'Do me.'"

"'Do me'? Or 'Draw me'?"

"Jesus, Jordie."

"It's not a trick question."

Ethan closed his eyes and sighed, like he was ready for this to be over. "I don't know. I don't remember."

"Okay. So Sophie takes her sweater off."

"Yeah, and I draw her. And everybody's, like, happy and Chris lights up another spliff and then all of a sudden he stands up, undoes his jeans, drops trou, and we're all kinda blown away but we're also wasted and the mood's mellowed out and it's just, like, go with it, you know? So I did. I drew him. Then Jen again and Sophie."

"Everybody's naked."

"Yeah."

"You?"

For just a second, the boy's face went blank. "No."

"Seriously." Skellenger cocked an eyebrow, feeling for the kid. The one who can draw. The different one.

"It was strange. It was almost like I wasn't really there. Or not like they were."

Skellenger could imagine. Hey, let's get naked. Except you. Not you.

Almost the exact opposite of Jacqi Garza. Come on, take everything off and show us. Show us what happened. Show us what he did.

80

Navarette—ripe with cologne, sleeves rolled up, hovering over Jacqi, who sat planted on the sofa—paged through a glossy brochure: pictures of horses in a bright green field rimmed with eucalyptus, a Tudor mansion with lush hills for background, a wind quintet in a sunny music room. No chain-link fences topped with razor wire, Jacqi thought, no husky men in off-the-rack suits and wraparounds. They wouldn't show that.

"It's called the Abrantes Academy," Navarette said, "after the family that founded it. Very powerful family, very influential."

And this, Jacqi guessed, is where they lock away the crazy bitch daughters. "What if I don't like it?"

"You'll like it." He held the pamphlet out for her to take.

"Or I'm free to leave?"

Dropping the pamphlet onto the sofa beside her: "You won't want to leave."

Don't push it, she thought, don't make a scene. Just go with it.

Despite the usual calm in his voice the man gave off an aura of checked intensity, a kind of tension rippling off his body like electricity. He'd lost a man he'd sent to find her. Another, Ben Escalada, sat in the kitchen, waiting to be needed, lucky to be alive. All because of me, she thought. Nobody causes that kind of trouble and doesn't pay.

"For once in your life," her mother said from across the room, "you'll be in a place where no one asks about the past." She sat in the wing-back armchair with the twill slipcover, her throne, coffee cup in one hand, saucer the other, legs crossed. "Follow the rules, people will leave you alone."

The rules, she thought. Act contrite. Give up.

Outside, Richie was loading the car. If things went right they'd be gone in a matter of minutes, heading wherever they wanted. Finally he was willing to break away, leave this house behind, and start over somewhere else. All they needed was the chance.

But what if Mamá came along? She looked ready for it, white silk blouse with ribbon collar, gray wool skirt, black flats—and yet she always dressed like that. Strangely beautiful, beautifully strange. If she came, though, Navarette would tag along for sure, and that meant Escalada too.

If she could get word to Tierney and Cass, maybe they could get the highway patrol to intercept the car somewhere between here and Chico, take her and Richie into protective custody. Was that even possible? Would Richie go along if it happened?

"How do you know," she said, trying for conversation, afraid being quiet made her suspicious somehow, "this academy'll be any safer than here? My name's all over the news, everybody's looking for me. I'm surprised the TV vans aren't still outside."

"You can thank the fire north of town for that." Navarette, still hovering, glared down at her. "Three more dead—Hector among them—on top of your famous fireman. Not to mention the arrest of all four *pinches jotos* caught on the video. The reporters have their hands full without you. For once. For now."

"They'll be back," her mother said. "Which is why we must leave soon."

"What I meant," Jacqi said, "is that unless they don't get TV or radio or the Internet up at this school, it's not like no one's gonna recognize me. There's the reward, remember. And sooner or later the cops'll put out a BOLO or APB or whatever they call it. Somebody's gonna pick up a phone, one of the other kids if not a teacher, a counselor—"

"You let us take care of that," her mother said. A dark sigh, brave smile. "There were dozens of others at the scene. Let them tell what they saw. It's not all up to you."

Navarette started wagging his finger, as if to prime some sort of motor in his brain. "What you were doing in that fireman's car, it shames you. It shames your brother. But mostly it shames that woman sitting right there. You don't owe a thing to that man. He was using you. The police will use you, the lawyers will use you, the whole city will use you. If you owe anyone anything, it's your mother. Time to begin repaying her, yes? Show some respect."

Because she's bagging you while my old man's inside?

"Live up to her example. Act like a lady."

Not a whore, Jacqi thought—a *puta*, a *zorra*—go ahead and say it. But he didn't. Everyone was reining it in, staying calm, setting the tone for the next few hours, the next few days and weeks and years. The future.

Except the only future she could visualize that resembled what they wanted of her lay in the past. She glanced across the room and wondered: Do you remember, Mamá? My seventh birthday. With Tía Loreta and Lucianna, before they moved away. Before Dad went to jail and I got taken and everybody stopped talking to us. All four of us wearing dresses and white gloves. You gave me a patent leather purse with a gold clasp, shoes to match. You said: You're getting to be a young lady now. The tablecloths at the restaurant so starchy and white, and crystal glasses like you were drinking from jewels. I had shrimp—first time ever—and a chocolate parfait and the waiters and waitresses sang.

I think of that afternoon a lot, Mamá, almost every day. Because I know nothing like it will ever, ever happen again. Not since I disappeared, not since that day at the hospital when you came into the examination room and locked the door. When it comes to you and me, Mamá, that is the future. Forever.

She closed her eyes, hot with tears, and pressed her fingers into them, tried to breathe—the air felt like tiny razors digging into her lungs—and she found herself wishing and wishing, something seemingly impossible, maybe not, if only, with all her heart—

The door swung open and quickly slammed shut.

Richie stood there, breathing hard. Something was wrong. He was boring a hole straight through her with his stare.

"The guy who's been looking for her," he said, not to her. "Tierney. He's outside. On his phone."

In the kitchen a chair screeched hard across the linoleum and shortly Ben Escalada stood there in the doorway. Navarette nodded toward the front yard. The small ex-boxer—with his scalded face and gauze-wrapped hands—buttoned his sport coat, wedged through the room, and headed on out.

Richie just stood there, eyes fixed on her, opening and closing his hands, like he didn't know what to do with them. "You told him," he said. "You weaselly selfish bitch—you *told* him."

81

By the time Tierney got off the phone with dispatch, he knew he was on his own. Too many questions, no promises, and that tone—the snotty, bunkered, put-upon edge all the operators had these days: At your service, sir. Please go fuck yourself. We're busy.

Tucking the cell back into his sport-coat pocket, he glanced up and down the block, hoping for a busybody at a window, a little backup, if it came to that.

Just as he placed his foot on the first porch step the front door banged open—one of the two jokers from yesterday, the small one, looking seriously the worse for wear.

Someone or something had torched the side of his face, the hair on that side patchy, the skin blistered and red, his ear glistening with ointment, and he held one hand—both were mummified—tucked close to his hip as he stepped to the edge of the porch, staring down at Tierney.

"You been told to leave these people alone."

The ferocity of small men, Tierney thought. "Are you the one who came to my girlfriend's house with Richie?"

"None of this affects you."

"I want to see her," Tierney said. "And you're wrong, it affects me plenty."

"Not telling you twice, *culero*. Turn around and walk."

Tierney dug out his phone, punched on the voice memo function. "You understand. Your protection, not just mine." He slipped the cell, now serving as a recorder, into his outside breast pocket. "Back to Jacqi—I want to talk to her. She was taken against her will from where she was staying, getting looked after—by me, my girlfriend, who's a nurse. Jacqi has a nasty gash on the side of the head—you know this already, you've seen her—she's at risk for concussion, I need to make sure she's okay. She comes out or I go in, either way works for me."

The small man's face tightened up like he was tonguing something to spit. "I done told you once already, okay? Leave this family be. They don't want you here. They want you should go. They'll look after Jacqi fine." He took a deep breath and his shoulders rolled with it. "Nobody was taken against her will—okay?—and I'm asking all nice, we're civilized people, but you're on private property. You been told."

Tierney took a short step back, cupped his hands to his mouth, and shouted. "Jacqi? Jacqi, come on out! I need to make sure you're okay."

He'd fault himself later for not sensing how quick the man could be, but in the snap of an instant he stepped down, plucked the phone from Tierney's breast pocket, and heaved it as far as he could. Arm like an outfielder. The thing landed with a clatter on the tile roof of the house across the street.

"Last chance. You get the fuck gone. While you still got both eyes in your head."

Skellenger said, "Once you drew everybody, where'd it go from there?"

"Nowhere."

It came out too quick, and he gave the boy a second to self-correct, but he just sat there. Waiting out the misery.

"Nobody touched anybody, that what you're saying?"

Ethan rubbed his eye with the heel of his hand. "Chris and Sophie made out."

"Made out as in necked? Or made out as in got lucky."

"For chrissake, Jordie."

"Nobody's gonna get pregnant," Ethan said, "if that's what you mean."

"Okay." Skellenger felt relieved. Not as much as he might've liked.

Rosellen said, "What about you and Jen, Ethan?"

"What about us?"

"Did you and she . . ." Like she was matchmaking. Like that was the point.

"No." He sounded apologetic, not defensive. "I told you, it was like I was, I dunno. Besides, her mom came home, everybody got dressed and we lit some incense."

"You're not serious." Skellenger bit back a laugh. People. "Incense? They can't be that stupid, the parents I mean."

"I dunno, we just did and her mom didn't even bother us anyway, just walked around upstairs. We played music. Jen asked if she could have one of her pictures and I said sure. I gave her the best one. Same with Chris and Sophie."

"You gave them pictures." Skellenger could imagine all three kids, late at night alone, looking at themselves. That's me, but it's not me. "Any idea if these kids still have those pictures?"

"No."

"They're gone, bet on it." The hall clock struck the hour, nine soft dignified chimes, and Skellenger clenched his teeth against an aching yawn. "Those pictures are gone and those three kids are getting their stories straight and you're gonna be the one left holding the bag."

Ethan's face quivered, a headshake, eyes cast down. "I don't see Jen doing that."

"I hope you're right," Skellenger said. "But I wouldn't bank on it."

"Jordie—"

"The McPartlands have to worry about how it looks, they turn a blind eye when their kid smokes dope, gets naked. Think they'll really cop to that? Think this Kelechava kid is gonna let his buddies know he stripped down to streak in front of another guy? And shy little Sophie, who blushes down to her neck. Oh yeah, she's a strong one."

"It's not like that."

"Ethan, I'm just trying to get you ready. They're all either gonna say you conned them into it somehow or it never happened. You just made up these pictures from your sick, twisted imagination and their parents are gonna wring their hands or pound the table and say their poor little dears have been wronged. They demand justice."

Ethan licked his lips, then said quietly, "Jen'll tell the truth."

"Someday, maybe." Skellenger eased up a little. "But it won't be up to her, not now. It'll be up to her lovely mother, who's too dumb to know reefer from incense, or pretends she is."

Ethan seemed lost for a second. "So what are you saying, we're back to lying?"

Like that's the worst thing imaginable, Skellenger thought. And yet, looking into the boy's face, he felt for the first time in a long while the cancer in it, the cowardice, not just the reckoning of odds.

"Listen to me." He reached out his hand. Ethan just sat there. "I'm *trying* to *protect* you."

Tucked up on the couch, Jacqi pivoted at the sound of Tierney's voice—outside, just beyond the porch.

Her mother, with a disgusted flip of her hand, said to Navarette, "What good are these *nacos* of yours?"

Navarette said nothing, just moved to the window, inched the curtain back.

"I'll tell him to leave," Jacqi said, and began to get up, only to meet a hammer, Richie's fist, pounding the side of her head so hard her eyes rolled back, her knees turned to ink. A spume of vomit launched into her throat and the world turned white and black and invisible all at once till at last, blinking, gagging, she caught her bearings, her vision zagged back into quasi-focus, and as she gasped for air she felt the fingers of blood threading down her face and throat.

"You *told* him," Richie said.

And then came the feel of his hands, on fire with strength and clenched around her throat, thumbs pressing deep into her windpipe, his hate total now—for her, for himself, for what he'd done, what they'd made him do—and that hate rushed into his grip like blood and though she pounded with her fists against his arms, struggled, kicked, secretly she saw no real point, a terrible knowledge filling her heart, telling her: he's not going to stop, he can't. Just as her mother, across the room, saw no point in pulling him off. She just sat there watching, too stunned to move, one child killing the other. Or secretly grateful, who could tell? Who would ever know?

Ironically it was Navarette who dragged him off. It took some work, they wrestled for a bit, but then the thick-bodied older man spun Richie around and slapped him across the face, the sound a thundercrack—"Act like a man for once"—and Richie's head snapping sideways, he almost fell. But then he stumbled to the end table near the door with their mother saying, "No, no," quietly at first, then shouting as he pulled out the gun she kept there.

From outside, Tierney still shouting, "Jacqi! What's going on? Come on out, talk to me." Then sounds of a struggle on the porch, the scrambling thud of men's bodies, as she tried to fit the jagged pieces of the room back together, take back her breath.

Richie held the gun at arm's length, first at Navarette, then his mother. His eyes seemed to melt and he began to tremble. A whisper: "I can't . . ." And he jammed the barrel in his mouth.

Skellenger's cell phone hummed in his pocket. He pulled it out, checked the display. "I've gotta take this."

He went into the kitchen, pretty sure everyone was as thankful as he was for the break. What else needed to get said? Wait and see, then go on the attack.

"Mayweather, yeah. What's up?"

The watch commander on the other end cleared the muck from his throat. "Got some kind of problem over at the Garza house."

Skellenger's viscera clenched. Nudes, now this. Like some kind of demented algebra—how many trains can simultaneously leave their stations and go off the rails and crash and burn and kill everyone onboard in screaming agony?

"We got a 911 call from some guy named Tierney, says Jacqi Garza was taken from his house and she's being held against her will at her mother's."

Jesus, he thought, thudding his hip against the counter, needing it for support.

"Had a similar call earlier," Mayweather said, "from the guy's girlfriend. Sounds a little loose on deck, to be honest."

If only, Skellenger thought. Taken, Christ. "Thanks, Roy. Yeah. Seems a little far-flung. Fetched, I mean. Far-fetched."

"Well now there's some kinda ruckus in the front yard, a fight maybe, we're getting calls from neighbors."

Oh fuck me. He dug at his eyes with his thumb and forefinger till jags of splintered light etched the backs of his eyelids. "What kind of fight?"

"Skelly, how the hell should I know? All the help we got yesterday's been remanded, started once you guys made your arrests. Fuckers checked out like there was free food someplace. I'm down to ten cars again except for a couple deputies out of Dixon—don't get me started on those two—and a few more guys checking in for OT in a bit. Been a goddamn jailbreak this morning. Some kinda minor riot at the high school, black gangs going after the Mex cliques on account of the arrests yesterday, everybody pointing fingers, snitch and bitch and fuck you. No guns thank God, not yet anyway. Plus I got two burglaries in progress, one at a pot dispensary downtown, hookers trolling the river road like it's raining men, a jackknife out on Blood Alley, and a bunch of mouth-breathers boosting everything they can get their hands on at the mini-mart right near where Verrazzo bit it."

Rahim Salaam, Skellenger thought. Payback. For not being a coward fast enough.

"And those are just the calls I can get to. Board's lit up like it's New Year's."

"I'll head over now to the Garza place," Skellenger said, thinking: Damage control. At minimum. "Do me a favor? Run the address and give me any 415s or DVs while I'm en route. And see if we've got any probies or violators in the neighborhood."

"I can't roll you any backup, not till—"

"It's okay," Skellenger said. "Sounds manageable. If not I'll let you know."

• • •

Tierney was already well on his way to getting his ass kicked—the small man had a savage right, even bandaged up, and it'd made its point twice to his midriff, once to his nose—when he heard the gunshot inside, followed by screams, two of them, Jacqi and her mother. The latter seemed barely human.

Navarette's man caught the sound too and stopped, fist poised in midair, head turned toward the house. Tierney saw his chance and with his left hand gripped the man's windpipe like he meant to rip it out, grabbed his crotch just as hard, slipped his left leg behind Escalada's right and took him down, kneeling quick for a strike to the soft spot at the edge of the six-pack, rectus abdominis. *You should teach math.* Cass's words. *You'd be brilliant at it.* He staggered and turned, pulled back the screen door as Escalada scrambled to his knees, barking out an airless cough. Tierney had one hand on the doorknob when he felt first the hold on his coattail, dragging him backward, then the other thing, more than a punch, hotter and deep, a blade launched upward, sinking into his back.

Confusion, then knee-weakening pain, then two more stabs and the small man, dazed and wheezing and shambling to his feet, pocketed his bloodied knife, pushed Tierney aside and down, kicking him for good measure.

As the door opened and closed he lay there, realizing a lung was hit, a sense like drowning, suckling in breath, and he remembered from somewhere the importance of lying on his side so the wound was down, keep the good lung blood-free, as he dug through his pockets for his phone, only to remember that it lay in pieces on the roof across the street.

· · ·

Jacqi watched her mother kneel over Richie's body, the back of his head a gruesome mess, brain ripped to pieces and exposed. His blood drained away, soaking the carpet, the woman keening, pulling the shattered head back, gripping the chin, forcing air into his mouth, into his irrelevant lungs. How much like a kiss, Jacqi thought.

Navarette stood there, a few feet back. Jacqi could not remember a time he'd ever looked helpless, and never like this. At last he dropped onto one knee, rested a hand on her mother's shoulder, but she shook it off violently, staring down at her dead son.

The rest went so quickly Jacqi could barely register it. Her mother collected the blood-caked gun from beside Richie's body, got to her feet, and fired two shots point blank, one into Navarette's chest, the other his face.

Not a second later, Ben Escalada burst into the room, gripping a knife, its blade dull and dark from use. Her mother lifted the barrel and stepped deliberately toward him and fired two more shots, same placement, like she'd thought about this moment, planned for it somehow, over who knew how many weeks or months or years.

Escalada jumped just a little from the bullets' impact, as though stung, face dotted with the wound over his eye that quickly flared with blood as he collapsed—first onto one knee, then the next, before sliding down crookedly onto his back—looking numb with concentration.

Skellenger didn't see a fight when he pulled up. What he saw was a man in slacks and a sport coat lying very still on his left side, halfway up the porch steps.

He thumbed his radio, waited through the squawks. "Mayweather. Skellenger here. I don't care what you've got out there, you've got to roll me some backup, I've got a possible 10-10 at the Garza house. I need code 3 medic and an ambulance to stage while we clear. Over."

He knew he should wait for at least one more unit but he got out of the car and drew his weapon, thumbed off the safety. Neighbors peered out from windows, some holding cell phones, calling in or catching the action on video. As he crossed the yard he could see it was the guy named Tierney on the porch, drawing ragged breaths, but alive.

Then the door flew open, Jacqi was there.

He lifted his weapon, sighted on her chest.

Jacqi saw the bloodstain on the back of Tierney's jacket as he struggled to draw himself up. There was more blood on the ground and his whole midriff was soaked in it. His skin looked waxy and damp. She knelt down beside him, wondering what to do, as he reached into his pants pocket, trembling all over.

"Go to my car." The words hissed through his teeth, he tugged out his keys, nudging them into her hand. "Lock yourself inside."

No, she thought, I won't, not again—trapped in a car, watching a man die. The inescapable pattern. "You need help, Jesus, what—"

"Go to the car, the neighbors, someplace, call 911. Just *go*."

She didn't really register Skellenger's presence till she started down the porch steps. He was easing forward across the yard, his gun drawn, and for a thousand reasons the fact it was him pissed her off, the anger filling up all the empty places scraped out by her fear. She felt light, like if she spread her arms the wind just might take her, over the mossy rooftops, inflated with rage.

"I want to testify, Skellenger." Her steps thudded on the ground like fists. "Help me, help my friend, he's hurt, he's been stabbed, and I want to testify, understand?"

The girl was talking—yelling, actually—but the words were just noise, a distraction from what was happening behind her. Nina Garza marched out of the house, onto the porch—dressed impeccably, caked with blood. Quickly, intently, she came down the steps and later he'd tell himself that the inexplicable oddness of that—the butcher-shop gore, even her face smeared dark with it, the eerie swiftness of her gait—it stopped him, confused him, and he didn't see the weapon in her hand, didn't register the movement as she raised it, aiming at her daughter's back.

He'd also tell himself that he didn't have a clear line of fire, not at first—even if he'd gone ahead, taken his shot, he might have hit the girl instead. It wasn't until the muzzle barked and the girl pitched forward that he had a clear bead, at which point he placed a three-shot group into the woman's torso, the place of largest body mass. She stopped with a jolt and a dull-eyed shudder and yet kept pulling the trigger, hammer clicking, cylinder advancing, even as she turned back toward the house, staggered, knees scissoring, then fell.

He'd had no idea her gun was empty when he fired. He believed she posed a clear and present danger. The proof was the girl.

For the slightest instant, he thought: We teach our children to lie.

He hurried to where Jacqi lay, saw the smear of blood on the back of her blouse, high left side, and gently turned her over. The exit wound on her chest was huge—hollow-point round, he guessed—and so near the heart. Her skin had turned ashen, her eyes rolled back, lips trembling like she was freezing cold.

"Stay with me," he said, applying pressure to the wound. Blood surged up through his fingers.

Her eyes fluttered and cleared for a second and with a weak smile she reached up, stroked his face with her fingers, her touch soft, like a feather. She whispered something, the words so faint he couldn't make them out, and as he bent closer, his ear an inch from her lips, he thought he caught the words "honest dime," but that made no sense, and she said nothing more.

Final Entry

Three a.m. and I was lying there wide-awake with this line from Iris Murdoch banging around inside my brain: "Love is the extremely difficult realization that something other than oneself is real."

It seemed to echo down every hallway of my life, and I thought of all the Something Others I'd not entrusted with reality. Like you.

I know, I know, how puzzling to say that to someone who's dead. But you know how it is. Sleep pulls a runner this time of the morning and I find myself in the dark and frightened, even with Cass sleeping so peacefully beside me, and I lie there wanting something to steady the nerves, calm me down.

It's not death that scares me so much as the sense that death is just a disguise for something else, something bigger. And not kind.

I've resisted this impulse to write for a while, as you know. I see the poison in it. So Irish, this business with spooks and fairies and doom, granting the greater reality to the dead and the misty wherever. Follow that path too long, you end up very alone.

So more and more I've tried to find my solace among the living. Those mysterious, Murdochian others. Not somethings. Someones.

But this morning, one last time, I felt a need to write to you.

I found this journal in the old house—we're cleaning it out, pitching the clutter, getting it ready for sale—found it in a drawer. Checking the pages, I noticed it's well over a year since I wrote last, the entry before this one dated not long after Cass and I first got together. Perhaps that's for the best. Perhaps I should stop now and just put this thing away. But there's much to report, and I need to get it clear in my own mind.

Recovery's not untroubled, but by and large we're fine. The lung itself has come along nicely—luckily I took a blade, not a bullet—but this odd nerve thing. Still get this weakness down the right side, the knee buckles for no conceivable reason. The ghost in the machine.

But I cut a rakish and Joycean figure, brandishing my walking stick—old maple, with an ivory lion's-head grip. Grady found it in an antique store near Union Square in San Francisco, his tribute to the wounded brother-in-arms.

The girl wasn't so lucky. The bullet tore her up pretty bad inside, eight hours of surgery, good 50 percent of one lung cut away, then post-op hemorrhage and shock.

The legalities were a mess—mother and brother dead, father in Soledad, an aunt living somewhere back east who first couldn't be found, then couldn't be bothered. Cass petitioned the court and got a temporary medical directive, power of attorney, and that gave the hospital a piece of paper to stick in the kid's chart so they were off the hook and everybody seemed happy.

It was rough, those first few months, fox-trot forward, cha-cha back, but little by little she got her strength, the lung cleared of fluid. Developed a bit of a dependency on the inhalers and the Percocet but, with Cass's help, she worked through that. Doing better than me, truth be told, oh boo hoo. Health, like youth itself, gets wasted on the young.

We filed the paperwork to step up as foster parents, even got her dad to sign off, but she turned eighteen before FCAS stopped dithering, so we just rented an apartment for her around the corner. Every now and then, she still talks about heading off for Mexico, but for now she seems content. She's close enough she's always welcome, far enough away nobody's snarling over bones. But she's at the house at some point almost every day, dinner at least, and some nights, when the nightmares are bad, she slips on over, lets herself in, curls up on the sofa.

Cass volunteered to coach girls' basketball at St. Catherine's and we got Jacqi enrolled, a second shot at senior year, and get this, she made the team. Small but mighty, Cass calls her, a beast in the paint, outhustling way taller girls on the boards—while missing half a lung. She has to come out every five minutes or so, sits there gasping and rasping, but it's impressive, her toughness. Not that she's the next LeBron. "Can't knock down a shot to save her soul," Cass says. "Posts up and lets it fly like she's trying to hit the wall." But she leads the team in assists. Imagine that. Jacquelina Garza. Team player.

Her testimony at Damarlo's prelim—talk about a media zoo— proved crucial, especially her testimony about Teddy Buker confessing to Verrazzo's murder. Cal Katsaros filed a motion for a 707 hearing and Damarlo got notched down to juvie. He took a plea for aggravated assault and got eighteen months, almost a miracle, really. He's doing the time at Chaderjian YCF in Stockton, not too far, his grandparents get over maybe twice a month.

As for the others—Mo Pete Carson, Arian Lomax, Chepe Salgado—they're heading into court one by one, the cases severed, as Grady predicted from the start, albeit cagily. No surprise, they can't jump on Jacqi's story fast enough, crowing they saw with their own eyes what Buker confessed to, a killing, just not theirs to own. Some of the kids Jacqi named who were there—not many, admittedly, just a few—came forward to testify and that's helped point everyone toward the exit, too. I think she had a hand in that, set an example they couldn't ignore. At least, that's what I like to tell myself.

Meanwhile the city continues its slouch toward Bethlehem. Verrazzo's murder seems to have made people stop, look at themselves and this place, back away from the abyss. Some, anyway. There's a tacit agreement to lower the volume if not the heat.

There's also a realization, thanks to Jacqi, that Teddy Buker wasn't just some crazed loon. An angry young man, sure, with a grievance most people can understand: kids with no future, adults without work, promises broken at the whim of money.

None of which has changed much, obviously. Things remain a bit of a train wreck around here, just less so, and that's about as good as it gets in America right now.

We had to put Noble down. Inside he was a mess, lesions and tumors everywhere, and the seizures started coming quicker and harder. Jacqi held his head and kissed him as Cass clutched him to her chest and, sure, we all cried. Good old dog.

I'm working, after a fashion. The ethics board cleared my bar card, but I'm not slipping back into that routine. Have the PI shingle as well, which makes me even more of a jack-of-all-trades—maybe I'll get a therapist's license, too, the trifecta. My business card reads simply "Professional Services." I help people start over. I'm not listed anywhere. The people who need to know who I am, know who I am.

Grady tosses me something here and there and the number of lawyers who get what I do call from time to time with a problem they think I can help with. Basically I go into my office, close the door, read my Spinoza and Schopenhauer or Ed McBain, maybe a bit of Hardy and Wright, *The Theory of Numbers*, and then go out and make the world safe for fuckups.

Which brings us to the real news, happened just two days ago, which may be why I can't sleep. Still rolling it around in my head.

Jacqi met with the detective, Skellenger, and asked me to come along. She still felt a need to tell the truth, come clean about her testimony against Cope, but the hang-up was how.

She'd thought about it good and hard, and we talked it out some too. I told her what I'd come to realize, that truth isn't an abstraction.

It's not in a book or a courtroom and it's not this big, airy, perfect thing hovering all around us like the ether. It exists between people. We share the truth, or we share a lie.

There was nothing at issue anymore with her mother or brother or Pete Navarette. The dead, like I need tell you, bear no responsibility. They're beyond that. And whatever happened to Clint Burkhead, poor Eastwood, is largely moot.

But what happened between her and Skellenger wasn't.

She picked the Chowhaus, this dive along the water where they slather everything in cornmeal—Christ, I'm surprised they don't deep-fry the silverware—but it's reasonably quiet and there's the river to look at, easing south toward the bay.

He looked better than I remembered, Skellenger I mean, and in passing, as I'd worked out his sitting down with Jacqi, he let it slip that he'd made some strides with his family, helped his son face some sort of jam at school.

I wondered if I should leave the two of them alone, but Jacqi insisted. She was a completely different girl the last however many times they'd spoken, and she wasn't sure how the new Jacquelina would hold up. Pointless worry, of course. She was stellar.

He began with an odd confession. He'd gone to the Office of Professional Responsibility—the local version of Internal Affairs—and admitted what had happened when he and his partner first interviewed Jacqi. He knew they'd had a duty to report any allegation of child abuse, but they'd hidden behind the fig leaf of deeming the girl confused, then waiting for the mother—an inexcusable lapse, letting the parent dictate.

The OPR held a hearing and it went pretty much as you'd imagine, from what Skellenger said. His word against his partner's. Men in uniform, like men everywhere I suppose, tend to hate it when one of their own starts turning over rocks. The most reliable evidence existed at the time, they said, and absent anything prima facie that would contradict the record, they saw no point in reinventing history.

"I didn't want to drag you into this," he said to Jacqi as we sat there at the table, the river ambling past the window. "I know what you've been through. But it won't go forward if you don't come in, give a statement, and—"

She reached out suddenly, gripped his hand.

"Yeah," she said softly. "There was maybe a thousand times I wanted to tell what happened, set the record straight. But whatever scores that'd settle, I think they're pretty much over and done with, don't you?"

"What I think," he said, "is I owe it to you."

"Anything you owe me," she said, "you've paid." With her thumb she stroked the back of his hand. "You ponied up when you walked into that hearing."

"There's still Cope."

"Believe me, I know." She squinted through the glare in the hazy glass, looking out across the strait at the old shipyard. "And maybe someday I'll go up to Susanville and talk to him, like this. Creeps me out to think about, but that doesn't mean I won't. I'll come clean. But just between him and me. He doesn't deserve another bite at the apple and nobody knows that better than him. He's right where he belongs."

Few minutes later, we're heading out to our cars, and Jacqi suddenly turns toward Skellenger and says, "This may sound awful, please don't take it wrong. But I've wondered—that day, you know, when it all happened. Outside, in the yard, when I was walking toward you, I saw something in your face. Something I couldn't quite figure. Like you, I dunno, hesitated."

She told me about this in private, her suspicion Skellenger had waited until her mother got off her shot before taking the woman out.

Solve God knows how many problems all at once. But given how gently she'd wrapped things up inside, I felt stunned she'd trot this out now.

Not half as stunned as Skellenger, apparently. He looked like she'd reared back and kicked him. "I didn't have a clear—"

She cut him off, reaching up, pressing her fingers to his lips.

"It's okay, really, it's doesn't matter," she said. "It's a stupid world. We do our best but we screw up almost always. Every now and then, it's okay, letting somebody off the hook."

Like I said, she's impressive. More to the point, she's real. So is Cass.

Wherever you are, if anywhere, I think you know where I'm going with this. There may be some weird logic to things and you actually need me to stay connected, like if I pray for your soul it will lessen your time in purgatory. Or maybe you continue to exist in some twilight limbo till the last person alive forgets you. I have no clue. What I do know is that Cass and Jacqi are alive and here and they need me. Full attention. Front and center.

I could have just left this book in the drawer where it was or tossed it, but though I don't believe much in closure I do believe in saying good-bye.

If there really is something on the other side, and it's not too lousy, maybe we'll reconnect when the time comes. Or not. You know the rules better than I do. Till then, thank you. Up until the day you died, marrying you was the single smartest thing I ever did.

Tanto la vita.

ACKNOWLEDGMENTS

One of the great myths of the writing life is that the writer, tucked away in his garret, hammers away in lofty isolation. Nothing could be further from the truth. Without the help of many other people, this book simply would not exist. Gratitude is particularly owed to Alan Turkus, Alison Dasho, Bryon Quertermous, Tiffany Pokorny, Gracie, Doyle, Jacque BenZekry, and everyone at Thomas & Mercer, who've worked so hard, so generously, and so thoughtfully to help bring this book into the world. Thanks to Johnny Shaw for introducing me to the T&M folks and to Barry Eisler, Bob Dugoni, and G. M. Ford for helping me seal the deal. Laurie Fox, Lisa Gallagher, and Kimberley Cameron selflessly provided professional guidance and asked for nothing but friendship in return. A particularly profound and warm offering of thanks is owed to Cornelia Read, Peter Riegert, and Don Winslow for supplying much-needed attaboys at crucial junctures. Opportunities to road test portions of the book were graciously provided by Peg Alford Pursell and Cass Pursell at their unrivaled event program Why There Are Words in Sausalito, and by Tom Jenks and Carol Edgarian, who both offered me the chance to read at Litquake, San Francisco's mythic weeklong book bash, and have agreed to print an excerpt in *Narrative* magazine.

Numerous people selflessly gave of their time to provide me with technical assistance. George Fong, former special agent with the FBI's Violent Crime Squad, as well as Captain James O'Connell, Lieutenant Syd DeJesus, and Sergeant Jason Potts of the Vallejo Police Department, in conjunction with all the officers and staff involved in the department's Volunteer Training Program, bent over backward to provide details about law enforcement strategy, tactics, and culture; they are a smart, dedicated, generous group. Similarly, thanks to Lee Lofland and everyone at the Writers' Police Academy—especially the remarkable Sarah Yow—for assisting me as I tried to tie up some loose ends in the police and paramedic procedure area. Dan Russo provided invaluable insight into local crime lore and the defense bar for the North Bay region. The ever-helpful, exceedingly unselfish, and too-smart-for-his-own-good D. P. Lyle as always provided on-point medical assistance, while Gail Lange-Katic, Eloise Hill, and Kris Anderson offered unvarnished insight on the work and life of nurses, which amplified what I'd learned twelve years earlier from the wonderful crew in the Oncology Clinic at Stanford Medical Center. Susie Foreman of Rosewood House graciously took time to discuss the invaluable and difficult work she does on behalf of young women trying to leave behind a life of prostitution and drug use. Stephanie Gomes gave me a crucial peek behind the scenes of municipal bankruptcy, and Mark Chubb, longtime firefighter and currently chief of King County Fire District 20 in West Hill, Washington, provided intimate insight into the firefighting profession and the inner workings of public service unions. Ann Smith, John Allen, Lony Meyer, and everyone at Fighting Back Partnership, the CORE Team, the Lamplighter, and the Neighborhood Watch Program helped educate me on bankruptcy from the community perspective, and the devastating effects of the foreclosure crisis. Gordon Harries has become not just a great friend but an invaluable guide to the Manchester music scene; he deserves sole credit for introducing me to Guy Garvey and Elbow, who in turn provided inspiration for the book's title.

Vince Keenan, Katy Pye, Theresa Rogers, and Leslie Schwerin all read early versions of the manuscript and provided invaluable advice on how to improve it. Whatever limitations, flaws, or errors exist in these pages are entirely my fault, and not due to any of the information or advice provided by these generous men and women.

Finally, thanks to Mette, my wife, who also read the manuscript in several incarnations, and whose patience, insight, and unflappable cheerfulness (except in Reno) steadied a ship that, all too often, seemed awash with uncertainty.

ABOUT THE AUTHOR

David Corbett is the author of four previous novels: *The Devil's Redhead*, *Done for a Dime* (a *New York Times* Notable Book), *Blood of Paradise* (nominated for numerous awards, including the Edgar), and *Do They Know I'm Running?* In January 2013 he published a comprehensive textbook on the craft of characterization, *The Art of Character*. His short fiction and poetry have appeared in numerous magazines and anthologies, with pieces twice selected for the book series Best American Mystery Stories. His nonfiction has appeared in the *New York Times*, *Narrative*, *MovieMaker*, *Bright Lights*, *Writer's Digest*, and numerous other venues. For more, visit www.davidcorbett.com.